D0179923

The Black Minutes

The Black Minutes

Martín Solares

Translation by Aura Estrada
and John Pluecker

Black Cat

a paperback original imprint of Grove/Atlantic, Inc.

New York

Published simultaneously in Canada
Printed in the United States of America

FIRST EDITION

ISBN: 978-0-8021-7068-2

Black Cat
a paperback original imprint of Grove/Atlantic, Inc.
841 Broadway
New York, NY 10003

Distributed by Publishers Group West

www.groveatlantic.com

10 11 12 13   10 9 8 7 6 5 4 3 2

To Vesta

Contents

The Black Minutes

CAST OF CHARACTERS

The Paracuán Police

- Rosa Isela, a beautiful girl doing her social service work at the Paracuán police headquarters
- Camarena and Rodrigo Columba: young graduates of the police academy
- Joaquín Taboada, El Travolta, current chief of Paracuán's municipal police
- Ramón Cabrera, also known as El Macetón (the Big Flowerpot, Shaggy)
- García, Taboada's predecessor
- Lolita, secretary
- Rufino Chávez, El Chaneque (the Duende): Taboada's right-hand man
- The forensic expert, Ramírez
- Jarquiel, El Profe (the Professor), police officer
- Wong, El Chino, police officer
- Salim, El Beduino (the Bedouin), police officer
- Zozaya, El Evangelista (the Evangelist), police officer
- José Tiroloco (Crazyshot), police officer
- Mena, Gordolobo (Fatwolf), police officer
- Luis Calatrava, El Brujo (the Wizard), checkpoint guard
- Dr. Ridaura, forensic doctor and respected biology professor
- Vicente Rangel González, detective
- Jorge Romero, El Ciego (the Blind Man): Rangel's *madrina, i.e.,* his lackey, his sidekick
- Emilio Nieto, El Chicote (the Whip), receptionist, prison guard, car washer, and courier
- Cruz Treviño, chief of the judicial police, previously a municipal police officer

The Locals

- Bernardo Blanco, a young journalist
- Don Rubén Blanco, Bernardo's father
- Johnny Guerrero, *nota roja* (crime-beat) reporter for *El Mercurio*
- La Chilanga, photographer
- René Luz de Dios López, imprisoned for killing four girls
- Fritz Tschanz, Jesuit priest
- His Holiness the bishop of Paracuán
- John Williams, influential businessman in the port, owner of Cola Drinks
- John Williams, Jr., called Jack
- Tobías Wolffer, local congressman
- Rodrigo Montoya, director of the Paracuán archives
- Lucilo Rivas, Bar León manager
- Raúl Silva Santacruz, witness
- Juan, El Chimuelo (Gaptooth) and Jorge, El Chaparro (Shorty), butchers
- El Lobina, fisherman
- Don Isaac Klein, restaurant owner
- El Profeta (the Prophet), ice-cream vendor
- Lucía Hernández Campillo, Inés Gómez Lobato, Karla Cevallos, Julia Concepción González, Daniela Torres, the victims of El Chacal (the Jackal)

The Visitors

- Lieutenant Miguel Rivera González, legendary policeman from Paracuán
- Mr. Traven Torsvan, writer

- Dr. Alfonso Quiroz Cuarón, internationally renowned criminologist
- Rigo Tovar, singer
- El Rey de los Marcianos (the King of the Martians), alien
- Cormac McCormick, ex-detective for the FBI
- El Albino, crime-beat photographer

The Narcos

- El Chincualillo (the Little Pain or the Little Measles), wholesale drug dealer
- El Cochiloco (the Crazy Pig), leader of the Colombians
- El Chato Rambal (the Flat-faced Rambal), head of the port cartel
- Vivar, the Paracuán cartel's lawyer
- Mr. Obregón, the Paracuán cartel's leader

The Politicos

- Licenciado Echaverreta, president of Mexico
- Juan José Churruca, government minister for the state of Tamaulipas
- José "Pepe" Topete, influential politician
- Daniel Torres Sabinas, Paracuán mayor at the end of the seventies
- Agustín Barbosa, Ciudad Madera's first opposition mayor
- Edelmiro Morales, leader of the professors' union in Tamaulipas

The Invaders

- The officers from the Federal Security Administration

I had the most important nightmare of my life so far while traveling in a bus down a highway flanked by pine trees. I haven't been able to figure out what it means, at least not entirely.

It was nighttime, but I couldn't sleep. Every time I started to nod off, the headlights of oncoming cars or the jolting of the bus jarred me awake. I knew I was finally asleep when I couldn't hear the engine drone anymore and the headlights turned soft and blue and stopped bothering me.

I was having a pleasant dream, one that was even, in certain respects, a musical one, when I sensed that a sarcastic person, someone who knew me fairly well, had moved into the seat behind me. The visitor waited until I was used to his presence; then he uncrossed his legs, leaned for-ward, and, breathing down my neck, said:

Isn't it true that in the life of every man there are five black minutes?

The idea frightened me so much I woke up, and since there was no one in any of the seats around me, I spent the rest of the night drinking water, watching the moon, and trying to calculate if I'd already reached my quota of black minutes.

That's what I was doing when we pulled in to Paracuán, Tamaulipas.

BOOK ONE

YOUR MEMORY
HAS A THOUSAND GAPS

1

The first time he saw the journalist, he reckoned him to be twenty years old and he was wrong. The journalist, from his perspective, reckoned the plaid-shirted rancher to be around fifty, and he guessed right. They were both traveling south. The journalist was on his way from the United States, after quitting his job; the man in the plaid shirt was coming back from a job in the northern part of the state, but he didn't say what it was. They knew they were getting into Mexico because the air on the bus was too thick to breathe.

When they crossed the Río Muerto, they saw a two-jeep convoy. As they got to Dos Cruces a pickup full of *judiciales* passed them, and at Seis Marias they ran into a checkpoint inspection by the Eighth Military Zone. A soldier with a lantern signaled the driver to pull over; the driver took the bus down a dirt road and stopped it in the beam of a huge floodlight, between two walls of sandbags. On the other side of the highway was a big canvas tent with a set of radar machines, and farther down three dozen soldiers were doing calisthenics. During the search of the bus, the journalist turned on his reading light and tried to read the only book he had with him, *The Spiritual Exercises* by St. Ignatius of Loyola, but just a minute into it he felt deeply uncomfortable and looked in the direction of the trenches. Just beneath him, behind the sandbags and the thicket of palm trees, two soldiers stared at him, full of resentment. He wouldn't have cared, if it weren't for the high-caliber machine guns they had trained on him. The rancher said he'd probably look the same, if he had to spend the night at the mercy of the mosquitoes, in hundred-degree heat, crouched behind a bunch of sandbags.

The inspection was carried out without incident. The sergeant who looked them over did it only out of duty and scrutinized the luggage lazily. Meanwhile, the young journalist took advantage of the wait to drink a yogurt, and he offered another to the rancher. In exchange, the fifty-year-old offered him some *pemoles,* the cornmeal cookies they eat in the Huasteca. The rancher asked if he was a student, the young man said no, he'd already finished his studies, in fact had even quit his first job, as a reporter for the San Antonio *Herald.* He was thinking of taking a year off and living down at the port; perhaps later he'd go back to Texas. He showed the rancher a picture of a blonde woman with her hair pulled back. The rancher remarked that she was very beautiful and said he shouldn't have left such a job. The journalist responded that he had his reasons.

The young man examined his fellow travelers: they looked to him like rough, uncultured types. There was the plaid- shirted rancher, shirttail untucked to hide his gun; a somber smoker, who traveled with a machete wrapped in newspaper; and, toward the back, one who seemed worst of all: a mustachioed giant who was eating oranges without peeling them. The young man was still looking them over when it came time for the second inspection.

Ever since he saw the pickups parked on the broken white line of the highway, he'd had the conviction that they would be rude and arrogant, but he hadn't guessed the half of it. They were pulled over by an officer with a walrus mustache, who raised his badge and his gun in the same hand. Behind him, the whole squadron was drinking beer, leaning against the trucks. They all wore dark glasses, even though it was not yet morning, and were dressed in black, despite the oppressive heat. For some reason their poise troubled him more than the arrival of the soldiers had. Keeping his devotional readings to himself, he thought merely, The world is so round and has so much room, and in it there are so many and such varied people. Soon enough he'd realize that the only thing pure about these souls was the white initials of the judicial police printed on their shirts.

The chief gave instructions, and a fat fellow climbed into the bus. He was followed by a kid with an AK-47. Neither of them was older than he was; the second didn't even shave yet. The journalist got the impression that this was the first bus they'd searched in their lifetime. The fat man displayed his badge as if he were going to bless them with it and requested that nobody move: they'd be doing a routine inspection—though it didn't turn out that way for anyone.

He walked the length of the aisle and looked twice at the other passengers, as if he couldn't believe he detected so many wanted individuals. He was a fat man of little faith and didn't even think of hauling them in. Then he brought in a German shepherd that sniffed at them one by one. As soon as the dog was on the bus, the journalist noticed a stirring in the back. Without a doubt the smoker was concealing the machete, the rancher was hiding his gun, and the guy with the mustache was tossing something out the window. All in vain: it was an extremely intelligent dog. It went to the very back of the bus, passed all the other passengers without pausing or doubting once, and stopped in its tracks before the young man who was reading *The Spiritual Exercises*.

"Get off the bus!" the fat man ordered.

They took him off at gunpoint, they searched him as if he were a member of the Paracuán cartel, they mortified him with raunchy cursing, and when he said he was a member of the press they made him take off his jacket—ah, so you're a reporter—and searched him for drugs. Then they emptied his suitcase on a table and the fat man began to rummage. The tape recorder and clothing grabbed his attention, but what he liked most were the sunglasses. The journalist said he had an eye condition and needed to wear them on doctor's orders, but the agent took them anyway. The kid with the AK-47 opined aloud, "Fancy-ass little prick," and spat in the direction of the journalist's shoes. The rest of them smiled.

"Here we go," boasted the potbellied officer, "now we've got the truth."

He waved a marijuana cigarette in his hand. The rancher, from his seat on the bus, shook his head.

"The cigarette is not mine," the journalist protested. "I saw when he put it there."

"No way, asshole," the fat man shot back.

When he figured the abuse was only going to get worse, the rancher said to himself, That's enough, and got off the bus. He walked straight to the judicial police chief, who was drinking a beer and leaning on his pickup. As soon as he saw him, the chief gave a noticeable start.

"Fuckin' Macetón, you lose something around here?"

"Screw you, Cruz, he's just a pup."

"He's old enough to vote."

"He's traveling with me."

The chief gave a distrustful grunt and yelled at the journalist, "What're you going to the port for?"

"Huh?"

"What're you going to the port for?"

"That's where I'm going to be living."

"Get out of here."

They put his things back in the suitcase, except for his jacket and the sunglasses. When he reached for them, the kid with the AK-47 blocked him.

"These stay here. And hurry it up, or the bus'll leave without you."

As the bus took off, the young man saw the fat guy trying on the sunglasses and the other had put on the jacket. Plus a thousand pesos were missing from his wallet.

"It's your lucky day, sir," the rancher said, "that was Chief Cruz Treviño, of the judicial police."

The journalist nodded and clenched his jaw.

Just before they reached the river's edge, two gigantic billboards welcomed them to the city: the first was an ad for Cola Drinks and the second showed the president with arms open wide. Both he and his campaign slogan were riddled with bullet holes. Where it read, A GOOD LIFE FOR YOUR FAMILY, the light shone through the perforations.

As they crossed the bridge, the rancher thought it strange that the journalist stared at the river with such curiosity: there were the same little boats as ever, and, in the distance, the immense cranes moved their dinosaur necks at the cargo port.

Once at the bus station, they made their way to the taxi stand and bought their tickets. As they waited their turn, the rancher observed, "If ever you want to transport weed, put it in a shampoo bottle, wrapped in a piece of plastic. Don't even think of putting it in a coffee can; that's where they look first."

The boy insisted that they'd planted the drug among his things; he didn't even smoke tobacco. Then he said he owed him and he'd like to thank him. A bit awkwardly, the plaid-shirted man handed him his card: AGENT RAMÓN CABRERA, MUNICIPAL POLICE. The boy looked at him dumbfounded, and the rancher insisted that he get in the next available cab.

After the car had turned the corner, he noticed the portrait of the blonde fluttering on the ground: it must have fallen out when the boy paid. Cabrera picked it up and put it in his wallet, without knowing what for.

He thought he'd never see the boy again, and again he was wrong.

2

For Agent Cabrera the case began on Monday, January 15. That day Chief Taboada had a meeting with the best member of his force, Agent Chávez. According to the secretary, they argued, and it seemed Chávez raised his voice. Halfway through the meeting, the chief peered out through the thick blinds that separated his office from the main room, looked over the officers who were present, and picked out the only subordinate who, in his opinion, could still be trusted. That is to say, Ramón "Macetón" Cabrera.

Cabrera was chatting with the social service girls when he was told the boss was ordering him to report. At the moment he entered the chief's office, Agent Chávez was leaving and jostled him with his shoulder. Fortunately, Cabrera was a peaceable sort, so he didn't strike back as he reported to his boss.

"Drop whatever you're doing and look into the deceased on Calle Palma for me."

He was referring to the journalist who'd been found dead the morning before. Sunday afternoon, some hours after the body was reported, Agent Chávez had managed to detain El Chincualillo in a lightning operation, with enough evidence to lock him up for fifteen years. To Chávez's mind, the guilty party had acted alone and the motive was robbery. But Chief Taboada wasn't satisfied.

"I'm missing information: find out what the journalist was doing over his last few days. Where he was, who he saw, what they said to him. If he was writing something, I want to read it. I need to know what was he up to."

Cabrera knew El Chincualillo was a dealer for the Paracuán cartel, and so his chief's request raised a problem of professional ethics. "Why doesn't Chávez do it?"

"I'd rather you took charge."

Cabrera hesitated. "I have a lot of work."

"Let the new guys help you."

Cabrera said no, that wouldn't be necessary, he could do it himself. He couldn't abide the new guys.

"One more thing," the chief added. "Go see the deceased's father, Don Rubén Blanco, and stand in for me at the funeral. It's essential for you to report to him, and for him to know you're going on my behalf, and for you to keep on the lookout until everything's over. It's at the Gulf Funeral Parlor, but hurry up; they'll be burying him at twelve. Don't you have a suit coat?"

"Not here."

"Have them lend you one. Don't show up like that."

"Anything else?"

"Yes: discretion. Don't let anybody know what you're up to."

Cabrera went back to his desk and asked the social service girls to hunt up the autopsy report. The girls, who didn't have that much work to do, squabbled over who would take it to him. Who brought it was Rosa Isela, a girl in her twenties with emerald-green eyes, who leaned on the desk and, after handing over the report, didn't take her eyes off him. Cabrera smiled, flattered, until she remarked that he reminded her of her father. When she observed the detective's discomfort, the girl became all smiles.

"I brought you a present." It was a ruled notebook.

"What's this for?"

"So you can get rid of the other one."

She meant the notebook he was using at the time. Cabrera's notebook was so full by now that he sometimes wrote over pages he had already filled at least twice before, a real palimpsest, as it's called in legalese. And it's true that he had had a lot of work the last few days.

"*Gracias, amiga.* Could you get me some coffee?"

Isela fulfilled his darkest desires and left the beverage on his desk. It should be noted that he brought his own coffee to brew at work, since he found the headquarters pot disgusting. Ten minutes later Camarena, one of the new guys, came in to chat with the social service girls. Camarena was a tall, cheerful young guy, successful with the ladies. That day he was flaunting at least three lipstick marks around his mouth: one of them could be Rosa Isela's. Camarena made himself some decaf and went to his desk. Cabrera wondered how anybody with half a brain could possibly like coffee without any coffee in it.

It was a hot, muggy day. He tried to study the report but couldn't concentrate and was reading through it unattentively when another rookie interrupted him.

"Hey, where's the concrete room?" He was wearing dark glasses in the office. These new guys know zip about the venerable institution of dark glasses, Cabrera grumbled to himself. Wearing them in the presence of a superior shows a lack of respect, and Cabrera's tone of voice was a reproach.

"What'd you lose in there?"

"Nothing." The young man lowered his glasses. "I was sent to look for mops. Your coffeemaker is leaking."

"Take the one in the closet, at the end of the hall; there's nothing for you to do in the concrete room, understood?"

His car leaked oil, the coffeemaker leaked water, what was next? Was he going to have prostate trouble, as his doctor had warned him? Perhaps, at his age, he should drink less coffee and more plain water. But could he live without coffee? After some depressing thoughts (a vision of a world without caffeine, the world as a long and boring blank space), he finally managed to concentrate on the text.

The report indicated that they'd sliced the journalist's throat from ear to ear, collapsing the jugular, and then extracted his tongue through the orifice. In other words, he told himself, they'd given him a Colombian necktie, so there'd be no doubt about who had committed the crime. Ever since the people of the port had been associating with the Colombian cartel, these things were happening more and more often. . . . He was thinking this over when, as he began to reread the report, he felt a burning sensation in his gut. Damn it, he said to himself, what did I get myself into?

When he was almost through reading the report, his stomach growled again and he told himself it was a sign that he shouldn't take the case. But his sense of duty was stronger than he was, and he went out to look for Ramírez.

In the entire headquarters there was only a single person who could have lent him a suit coat in his size, and that was the forensic expert, Ramírez. Not that Cabrera was fat, it was just that he was very broad-shouldered. As for Ramírez. . . .

In the port city that we're discussing, when people get upward of forty they face a dilemma: either they find something interesting to do or they take up eating, with the universally acknowledged outcome. The expert Ramírez belonged to the second category. He had not a double but a triple chin, and his belly spilled out over his belt. Cabrera went in to say hello and noticed a young man wearing glasses typing on a computer at the desk in the back.

"So who's that?"

"My assistant, Rodrigo Columba."

Ramírez had no idea what they wanted from him. In the journalist's house not a manuscript was found, no drafts, nothing. Only a notebook, of no real interest.

"Let me see it."

"Handle with care. . . ."

"Yes, I know." They had found Cabrera's fingerprints at a crime scene once, and since then no one let him off without a good ribbing.

Ramírez handed him the evidence and Cabrera examined it with gloves and tweezers, so as not to worry his colleagues. It was a black notebook: a journal, which at first glance revealed nothing of importance: two or three dates, a poem about Xilitla, and a name, Vicente Rangel. . . . Cabrera felt his gastritis flare up again. Son of a bitch, this can't be happening. He read the poem, which he thought terrible, but found no other written mark. How strange, he thought at last. He couldn't imagine a journalist who took no notes . . . a journalist who didn't write. And that name, Vicente Rangel. He said nothing to the forensic expert, but taking advantage as he looked away, Cabrera tore that page from the notebook and put it in his pocket, under the astounded eyes of the young agent. It wasn't the first time he'd had to "erase" a little evidence. Cabrera completely ignored the young man's look and spoke to fat Ramírez.

"Did he have a computer?"

"Did he have a computer? Strictly speaking, yes, he owned one, but we can't access it. It requests a password, and there's no way of guessing it."

"Get a technician."

"That's what my colleague Columba here is doing; he's the next generation of policemen—not like you, Macetón, still using a typewriter."

The young man in glasses smiled at Cabrera, who looked away.

"And cassettes? Did you find any?"

"Audio cassettes? No, we didn't."

"No, not audio cassettes but, like, cassettes to save information."

"They're called diskettes," Ramírez said, "or CDs."

The specialist bent over the evidence, pulled a diskette from a plastic bag and in one sweeping motion handed it over, more gracefully than Cabrera would have expected.

"This is what we found. Let Columba help you."

The young man in the glasses inserted the diskette in the computer. On the screen an empty window appeared. "It's blank."

"Let's see it." Cabrera looked at the blank image. Yes, the diskette had nothing on it.

"Or maybe it's not formatted for a PC. I'd have to look it over on my Mac. If you want, I'll examine it later, with another operating system."

Cabrera answered with a growl. "Give me a photocopy of that notebook, butthead," he ordered the kid. "And wear gloves."

"Hey"—it suddenly dawned on Ramírez—"why are *you* working on the journalist? Wasn't this El Chaneque's case?"

Cabrera motioned for him to lower his voice. They went out to the hallway, and Cabrera said, "Chief's orders."

Ramírez heaved a deep sigh. "If I were you, I'd get out of it; this smells very weird."

"Why? Or what? What did you hear?"

"Haven't you ever wondered if the chief is just using you?"

"What are you trying to say?"

At that moment another colleague came in to ask for a report and Ramírez took the opportunity to end the conversation. "I'll hunt down what you asked me for later, OK? Right now I've got a lot of work."

3

Before he got into his car, he noticed that he had a flat tire and his head hurt. He didn't know if the tire caused the headache or if the headache caused the tire, but it was clear that if he stopped to change it he was going to miss the funeral. Besides, he'd end up sopping because at that time of day the sun was broiling.

Fortunately, there was a tire-repair place two blocks from headquarters; Cabrera went to see the manager and gave him the keys. Since there weren't any taxis in sight, he stood waiting for one in the middle of the street, deliberating whether it might not be better to walk—the funeral parlor wasn't very far—but he had other things on his mind, a couple of ideas he couldn't quite make sense of.

Minutes later, he saw a rickety old boat of a taxi approaching, a disco ball dangling from its rearview mirror. He told the driver to take him to the dead man's house, the house fronting on the lagoon, where he thought he'd find more information. Cabrera was a methodical man; now that he'd reviewed the autopsy, he wanted to see the scene of the crime. The driver had on dark glasses and he'd purposefully greased down his hair with Vaseline. He was wearing a green shirt, military style. For quite some while now, Cabrera said to himself, everybody's been wearing military-style clothing.

At first the address—No. 10 Calle Palma—meant nothing to him but as soon as he saw it he remembered. Look at this, who would've thought a crime would take place here? A long time ago, some twenty years ago at least, 10 Calle Palma was one of the few buildings in that neighborhood. At first, the good drainage system was bad and the electricity would go off; on the whole block there were only two or three houses, and the asphalt ended a few hundred yards farther down. Cabrera had always liked driving, to go tooling around, and when he was young he used to park nearby at nightfall, facing the lagoon, sometimes by himself, sometimes with one of his girlfriends from back then. He had a fleeting moment of happiness, remembering the things that happened there with his girls. How long has it been since I was here last? he wondered. The area had become an exclusive neighborhood, full of fancy houses, and because of the new buildings it wasn't as easy to see the lagoon. If I weren't here on an investigation, he thought, there'd be nothing for me to do around here.

The crime scene was an unpretentious house. It stood between two lavish mansions, but that wasn't what most drew his attention. On the façade of the house, bands of police tape blocked access to the front door; beneath it, toward the entry, they'd drawn the outline of the body. Something was off and Cabrera's expert eye caught it immediately.

He asked the cabdriver to wait and got out of the car. Examining the bloodstains confirmed his worst fears; the carelessness with which the journalist's outline had been drawn didn't hold out much hope for a solution to the case. It looked as if he'd been finished off inside and then dragged out here, though the report didn't say that. Holy shit, he thought, what did I get myself into? Do I tell the chief or not? He kicked at a flowerpot, insistently, until he shattered it. The cabdriver asked if he was ready to leave. Cabrera yelled back to him, "Wait for me here!" and walked around behind the house to see if he could get in through the back.

At the far end of the garden, where the lagoon began, sat a huge bulldozer. No trace remained of the yard's trees, and in their place one of those mammoth gas pipelines had been installed. At the very back, an Oil Workers' Union sign warned caution. Do not dig, and topping it all off was a big skull and crossbones.

Three impatient honks of the horn brought him back to earth. "I'm coming, motherfucker!" he yelled to the cabdriver. "What's the hurry, man, if I'm gonna be paying you?" The driver didn't answer him and tuned the radio to *Classics of Tropical Music.*

At the mansion next door, an indigenous maid was scrubbing at the stream of blood that had drained all the way over there. The maid, who was attempting to wash away the stain with soap and a brush, got unnerved when she saw him come up. He wanted to ask if she or her employer had seen anything suspicious, but the maid thought he was going to assault her, and from the way she gathered up her things he guessed she meant to run away. Cabrera showed her his badge, but the girl was so alarmed it was impossible to get a word out of her. So he told her good-bye and got back into the boat.

As the cab pulled away, the maid went back to scrubbing at the young man's blood. Soon there wouldn't be a trace left of him. Cabrera looked back at the crime scene, and the wind blew the police tape.

4

"Where to, boss?"

Cabrera looked at his watch and told the driver to take him to Gulf Funeral Parlor.

"The small branch or the big one?"

"The big one, and step on it; I'm really late."

The driver took the avenue downtown. Around the military hospital, after a brief contest for dominance, the taxi passed a pickup with polarized windows, which was taking up two lanes simultaneously.

"Hey," the driver said to him, "that was the dead man's house, right? That's where the journalist they killed lived."

"That's right."

"Are the rumors true?"

"What rumors?"

"That he was running with the dealers, that he was friends with El Chato Rambal."

He was about to reply, but before they reached the light the pickup cut them off. The cabdriver slammed on the brakes and stopped in the middle of the street. The first thing they saw when the pickup door opened was a leather boot with metallic studs. Cabrera imagined a six-foot-tall rancher, nasty and riled up, but instead the pickup spat out a five-foot-tall kid. Even that height was largely thanks to his boots. He couldn't have been more than twelve, but he already sauntered with drug-runner arrogance. He had on a sleek leather jacket and his gun was in sight.

At first Cabrera didn't understand, because the youngster was talking too fast, but soon he realized that he was angry with the cabdriver for passing him.

"Are you in a hurry, asshole? What's the rush?" He talked straight at the driver. "You won't be in a hurry when I'm done with you, you fucking dickhead." Then he realized the driver wasn't alone. "And you, asshole? Someone talking to you?"

In this city, if you don't know how to keep your mouth shut you don't last long. Luckily, Cabrera was a pacifist and responded with a friendly smile.

"It's no big deal," he said calmly. "I'm on my way to a funeral."

"Well, you can walk," the kid provoked him. "Get out of the car." He lifted his jacket to show his gun.

Of all the cars on the road, the detective said to himself, this kid had to pick me to tangle with, an honest citizen just doing his duty. As Cabrera was getting out of the car, the kid slapped the cabdriver. Shaking his head, Cabrera turned the tables on him. One slap knocked the kid's face to the side.

"Hey, asshole! Fuck off!"

"You fuck off. Act right or I'll make you."

When Cabrera saw the kid was about to pull his gun, he twisted the kid's arm with one hand and grabbed the pistol with the other. Then he raised it to look at it closely. It was top of the line and sported in gold plating the initials C. O. Since the kid kept on jumping around and wasn't listening to reason, Cabrera slapped him again.

"I said stuff it, asshole. Do you have a carry permit?"

"No," the kid answered, "but it's not mine. It's my dad's."

"If you don't have the permit on you, I'll have to confiscate this. Tell your dad to pick it up at the police station."

The kid just laughed. "My dad is a friend of the chief."

"Well, when he drops in to say hi to his friend, he can stop by my desk and pick up the gun. Now get out of here, you fucking punk. If you keep messing with me I'll tell your father on you."

The kid was red in the face, he was so angry, but he faked politeness. "Yes, sir. And who might you be?"

"Agent Ramón Cabrera, at your service." As soon as he said it, he knew he'd said too much.

"I'll remember that."

"And now, get a move on." He tucked the gun into his pants.

The kid stepped on the accelerator, his tires squealing, and pulled in to the curb a couple hundred feet farther down.

"Oh, God," said the driver, "he's waiting for us."

"Do you know him?"

"I've seen him coming out of the clubs. I think he's El Cochiloco's son."

Cabrera thought it over for a moment and finally said, "Could be."

He tried to persuade the cabdriver to follow the kid, but the driver was entirely freaked out. "Give me a break, sir. Let me just take you to the funeral home. I don't want the kid to get mad; these guys'll shoot you for less than that."

"Well, all right," he agreed, but he didn't like it. It was one thing to avoid violence, but something very different to let the dealers do whatever they wanted.

When they passed the truck, its engine revved five times, but it didn't follow them.

5

Almost everyone gaped at him when they saw him come in: the blue suit coat was far too big for him and the multicolored tropical shirt he wore underneath it was all too visible. The first person he saw was the deceased's father, Rubén Blanco, talking with three respectable elderly gentlemen. The mother and sisters wept on some nearby couches. At the other end of the room, four ranchers stood guard next to the coffin.

Cabrera nodded to the dead man's parents and approached the coffin to pay his respects to the departed but actually to examine things in detail. That's when he recognized him. Damnation, it can't be, he thought, it's the kid with the yogurts, the one who'd been living in San Antonio. What the fuck happened to him?

The cut on the neck was covered with a scarf but what he saw was enough to raise his suspicions. This wasn't a regular Colombian necktie: either the attacker's hand was shaky or the killer was no expert, otherwise there was no explaining the erratic trajectory of the cut. He then took a look at the body, and confirmed that he couldn't be more than twenty-five. Poor boy, he thought. What could he have possibly done to be taken out so young? According to Chávez's report, El Chincualillo was breaking in to rob the house when the journalist surprised him. No, he thought, it doesn't fit. Why would a member of the Paracuán cartel break in to steal? As if they needed the money! With what they earn in a day they can live for months without working.

"Sons of bitches," a mourner behind him murmured. "He was a defenseless kid."

He felt as if he were the one they were complaining to; their eyes were on him, and he thought, As if I had anything to do with this.

As soon as he could, Cabrera gave his condolences to the victim's father and, on Chief Taboada's behalf, asked if they could talk privately.

"In a minute," the man answered, and shook his head disparagingly.

Cabrera didn't like being treated like this, but he told himself that Don Rubén was going through a difficult time and you had to be understanding; so he stepped outside and waited for him at the end of the hallway. There was a vending machine with instant coffee, but it was out of order, and his longing for a coffee made the wait seem many times longer. Since he had nothing else to do he took out the confiscated weapon and inspected the initials for a second time: C. O. *Damn,* he thought. If the gun belonged to Cochiloco, he had problems.

He was still considering the gun when in walked one of the most attractive women he'd ever seen in his life. She was an impressive blonde, her head full of fierce curls. She wore a black dress, and even the most discreet of the men there followed her with their eyes. She was the woman who'd been living in his wallet since he picked up her picture at the bus station: the journalist's girlfriend. Before Cabrera could react, the woman walked by him and at the sight of the gun opened two delicious lips. Troubled, Cabrera cursed himself for his slipup and put the gun away. The woman walked on by, pretending not to have noticed a thing, and went into the viewing room. She left behind a flowery scent that made Agent Cabrera tremble. *Sweet Jesus!* a voice inside him said.

Five minutes later, Mr. Blanco still hadn't come out in search of him. It's only natural, he told himself. In cases like these people take their anger out on the police; if we did our job right, these things wouldn't be happening. At eleven-fifteen, he thought he'd waited long enough and went downstairs to the lunch counter, to see if he could find some real coffee.

There was a brew from Veracruz that seemed tolerable. The lady at the counter was handing him a steaming little cup when he felt his cell phone vibrating: it was his boss's secretary.

"Cabrera? Are you at the funeral? I have one of the mourners on the other line. She says there's a suspect in the area."

"Tell her I'll be right there. I'm down the hall."

He left the coffee on the counter without even tasting it.

"She says he's right there! He's walking into the room."

"Ask her to describe him."

"Sky-blue Hawaiian shirt and sunglasses."

"Gimme a break, Sandra, tell her the suspect is me."

He watched the blonde woman nodding her head, and acknowledged her with a wink. The young woman blushed. In different circumstances, Cabrera would've been irritated, but not that day, even less with a woman like her. People get nervous in situations like this; it's natural, he told himself. Later, when things calmed down, he thought about returning the picture to her, but his shyness got the better of him.

Seeing him looking in again, the dead man's father stepped out to give him a piece of his mind. "If Chief Taboada sent you, you've got no business here."

Cabrera explained that he was just following orders and expressed his sincerest condolences. Don Rubén looked Cabrera right in the eye for a moment—just for a moment—and shook his head, but less intensely.

"How many times do I have to make a statement? I already told Agent Chávez everything I know."

This took him by surprise. He hadn't been aware that Chávez had interviewed the man. "When was that?"

"Last night."

That smelled all wrong to him, because not a sentence of Don Rubén's had appeared in the report.

"And another thing: I'm not at all convinced that my son's murderer is the person they arrested. I've got friends in the state government, and we're going to open a new investigation."

"That's what I'm doing right now," Cabrera explained. "They put me on the case."

"Well, we'll see how well you gentlemen do your job," said Mr. Blanco, and he went back to his family.

Over the next half hour, old business associates and family acquaintances, classmates of the deceased, and friends of his sisters paraded through. Cabrera was surprised to see Ramírez's assistant.

"And what are you doing here?"

"I was a friend of Bernardo's. I studied with him in high school."

Cabrera had forgotten his name. "Ricardo?"

"Rodrigo, Rodrigo Columba."

They sat down at the end of the hall, where nobody came up to bother them. Cabrera asked him how well he had known Bernardo Blanco, what kind of reporting he'd done. The crime beat, the young man said. Cabrera thought it strange that Bernardo would have been interested in that, he looked so mild-mannered, but Columba said yes, it had always interested him.

The deceased had prided himself on reading crime reports with the same thoroughgoingness with which others read the Bible or *Don Quixote*.

"Was he bad at his work?"

The young man shook his head. "No, they even gave him a prize."

When he was living in the United States, Bernardo bought himself a motorcycle and a shortwave radio to listen in on the San Antonio police communications. Little by little he deciphered the local slang and memorized the codes they used in the city to designate each crime. A number of times he reached the crime scene before the patrol cars. He got to witness the chasing down of a drug dealer, the beginning of a shoot-out in a bank, and the day he decided to quit, it was he who had gazed into the eyes of a man with a gunshot wound as he died in a shopping mall. Bernardo watched the man die, he complained to the paramedics about their late arrival, and after he gave his statement he had no memory of anything he did, from that moment on to the end of the day. What's impressive is that after giving his evidence he went back to work, wrote a very detailed and succinct article, and said some incoherent sentences to his editor. When he finally snapped out of it, he found himself standing on an avenue that led downtown, in the moments when the sun was beginning to set and the windowpanes and asphalt were reflecting an orangey brilliance. Rodrigo Columba told him this, then interrupted himself.

"Look who's coming; it's Father Fritz Tschanz."

Since he wore his cassock they supposed he was going to say mass. The young man asked what kind of relationship Father Fritz had with the police, why he was always seen coming and going at police headquarters. Cabrera explained that the priest taught at the Jesuit school, and in the afternoons, or at need, offered his services to the community: he gave psychological counseling to the policemen, confessed them, and, when necessary, reprimanded them. When they were about to arrest a member of the Paracuán cartel and worried about the possibility of gunfire, the agents were in the habit of inviting Father Fritz to serve as mediator. Before the shooting started, the priest would talk to both sides and try to persuade the guilty party to turn himself in. He'd prevented a lot of bloodbaths that way.

"It looks like they want you," the young man said, and he was right.

Once he'd said hello to the people in attendance, Father Fritz had recognized Cabrera and gestured him over. The last time they'd met up, the padre had devoted his time to criticizing the department Cabrera worked in, and they didn't part on good terms. Cabrera's resentment was tattooed on his forehead, but that's normal; nobody likes to have his work criticized, especially if he tries to be good at his job. As soon as he could, Father Fritz stepped away from the crowd and took him by the arm.

"Are you in charge?"

Cabrera nodded yes.

"That seems like a great idea to me. Bernardo left some things in my office. Stop by for them, they'll interest you."

Cabrera was about to ask, What things? but a young woman came and interrupted them, and despite efforts to shoo her away, she insisted on making her confession with the priest. A woman walked up behind her, followed by another, and yet another, until a surge of unwelcome visitors had separated them completely. At that moment the first of the odd things that followed the journalist's death took place.

The crowd parted and in walked the Lord Bishop. Cabrera, who remained trapped between the wall and the crowd, managed

to see the prelate approach the Blanco family, give them his condolences, and start as he met up with Father Fritz. With the firm-
ness for which he was notorious, the bishop dragged the Jesuit
toward the coffin, and they bent forward as if to pray, but Cabrera
had the impression that the bishop was giving Father Fritz an order.
Fritz pursed his lips until they whitened but made no attempt to
reply. He made a show of praying with the prelate, blessed the
dead man's corpse, and bent over the coffin in tandem with his
superior. When the rite ended, the bishop took his leave of the
relatives, showered a last sprinkling of holy water upon the at-
tendees, and left as quickly as he had arrived. Fritz stayed behind, head bowed, and set himself up in a corner, ready to hear
confessions.

The rest of the morning was extremely difficult, especially for
Cabrera, who couldn't stand funerals. He listened to every kind
of idiotic comment, along the lines of "He got what was coming
to him, that's the risk of the profession," "Who told him to come
work here in the port when he had a job in San Antonio?" and "If
only he'd worked in his father's business." There came a moment
when he found the comments intolerable, and he went out to look
for a cup of coffee.

In a law-enforcement setting, the first impression is what
counts, and Cabrera was no exception in believing this. As soon
as he saw Agent Chávez walk in, he knew his colleague was worried about something, for he looked on edge and irritable. Like
Cabrera, Rufino Chávez, aka "El Chaneque" was a survivor from
the seventies. You had only to look at his wide tie, his salt-and-
pepper sideburns, and his gangsterish mustache. Despite his fifty
years, he kept in shape, like those featherweight boxers who stay
in training their whole lives. One of the new recruits had accompanied him, in point of fact the one in the dark glasses from before:

pistol in his waistband, glad of being on an official mission, unaware of what kind of prick he was keeping company with. Chávez customarily took on the new guys as apprentices—and too bad for them, thought Cabrera, because, honestly, what could they possibly learn from El Chaneque?

Chávez went up to Cabrera like someone getting ready to drive off a dog.

"Did Taboada send you?"

"Yep."

"Tell him I'm taking charge, and you make tracks. You've got nothing to do around here."

Cabrera counted to ten and made an effort to answer like the pacifist he was. "If you don't like it, complain to the boss. Got it?"

There was an audible *click,* and Cabrera found that Chávez was holding a switchblade against his paunch. The harder he tried to avoid it, the deeper it impinged on his belly. Cabrera felt himself turning pale. This is it . . . this is it . . . When Chávez decided it had been enough, he put the blade away and walked off. Cabrera breathed a sigh of relief.

In the hall, he gave his full attention to recovering, but then he saw that Father Fritz was headed for the exit and he approached him. The priest's head was bowed, and he displayed not a trace of his customary optimism. Cabrera called him by name twice but had to tap him on the shoulder to get him to respond.

"Oh, right, the things." He sounded depressed. "It's not important in the least. I can throw them in the trash myself."

"Certainly not," Cabrera insisted. "Tell me when I can come by for them."

Fritz regarded him for a moment. "Today at five, in my office."

"The same one as before?"

33

"The same as ever," he said with a grunt.

It was going to be an awfully difficult talk. Since the last time they'd seen each other, the priest's personality seemed to have worsened.

"Now you'll have to excuse me." He stepped to one side. "They're taking him off to the cemetery."

6

When he found out Cabrera didn't have a car, his young colleague insisted on giving him a ride to the cemetery. Cabrera suggested that they pass the funeral procession.

They arrived long before the cortege and sat down to wait beside a wall. Immediately they began to sweat. The few palm trees around provided no shade, and it was hard to see into the distance with the sun rebounding off the whitewashed tombs. Cabrera's shirt was sopping, and sweat trickled down his back.

The first to arrive was a fat fellow of about fifty, who wore suspenders. He asked if they were waiting for Bernardo Blanco, and the young colleague said yes. Before he sat down with them, the man looked the detective over.

"You're Ramón Cabrera, right? The one who solved the fraud at Gulf Insurance?"

Cabrera tried to avoid it, but the fat man sat down facing them. "I haven't heard anything about you in the news since then. It's been quite a while since you were at the press conferences."

"The best policeman is an invisible one," he growled.

The fat man handed them his business card. "Johnny Guerrero, crime reporter for *El Mercurio*." He asked if they knew anything about the case.

Cabrera didn't say boo, but countered with, "Why don't you tell us what the rumors are. You must be better informed than I am."

"I haven't got anything for a fact," Johnny explained. "I think it was the Colombians. They're squeezing out the local dealers. First they did business with them and learned their routes and contacts into the United States, and now they're eliminating them, only instead of marijuana, they're thinking of transporting cocaine. The deceased knew all that, I hear, and maybe he was going to be writing on the subject. What's your opinion?"

Cabrera was intent on wiping away the sweat that trickled into his eyes. As much as he tried, the journalist couldn't get the detective to put forward a different motive for the crime. Cabrera lost interest in the conversation and would have kept answering in monosyllables, when all at once the reporter said something that got his attention.

"Do you know what Bernardo Blanco was writing about before he died?" Cabrera asked, and he scrutinized Guerrero closely.

"I haven't a clue," the reporter confessed. "That's the question, isn't it?" he said in English. "That's the key to the crime."

Seeing the procession approaching, the journalist got up.

"Uh-oh, here comes Father Fritz. That priest is crazy, and he can't stand the sight of me." And Guerrero walked off in the opposite direction. Cabrera noticed he limped on his left side.

"Hey," he asked Columba, "do you know who the blonde was who came in at the end?"

"The blonde? Cristina González, Bernardo's ex-girlfriend."

By his account, Cristina and the journalist met in San Antonio, when the two were studying there, and were together all through college. Then Bernardo decided to return to his hometown and broke off the relationship. "Why would he do that?"

"I have no idea."

How strange, he thought. If I were in his shoes, I would never have left a good job in San Antonio to come back to this port town. Or left a woman like that.

"So what have you heard?" Cabrera asked his young colleague. "Was it the dealers who killed him?"

"I don't think so." He shook his head. "Didn't you hear about the Chato Rambal business?"

"What was that?"

"El Chato, of the port cartel. Bernardo interviewed him a year ago, because he was writing a piece about drug trafficking here."

According to Columba, El Chato wasn't at all upset by Bernardo's article, since it was critical but objective, and from then on Bernardo had become the cartel's protégé.

"Once, he was about to be mugged in the market—you know how dangerous it is in Colonia Coralillo—and Bernardo told me the muggers suddenly stopped, their eyes bugging out, and slunk off, all apologetic. When Bernardo turned, a cowboy with a pistol tipped his palm-straw hat and walked away without a word. With protection like that, nobody would get up the nerve to do him any damage. I don't think it was the dealers."

"Who knows, don't jump to conclusions. Maybe he wrote another article, attacking El Chato."

"That's impossible."

"How do you know?"

"Because Bernardo stopped writing for the paper. Over six months ago."

It seemed to him that at the grave site, a small cloud took shape in that section of the cemetery and rose elegantly into the sky.

"And do you know why he quit?"

"I couldn't tell you."

"If he wasn't working for the paper anymore, what was he doing at the port? How was he making a living?"

"I don't know . . . I suppose he had savings. . . . Bernardo was a hermit: just like that he'd disappear for weeks on end and hole up to write. I hadn't seen him for over six months when I found out he'd died."

"And you don't know what he was writing?"

"No idea."

"Did he know anybody with the initials C.O.?"

Columba shrugged and, as Cabrera said nothing, stood up. There was a stir among the funeral party.

As they were lowering the journalist's body, a tiny nun who looked to be a hundred years old shouldered her way through the crowd to the center. She tuned an ancient guitar and, as the coffin descended into the grave, began to sing, before anybody could stop her, a Christian version of "Blowing in the Wind," in an adaptation so free that the only thing left of Bob Dylan's song was the original melody. In place of Dylan's lyrics the sister sang a song of protest, religiously inspired. Something on the order of "Know ye He will come / Know He will be here / Meting out His bread to the poor." Her voice was no good, but she did sing loudly, and as she repeated the chorus some of the mourners wept, especially the dead man's relations. Cabrera was a roughneck, but even he felt a lump in his throat: burials depressed him. To change the subject, he said to Rodrigo Columba, "If the deceased were here, he'd request a different song."

"Don't be so sure," the young man answered. "Bernardo loved Bob Dylan. He loved anything that had to do with the sixties and seventies; he was obsessed with all that."

None of this jibes, thought Cabrera: Bernardo Blanco had a job and a girlfriend in Texas, a promising stable future, and suddenly he decides to leave it all to come here, write tabloid journalism, risk his life. Cabrera would've liked to know what the reporter was really up to, though most likely he'd never find out. As Bob Dylan's song echoed through the cemetery, the cloud above broke up into ever smaller pieces, until it dissipated completely.

"Time to get back to work," he growled.

7

Columba dropped him off at the tire-repair shop, where the manager was waiting for him.

"I had to put a new tire on."

"Why, isn't the other any good?"

"No way, not even with Viagra. Look here, officer." He showed him what was left of the tire. "How can I fix that? It's impossible. Who did you get in a fight with?"

The tire had been cut. Slashed, actually.

"That isn't a tire," the workman said, "it's a warning."

Cabrera's stomach growled again.

He went looking for Ramírez twice, but the forensics expert had an assignment at the docks and hadn't come back. Meanwhile, the kid who'd had the pistol started calling; Cabrera hung up on him a couple of times, thinking Go change your diapers, fucking snot nose. If you want your piece, let your daddy come get it.

At 3:30 he decided to go have lunch at Flamingos, well aware that he had an important date at five. He rummaged through all his desk drawers until he found a very battered book and went out to the parking lot. After he'd made sure the car didn't have another flat tire—the last thing he needed—he headed to the restaurant: all the troublemakers from the office were there. He caught sight of Ramírez eating in a corner and went to sit down at his table.

"OK, Fatso, out with it! What were you going to tell me?"

In front of Ramírez were two orders of enchiladas *suizas* and another of *cecina*-style dried beef, waiting its turn. The expert swallowed a mouthful and wiped his lips with his napkin.

"Don't get into that, butthead, it's a minefield." Ramírez spoke in a low voice.

"I'm not in it for pleasure, dude; the chief gave me the assignment."

"It's really weird, really weird. If I were you, I'd drop it. You're getting in way too deep. I wouldn't, and"—he took a deep breath, wiping sweat from his forehead—"nobody else would dare take on a case that had been El Chaneque's."

Cabrera noticed two of the new guys sitting a few tables away, with Agent Chávez, nodding in agreement at everything he said. What a pity, thought Cabrera. These kids just got here, they've got nothing to regret, but with Chávez as their role model they soon will have. El Chaneque had been assigned to this post by Durazo, the worst specimen ever spawned by the national police. That's why he was still here, showing these kids the ropes.

"What're you going to do?" Ramírez asked.

Cabrera didn't answer. A kid in filthy clothes had sneaked into the restaurant and was handing out flyers at all the tables. Soon he handed one to them. What if today was the last day of your life? Come enjoy it at El Cherokee Music Disco! This was a club that had once belonged to Freaky Villarreal, which they'd turned into a table-dance bar. A customer stood up to go, leaving a copy of *El Mercurio* on the counter, and Cabrera grabbed it. Johnny Guerrero's column was on page three. Fuck: the bugger worked fast. After mentioning the "deplorable" death of Bernardo Blanco, "the promising young journalist back from San Antonio ," he observed that, according to some rumors, Bernardo had disturbed "prominent residents of the area," and investigators in charge were speculating about the possibility that "the lately deceased" had perhaps died for attempting blackmail. He went on to say that a respected officer of the secret service was carrying out a parallel investigation—Oh, shit, I'm that officer! This is totally fucked, he thought. He asked for the menu. Nothing looked good to him, and he burned his mouth on his coffee.

At a quarter to four he recalled he had an appointment and went out to his car. He made sure all four tires were in good shape, then took the main avenue down to the Paracuán Cultural Institute, the Jesuits' school, and parked in front.

He knew for certain that school was in session because he had studied there. Everybody had studied there, even Bernardo Blanco! For years the Jesuit brothers' school was the main educational institution in Paracuán. As was to be expected of such an institution, the majority of the students were scholarship kids. Bernardo'd had a full scholarship; Cabrera had had only half, because he never had the grades to get the other half. Aside from having been expelled during his freshman year, he had nothing but good memories of his time there: the field trips, the spiritual retreats, the arguments about social injustice, the insistence on getting better grades, and the steely discipline that strengthened moral fiber.

He knew very well this wasn't going to be an easy chat. Fritz had studied in Rome: theology and law. He'd lived in Nicaragua and been transferred out, owing to his sympathies with the liberation theologists, but all the moving around never managed to lessen the priest's activity. Ever since Cabrera could remember, the padre had offered psychological orientation to the local policemen and organized social services in the local prison. But mediating between police and criminals is no easy task, so—to avoid endangering the rest of the Jesuits—the provincial superior had decided that Fritz should move into the bishop's residence, a secure bulding, with two guards on duty. Cabrera knew for certain that Fritz could be found at the school in the afternoons, because he taught his high-school classes then. He knew all this for certain, because Fritz had told him.

8

Testimony of Father FritzTschanz, Jesuit Priest

I saw Macetón again the day of the funeral, in among the throngs of people, and he came by my office that afternoon. He arrived too early. "I said five o'clock."

"I ended up being early. I hope you don't mind."

Of course I minded, but I couldn't tell him that. At my age, seventy-five, I have to watch my back. Since I was caught in flagante, I remember I went on the defensive, arranging the various little objects on my desk: pencils, cards, pens, as if I were building a wall between the two of us. But Macetón got the jump on me with a surprise gambit. He took out a copy of *The Spiritual Exercises* and placed it in front of me.

"I finally read it. Let's see if we can talk now."

He was referring to a conversation we had begun years before, the last time we argued. Ramón "Macetón" Cabrera was never one of my best students. This is the opinion of a Jesuit who taught six leftist congressmen, at least one Sandinista battalion, one great reporter, and the best political columnist this country has produced. Compared with them (and compared with practically anyone), Macetón Cabrera's merits paled. Once I scolded him about his reading matter. Ramón was with a girl at recess, chatting about a detective novel. I recognized the cover and walked over. As soon as I heard him say, "Be very careful with this book," I stepped up.

"I don't know why you waste your time reading things like that," I said.

He blushed, but the girl was on the verge of fainting, because I've always been known for being a crab, and for talking to students outside class only to report them. To cut their agony short, I showed him my battered copy of *The Spiritual Exercises.*

"Now, *this* is a truly dangerous book. On every page the reader runs the risk of feeling recognized and humbled. When you've finished reading it, we'll talk again."

Later I found out, putting two and two together, that the book jacket actually hid an erotic novel, which Macetón was in the process of lending to the girl. I considered calling him on the carpet, but I didn't see him again one-on-one until the end of the school year, the day we gave him his diploma. Every time I ran into him in the library, he pointedly ignored me; in class, he sat all the way in the back and pretended to be invisible. That went on over thirty years ago and now Macetón had come to remind me of it.

Unfortunately for him, the day before I had taken up drinking again. The reason I'd asked him to come to my office at school and not to the bishop's residence was that I needed a good stiff drink, and the day before I had confiscated a bottle of vodka from one of my students. When Cabrera arrived, I was about to pour myself the first drink of the afternoon, but I couldn't do it in front of him. What's more, the bottle was behind him, in the bookcase where I keep my files. I kept glancing over there, worried that Ramón might discover one of my secrets. That afternoon's conversation was a battle between someone who always knew everything and someone who never understood anything. That's why, when he pulled out our holy patron's book, it took me a while to react.

"Ah, yes . . . St. Ignatius's *Exercises*. . . . And did they answer?"

"With two nightmares."

"What?"

"As of today, it's given me two nightmares. You said it was a dangerous book."

He had skimmed through it over the last few weeks. I replied with a growl. My students permit me such outbursts, which they accept as an eccentricity. And just like that, I succeeded in going on the offensive.

"And so, then, Cabrera? What can I do for you?"

"I've come to pick up the deceased's things."

Your mother! (as my students say). I'd forgotten our conversation at the funeral. You see, Fritz?—I do sometimes talk to myself—this is all drinking is good for! You went astray again, *Saüfer!* But I tried to conceal the dilemma. I went over to the second bookshelf, the one that is forever near collapsing under the weight of my books and magazines, and sought to pick up something at random, but my unconscious betrayed me. The book I took out was the *Treatise on Criminology,* by Dr. Quiroz Cuarón. When I saw what it was, I almost fell over. I gulped, worried sick, but Ramón was admiring the large portrait of Freud that took up the entire left wall and didn't notice my hesitation. Then I took up the next book over: *Black Past,* by Rubem Fonseca. The devil you say—I thought, do all books lead to the dead man? In a state of nerves, I pulled out the three books beside them: *In Cold Blood,* by Truman Capote; *The Judge and His Hangman,* by Friedrich Dürrenmatt; and *Dr. Jekyll and Mr. Hyde.* . . . When I experience coincidences like these, in which the harmony of all things is revealed, I fall to trembling before the divine plan, and Ramón noticed.

"Father? Are you feeling all right?"

Nothing irritates me more than pity, especially when it's directed at me. So I responded thoughtlessly. "It's nothing, nothing. Here you go."

Macetón lowered his gaze, and I began wondering how this man could possibly be in charge of investigating Bernardo Blanco's death. Young Bernardo had had a brilliant mind, astute and inquisitive; his reporting work was a wonder, particularly his crime pieces, and Macetón. . . . You could expect nothing from Macetón, I thought; he was a vulgar imitation. But I was wrong.

"Is this all?"

"What do you mean?"

We'd gone back to square one. He was once again the hound and I the fox.

"My impression a while ago was that you were going to give me something else."

"Like what?"

"I don't know," he replied. "Something very important."

"These books are important; they were very important to Bernardo," I insisted. How I needed a shot of vodka!

"But you gave me to understand it was urgent."

"Well, of course." I gestured at the bookshelves. "I never have enough room in this place! Every student who comes in forgets a book in this office! I am not a public library!"

He frowned and I understood that since I'd seen him last he had sharpened his intuitive capacity (quite dilute, but there it was). Cabrera looked at me the way Bernardo used to look when he knew people were lying to him. For a moment, I thought he was about to come straight out and interrogate me probingly, just as the dead boy once had, but his reaction was crueler. He prolonged the torture, speaking of trivia, until he was set to attack.

"It was a pleasure to come to the school. I see they built more classrooms."

"Yes," I answered. "Every day more illiterate people are being born. How long has it been since you were here last?"

"Oof . . . like twenty years."

"Ah, I see." And before Ramón could barrage me with further questions, I tried cornering him. "When did they give you the case?"

"This morning."

"They bumped El Chaneque?"

"Yep," he said. "By the way, Father, last week I saw you talking with the very man. What did you want with him?"

"It's part of my job, as you know."

"You don't work with the prisoners anymore?"

"I do both. The Lord Bishop ordered me to close the loop and mediate between the two camps. It's the only way to stop the violence."

His questions put me on guard. At this moment, my main concern was finding out how much he knew. The way he frowned, it seemed he had some idea of what Bernardo Blanco had been working on. We both passed an awkward moment and fell silent. What must have been going on in Ramón's mind? If he was expecting me to confess, he was very mistaken. But he stayed on, and meanwhile the bottle of vodka, like a seductive woman, enticed me from the bookshelf. You deserve it, *Saüfer,* I told myself, nobody's more to blame than yourself. I put on an angry face, but Ramón made it clear he was just getting comfortable. I wanted him out of my office this minute! Since he had arrived too early, I'd had no time to clean up. My office was full of telling evidence, right there for him to find. To begin with, he noticed the chessboard to one side of my desk, an unfinished game on it.

"Was Bernardo a worthy opponent?" he asked.

"He was incredible," I said, "but he always lost on account of the queen." I immediately regretted having opened my mouth. Fritz, you did it again! You got yourself into a corner now! Ramón shot me a look of amusement, perhaps suspecting what happened. But instead of asking me further malicious questions, as Bernardo would have done, he looked down at the Robert Louis Stevenson book.

"Did you see him often, Father?"

"Not that often," I said and, to change the subject, added, "How's everything down at headquarters?"

"Same as always."

"It's a shame," I replied. Before Ramón could react, I put the chessmen away in their case. Later, I'd get rid of Bernardo's remaining fingerprints. One of the pieces went tumbling and, instead of impounding it, my visitor handed it back to me.

"Here you are, Father."

I favored him with a growl. Lord, forgive them, for they know not what they do! They have eyes and do not see, ears and do not hear. While Bernardo had admirable intelligence and a deep curiosity, Ramón Cabrera was the diametrical opposite. What if suddenly . . . ? I said to myself. What if, instead of keeping silent . . . ? But no, it wasn't possible. I told myself it wouldn't work, but I kept getting my hopes up; one is always getting one's hopes up, since that is what we are taught to do.

"Father, I need your help."

I pretended to clean my glasses. "I'm listening."

He gave a summary of his wanderings and I merely shook my head.

"Awful, simply awful. Terrible."

"Did you hear the rumor about the port cartel?"

"Yes."

"What do you think?"

"With all due respect, it's bullshit. Bernardo had nothing to do with it."

Cabrera didn't flinch. This could go on to infinity, I said to myself, and so looked at the clock and gave him to understand that he ought to be leaving. I had to get him out of there at the first opportunity.

"One last thing, Father. Did you know that Bernardo had given up journalism?"

The Church Fathers, who prohibit lying, never did counsel telling the whole truth, especially if the inquisitors haven't asked the right question. "Yes, I did know."

"And can't you tell me why?"

"Interesting question. No." I was silent for a second. "It's a shame!" I said. "If you knew how to read between the lines, we could talk for hours in great detail. Bernardo was an expert at that. It's an extremely complicated situation, Cabrera. But first tell me something: What did I give you in Logic?"

"A *C*."

"A *C*? That seems too high. I've given only one *A*-plus in all my career as a professor, and that was to Bernardo Blanco. Are you sure it was a *C*? No, it couldn't have been that high; I'll look through my files."

"Father," he insisted. "Tell me what happened to Bernardo."

"Not even I know that," I said.

And I was telling the truth, only he was talking about Bernardo's earthly fate and I was talking about the salvation of his soul. Then he turned and looked at the bookshelf. *Your mother!* I said to myself again, and from the way he looked at me, I knew he had seen the bottle. Surely he must think I still drink the way I did during his time in school. Fritz, I said to myself, you need to calm down; if you go that route you'll ruin everything. Stop worrying about the fucking bottle. What does anyone care about a fucking bottle? It could be a gift from a student or what it is: an object confiscated at the Institute. I thought he would get tired and leave, but he kept examining the bookcase and then he came alive again.

"People told me three things about you, Father."

I began to sweat. "What things?"

"Should I tell you in order or——?"

"However you damn well please. What did they tell you?" "That you counseled Bernardo."

"It could be," I commented.

My hands were shaking, and Ramón noticed. "Forgive me," I said, "but some people are about to come by, and I don't want them to see you here."

That set him on the defensive. "Don't you want to hear the second rumor?"

"Go on, tell me."

"That you don't get along with the bishop."

"That's a lie. And the third?"

"It's that you have a bad relationship with the bishop but a great one with the port cartel."

I remained silent for a second, then burst out laughing. Ramón must have thought I was crazy. When I was done laughing, I had to dry my tears with a handkerchief.

"Anything else?" I asked.

He looked furious, and rightly so. "No," he said. "Now it's your turn. I need you to give me some actual information, or did you make me come here for nothing?"

I leaned forward, and the copy of Dr. *Jekyll and Mr. Hyde* was once again in my line of sight.

"Three things," I said to him, "and that's it, because my visitors are about to arrive. One: Bernardo was writing a book. Two: it was about the history of this city in the seventies. Three: yes, he did receive death threats. And a fourth thing: stay out of this, Macetón. You're a good officer, but you should just walk away. As the Buddhist monks would say, *When you gaze into the abyss, the abyss is gazing into you.*"

He tried to get me to talk further, but there was no way I was going to give him the name of a suspect. I explained that at another time I would have given him the information without hesitation, but that morning I had had a problem.

When I went to Bernardo's burial, I unexpectedly ran into the Lord Bishop. He was surprised to see me there, too.

"What are you doing here?" Once he was near, he smelled the alcohol on my breath. "You're drinking again, aren't you? As soon as the service is over, go straight back to the residence."

"Am I allowed to decline?"

The bishop knelt before the cadaver, making a show of murmuring the *Ora Pro Nobis,* but as he rose from the floor he was really saying, "Enough. Your fourth vow is to express obedience to the pope, and as his representative around here, I forbid you to talk about this with anyone, under penalty of suspension from your duties. Do you understand?"

"Yes, Your Excellency."

Fritz! I said to myself, for thirty years you've known this fellow, and you still forget his fondness for simple solutions! He doesn't listen to reason in public and you, of course, instead of talking to him in private, challenge him in public: impatience is a poor counselor. At such times, the two years we spent together at the pontifical seminary in Rome, my having invited him to spend

Christmas at my parents' house outside Berlin—all this avails us nothing. There are things that friendship can't weather. Fritz, you're an animal; instead of resolving matters in a civilized way, you confronted your superior and got what you deserved. Now your hands are tied and meanwhile Macetón is all over the place, digging into Bernardo's death.

Well. Then I saw it was four thirty and I got to my feet.

"Please forgive me, Ramón, but I have another appointment. Be very careful."

And I opened the door, not giving him time to respond. He looked dissatisfied. Watch out, I said to myself. This guy is going to be back.

At that moment, and unfortunately for everyone, Cabrera ran into Chávez, who was just arriving. Chávez said nothing until we were alone.

"What were you telling Cabrera, Father? Are you going to be counseling him now, too?"

"Calm down. The bishop got on his high horse and forebade my getting mixed up in the matter. It will work itself out without my getting involved . . . for a second time."

Chávez burst out with that hateful laugh I'd heard before. "The chief will look to find a way to thank you."

"And if he hadn't done it?"

"It's late," he said. "I have to go buy some knives."

I didn't want to imagine what for. Coming from Chávez, that could be a threat, but I didn't flinch. When one works with this kind of people, one gets used to their rudeness. "Don't worry about me," I told him, "worry about yourself and the salvation of your soul."

Chávez looked at the bottle with an expression of disdain. What a disaster! I said to myself. Cabrera couldn't have been more troublesome, and now they were surely tailing him. I wondered if there was any way to warn him. Later, Cabrera did things one would never have expected of a person like himself, and there wasn't a way on earth to prevent it.

Fritz, I said to myself, everything has been in vain. You ought to retire. Look at the agents: you've spent years working with them, and they're just the same; it wasn't so easy to raise their consciousness. And since I was feeling worse by the second, I took up the bottle of vodka and went off to the bishop's residence.

That night Sister Gertrudis came and knocked on the door of my room. I didn't answer and went on staring at the ceiling, lying on my bed. Since I didn't answer, she opened the door a crack and said, "We made *chucrut*."

Sauerkraut, I thought, sauerkraut! The sisters cook German food every time they see me overwhelmed. I enjoy this twofold because His Excellency doesn't like *chucrut*. He says, "Cabbage again?" And during supper he spreads the food all over his plate in an attempt to conceal his aversion to German food. At such times, as I serve myself a second or third helping, I tend to ask him, "Are you done with your plate? Shall we serve you a bit more, Your Excellency?" He invariably says, "No, a morsel more would be gluttony." I reply, "It's a shame, the sisters deserve some recognition." And the Lord Bishop, with a queasy expression on his face, picks up his utensils and goes back to playing with his food. But there are days when not even the culinary guerrilla war can succeed in lifting my spirits. And still less on a day like this, with a dead man on my conscience and another ex-student risking his life. All of it my fault, and my guilt materializes darkly, in Sister Gertrudis's habit, still waiting at the door.

"I'm not having dinner."

"No?"

"No."

And the sister leaves. I wish my worries were so obedient. What are you doing, Fritz? I reprimand myself. Don't you find your attitude childish? At your age you can't abuse yourself like this! Put something in your stomach, *mein Gott!* You'll pass out! I say to myself, I'm on a hunger strike. Resist irrational bishops, *und ihre unterdrückenden Maßnahmen!* I told myself this, but I wasn't convincing anyone. In my head was a mob of people allied against me. One of them stood up and rebuked me. Fritz, you sinner, you've got blood on your hands and you must do something. Can't you hear Bernardo's soul crying out for justice? Yes, I've heard it, I tell them, I've heard nothing else these last few hours. Well, then? Well, then, just wait. And there the colloquy ends, since talking to yourself is bad for your mental health.

I asked myself, What are you going to do if Macetón comes back with a search warrant for your desk? He could do that. . . or worse. What makes you so sure that Macetón isn't closing in on the Williamses or old Romero right now, putting his life in danger? That would be *two* dead people on your conscience. El Chaneque's words still tormented me— "I have to go buy some knives"—and I thought about Macetón, risking his neck in vain.

Around eight I heard the Lord Bishop's car pull in. I heard him walking into the kitchen to check the dinner menu and yelling, "What? *Chucrut?*" and then muttering something incomprehensible.

A minute later he knocked twice on my door and I yelled back, "Silence, damn it! I'm praying!"

But he opened the door anyway. As always when he oversteps in reprimanding me, he wanted to tender a veiled apology, but I was too angry.

"What do you want, Your Excellency?"

"You're not coming to dinner?"

"No."

"They made that thing you like . . . the cabbage."

"No. What you said has set me thinking. I have to meditate on my mistakes, and for that one must be alone."

My answer succeeded in making him uncomfortable.

"Fritz, you're not a little boy anymore. Come along and eat that stuff. One of the women from the Church Council brought us a case of that German beer you like so well. If you don't come, I'll drink every bottle all by myself." And he wasn't joking.

"The Lord punishes excess," I said to him.

"Whatever you please." And he closed the door.

For twenty minutes I listened to the noise of the dishes. I thought I heard him opening one, maybe even two of my beloved beers. It would have been the ideal time to make the call, but I hadn't yet come to my decision. When I was at my most anxious, I went to my desk. I took out my copy of *The Exercises* and opened it at random. Christ Jesus never preached divination by the book, but it never fails me. Loyola seemed to advise: "Be ye therefore wise as serpents and harmless as doves." Speed and agility, my holy patron was telling me that if I wanted to overcome this problem I'd have to act without the bishop finding out, and to conceal my role in the case.

I looked over the names in my address book and in less than a minute had selected one. I mentally sketched out a plan and achieved a moment of inner peace, in which part of my mind went in one direction and another part in another. When at last these parts met up again, in some surprise, one asked the other, Fritz, you scoundrel, I'd like to know what's on your mind. Right this very moment, I said, I'm thinking of *chucrut* for dinner.

So I waited until the bishop had got up from the table and gone into his studio. I have to put an end to this, I said to myself. I went out to the hall and picked up the phone. I was startled by a horrible noise, a resonant shriek, and understood he'd used his modem and dialed on to the Internet, as he did every night. I'd have to wait half an hour at least, while His Excellency communicated with his colleagues all over the world, so I returned to my cell to listen to the sounds my stomach was making. As I sat at my desk, I heard the voice of my moral conscience: "It smells like food. Aren't we going to take a break?" Not now, I told it, we have work to do. "That's a shame," it said to me, "the sisters spent all that time preparing cabbage . . . and the German beer, brewed strictly in accordance with the Treaty of Bavaria—" I was about to come up with a smart retort when I heard the bishop hanging up and darted to the phone at the end of the hallway. There, I dialed El Chícharo's work number.

"La Tuerca here." La Tuerca is the hardware store where he works.

"*Carnál?*" Speaking in *Caló* street slang doesn't come easy to me, but Chícharo won't understand you otherwise. "I got a fourteen for you."

He took a while to respond and I deduced that he was dragging the phone to a secure corner.

"What's up, *vato?* Another fourteen?"

"Yes," I said. "This one's more complicated."

"That's what you said about the last one, and look what happened. Did you see his picture in *El Mercurio?*"

I felt insulted. "Can you do it or not?"

"Right now I don't know. It's gonna be tougher, 'cause they're gonna be tailing him." He went quiet, before adding, "I think we're out of those size-nine washers."

"Ah, you can't talk, I see. Will you do it? Answer yes or no."

"I couldn't tell you. I gotta check the invoices."

I should've known. "Is it a matter of twenties? *Du willst das Doppelte, oder?*"

"Wha'?"

"You want double, right?"

It seemed that El Chícharo had covered the receiver with cellophane; it was clear they were keeping an eye on him. And I was sweating. The bishop could pick up the phone any time.

"*Carnál?*" I pushed him.

El Chícharo removed the cellophane or whatever it was from the receiver and finally answered. "It's just we've got an order coming in. Leave me your number and I'll call you."

"Negative," I burst out. "I'm being watched."

"I'm gonna see if I can find your washers. Talk to me in fifteen minutes."

And he hung up. Obviously, I wasn't going to wait fifteen minutes in that hallway, so I counted to a hundred and dialed again. El Chícharo picked up.

"The news is that I found your fuckin' washers. Where do you want 'em delivered?"

"I want you to settle in at the front door of his house."

"And that is?"

I didn't need to look in my address book, I knew it by heart. "It's 32-A Emiliano Contreras Street, next to the Hotel Torreblanca. On second thought, why don't you watch him from the hotel; wouldn't it be more comfortable for you?"

"OK, I'm on my way. You really think I'm gonna go in the hotel? The guy at the door is my brother-in-law."

"And what's the problem with that?"

"He'll be telling my old lady he saw me go into some transient hotel. Don't you know anything about women?"

These local fellows, I thought. Everything would be much easier with a professional from Germany.

"But don't worry, I've got the experience you need. I'll find a way to follow through on the order."

"I hope so."

"Aren't you forgetting something? How will I recognize him?"

"Easy as can be. It's Macetón Cabrera."

"Ah!"

"And we'll see if you do a better job this time."

"Balls. I'm a pro at this stuff."

"You'd better be."

I hung up discreetly and walked to the kitchen. With a little luck, I told myself, they may have left me some *chucrut*.

9

Cabrera spent the rest of the afternoon doing paperwork. He wrote a report on his investigations and left it on the chief's desk. At eight sharp, he said to himself: Another day, another dollar, and went home to relax. He had a date with his wife, and he didn't want to stand her up.

Their relationship had deteriorated in the last few months. Since December, she had been living in one apartment and he in another, but they still slept together most nights. Their last fight was over the remote control. His wife complained they never talked anymore, that he was always quiet, that he only wanted to make love and then watch TV. Cabrera denied this and then made love to her. Afterward, he turned the TV on—he couldn't help it; it was a reflex—but she started screaming, and he ended up sleeping in the living room. He can't remember when that happened, but without a doubt she does; she has a record of all their arguments. Unlike her, Ramón was a pacifist and forgave her whatever she did.

That night he went to his wife's apartment, thinking he was going to keep himself in check. He found her in a suspiciously good mood: I'm glad you're here; I was waiting for you. She sat him down on the sofa in the living room, and his hand almost cramped up when he couldn't find the remote.

Where's the remote? Hidden, she said, it's killing our relationship. Gimme a break—he lifted up the cushions—give me the remote; if you don't give it to me, friggin' Mariana, there's going to be trouble; you know I'm a pacifist, but if you're looking for trouble, you're gonna get some.

I'll give it to you, she promised, but before that I want to give you a massage.

A massage? Why?

A massage, come to bed.

Ah . . . bed; he liked that word. It's a double feature: bed and TV?

You're a macho pig, shut up and come to bed, take off your boots and lie on your back. Whatever you want, just don't tie me up, I can't stand being tied up.

Don't you worry.

She showed him a small bottle of oil that smelled really, really good.

What's this?

Aromatherapy, you'll love it. With just a sniff, El Macetón felt relaxed, and a silly grin lit up his face. He went to the bed and lay down on his back.

Naked, his wife demanded. El Macetón protested. And you? Why don't you take off your clothes? It took a while to convince her, but finally she removed her blouse, her skirt, and then her bra. They were listening to some down-tempo soul music, and the massage began. First chance he got, El Macetón tried to grab her breasts and she slapped his hand: You just want to make love! Treat me like a lady, you miserable pig! She massaged his neck, his arms, and his shoulders and he let her do whatever she wanted; obedience was the shortest way to the remote. But the massage turned out to be really, really nice, and El Macetón ended up getting used to her hands pushing into his flesh and he smiled more and more.

Suddenly, the movement stopped and El Macetón looked at her, intrigued: What's up? She rubbed some oil onto her neck and shoulders. She tilted the bottle a little and a drop fell between her breasts, toward her belly. That's not how a lady should act, El Macetón chided her.

Do you think this is wrong?

I do, but I can manage, we pacifists are very tolerant.

She let a second drop fall in the same place. What's up? The oil's going to run out. Weren't you going to use it on me? Hold on, she said, and let a third drop fall on her right breast; El Macetón watched it trickle down. The drop made its way slowly but didn't slide off her breast.

Don't you need some help? If you want an assistant, I can lend you a hand.

Quiet, she ordered him, or I'll get dressed and leave. Then she let another drop fall on her left breast. She looked him in the eyes, smiling. . . .

A little while later, Cabrera got the nerve to say, That's the best demo I've ever seen, I want a box of that product.

You liked it?

Well, yeah, I want to give it to the social service girls.

You shameless pig, she chided, you macho pig.

In the end, it was a quiet evening. It helped him to do the right thing.

10

In the morning, El Macetón was brushing his teeth when he heard the doorbell. The Bedouin was waiting on the doorstep.

"The chief wants to see you. It's urgent."

He practically dragged him the few blocks that separated them from headquarters.

"What's the rush, *cabrón?*"

But his coworker didn't answer. Like everybody knows, the police offices are located in the historic downtown, in a whitish building, under a giant pecan tree swarming with ravens. In the morning, the noise they make is deafening.

There was the usual hustle and bustle at the front door. The Bedouin asked for the chief, and a new agent, who had someone in cuffs, motioned with his chin and signaled down a hallway: He's back already. Hurry up, man, they're waiting for you. They walked down the corridor. The walls were covered with official announcements, composite sketches, photographs of missing people, messages from one cop to another, ads for cars or apartments for sale, and several maps of the city, neighborhood by neighborhood. Finally, they reached the reception room. Two new guys were on duty. The chief's secretary said hi to Cabrera, ignoring the Bedouin. Obviously bothered by this, the Bedouin made his way between the two guards and reported to the chief.

"Here's Cabrera."

Inside, it was as cold as in a glacier, though the chief didn't seem to mind at all. He was wearing a white guayabera, like the ones in fashion when Echeverría was the president of Mexico in the seventies, and a black leather jacket, extra large. When Cabrera walked in, the chief was on the phone. The Bedouin approached him to whisper something in his ear, and the chief did nothing to welcome them. Cabrera had enough time to examine the office furniture, the official photograph of the president of the republic, the TV with the news on, two pictures of the chief with the current governor (one eating with him, the other hugging him), and, underneath them, three glass display cases packed with standard-issue firearms. There were few personal items in the office and all of them had to do with hunting: a Winchester shotgun, a deer's head, and a wild boar.

While the chief was on the phone, Cabrera took a seat in one of the two chairs in front of his desk. The Bedouin hit the back of the seat twice and whispered, "You better wait for his permission, *cabrón*. Who knows what you did?"

Cabrera replied, "No mames, buey." And he didn't stand up. Even though the thick blinds blocked all the light out of the office, the chief kept on his dark aviator glasses. When he hung up, he looked at the detective and asked him point-blank, "You confiscated a gun that belonged to Mr. Obregón?"

The kid's pistol. . . . He'd forgotten about that.

"Yes, it's in my desk. It's Mr. Obregón's?"

The chief didn't answer.

"Come on, Macetón, who do you think you are?"

"It was a mistake: the friggin' brat. The kid was threatening a civilian with the gun, without identifying himself." If the kid could lie so could he.

Chief Taboada shook his head. "Do me a favor and give it back right away. And one more thing: Why didn't you tell me about this?" He threw a copy of *El Mercurio* at him.

There wasn't much news in the port, and the really important stuff happened in the crime-beat section. That's where the results of all the scheming and rivalries showed up. After every power struggle, the ones who were convicted or murdered ended up on those three pages. The secret history of the port was in there, and if there was somebody who knew how to read it, it was the chief.

Johnny Guerrero's new column was on page three. Damn! Goddamn that Johnny and his stupid gossip. Just like the afternoon before, it wasn't really an article, it was an editorial. The journalist commented once again on Bernardo Blanco's death, writing that the officer in charge of the investigation was following a solid lead to track down the killer.

The chief looked at Cabrera without blinking or moving, using one of the oldest tricks of the police force: Whenever you want a suspect to talk, stay quiet. A couple of minutes of silence from a cop applies more pressure than a couple of good questions. Generally, people feel uncomfortable and start talking on their own, just like Cabrera did.

"The journalist is making up—"

The chief interrupted his explanation. "What have you found out?"

Cabrera explained there wasn't much to go on. Before his death, Bernardo Blanco met with Padre Fritz Tshanz.

"What did they talk about?"

"I don't know yet. Padre Fritz was very evasive. You know how he is."

"What about the diskette?"

"There was nothing on it."

"Are you sure?"

"I'm sure, Chief."

Taboada exhaled, grunted, and stared at him. He didn't like his answer. "I think your time has come, Officer. Hand over the case to the new guys. Talk to Camarena and fill him in on your investigation."

He had never been humiliated like this before. The worst thing, the absolute worst thing, that can happen to an agent is to be replaced when he's on the verge of solving a case. And to be replaced by Camarena! It wasn't fair!

"I want three days off," he said.

The chief looked at him angrily. "Who do you think you are?"

"Nobody. It's just that I haven't had a day off in two months, and I need a break."

It was true: for the last two months, he had practically been living at police headquarters. His failing marriage was the proof.

"OK, I'll give them to you, but watch out." The chief made himself clear. "You have nothing to do with this case."

"Thanks, Chief."

The Bedouin looked at him disdainfully, and on his way out he bumped him with his shoulder.

He went to eat at his wife's apartment, and miraculously he found her organizing his papers from work. To be cautious, he didn't tell her about his days off; she would have insisted on using them to go visit her sister, and Cabrera didn't feel like being a chauffeur. He tried to take her clothes off, but she slapped his hand. "Respect my space; I'm working."

Cabrera looked for the remote control, and his hand almost cramped up again when he couldn't find it. It was still hidden. He shouted, asking for it, and his wife got offended. He threw himself on the couch and stared out the window. After fifteen minutes of silence, his wife asked, "What are you thinking about, Ramón?"

"A lot of stuff. About Padre Fritz Tschanz, about the dead journalist, about Xilitla, and about a suspect whose name is Vicente Rangel."

His wife, who was still organizing the papers, dropped a stack of them. Cabrera noticed it and walked away to the kitchen. He was in an awful mood.

He fixed himself a grilled fish with lime juice and sliced onion— bachelor food, since his wife didn't like onions. She asked him if he was OK, and he told her about his argument with Chávez and his doubts about the Paracuán cartel's responsibility. His food was almost ready when his wife suggested he should let the new guys handle the case, and he grabbed the pan and threw it against the wall. They yelled at each other and he ran out, slamming the door behind him.

He spent the next half hour driving around aimlessly in his car. His rage ended up leading him to the beach, where he ended up whenever he needed to think. He stopped at El Venado's stand and bought two Tecates and six beef tacos.

There were no cars on the beachfront highway, and he parked in the dunes. The sea was rough and choppy, and the sand was stained with oil: maybe there was an accident at the refinery or another leak on the platforms. He ate the tacos with salsa, drank the Tecates, and smoked a cigarette: the perfect recipe for a bad case of gastritis. He had to go pee twice. If things kept up like this, he'd have to see a doctor.

He would've paid to find out what had gotten into the chief. Why'd he ask him to investigate the murder and then change his mind? But even more, he was wondering what was happening between him and his wife. Were things between them coming to an end? Was he so blind he couldn't see it? It was no secret that of the two of them he had more to lose. His wife was still beautiful, she had admirers; he felt old and clumsy, with nothing going for him. Except for Rosa Isela, he had to work hard to make the social service girls look at him twice. There were two seagulls next to his car, and he asked them if his wife was about to leave him. As if to answer his question, the more capricious of the two seagulls flew away, leaving the other one alone next to the car. *Ay, cabrón.* Never try to tell the future with seagulls.

In the last few weeks they had fought more than the whole time they had known each other. He asked himself if they had a future together, if they worked or not. Perhaps he was the only one really interested in the relationship. He said to himself, Maybe it's finished, and felt a knot in his throat. Bueno, if it's over, it's over; there's nothing I can do about it. He had to be mature, he said to himself, and accept these things.

After analyzing everything he had heard and seen that day, he decided that she might have a lover. It was definitely a possibility. He was on the street all day, he only ate with her every now and then, sometimes he got home so exhausted he only wanted to watch TV. He imagined her making love with someone else and felt queasy in the stomach, that anxiety that comes when really important things come to an end.

He looked at the rough water. The sea was as black as the oil-stained sand. He was so focused it took him a minute to respond to a kid carrying a foldable table who approached to offer him coconut candies.

"*Condesa? Cocada?*"

How was it possible for a candy seller to appear next to his car in the most deserted area of the beach? He said no thank you, started his car, and drove back to the city.

11

He pulled up to the city archives as the employees were getting back from lunch. Now that he had three days off, he would do things a little more slowly. When he asked for newspapers from twenty years ago, the clerk didn't know what to answer.

"I'm new here. Let me see where they are."

Cabrera wondered what case from the seventies had caught Bernardo Blanco's attention. Was it corruption in the Oil Workers' Union? The activities of the September 23rd Terrorist League? The founding of the Cartel del Puerto? Any of those three subjects would mean some thorny territory.

The girl came back with three dusty tomes tied together with a rope, and he could see the job was going to be grueling and long. Literally, he was going to dust off a case that others already considered buried and forgotten.

He examined the first volume: January through February 1970. The majority of the articles seemed to repeat themselves in the same stilted, overwrought language of low-budget provincial newspapers: SEASONED SMUGGLER; OBSTINATE THIEF; PICKPOCKET ARRESTED; IMPRISONED FOR STEALING LIVESTOCK—invariably followed by a picture of a guy looking sad and, next to him, a thoroughly outraged ox—and, again, SKILLED SMUGGLER; OBSTINATE THIEF; PICKPOCKET ARRESTED; IMPRISONED FOR STEALING LIVESTOCK and then the picture of another sad guy, another cow.

Since Cabrera didn't have an exact date for the issue Bernardo was interested in, he began by examining the papers from 1970 and then the following year, advancing year by year. An hour later he thought he'd found something. By six that afternoon he had no doubt: eight months of newspapers confirmed his fears. *Puta madre,* he thought, what have I gotten myself into? At times, he felt like reality actually consisted of several layers of lies, one piled on top of another.

Back then there were two newspapers that copied each other's designs, logos, and corporate colors. The leading one in sales was *La Noticia,* owned by General García; it was a weak newspaper, and obedient, always backing the dominant Institutional Revolutuionary Party and critical of its enemies. Its competition was *El Mercurio:* an independent paper, faithful to the official version of events and, more than anything else, utterly sensationalist. It was easy to confuse the two, because both were tabloid size.

Judging by the pictures, the city went through one of its most prosperous periods in the seventies. New oil reserves were being discovered, the government promoted private investing, and there was a boom in commerce. During that time of growth, the dollar exchange rate was at twelve pesos and fifty centavos, and because of the proximity of the United States, people would go to "the other side" as if they were picking something up at the supermarket.

Kraft cheese was everywhere. Brach's candies. Levi's jeans. Nike tennis shoes. Gringo aspirins. New neighborhoods were built in front of the lagoon. Hotels and restaurants were opened. A new hospital was built with the most modern equipment for the Oil Workers' Union.

One night Mr. Jesús Heredia killed a tiger weighing more than four hundred pounds at his ranch. His horse reared when it saw two eyes stalking it in the bushes. Heredia barely had time to turn his flashlight on and shoot at the shape. They needed two donkeys to hang the cadaver from a tree and take the picture published in the papers.

The article next to that one reported on a young mechanic who tried to abuse two teenage girls. One of the girls managed to escape and get help. The passersby almost lynched him. The image showed the mechanic with his lips swollen and a black eye. The headline read: VICIOUS JACKAL and it was the first time the word, jackal, popped up that year. In tabloid slang, jackal is used to refer to people who attack those smaller than them, like a predatory animal. The case didn't cause any great commotion. Back then, three rapes a week made the news. The rest didn't make the cut.

A hurricane hit that year and killed hundreds of livestock. Many of the businesspeople in the area lost everything they had. There was a minor fire next to the refinery, which was at first kept secret.

A livestock farmer was kidnapped, and two secret-service policemen liberated him three days later. It was the first time the paper mentioned officers Chávez and Taboada, Cabrera's longtime coworkers. Remember, he said to himself, that journalist in suspenders, Johnny Guerrero, wrote that the agents following the case were in cahoots with the kidnappers.

Then a new governor came to office, José "Pepe" Topete, a fan of spiritualism, pyramids, and herbal medicine. He only trusted a few of his staff members: the deplorable Juan José Churruca, his government minister; and Licenciado Norris Torres, member of a dynasty of dinosaurs in the office. The beginning of his term coincided with that of two mayors: Daniel Torres Sabinas in Paracuán and Don Agustín Barbosa, the first opposition mayor of Ciudad Madero. A little while later, the governor would put one of them in prison. That year, 1978, Don Daniel Torres wanted to put on an unforgettable summer carnival, the port's main celebration commemorating the second founding of the city of Paracuán.

Kojak was on television.

In the movie theaters, 007's *Live and Let Die, Papillon, The Exorcist, El santo oficio* by Arturo Ripstein, and *El llanto de la tortuga* with Hugo Stiglitz.

There was a porn movie theater, the Hilda, that had *Emmanuelle, Bilitis,* and *The Story of O,* but most of the time they were showing the same movies over and over again: *Elsa the Pervert; Ubalda, All Naked and Warm; The Gestapo's Secret Train, College Girls Have Fun, My Lover Is a Puppy* (parts I and II), and other movies that mixed sex and geography: *Asia the Insatiable, Khartoum, Sensual Nights; Samsala, Voracious Tongue.* Understandably, the bishop attacked these movies during his Sunday sermons.

These are the ads: Rigo Tovar Premieres his New LP; Listen to *La Hora de Roberto Carlos* on XEW; José José and His Friends, Juan Gabriel and Guest Stars; Come to the Cherokee Music Disco Nights and dance to the sounds of the Jackson Five, Donna Summer, Stevie Wonder, and the Bee Gees. Meet the pretty people and dance to the YMCA.

Social News, January 8: "The distinguished beachgoers in the photo have arrived from Germany. The tanned young ladies have traveled all the way from the Rhine to visit our greatest tourist attraction, Miramón Beach. They are, from left to right: Inge Gustaffson, Deborah Straus, and Patricia Olhoff."

Local news: GREAT RISK OF MALARIA INFECTION: VIRUS MIGHT COME IN A TOMATO TRUCK.

Sports: CASSIUS CLAY SHOWS OFF AT A PRESS CONFERENCE.

International: KISSINGER THREATENS ECONOMIC EMBARGO. ALARM IN THE MIDDLE EAST.

Local news: "For four consecutive days, Paracuán PRI supporters distribute pamphlets condemning the stones thrown at President Echeverría at the National University."

Social news, airport: "John and Jack Williams travel to our sister city, San Antonio. Family and friends see them off."

Local news, blood and gore: QUINCEÑERA ENDS IN BESTIAL BRAWL; DISGRACEFUL MAN BEATS HIS OWN MOTHER; HUSBAND ABUSES WIFE FOR NO REASON; EPILEPTIC MAN RUN OVER BY BUS; SHADY CHARACTER WITH STUNTED MIND SPENDS FREEZING NIGHT IN THE SLAMMER.

That was the situation in the progressive city of Paracuán, state of Tamaulipas, always interested in the more spiritual aspects of life (while at the same time condemning the more carnal side). But then the port's two papers begin to take different tacks: in the following days, their coverage was almost identical, except for the tone of the articles and the style of the headlines.

The first news related to the killer appeared on Thursday, January 1 2, as a small paid insert, along with the day's television programming: DIFFICULT SEARCH: A GIRL IS MISSING. A photo was included, taken from a yearbook, and next to it appeared the following text:

The young girl in the picture, Lucía Hernández Campillo, disappeared last Monday while on her way to Colegio Froebel. She was wearing a blue skirt and a white shirt with black shoes. Her distressed parents, Everardo and Fernanda, will provide a reward to anyone with information on her whereabouts.

Twenty years later, the headlines from the following day actually seemed more like omens: LA SIERRA DE OCAMPO BURNS; DROUGHT CAUSES ANXIETY IN PORT; DAMAGE EXPANDS TO CENTER AND NORTH OF TAMAULIPAS.

TWO SECRET AGENTS ACCUSED OF ROBBERY. Once again, agents Chávez and Taboada. Cabrera shook his head. *El Desconocido* premiered with Valentín Trujillo.

At two o'clock in the afternoon of February 17, there was a horrendous discovery at El Palmar. A couple rowing around the lagoon found the body of a little girl, Karla Cevallos. The body was badly hidden under branches and dead leaves on a little island, just a few yards away from the busiest avenue in the city.

Ah, Cabrera concluded, so this is what it was. How could I forget? We were working forty-eight-hour shifts to find the killer; I'd just joined the police force. Unfortunately, all the work led nowhere, and the newspapers published a number of editorials about the first girl's disappearance: LUCÍA STILL NOT FOUND: PARENTS DISMAYED.

On March 17, thirty days after Karla Cevallos was found, *El Mercurio* noted, GRUESOME DISCOVERY DOWNTOWN. On his way into the bathroom at the Bar León, right in front of La Plaza de Armas, office worker Raúl Silva found the remains of a second girl. But it wasn't Lucía, it was Julia Concepción González, who had disappeared just a few hours earlier. The resemblance between the two deaths was obvious, and the police had to accept the existence of just one killer. POLICE LOOK FOR INDIVIDUAL ACCUSED OF SERIOUS CRIMES.

JACKAL STILL ON THE PROWL: Agents of the Secret Service focus all their resources on the difficult search for the person who carried out kidnappings and attacks on several young girls in the last few days.

Newspapers speculated that the offender was passing through the city. It was said he was mentally ill. Both papers interviewed Dr. Margarita López Gasca, a psychiatrist from the health center in the nearby city of Tampico, and at their request she worked up a profile of the killer:

> We are dealing with a person unable to function socially, who lacks a moral conscience and who repeats the same acts compulsively, because his greatest satisfaction is to be found in the punishment awaiting him.

She is credited with another comment, obviously inserted by the journalist at *El Mercurio:* "All evidence suggests he will attack again."

Collective hysteria unleashes in the harbor. Teachers warn their students about the danger, and surveillance is doubled.

That same week in March, when the police announced they had a firm lead in the case, another singular fact occurred, but due to the horror of the crime it went by almost unnoticed: the French archaeologist René Leroux announced he had finally discovered the exact location of the legendary and mysterious pyramid of a thousand flowers and a conch shell. Anyone who has lived in the harbor knows that the legendary pyramid of a thousand flowers and a conch shell was located in the garden behind Mrs. Harris's house. The mound was about thirteen feet tall and covered by a thick layer of grass. According to the French archaeologist, those thirteen feet were just the tip of the iceberg. According to the legends in the area, the pyramid was four thousand years old and over three hundred feet high and might be home to important treasures. To support his claim, he said all you had to do was ask the residents of the neighborhood how hard it was to build their houses' foundations and have them show you the clay objects found during the construction work. The mound's neighbors, including Mrs. Harris, didn't want to hear a thing about it, so the pyramid stayed buried for more than twenty years.

Just a few days apart, both papers published incendiary editorials, demanding that the killer be arrested and suggesting that if the offender were still free it was because he was a person with power. As popular resentment increased, the weather report augured that the situation would remain the same for the next few hours: "Threat of rain. Gale-force winds blow in from the northeast."

At the beginning of March, an anonymous donor had offered twenty-five thousand and then later fifty thousand dollars to anyone who helped find the jackal. Attracted by the reward, amateurs, ex-cops, and detectives had invaded the city. The race for the reward began.

Popular anger had not subdued when, on March 20, a group of Boy Scouts, entering an abandoned construction site, found the bodies of Lucía Hernández Campillo and Inés Gómez Lobato. *El Mercurio* spared no details or unpleasant pictures, and general rage was unleashed: TWO MORE GIRLS FOUND; TODAY AT 5, PROTEST IN THE PORT.

From Mexico City, the head of the National Professors' Union announced that, if no one intervened in the matter, they would call a national strike. The union, with four hundred thousand professors, was one of the most powerful in the country. The governor intervened in the case, and finally, on March 21, the killer was arrested; he gave an immediate confession. Cabrera could only follow the story up to this point, because the files in the archives were incomplete. Judging by what he read, it was obvious that the trial was full of irregularities. The defense attorney insisted important evidence had been covered up, evidence that would have led the investigation in a different direction.

A few days after the trial began, *La Noticia* stopped covering it, and *El Mercurio* did the same a day later. That weekend *La Noticia* published a photograph that had impressed Cabrera a great deal back then. It was the image of a bearded man, dressed in white like an ancient Christian, with a gigantic piece of fabric over an immense expanse of water: "Bulgarian artist Christo Javacheff covers King's Beach, Massachussetts, with over 40,000 square feet of white fabric."

From that moment on, the papers didn't mention the subject again and the crime section went back to normal: JAWS OPENS; CONSTRUCTION WORKER'S DRAMATIC SUICIDE; THIEF NEVER GIVES UP; SKILLED SMUGGLER. On June 20, the minister of health, on a visit to the port city, confirmed that the region was no longer at risk of malaria. But looking through the crime section for the following months, it was clear that even though the killer was tried and locked up, the bodies of little girls kept turning up in the northern part of the state. Cabrera tried to get more information, but the files in the archives stopped there.

12

When Cabrera asked for the volume with the newspapers from May and June, the attendant came back empty-handed.

"That's strange! They're not where they should be or anywhere in the stacks. It must be misplaced. I'm very sorry, but I have to go now. You should report it to the director, Don Rodrigo Montoya."

The director turned out to be one of the people from the funeral; he had been talking to Bernardo's father. Cabrera's request seemed to surprise him.

"Excuse me?"

"I need to see the fourth volume from 1970, the book that has May and June."

"It wasn't there?"

"No. I read though March but they couldn't find the next one."

"It's very odd that it's not where it should be. I'm obsessive about organization. It's probably the social service people, they mess everything up."

He called the attendant in charge on an intercom and ordered her to look for it again. From his window, the lagoon was visible, surrounded by cranes and bulldozers.

"They're checking on it right now."

He was about to say something else when the attendant called back. "I already looked, Licenciado, and it's not there."

"Keep looking, Claudina." He looked out the window again at the bulldozers, and after thinking for a minute he turned to Cabrera. "Not many people come to the archives. Now that I think about it, only one other person ever asked me for that volume, and we buried him this morning."

Cabrera explained that he was in charge of the case, and the director looked at the bulldozers.

"Look," he said, "three months ago, Bernardo came for the first time. He said he was researching the economic history of the city. I warned him he wasn't going to find much, because things here have never changed, but he came anyway to read in the archives every day for three weeks, and it took me a while to understand what he was looking for. He was very discreet. One afternoon I found him making copies of some pages that definitely had historical value but had nothing to do with the local economy, or at least not in an obvious way, so I stood next to him and said, 'There are a lot of people who would be very angry if they found out you were poking around in that case; it's a very delicate issue.' And he asked me, 'What would Dr. Quiroz Cuarón have said?' That comment made me realize that Bernardo knew about my humble participation in the case when I worked for the police force more than twenty years ago, so I answered, 'If you want to know what the doctor said, I have his testimony, and you can see it if you like . . . but if you want to get even more information on the case, there's someone else who could tell you more interesting things, things that have been forgotten.' I warned him it could be dangerous, because that person lives at the margins of the law. He was a cop back then, and he knew how everything went down. Bernardo made a note and told me, 'I'll think about it.' He disappeared for several weeks, and then ten days ago he came looking for me to ask me the informant's whereabouts. I got him an appointment and found out they met together. I thought that since this person had some unresolved problems with the law, they would pin Bernardo's death on him, but as you know, that's not how it happened: they blamed El Chincualillo. But I'm absolutely certain that the informant is innocent: I can vouch for him."

"I'd like to talk to that person," Cabrera said.

"I'll do what I can. In the meantime"—he unlocked a drawer and took out a notebook that had a blue cover with psychedelic drawings all over it—"It's my account of what happened twenty years ago. Bernardo read it, too."

He called the attendant and asked her to make a copy, and while they waited, they stared out the window. In the distance, the bulldozers worked incessantly. Then the secretary came in, handed back the original and the copy, and Cabrera left. He had a lot to do and only three days off.

13

The prison in Paracuán is on the road headed into the city, on a hill looking down on the river. Originally, the building belonged to a Spanish hacendado. Now its towers are used by eight armed gendarmes to watch over the inside of the penitentiary.

To go in, all personal items must be left in an envelope; belts, shoelaces, and anything that can cut or be melted down must be removed. A sign written on a cardboard box warns that alcohol, food, sharp objects, bananas, mangos, or soursops are not allowed, since the inmates will ferment the fruit to make alcohol. At the entrance they ask you for an ID, they ask your relationship with the inmate, and then they let you in.

René Luz de Dios López was not called the Jackal by many people anymore. Everybody just used his first and last name. When Cabrera asked for him, one of the guards said, "He's the one over there with the guitar. Hurry up, they have to go eat dinner; it's time for mess hall."

The man known as the Jackal was playing the guitar and singing a religious song with some other inmates. Cabrera didn't want to attract any attention from the guards so he interrupted him discreetly. "René Luz de Dios?" And he explained why he was there.

López wasn't surprised. "Two interviews in two weeks. I'm getting famous."

And Cabrera knew he was getting closer.

14

The story of René Luz de Dios López is the story of a scapegoat. In 1975 he was a delivery driver for a processing plant that made cold cuts. When the first three girls were murdered, he was in Matamoros, a full day's drive away. Every fifteen days, his boss sent him to the northern part of the state to supply the clients in that area. He even had a receipt from the hotel where he stayed, stamped and signed by the cashier, who remembered him well. Unluckily for him, the morning one of the little girls was found, he was in Paracuán. A random chain of events led the police, who were actively looking for someone to blame, to the conclusion that René Luz de Dios López was their ideal candidate. For the last twenty-five years, he's been locked up for four murders he didn't commit.

When the State sets out to hurt somebody, nothing can be done to stop it. Eighty Jehovah's witnesses—who by religious law cannot lie— were willing to declare with the vehemence of the converted that the day the second girl was murdered René Luz de Dios had been with them from ten in the morning until at least six. There was no way he could have left without their noticing, but the judge ignored their testimony. He didn't take stamped and dated receipts into consideration either; these were provided by the owner of the plant and showed that René Luz de Dios was delivering merchandise in Matamoros and Reynosa on the days when the first three girls were murdered. The day the first victim disappeared, for example, he was on the border from the night before. When the second girl disappeared, he was working in Reynosa, and the day the third girl was killed he was shopping in McAllen for his wife's birthday present, as his stamped passport showed. And yet the prosecutor suggested that the receipts were forgeries and that, if he had wanted to, the defendant could have traveled round-trip from the port to the other end of the state, just to murder the three girls without provoking any suspicion.

The photos of the day his sentence was read show him to have been depressed and inconsolable. He was about to turn twenty-five when he went in. If he managed to get out alive, he would be a seventy-year-old man by the time he finished his sentence. He left behind two baby girls and, above all, his wife, to whom he'd been married almost three years. His public defender, a lawyer who was an activist in the opposition, appealed to the higher State courts and called a press conference to decry the handling of the case. A month later he published a book with his own funds, in which he laid out the injustices the driver suffered. The public defender kept making public statements until he had a car accident on the highway. He died five years later from his injuries.

Inside the cellblock reserved for murderers, the ceiling was made of a thick metal mesh, on which the guards paraded, ready to shoot rubber bullets or throw tear-gas grenades; the inmates' cells were concrete boxes, many of them with plastic curtains instead of doors. Ever since they sent him to the murderers' block, the guards had warned René Luz to be careful. When a guy who murdered a woman, or a child rapist, arrived, the inmates would normally get together to kill him, while the guards pretended not to notice. Everything the guards said was dripping with cynicism, since if they did attack him, nobody would come to his rescue. The inmates could tolerate anyone, except for a rapist.

René Luz wasn't planning to sleep the first night. When he noticed how his neighbors were looking at him, he started to get worried, and when he saw his cell door was just a simple piece of fabric, he thought he was going to pass out. Even though he tried to convince the guard, pathetically appealing to him for help, the man who was in charge of keeping watch over the block from the ceiling not only didn't answer him, but also moved away to a corner on the far side of the roof to sleep more comfortably. The guard watching the door at the end of the hall told him to go away. At nine, they turned the lights off.

As soon as the moon was hidden, they went to see him. There were only three: one stayed by the door and never went in; the other two were thin, dark-skinned, and barefoot. *Buenas,* the thinner one said to him. He was a mulatto with a scar on his neck and a hard stare. René Luz de Dios López must have thought they were the eyes of the man who would kill him. So, you're René Luz? The one who killed those three girls? About to pass out, the scapegoat, knowing he was on the verge of being sacrificed, tried to tell the inmates about the injustices committed against him. But it was useless. If the civilized people didn't want to hear him out when he had all the evidence in hand, what was the point of telling the same story to three convicted murderers?

As best as he could, with a voice as thin as a thread, he recounted the story of his trial. His account didn't seem plausible to him. Compared with his testimony before the court and his family, this sounded terse and unbelievable. Occasionally, some-one would stop him with a question or a monosyllable, to which René Luz would respond in his weak little voice. He could barely string two words together, and he felt his ears buzzing. When the moon shone through the metal grating, he noticed the thin guy was hiding the tip of a metal blade under his clothes.

Right then, he noticed the one at the door motioning to the others. He remembers thinking: this is as far as I get. The skinnier one stood up and took a step toward him, then another and another, pretending to check out his personal items. When he was almost on top of him, he grabbed a bag of coffee René Luz's wife had sent him. *Ca-fé de Co-mi-tán,* he read under the moonlight. And where's that at? In Chiapas, René Luz said. He didn't think he was going to make it out alive. It must be good. Could you give me some? Take it all, he said, but the inmate said that would be wrong. Despite how much time his visitor was taking, René Luz expected to receive the first blow any moment now and asked himself if they'd start on his neck or his stomach. When the inmate pulled out his weapon from his shirt, he closed his eyes reverentially, like a lamb offering himself for sacrifice. He didn't see the inmate cut the bag with the tip of his blade, and he opened his eyes when he heard something being poured softly: it was some of the coffee falling onto a handkerchief. Then he heard, *Gracias, amigo,* and all of sudden they were gone.

He didn't know what time he fell asleep. He dreamed that a pack of dogs came around to sniff him, and then they left.

The day Cabrera visited him, he wasn't holding out any hope. Fifteen more years till he'd get out, the sentence had already been shortened, why would he risk that? Cabrera had to push him hard to get him to speculate on who might be the real killer.

"People said it was the owner of Cola Drinks and that President Echeverría was protecting him."

René Luz stared at the floor, as if resigned to the fact he'd never find out anything about the guy who should have been in prison instead of him. The room darkened. Cabrera noticed clouds had filled the sky.

15

At night, in the middle of a heavy downpour, Cabrera called Padre Fritz at the bishop's offices.

"Why didn't you tell me Jack Williams was the main suspect?" He sounded annoyed.

"Because it wasn't relevant," the priest explained. "Mr. Williams has been trying to clear his reputation for twenty years, and I wasn't going to give any more life to those stories."

"How are you so sure it wasn't him?"

"Because I know him. I was friends with his father."

That changed his perspective completely. What side was the Jesuit on? He didn't know what to think anymore.

Cabrera called the archive director, Rodrigo Montoya, at his home and asked if he was able to locate the informant.

"He'll be waiting for you tomorrow at eleven by the lighthouse at the beach," and he specified the exact place to meet him. "His name is Jorge Romero, and he worked in the Secret Service."

"His name sounds familiar. How will I recognize him?"

"Don't worry, he'll recognize you; he has eyes everywhere. On the other hand, you could never identify him. He's very good at disguising himself."

"And why would he be in diguise?"

"There are a lot of people here who don't like him, starting with the chief of the judicial police. I already told you this was going to be complicated."

"And how will he recognize me?"

"It won't be hard. One more thing: If you have some extra pesos, give him some cash. He doesn't have much money."

"I don't have much either."

"Two hundred pesos would do."

He called headquarters to check in and found he had six messages from Mr. Obregon's son: Give me back my gun, assfuck. Damnit, he said to himself, I'd completely forgotten; I should take it in right now, I don't want any trouble with Obregón. But he was completely exhausted and he figured a few more hours wouldn't make a difference . . . and he was wrong again. Since he'd argued with his wife, Cabrera went back to his own apartment, which needed serious cleaning. When he collapsed into bed, he made an attempt to read Rodrigo Montoya's testimony but it was impossible: too many things had happened in one day already. He stood up for a glass of water and saw the sunset: dusk had begun and darkness descended over the city. Near the refinery, the horizon turned the same color as the gas burn-off stacks; the clouds were lit up with that reddish, anxious color he hated so much. He needed rest. What a day off! he said to himself, and fell asleep.

16

With the weather like it was, there were only three crazy people at the beach: a group of kids wrapped in thick blankets trying to grill some meat on a barbecue. Following Montoya's instructions, he took the beachfront boulevard up to the Hotel Las Gaviotas. As soon as he saw the Cola Drinks ad, he parked by the dunes and walked to the shoreline. A freezing wind rustled the empty *palapas* and rushed all the way up to the seawall. He wondered why the hell he hadn't grabbed his jacket on the way out.

Once in a while, a hermit crab would spit a handful of sand on him. Right at the water's edge, a tiny seagull hopped around a few feet away. Every time the waves receded, the seagull would chase the silver fish swimming in the current. They walked in the same direction for a few minutes so as not to freeze, until a second seagull arrived to pick up the first one, and he realized even seagulls had better luck than him.

Cabrera didn't know how the *porteños* managed to have a stand selling candies all the way at the farthest end of the beach, but there was one. Before he saw him coming, a vendor had already offered him coconut and milk candies. He thought that if a vendor with a portable glass showcase could walk up without him noticing, anybody could. What kind of detective was he? He wasn't made for this, being out in the streets; he should stay in the office, chatting up the social service girls. When he noticed the three kids get in their cars and leave, he realized the beach was now deserted. It was like someone had taken the blindfold off his eyes: What if this little meeting was a trap? This sucks, he thought. There was no one to turn to if he got into trouble. The deserted beach was an ideal spot to hide a body. The whole thing might be a trick! The archive director was in cahoots with Chávez! He was going to end up buried up to his neck in the sand, like a victim of the Chinese mob. He was thinking about all that when he saw a bus stop on the boulevard. Just two people got off the bus, one of them, a child, looked at him, and he knew he was the one they were looking for.

It was a blind man with a cane and a little girl who was helping him along. The girl guided him toward Cabrera and, before he could say his name, the blind man said, "Yes, I know who you are. Don't be frightened, amigo, I'm not going to kill you."

He took them to the only open restaurant: a cement-block food stall, which at the very least protected them a little from the weather. They sat in chairs so cold the child was shivering. She carried a metal lunchbox, rusted, with some pictures from *The French Connection*. She was around ten years old and wearing a torn windbreaker. As soon as they were inside the restaurant, the blind man sent her away to the farthest corner of the place.

"Go play, Conchita. Don't interrupt us." She moved to a different table, pulled out some papers and colored pencils, and started drawing. She was a very obedient girl.

His name was Romero and he'd worked in the Secret Service. At first glance, he looked like he was homeless; under his jacket, he was wearing a shirt that was missing several buttons. His hem was stapled, and he hadn't shaved in several days.

"Did I frighten you? Don't be scared, I managed to lose the guys who were following me. You don't have people following you?"

"I don't know. I hadn't thought about it."

"Conchita says there's no one else on the beach, but be very careful, El Chaneque is serious about revenge, and this case is particularly important to him. Let's just say he built his career on it. He owes everything to this case."

The blind man was extremely tense, as if he were constantly expecting danger. According to the archive director, Romero had been a cop more than twenty years ago, and then he became a well-known detective. Just one mistake was enough to ruin his life forever. Cabrera asked him how long ago he knew the archive director, and after a few trivial remarks Romero said, "Whenever you like. I'm at your service."

"*Bueno,*" said Cabrera. "Let's cut to the chase. Do you know who killed the journalist?"

"Just like that? Let me have a drink first, or, what, you're not going to ask me to eat?"

That morning, the blind man was in danger for two reasons: a group of *judici ales* was making his life miserable because of some business about stolen cars, and Chief Taboada was looking for him. Ever since his colleague disappeared, and especially now, with the opposition government at city hall, Romero had had no place to stay, and every week there was another charge brought up against him. There's nothing worse for a *madrina,* or lackey, than to lose the people who protect him. For three years, he'd had no permanent address; often he had to hide for months, and twice he had to run away to the United States. On the morning they met, he was scratching his scraggly white beard and swore he hadn't eaten in two days.

Romero ordered the two dishes on the menu with the most food, one for him and the other for the girl, and, on average, he finished off a Cola Drinks every ten minutes. At the same time, he ordered a block of hard cheese and devoured it in chunks, as well as his incomplete set of teeth allowed.

As the blind man finished his food, Cabrera was able to get him to say a bit more than monosyllables, and by dessert he was a different person entirely, completely unlike the aggressive, crafty bum who had first come into the food stall. When he looked more intently at Romero's profile, he remembered having seen him at police headquarters, many years before, when Cabrera was still a young man, inexperienced and just starting out on the job.

Romero was sitting very stiffly in his chair with one hand on his cane. Cabrera couldn't forget he was looking at a former torturer, though he didn't seem like one: he looked more like an animal tired of running away. Once he felt more comfortable, Cabrera asked him if he knew what Bernardo Blanco had been writing about. He nodded, humbly.

"How could I not? I was his main source. You see this?" And he pointed to his eyes.

Don Jorge Romero wore dark glasses for just one reason: he had no eyes. They'd been torn out.

"In order to solve this case, you have to know what happened twenty years ago: I'm talking about the Jackal."

After beating around the bush, Cabrera went so far as to say, "Yeah, I remember some things about the case. I was reading about it, too. People said Jack Williams was the killer, right?"

Romero asked Cabrera for a cigarette and Cabrera gave him his almost full pack. The blind man expertly lit one and shook his head as he exhaled a cloud of smoke. "Jack Williams had nothing to do with it."

"Why are you so sure?"

"Because I caught the real killer."

17

They were there for three hours. The whole time, Romero referred to his partner, and when Cabrera asked the partner's name, the blind man said, "Vicente Rangel."

Cabrera felt a chill surge up his spine, and he asked to meet Rangel as soon as possible.

"That's impossible. He disappeared; nobody knows what happened to him." Romero filled his jacket pockets with free sugar packets and said he had to go, but first he asked for a second pack of smokes.

"What about the murderer?"

"That'll cost you. I have to make something out of this, *chingá*. I'm not doing it for love of country."

Cabrera handed him practically all the money he had on him. In exchange, Romero called to the little girl, "Conchita: give the piece of paper to the gentleman," and she handed him a wrinkled piece of newspaper from the section with local society news. There, two men in ties and jackets, surrounded by bodyguards, looked at the photographer intently.

"The murderer is the one in dark glasses."

As he left, Romero said, "Wait a while before leaving. If we *are* being followed, it's best if we don't step out together."

Cabrera waited for as long as he could. When it seemed like he'd waited long enough, he asked for the check and went out.

Romero was still there, waiting for the bus on the other side of the street. The little girl noticed him, and, so as not to cause them concern, he went to waste some time on the beach.

What Romero had told him was a real bombshell. *¡Carajo!* What should I do now? He was close to the refinery, and the wind had the rotten smell of sulfur.

To calm himself down, he spent a little while contemplating the barrier made of pine and palm trees that signaled the end of the beach. But despite the roiling sea of thoughts in his head, he suddenly remembered the gun. Yeah, I did: I forgot to return the gun. If he wanted to stay out of any more trouble, he would have to go pick it up at the office.

18

Rosa Isela was waiting for him at the door; she was obviously distressed. As soon as she saw him, she ran toward him and took him by the arm. The Bedouin and the huge Fatwolf were two steps behind her. The Bedouin shouted at him.

"Cabrera! Chávez is looking for you."

Isela tried to drag him in the opposite direction, but Cabrera pulled free. "Wait a minute, *mi reina,* I'll catch up to you."

"No, sir, please, don't go over there."

When he heard this, he understood what he was in for.

"Chávez wants to talk to you," Fatwolf insisted.

As soon as he walked in, he noticed the desks had been pushed to the sides, making an empty space in the middle of the office. And the civilians, who normally were everywhere, were nowhere to be found. Isela was the only one trying to get him out of there. At some point, Fatwolf pulled her off his arm, and Cabrera agreed to go into headquarters.

Chávez was sitting behind a plastic table, playing with his car keys.

"What's up, Chávez, what can I do for you?"

Chávez looked at him and said nothing. His left hand was hidden behind his back.

In this line of work, if you get distracted, you lose. Chávez slowly looked him up and down, and Cabrera did the same to him. It went on like that until Chávez laughed and tugged on his little goatee.

"You've been very busy."

"Yep."

"I heard you met with Romero. Are you looking for Rangel?"

Hearing that name, for the third time in two days, gave him a bad feeling. "Why? Are you looking for him?"

"No." He mocked him. "But if *you* want to find Rangel, go ask your wife."

Rosa Isela knew what was going on, because she tried to intervene— "Mr. Cabrera, Mr. Cabrera, come on, please"—but Fatwolf and the Bedouin were guarding the door.

"Stay out of it, miss, leave them alone."

Cabrera walked toward Chávez. "What did you say?"

"Go ask your wife."

"Do you want me to beat your ass?"

"No pues. If you're going to get all upset, *don't* ask her. But if you want to find out where Vicente is, go ask your wife."

Cabrera kicked the table up into the air. Chávez pulled his hand from behind his back, brass knuckles covering his fist, and brandished it in Cabrera's face. Cabrera took a step back. While Chávez waved his hand around, Cabrera took the chance to punch him in the jaw, a direct hit as hard as he could, and Chávez fell down face-first. He was on the floor, but he wasn't giving up; Cabrera guessed that he was about to jump up and hit him back, but as Chávez started to stand up, Cabrera kicked him right in the solar plexus. Unfortunately for Chávez, Cabrera was wearing cowboy boots. Chávez went up in the air, flipped over, and fell behind the table. He tried to get up but his legs gave out. It was already too late: Cabrera's pacifist spirit was completely gone. The Bedouin and Fatwolf had to grab him by the arms so he wouldn't kill Chávez: "Take it easy, dude, take it easy."

"Ah, *now* you interrupt me, fucking *pendejo?* Fuck your mother!" he screamed, and pulled himself out of their grip. Then he saw Chávez arch his arm and he felt a pain in his right leg. "Son of a whore!" he spat out. The asshole had thrown his brass knuckles without even looking and got him square on the shin. Cabrera pushed Fatwolf off him and he was about to go finish what he had started, but Isela hugged him, bawling, "Mr. Cabrera, please calm down!" When he saw her, he pulled himself together and walked out, gasping for air.

By then a crowed had gathered at the door; all the new guys were there. Goddamn nosy people, he thought. The problem was that in order to leave he had to walk by Chávez, sprawled out on the floor. Rosa Isela dragged him by the arm, trying to get between the two, but when Cabrera went by Chávez, he heard murmuring and went back.

"Repeat what you just said!"

"You're dead," Chávez said. "You're dead."

"Learn from this," Cabrera told the newbies. "If you're going to kill somebody, just kill him and be done with it, don't run an announcement in the society pages."

Chávez squinted his eyes like only he knew how to do and Cabrera understood he was serious.

Leaning on Isela, he went out into the street.

"Please, get out of here. Chávez is going to be after you."

"Don't worry," he told her, "nothing's going to happen to me."

"Do you want me to call an ambulance?"

"Yeah, but for Chávez. He's probably spitting his teeth out right now."

"Have you seen how *you* look yet? They hit you real bad."

It was the truth. When Chávez hit him the first time, he must have grazed the tip of his nose, because it was bleeding. He was so enraged, he hadn't noticed. And he noticed his leg was starting to go numb.

"You have to see a doctor. It might be broken."

Where his leg had been hit, a dark black mark had begun to form. Rosa was right. He wasn't going to be able to do anything like this, it would be better to head home.

"Here he comes. Get out of here, please!" The girl was incredibly anxious, "Chávez is coming."

And, in fact, Chávez was walking out, leaning on Fatwolf. Cabrera saw him say something to one of the new guys, giving him instructions, and the kid got into a patrol car, staring at Cabrera the whole time. I can't believe it, he said to himself. What has this fuckin' world come to when other officers are following me?

"Thanks, sweetheart. You should go get some rest, too. Your work here is done." He hugged the girl and said good-bye.

Just walking caused sharp, shooting pains, but he couldn't stop; the youngster had already started his car. We'll see if you get me, you son of a bitch.

Instead of getting into his car, he took a bus downtown. Disconcerted, the kid followed the bus at a prudent distance. At the third stop, Cabrera got off and the kid slammed on the brakes. OK, he said to himself, we're going to find out how smart you are. He grabbed a taxi headed in the opposite direction and watched the kid struggle to complete a U-turn in the middle of the avenue. This was fun and games for Cabrera. He asked the taxi driver to take him to the Rosales Supermarket.

"But it's right over there."

"Exactly."

The driver groaned and turned and the kid did, too. Cabrera got out of the taxi and limped into the main entrance; then he walked out the back door and walked back to headquarters. The patrol car was caught in the thicket of señoras in the cars looking for parking spaces. Too bad, he said to himself, he's got a lot to learn. He walked around the block and said hello to everyone there before getting into his car.

"Good afternoon!"

Chávez was so angry he was red in the face, and Cabrera was dying of laughter. *Pobres pendejos,* he thought, missing the mark can be really frustrating; I hope they won't build up a lot of negative energy on my behalf. He was saying this to himself as he drove down the street; accelerating hurt a lot, but he would be able to make it home on empty roads. When he got to the intersection with the avenue, it was a red light. His leg was throbbing. A movement as simple as depressing the accelerator caused shooting pains. As he waited for the green, a pickup with blacked-out windows that had pulled up on his left side suddenly went in reverse. He didn't pay much attention because the pain in his leg was killing him. That's weird, he thought, going in reverse in the middle of the street; at least there aren't many cars. If there were, he could cause an accident. Then the guy in the pickup slammed on the accelerator and ran right into the driver's side of his car.

Cabrera's head went right through the window, breaking it into a million pieces. Of the chaos that followed, he only remembered leaning out the window of the car and repeatedly reading the words on the side mirror: OBJECTS ARE CLOSER THAN THEY APPEAR.

As he asked himself who he was and why he was there, he saw the pickup pulling into reverse again, this time all the way back to the end of the block; he was going to ram right into him again.

Cabrera couldn't move. For a second, he was under the impression that there was an argument going on in his head, but then he looked in the rearview mirror and saw that no, he wasn't the one arguing, it was two girls sitting in the backseat: a dark-skinned girl and a redhead. The first girl, the *morena,* was saying, Here comes the pickup, we gotta move. The redhead was really distracted, or maybe just in shock like he was because of the accident: Move? Why should we move? We're fine right here! Meanwhile, Cabrera watched the pickup coming closer and heard a Rigo Tovar song on the radio: *Oh! It's so good to see you again! / To say hello and know you're happy. / Oh! It's so good to see you again. / So pretty, so beautiful, and so happy.* When he asked himself why he could hear it so clearly, he realized it was none other than Rigo Tovar himself in the backseat. The best singer of *música tropical* on the planet was there, right next to the girls, behind the driver's seat! Rigo, who was wearing a white suit and dark glasses, was playing the guiro with a lot of feeling. Cabrera smiled at him: Man, what a huge honor, Rigo Tovar in my car. Rigo sang: *That day when you left / I found myself alone and sad in the park / trying to figure out a reason / why you were so angry.*

The only thing was, the pickup was still moving toward them, and the *morena* mentioned an important fact: *It's getting closer; it's dangerous.* And the redhead said, *Dangerous? Why dangerous?* The redhead was not known for her intelligence. Suddenly, Rigo leaned forward and said in a haughty tone of voice: *You know what, my friend? I think you need to move your car; otherwise they're going to run into you and you won't be able to sit in the park under the flamboyants and the rose bushes, you won't see the social service girls or be able to dance to my songs, and I'll feel sad.* No, not that, Rigo couldn't be sad. *Don't worry,* Cabrera said to him, *I promise I'm going to move the car,* and the musician smiled condescendingly. *No problem, Rigo, it's an honor to be here talking to you,* and Rigo laughed, and suddenly he and the girls had vanished into thin air.

Then it was just Cabrera and the pickup left. Not quite conscious of what he was doing, his hand shifted into reverse and his foot found the accelerator; his car jerked backward with a loud screech. The pickup grazed the bumper, just barely touching him and jumped over the median. Unfortunately, at that same moment a double tractor trailer was headed down the other side of the road. It dragged the pickup almost a thousand feet and then rolled up on top of it. That's why I don't run stop signs, he said to himself. You never know when there'll be trouble.

The last thing he remembers is his car hitting the sidewalk behind him and coming to a halt. Then he turned off the engine, got out of the car, and passed out. The rest is what's expected: ambulance, fractured arm, broken ribs, concussion.

BOOK TWO

The Equation

Part I

1

There are two kinds of police officers in the world: those who like their job and those who don't. I liked my job, Agent Chávez liked his job, and of course Chief García liked to investigate and solve a case, but his best detective did not—and he was the one who received the crime report first. He tried to pass it on to somebody else, like a hot potato, but there are leads that get under your skin and don't leave you in peace until you follow up on them. They say that a kind of obsession takes over, like a dog dreaming about the scent of his prey, even when the hunt is over.

Well, I have to start somewhere. On March 17, 1977, Vicente Rangel González, nearly thirty, a native of the port who lived in a house by the river, a musician turned detective, was the one in charge of following up on the crime report. Rangel had spent six years on the force, the last four trying to resign. He was always saying he was going to resign, but every time he was on the verge of doing so he got involved in some difficult case and ended up putting it off again.

The day it all began, El Chicote—receptionist, guard, car washer, and errand boy for the entire department—passed him the call. "It's for you."

"My uncle?"

"No, what do you think? It's somebody reporting a crime."

That bit about the uncle was something of a joke between them, if you could say that Vicente Rangel liked jokes. . . . He didn't, really.

He picked up the heavy black telephone in the middle of the office. On the other end of the line, an exasperated voice was shouting. "Hello? Hello? Hello?"

"Headquarters."

"Finally! This is Licenciado Rivas at the Bar León. We found another girl, like the one in El Palmar."

"One moment," he said, and covered the mouthpiece with his hand. "Where's El Travolta?" he asked El Chicote.

"He hasn't come in."

"Why'd you transfer the call to me?"

"Lolita told me to."

Two desks away, Lolita was chewing her nails. She was the chief's secretary.

"Hey, Lolita. What's going on? This case belongs to El Travolta."

"But he's not here, you know he's always late. Why don't you go?"

"Is it an order?"

"Well . . . yes. No? Which would you prefer?"

Rangel let out a huge sigh and filled his lungs with the hot, heavy, unbreathable air; then he uncovered the mouthpiece and said, with as much authority as possible, "Are you the manager?"

"Yes."

"Don't touch anything and don't let anybody leave. They'll be right over. "

"Do you know where it is?"

"Sure, man, they're on their way."

Everyone knew where the Bar León was: in front of the central plaza. It was one of the oldest bars in the port, as old as the second founding of the city at the end of the nineteenth century. Although its golden age was past—sometime in the thirties, just before the Second World War—its air of a grand bar fallen on hard times still attracted tourists and, above all, a sparse but loyal clientele of neighbors and government office employees who worked nearby.

Rangel noted the time: a quarter past two, and let it be on the record that I didn't want to go, he told himself. As he hung up the phone, Rangel had to admit he felt nervous. Could it be the same guy? he wondered. He felt like the palms of his hands were on fire again and he told himself: Motherfucker, I bet it is. He thought of applying the medicinal ointment prescribed by Dr. Rodríguez, but he wasn't sure. He didn't want anyone to see him using it; ointments and makeup seemed like fag stuff to him, nothing to do with a tough cop about to turn thirty, but it was true that Dr. Rodríguez Caballero was the best specialist in the state. OK, he told himself, what's the harm in using just a little bit? He was opening the box, he'd already pulled out the ointment and was about to rub some onto his left hand, when he realized that he was being watched by a guy in a plaid shirt wearing thick coke-bottle glasses, a lowly type but very clean, who was waiting in a chair by the entrance to the corridor, maybe just another aspiring *madrina,* like so many others who turned up there. They all wanted to be lackeys, gofers for the police officers. Annoyed, the detective put the ointment away in his pocket.

Vicente Rangel González pulled out the twenty-two caliber pistol he'd paid for in ten installments, undid his belt, and put on the holster. He preferred the twenty-two caliber to the heavy regulation forty-five caliber the department offered. As it was a small city, there weren't enough firearms for everybody, and the few they had were kept in Chief García's office, under double lock in a case, but the chief wasn't there and he had the key. Rangel didn't like to carry a weapon and was sure he wouldn't need it, but he took it anyway; don't want that guy to find me first. When he'd closed the holster he conveniently and discreetly scratched himself, and when the itch had diminished he turned to El Chicote.

"Tell the forensic guys, and send me Cruz Treviño, or Crazyshot and Fatwolf. Tell them to do a complete search of the plaza and the docks."

"What? Can you say that again?"

Rangel would have liked to give an explanation, but he couldn't discard the possibility that the man in the plaid shirt was a newspaper spy, and so he made a gesture that said *Don't ask* and went out of the room.

El Chicote silently obeyed. Experience had taught him not to argue with nervous policemen, so he picked up the yellow pages, looked up the Lonchería Las Lupitas, and set to work trying to track down Crazyshot.

Rangel crossed the gravel parking lot, trailing a dusty wake that accompanied him to the car. As he'd feared, the metal was broiling: waves of heat rose from the hood. Fuck, he said. If only he had air-conditioning. He stuck the key into the red-hot lock, rolled the window down, flipped the driver's seat cushion over, and got in. Before he could reach across to lower the right-side window, he was already sweating, rivers flowing down his face. I surrender, he thought. Turning on the car he burned his fingers again, so he pulled out a handkerchief and a red bandanna from the glove compartment, draped one over the steering wheel, covered the stick shift with the other, and drove in the direction of the bar. Back then the department only had three vehicles: La Julia—a covered pickup, adapted for transporting "suspects"—and two patrol cars painted in the official colors; one was used by Chief García and the other was driven by El Travolta, otherwise known as Joaquín Taboada, García's second in command. All the other agents had to use their own cars if they had them, as was the case with Vicente Rangel.

He looked at the thermometer. One hundred and three degrees, and it wasn't going to get any cooler. Since buying the Chevy Nova he'd tried to avoid driving at the hottest hours, during the port's interminable midday, when the buildings seemed to be boiling, and hazy mirages rose from the pavement.

Today he had the impression he was entering another reality, the epicenter of fear. To distract himself from such macabre thoughts, he turned on the radio, where the announcer was suggesting it was the Martians overheating the earth: "First they're gonna finish off the ozone layer and deforest the planet, and then they're gonna melt the ice cap at the North Pole and flood the cities. Their plan is to mercilessly extinguish the human race." Fucking Martians, he thought, they must be *putos.*

As he passed the Tiberius Bar he slowed down to see if El Travolta was there, but no luck. Fucking fat ass, he thought, and to top it all off he's going be mad at me.

He took the Boulevard del Puerto to Avenida del Palmar and only had to stop for the light at the Texas Curve, and since there was a tractor trailer in front of him and he had no siren, he had no way of making himself heard. OK, he told himself, I can wait a second. Honestly, he didn't want to take on this job and he still held out hope that El Chicote would find El Travolta and he'd be relieved of the investigation. Thirty seconds later he felt sure it wouldn't happen that way, at least not right away. There was no way out of this situation. Who cares? he thought. Let the fat ass get mad, so what. One more stripe on the tiger.

He looked at the enormous billboard for Cola Drinks, with a woman picking up a glass of petroleum-colored liquid overflowing with ice. While he waited for the light to change, like the good anti-imperialist he was, he thought mean things about the company and even about the model in the ad. Fucking gringo assholes and fucking bitch in hot pants, she must be a big whore. Every time he saw a cola drink he associated it with the war in Vietnam, the tension in the Middle East, the Cold War, the fall of Salvador Allende in Chile. Since he'd joined the police force, these explosions of overt rancor had become less frequent, but they persisted. His internationalist conscience wouldn't die. But there had to be some explanation for that stuff about the girl found dead.

He reached the Bar León in ten minutes—back then, you could traverse the whole city in half an hour—and as he approached, he recognized Dr. Ridaura's car, which meant Ramírez would be there, too. In the mornings they gave classes in chemistry and biology at the Jesuits' school; in the afternoons, or in case of an emergency, they were the only forensics specialists in the city.

Strangely, the forensic expert, Ramírez, was waiting for him in the street. He looked seasick and his eyes were red. This guy can't take anything, Rangel thought. Looks like whatever he saw made an impression on him.

"Finished?"

"Getting some air."

"Hurry up, because the ambulance is coming," he ordered, and added, as a large group of curious onlookers was forming, "Open a space in front of the door. Don't let anyone in or out."

Before he could take another step, Ramírez confessed. "Mr. Rangel?"

"Yes?"

"The manager let one individual leave."

Rangel nodded. "An individual? The manager? I'm going to see that asshole right now. Fuck him for obstruction of justice."

He was about to resume walking but the voice of intuition stopped him. He knew Ramírez well enough to know he was hiding something.

"Do you know who it was?" Rangel guessed he did, judging by the forensic specialist's hesitation.

"It was Jack Williams. He was with his secretary and four gringos."

Son of a whore! An influential person. He didn't like dealing with influential people, and the person who'd left without waiting for them was the son of the richest man in the port, owner of the local Cola Drinks bottling plant. Ramírez was sweating, and it wasn't on account of the 103 degree in-the-shade heat.

"Where's the body?"

"At the back, in the bathroom. The doctor is there."

When he stepped through the doorway he had to wait a minute to get used to the dark. Three dark shapes approached him, with each step a little less blurry; the manager must be the one with the biggest potbelly. No need to pull out his badge—there never was, and much less now; nobody wanted to be in that place.

The manager's name was Lucilo Rivas. Rangel recognized him immediately; he'd seen him many times at a distance, whenever he went to the bar as a customer. He always wore tight-fitting light-colored suits, at least one size too small. Seeing him, the manager made it obvious he recognized him as a regular customer. It was like he was saying: Well, damn, I didn't know he was a detective. They called him La Cotorra, the Chatterbox, but today he was keeping his mouth shut. Oh, goddamnit, Rangel said to himself, this asshole is going to give us a hard time.

"Is everyone here?"

"If they'd left without paying, I would have noticed."

"That's what we're going to find out. Do you have all of today's receipts?"

The manager's expression changed. There you go, thought Rangel, he didn't like that one bit.

"We just opened."

"Don't dick me around. No way they took their checks with them. You must have some record."

More taciturn than ever, the manager pulled opened a drawer and turned over the receipts. Rangel took the one on top and found what he was looking for. Junior had paid with a credit card:

Cola Drinks Group—Paracuán
John Williams, Jr.
Assistant General Manager

Rangel didn't have a credit card. If he couldn't even get to the end of the month with money in his pocket, how could he afford one? For him the cards were like titles of nobility, glimmers of an impossible country, a dream as remote as a Ford in your future.

"What?" The voice of the manager had broken his concentration.

"I said I let him go because he was in such a hurry. He was with some gringo investors, and he had to show them around the city."

Rangel shook his head. "You and I are going to continue this conversation. What you did is enough for me to haul you in. . . . I'll take this." He took the receipts. "Who found her?"

The bartender gestured toward a young man who looked like a bureaucrat, seated at the bar, pale as a ghost. "Oh, man," said Rangel, "he's going to faint."

As usual, Raúl Silva Santacruz had gone to have lunch at the Bar León at two on the dot. Every third day, he came with two colleagues during the hour when they gave away free food; he'd order one or two beers and in exchange they'd serve him a dried shrimp *caldo,* crab or pork tacos, or a *guisado* with rice. On the 17 of March, 1977, he finished his two beers, shared one last dumb joke with his friends, and went to urinate. It was 2:40. Although the bar had urinals in back, usually flooded miasmas, Silva Santacruz preferred to go through the door behind the bar and use the other, better-ventilated, bathroom. It was a room with white tiled walls about four meters high, a rectangular communal urinal, and two stalls, each with a toilet, illuminated by a large window. That day, as he stepped toward the urinal, Raúl Silva Santacruz noticed an object on the floor in front of one of the stalls. He remembered the homeless guys who hung around the plaza and thought, Fuckin' bums, they just come in here to make a mess. It was normal for vagrants to come into the bar to use the bathrooms and then leave behind their soda bottles, french-fry cartons, and the needles they used to shoot up. He was about to lower his zipper when he noticed that the discarded object was a tiny shoe. He lifted his gaze a few inches and discovered, just inside the stall door, a little kid's foot poking out.

What he found caused a nervous breakdown. Although the bartender served him a shot of liquor in a tequila glass, his movements remained slow and swaying, as if he were following the rhythms of a waltz. Rangel would have preferred that the witness not drink, but he couldn't reprimand him: if he weren't on duty he would have had a shot of rum, too. He didn't like the job that lay ahead of him one bit, but there was no avoiding it.

A lightning flash illuminated the inside of the restaurant, and the agent knew the journalists had arrived: in this case El Albino, the crime-beat photographer always first on the scene. For quite a while, Rangel had felt uncomfortable whenever he ran into El Albino, and every time he went to investigate a homicide, he knew he was going to find him. Fuckin' vulture, who knows who tips him off? he thought. He must have an informer in the department, otherwise there's no explanation for how he's always the first one on the scene. It wasn't that El Albino was a bad person, but it still perturbed Rangel to watch him at work: he was the silent type, with white hair and white eyebrows, always dressed all in white amid the sea of blood. If he'd just make some effort to be amiable, Rangel thought, but he only stirs things up. After him, it wasn't long before La Chilanga turned up, a graduate of the Carlos Septién García School of Journalism, expelled from the Ibero for her leftist ideas. Whenever she was denied access to a crime scene, La Chilanga usually launched into a long and painful harangue, full of Marxist vocabulary that Rangel didn't always understand. "Fourth-class materialists, shitty dogs, you're the armed branch of the bourgeois government." Rangel didn't know how to treat her: she used the fact that she was a woman, beautiful, feminist, and educated. Fucking bitch, she's got me all figured out; she ought to stay in her house. To Rangel it was obvious that reporters got in the way of police work. If it were up to him, he'd forbid them from getting mixed up in investigations, but not everybody thought the same. The chief liked to show off, and Crazyshot liked to show off, and El Travolta—don't even talk about it, he was practically a *vedette,* a showgirl. And then El Albino tried to cross the security perimeter—in reality, just a pair of chairs in the entranceway to the bar, put there by Ramírez—"Listen, *cabrón!*" Rangel shouted at him, "get the hell outta here!" But El Albino stayed quiet, like he was playing dead or like an animal who didn't understand human language. Rangel gave the order to lower the blinds. A minute later, the waiters had shut out the light from the street and the detectives were enveloped in darkness, in the most literal manner.

2

From the moment he entered, the regulars had stared at him like he was a priest about to perform a secret rite. Fucking assholes, he thought, as if I have any idea how to solve this thing. He figured there were seventy people. Damn, he thought, I'm going to need backup; no way I can interview them all, I didn't bring a pen, paper, nothing.

"Where is it?"

"There in back, behind the jukebox," explained the manager, and led him to the main restroom.

The agent shoved aside the tables blocking his path and noticed Rivas paused in the doorway, letting him go by. In that instant he asked himself: What am I going to do when El Travolta gets here? He's going to give me shit, for sure: What's up, dude, stepping on my toes? No way, *cabrón,* this is just the way it happened; if you don't believe me, ask Lolita. And if he gets pissed off, it's his problem, fat fucking piece of shit; this is his case, not mine.

Rangel had been on the police force six years. He'd seen people killed by bullets, shot at close range, poisoned, drowned, strangled, and run over, heads smashed in with blunt objects, a suicide who'd jumped from a sixth floor, and even a man butted to death by a zebu. But he was completely unprepared for what he was about to find. What he saw before him was the worst thing that had happened to the city since the nineteenth century. And it was just getting started.

Paracuán was the third oil port on the gulf. The only time it had been on the brink of fame was in 1946, when John Huston came through scouting locations for *The Treasure of the Sierra Madre*. According to the old guys, they were on the verge of filming in the port, but the cinematographer insisted that another city farther north was more photogenic, and the film crew took off for Tampico. That's the story of Paracuán: everything good disappears right when it's about to arrive. In its five-hundred-year existence, it's suffered every kind of catastrophe. It was the center of indigenous commerce until the Spaniards destroyed it, it became a prosperous mercantile center until the invasion of the French, it had an important stock exchange until the Depression of 1929, and it had great oil fields until they shut down the Oil Workers' Union. Being in an oil-producing region, it is plagued by the same curse as are the mining towns: great wealth is produced but little or nothing ends up benefiting its residents. Sensational bloody battles happen more or less constantly: when it's not the sailors, it's the ranchers, and when it's not them it's the unions or the smugglers. They've used switchblades, grappling hooks, harpoons, fishhooks, machetes, ropes, cords, frying pans, hydraulic jacks, car bumpers, and even freight cars—all to cause or to fake falls, crashes, work accidents, suicides, drunken deaths. At the political level, the only thing worth mentioning is the incipient opposition, both on the left and on the right. The left continues despite the infighting practically tearing them apart, and saying *right* in Paracuán is the equivalent of saying *far right*: ignorant people, racist and unaccustomed to actual thinking.

Another girl had been found in El Palmar a month before. Her name was Karla Cevallos. A pair of young lovers, whose names were left out of the papers, were crossing the lagoon in a rowboat when it occurred to them to stop and get out on a reed-covered islet. The woman was the first person to find her. It smells awful here, she said, it really stinks. As she was exploring in the underbrush, her heel got caught on a plastic bag, and when she tried to pull her foot free, she discovered the girl's remains. *El Mercurio* didn't spare its readers any unpleasant details or photographs: BODY FOUND AT LAGOON. The article said she appeared to have been chopped up into pieces and that wild animals had started to gnaw on her flesh. Ten days before, her parents had reported her disappearance. The last time she was seen alive she was leaving Benito Juárez Public School.

As he stepped through the doorway, he recognized Dr. Ridaura's white hair. Despite her seventy years, the old lady was on her knees, conducting an exhaustive examination of the stall. She's even more cold-blooded than Ramírez, Rangel thought. She was from Spain, an immigrant. They said she'd left her country at the end of the civil war. How had a biology professor ended up doing autopsies? Rangel asked himself. For years, her husband had worked at headquarters as their forensic expert, but for the last five years she'd taken over. The day they hired her, the chief asked if she felt capable of taking on her husband's job, if she thought it would be hard for her to work with corpses. She had replied: "I've been a physician for forty years. You let me know if there's something that can still shock me." Rangel wondered if she thought the same thing after five years on the force.

When she noticed him, the doctor turned around and lowered her mouth mask.

"Ah! I'm glad you came! I don't know where to begin. How do you want to proceed?"

She got to her feet and walked toward the agent. The toilet stall door slammed shut before Rangel could get a glimpse of the corpse. Up close, the doctor no longer seemed so calm. She had a pair of tweezers in her right hand and a plastic bag in her left, which amplified her hands' barely perceptible trembling. *Ay caray,* I can't let her get me nervous, Rangel said to himself, so he answered her in his calmest voice.

"She hasn't been moved, right?"

"No, God forbid."

"Don't move her until they've taken photographs. You have any opinion?"

"It's too early," she answered. "I was just getting started, studying the scene. At first glance, she wasn't killed in situ, they just tossed her here."

"You sure?"

"It would be impossible to do this without leaving blood all over the floor. And look, there are no stains, and the bag is intact, except for that little hole. . . . You be the judge."

The doctor moved to one side to let him past. Rangel hesitated, as if avoiding having to look, but was dissuaded by the expressions on the faces of the woman and the manager, who'd come through the door. It was as if they were saying, Do something, *cabrón*; you're the law, well, show us; you're supposed to protect us, get moving, don't be useless. What the hell, Rangel told himself, this is supposed to belong to El Travolta . . . and he decided to go ahead.

He pushed open the stall door with one hand, and the first thing he saw was a black trash bag . . . something that looked like hair . . . strips of a white blouse and a plaid skirt. . . . All of a sudden, he saw the head. How awful, he said to himself; he couldn't think of anything else to say. He remembered the time they sent him to the town of Altagracia to pick up the remains of a man devoured by a tiger. Ah, *cabrón,* he thought, who could've done this? He felt he hadn't quite woken up yet, the forty-eight-hour shifts with no sleep had messed with his sense of reality. Oh, God, he said to himself, oh, God, I'm getting dizzy. But he had to get a hold of himself. He was the one conducting the investigation.

He pushed the crooked door open again and noticed a thin layer of dust on everything and a fine fuzz floating inside the stall, visible in the sun's rays; however, more than anything else, what grabbed his attention was the state of the body. Damn, what's going on here? Why does this get to me so much? There was something strange in there, but he couldn't figure out what it was. Let's see, pay attention, man; what's getting to you? I know it's a gruesome scene but pay attention; you have to do something.

He looked at the bag again. If there was a clue there, it escaped him. Then he asked himself what his uncle would have done, the legendary Lieutenant Rivera who had died two years before. If his uncle had been there, no doubt he would have said to him, "You look like a faggot, not my fucking nephew. Your hands all slimy and sweaty. Let me through, get out of the way." He could almost see his uncle walking up to the body and carrying out his detailed examination of the crime scene, even the floor tiles in the stall and in the one beside it. "Aha! Yeah, I get it." He observed everything just to get an accurate picture of the place. "Aha. Aha. Aha." Then and only then did his uncle move in closer to the cadaver, once he was sure he wasn't destroying any evidence. It wouldn't take him long to come up with his first explanation: "It reminds me of the El Palmar girl. I know they're different circumstances, but that's what I think. . . . Remember, the first impression is always the most important, always ask your gut what it thinks; don't forget the sys-

tem, nephew; it's like you only got this job 'cause you knew somebody: I go through so much bullshit with you."

As he half closed the door, Rangel caused a draft of air that
stirred up a cloud of dust and fuzz.

The doctor sneezed. "Excuse me, I'm getting a cold."

He noticed that the bars on the front door shuddered as someone kicked it on the other side. Don't let anyone in unless they're
a detective, he ordered the manager.

When he was alone with the older woman, he asked her,
"What did they use to do this?" He pointed to one of the wounds.

"The one on top? I'd say a hunting knife, a little more than an
inch wide. I'll tell you exactly how big when I take the body to
the morgue. Yeah, for sure it's a hunting knife."

"About an inch wide? Like the other one?"

"At first glance, yeah. I'd say that's correct."

All evidence seemed to point to the fact that it was the same
guy. The idea wasn't at all pleasant, and both Rangel and the doctor fell silent. Finally, Rangel said, "Before going to the morgue,
look for initials on the clothes. Our first priority is to find out who
she was and what school she went to."

He heard a voice saying, "Right this way." Finally, he thought,
it's Wong and the Professor, but it was just Ramírez coming back
in from outside. The photographer walked toward the bathroom
and just as he was about to go in, Rangel grabbed him by the arm.

"Before you go in there, you need to take pictures of the floor."

"Sorry, but I don't work that way with Mr. Taboada."

Don't fucking mention El Travolta, he thought; I already know
how he runs his cases. "Today you're working with me, *cabrón,*"
he shot back at him.

"What do you want me to look for?"

"Evidence, any kind of evidence. It's like you don't know how to do your own job, Ramírez!"

"I'll tell him what to do," the doctor answered coldly and started to give instructions.

As they waited for the ambulance and backup, Rangel interviewed the staff. No chance the perpetrator was one of them: the cook hadn't left his area since eleven, the manager was watching over the cash register, the bartender wasn't allowed to leave his spot behind the bar, and the waiters had never left the main room. Raúl Silva found the body a little before 2:50. I'll be damned, Rangel thought.

The first thing he had to do was figure out what time the body was left there. Once he'd cleared that up, Rangel had to check to see if anyone present at the scene was a suspect, arrest him if necessary, and reconstruct what happened in the last hour. All of this while under pressure from the reporters just starting to arrive and, of course, not even mentioning the threat that El Travolta represented. Taboada wasn't going to like the fact that another dog was sniffing around his territory. Fatwolf handled drugs and sex crimes. Rangel was homicide and kidnappings, especially kidnappings, but he also investigated robberies occasionally, using the contacts his uncle had passed on to him. Fucking fat ass, he thought, he should thank me for covering his back. For now, though, he had to hurry up. An angry crowd was milling around outside; they were demanding results and the ambulance lights were nowhere to be seen. He looked at his watch: it was 3:30. From now on, every minute counted.

Let's see, he said to himself as he looked over the people who were present, could one of these guys be the killer? Knowing he was about to ask them questions, the majority of the people looked

off into space, as if the ceiling were suddenly intensely interesting: Damn, you seen those huge stains? How'd they get there?
Trying not to wear himself out for no reason, Rangel looked at
the tables and picked the one with the most bottles on it.

Twelve minutes later, he'd established the killer must have
left the girl there after 2:20. Usually, Rangel would have arrested
the office worker, but everyone had seen that Raúl Silva Santacruz
wasn't carrying a plastic bag when he went to the bathroom.

"Listen to me good," he said to Raúl Silva. "You aren't under
arrest, but you have to go to headquarters to finish your statement."

A waiter told him another person had gone into the bathroom
before Silva: "That guy next to the door."

The suspect was a traveling salesman, a guy named René Luz
de Dios López. He was eating with his boss, a Mr. Juan Alviso,
owner of a local chain of candy stores. The waiter stated that he
saw him go to the bathroom after ordering his drink. He didn't
have anything in his hands or take more than a minute in there.
René Luz de Dios explained he'd just finished loading boxes and
it was normal for him to wash his hands before eating. His boss
confirmed his alibi: "He was loading the orders into the truck,
'cause it was going to Matamoros in a little while. My distributor's
there." One look at the guy was enough for Rangel to know he
was innocent, but he still had to take him in to get his statement.

"Officer," Mr. Alviso explained, "my assistant came with me,
he was in the office all morning, and we came together. There's
no way a man sitting by the door could walk across the entire bar
with a girl in his arms, is there?"

Rangel knew Alviso was right, but he couldn't let the driver
go. René Luz de Dios would have to go through the purgatory
that the legal process is for innocent people. It was clear to him
after six years on the force that no one ever left headquarters

unscathed. The experience of being guilty until proven innocent changed people. Besides, while he was waiting to be called in, René Luz ran the risk that any one of the guys there, even El Chicote, would try to extort money from him. Most likely, El Chaneque or El Travolta would handle it. Rangel didn't like that part of his job, but if he didn't do things by the rules, it'd seem like he was protecting the driver; in the unlikely case that René Luz turned out to be guilty, he himself could face jail time. So he held fast.

"I'm sorry, but I have to follow procedure. If I don't, I'd be under arrest," and he put the driver's ID in his pocket.

"Right, but you let the big shots go, don't you?" Mr. Alviso shot back. "Even though they were in the bathroom longer. It's obvious whose back you've got."

Rangel stared at the businessman. "What? What'd you say?"

"Mr. Williams was in there for half an hour, right? And my driver here, who was only in there for a minute, just to wash his hands, you want to arrest him? That's outrageous."

Rangel made a note to ask Junior a few questions, but in any case he'd have to take the driver in.

"Look." He lowered his voice. "I give you my word that this is a routine procedure. I'm sorry," he said. What a fucking joke, he thought, this job is bullshit.

The Professor and Wong arrived at 4:05. The first one interviewed the drunks waiting their turn at the bar, and Wong used his irritable oriental look to interrogate the regulars at the tables in the back. At 4:30, Rangel went to see the forensic experts.

They'd already placed the body on the ground, and Ramírez was taking the last pictures. They'd laid it out on a yellow tablecloth with the Cola Drinks logo on it, provided by the bar's owner.

Rangel was an experienced police officer, but he couldn't keep his stomach from turning. When they emptied the remains from the bag, a leg came out and almost fell off the tablecloth. Rangel and the doctor stared. In view of the fact that the extremities were separated from the torso, there was no doubt it was the same perp.

"Hurry up," he told Ramírez. "I want to get this done already."

They were examining the marks on the body when a strange phenomenon caught their attention. Every time Ramírez pressed the shutter of his camera, it seemed like the lightning flash had a kind of echo effect that made it last longer than normal. The phenomenon was repeated twice, until they raised their eyes and discovered La Chilanga was focusing her camera on them through a window. Fucking nosy bitch, Rangel said to himself, I can't believe it. Rangel pointed a finger at her.

"Hey, you; stop!"

La Chilanga made like she was going to leave, but her shirt got caught on the window. When she tried to get free, the window moved a little and Rangel understood everything: Of course, he said to himself, I look like such an idiot. The girl was understandably upset and shot back at him with some Marxist rhetoric, but Rangel ignored her.

"What's on the other side of those windows?" he asked the manager.

"Customs Alley."

Sure, he said to himself, it all made sense.

"Wong," he said, "you take charge for a minute, OK?"

Three dozen onlookers had gathered at the bar's front door. They asked him what was going on, but he didn't respond. He went around the block, all the way to the alley. He didn't want to run into El Albino. When Rangel went into the alley, the photographer came out, but the officer didn't do anything to stop him.

Maybe he didn't want to accept it, but he was always a little freaked by the albino. Maybe he was intimidated by the guy looking at him; he was always so quiet, and his eyes were so pale. El Albino shot him a calculated look, like a gravedigger taking measurements of a body, and left without saying a word. Rangel didn't breathe until he saw him move away. Then he noticed the photographer was rewinding a roll of film. *Ay, caray,* he guessed: he took snapshots of the girl and I didn't even hear him working. Rangel didn't know which paper El Albino worked for, but he didn't want to ask. Deep down, he was afraid he didn't work for any newspaper at all. One time, he asked his uncle about him: An albino? Who? I don't know him, and Rangel left it at that.

The alley behind the Bar León was a trash dump for all the buildings around it. There were six dumpsters, countless cardboard boxes, and the metal skeleton of an old rusty refrigerator, abandoned there a few decades before. La Chilanga was struggling on top of it with one of her sleeves caught on the edge of the window. Fucking broad, he thought, she might *say* she's a Marxist but she needs a lot more experience; you can tell she just got out of college.

There were three different routes to get to the back window of the bar: one was coming from Calle Aduana, another from Calle Progreso, and the last was from the Avenida Héroes de Palo Alto. Sure, Rangel said to himself, three buildings come together here, the killer could've gone in and come out on any one of the three streets; he just had to climb onto that refrigerator and throw the body through the window. But why leave the girl's body in the bar if he could throw it away outside with no danger of being seen? There was something very strange about all this. It doesn't make sense.

He helped La Chilanga down; she was raging mad. Assholes, gangsters, *cabrones!* He climbed onto the refrigerator. He immediately realized the window was only half-open. From inside the bathroom, Wong and Dr. Ridaura were watching him.

"Of course," he said to them. "He put the girl in through here."

He looked over that section of the alley quickly and determined that there weren't any other bloodstains. He didn't kill her here; however, as he examined the window, he discovered there was a dark stain on the outside edge. Ramírez has to check this out, he said to himself; it's too bad the metal's so rusty, I don't think he'll get any fingerprints. Fucking sea air destroys everything. He was examining the stain when he heard the sound of the shutter click.

"Listen, smart-ass, who do you think you are?" he asked the girl.

"I'm doing my job!"

He was trying to think of what to say when he saw the department pickup truck, La Julia, drive by. Finally, he said to himself. He was sure that Fatwolf had recognized him. The truck ground to a halt a few meters farther on, went in reverse, and stopped so Cruz Treviño could get out and go into the alleyway. The huge guy looked at La Chilanga suspiciously. I should have run her off, Vicente said to himself, this guy's going to think I was the one who leaked the news to her.

Cruz Treviño was incredibly rude. "Get out of here," he ordered. "You can't be around the crime scene."

The woman spit out a slew of insults at him. When she walked by, Treviño watched her angrily and then said hello to the detective.

"Another girl?"

"Like the El Palmar one."

Cruz Treviño took a step back. "That's Taboada's case."

"They sent me. I was on call."

"Okay, it's up to you." He shrugged his shoulders. "Everybody gets the same treatment?"

"It's your decision."

The huge guy nodded and went to leave. Before turning halfway around, he patted his pants. "You got cuffs?"

"I'm gonna use 'em."

"I need 'em more than you do."

Reluctantly, Rangel stuck his hand into his right pants pocket and threw him the handcuffs. Cruz Treviño was right: what he found out about the window made it practically impossible that one of the regulars was the killer. If they were going to arrest a suspect, they wouldn't find him in the bar. He said that to himself and then went to coordinate transportation for the dead girl's body.

All in all, they were there for two hours. During that time, Fatwolf and Cruz Treviño picked up all the suspects they could find in the area. Cruz Treviño parked La Julia a block away from the Bar León, and the two officers walked to the historic center of the city. They walked around the Plaza de Armas, paying attention to every detail, and when they found a bench full of gang members, Fatwolf went up to them and dragged them to the truck. One of them tried to get away, but Cruz Treviño caught him by the arm and knocked him to the ground in one fell swoop. Cruz Treviño could throw a good punch. Then they went down to the train station, where they picked up the bums sleeping on the benches; after that, they stopped at the black market stands and repeated the same operation.

Cruz Treviño was from Parral, Coahuila. A good friend of El Travolta, Cruz Treviño was in a very bad mood whenever it was hot out.

That day, Cruz and Fatwolf put all the prisoners into one cell, including two hippies who were on their way to Acapulco. Fatwolf wrote the suspects' names in the registry, while Cruz Treviño rolled up his sleeves and got his arms warmed up. When he was ready, Cruz went into the cell with the prison guard behind him.

"Door." He was asking them to open it. "You." He pointed at one of the hippies and made him come out.

Once in the hallway, Cruz took a step toward the prisoner— he had a John Lennon look, long hair, sideburns, round glasses, and shoved him.

"What's the deal with the girl?"

The hippie—a political science student from the Universidad Nacional on vacation in the port—adjusted his glasses and replied, "What girl?"

He never should have said that. The punch took the wind out of him; at least that was the guard's judgment. The guard was named Emilio Nieto, aka El Chicote, and he elected to study the ceiling as Cruz Treviño got ready to repeat the treatment in controlled doses. The prisoner panted until he could gather enough air to ask again, "What girl?" and take another punch. Meanwhile, the prisoners started to whisper "Assholes," and the second hippie's face went pale.

Then Cruz Treviño shouted, "Door!" and the suspects, like sheep in a flock, scurried out of the way.

Identifying the body took half an hour. One of the waiters confirmed that the uniform was from Public School Number Five, which wasn't too far from there. The Professor telephoned the principal and found out that the mother of one of the girls had called asking about her daughter.

"Send her over here."

The mother arrived, escorted by two female neighbors. She was carrying a rosary and a few holy cards in her hand. What a shame, Rangel thought, those aren't going to help her at all. The woman erupted in tears as soon as she saw the shoes, and there was no way to calm her down. Finally, they injected her with a tranquilizer and she left in the same ambulance as her daughter. They found the husband an hour later, thanks to the neighbors who came with the mother. His name was Odilón and he worked in the refinery. It's always painful to see a grown man break down.

"Yes, that's her," said the man. "It's my daughter."

The girl was named Julia Concepción González. Once they were at headquarters, the father mentioned that his daughter was in her second year in elementary school and was about to turn nine years old. Nine years old, thought Rangel. Who could attack a defenseless little girl? Only a sick murderous bastard.

"Taboada's not back?"

It was the second time in an hour that Chief García had asked for him. For the last few months, the fat guy had become the chief's favorite, so much so that he even let him take the patrol car for personal business for as much time as he needed. Anyway it doesn't matter, Rangel thought, as soon as he gets here, they're going to screw him. Supposedly, El Travolta was the one in charge of the case, since he was the one who picked up the first girl's body. But, knowing his coworker's ways, Rangel doubted the chief would find him that day. On Fridays, after eating lunch, El Travolta would head to the docks, perhaps to the Tiberius Bar, pick up a prostitute or two, and go party.

When Rangel got back to headquarters, they told him Dr. Ridaura had called. Rangel pulled out his tiny phonebook from his back pocket and dialed the university morgue. It was six in the afternoon.

"Doctor? It's Rangel. You got something?"

"I'm finished already. But before I say anything, tell me something. Did you send a photographer over here?"

"No."

"That's what I thought."

"Hold on, hold on, what do you mean?"

"A guy with a *norteño* accent called and told me you ordered him to come. "

"And you let him in?"

"Of course not, even though he tried to intimidate me. I told him I was going to confirm what he said, and he hung up."

An accent from northern Mexico, Rangel thought. It must be Johnny Guerrero, that fucking piece of shit.

"Thanks, Doctor. Did you find out anything?"

"Yes, but I'd rather tell you in person. They're probably tapping our call."

He got to the morgue at nine P.M. on the dot. Rangel parked at the university medical school and walked down the wide staircase leading to the student amphitheater. He had to knock hard for someone to open the door. A sweaty young man led him to the laboratory, a room covered in tile where the smell of chemical products was particularly strong. The doctor was still working. As soon as she saw Rangel, she sent the young man away and let out a tired sigh.

"Welcome."

"You've been at it a long time."

"If I don't do it myself, someone else will do it worse," she said. "Can you imagine El Travolta managing all this?"

Rangel didn't respond. He didn't like to talk badly about other officers, even though he agreed with her.

"Do you have any news?"

"I'm almost finished typing it all out." She pointed to a hefty Olivetti typewriter. "The first thing you'll be interested to hear is that it's the same weapon they used in El Palmar. See? This cut here, and see this photo?"

"Was any organ in particular affected?"

"What are you looking for?"

"Do you think it was a doctor, a butcher, a medical student, or an employee at the city market? Did the person know where to cut to cause harm?"

"I don't think so. Do you remember the sailor?" The doctor was referring to a drunk sailor who stabbed a prostitute two months previous. "I'd say it's the same: mindless violence, completely irrational. If he had started cutting here, for example," she pointed to a specific point on the torso, "the knife would have traversed the heart and death would've been instantaneous. Instead of that: look. See? And again, look."

"Right-handed?"

"Yes, without a doubt." Using a metal rod, the doctor lifted the skin away from the cadaver. "Look at the trajectory. The cut slants to the left as it moves down; I think he cut her like this." The doctor lifted the little rod and swiped it downward. "But first he had to lay her down on the ground."

"Was there sexual violence?"

"Just like the other."

"The same way?"

The doctor nodded.

"Before or . . . ?"

"No, after she was dead, like before. And this. You remember the first one? I asked myself, How could someone hate a little girl this much? And now I'm saying to myself, How could someone do this to two girls in a row? I can't understand it." She sneezed.

Rangel asked if she could do a blood test on the two girls. The doctor wrinkled her nose.

"What're you looking for?"

"Anything that would put them to sleep. I'm wondering if he sedated them."

"I'll have it for you tomorrow. I need reagents that only Orihuela has in his lab."

A moment later, she handed him the report, which Rangel read immediately. When he was almost finished, the doctor interrupted him again:

"Is that all, officer?"

"Huh?"

"I'm asking if they can take her already. The father's called twice."

"Tell him they can; we're finished. But one thing: no one's authorized to photograph the body. Tell the parents. Only family gets to see."

"Yes, of course."

Then the doctor did something Rangel would never see her do again. Already a black blanket covered the girl's body from the neck down, but the old woman took out a white handkerchief and used it to cover the girl's face.

"Poor thing. Here, *chiquita*, it's all over now. Your parents are on their way."

3

He was up writing his report until three in the morning. Like usual, he hit a wall eventually; he couldn't do anything else and there was no other choice but to wait. El Chicote was snoring at the front desk, and Crazyshot had gone to sleep in his car. The last person to come in was at one o'clock, when Wong came back from interviewing the parents at the funeral home.

"The parents don't suspect anyone, the father doesn't have any enemies, and no one has seen anyone suspicious on the street. It's the same thing as El Palmar."

Wong was a good officer. He identified leads quickly and pointed them out so the investigation could proceed. Thanks to him they were able to establish the approximate time when the killer went into the bathroom. As soon as Rangel proved the murderer had climbed through the window, Wong had found out that two of the regulars had heard a noise around 2:30. It was the psycho, thought Rangel.

Now we're getting somewhere, Wong cheered, we can move forward. Rangel said yes, even though deep down he had the feeling that the investigation wasn't going anywhere. All he had to do was close his eyes and remember the bizarre way the body was found. There was something about all this that was irrational, hidden, reminiscent of something else; as if someone were sending a message he couldn't decipher. Shit, he said to himself, how could he break the code?

As Rangel wrote his report, El Chicote dropped off the latest edition of *El Mercurio,* hot off the presses: THE JACKAL IS BACK. Ah, *cabrón*— and he suddenly felt sick to his stomach—how irresponsible can they be? Now they had really gone too far giving the murderer a name: the Jackal. In the article, the reporter wrote he was shocked by the number of rapes in the city: "At least three every month, according to official statistics." I didn't think there were so many, Rangel thought. The reporter argued that the guilty party was "a real-life jackal." They said men who attacked minors were like jackals, predators that hunt in a pack and when they're sure their prey is small and defenseless. "The authority's ineptness is what laid the foundation for the Jackal to emerge." Just a second here, Rangel said to himself, I don't like this one bit.

The article was by a new columnist, Johnny Guerrero, a guy from Chihuahua. Rangel didn't like his style. From the first day, he was writing articles attacking the chief, like he was on the mayor's payroll. He interspersed his opinion with the facts and he exaggerated things, but more than that he seasoned his writing with flowery words: he made a bum into a *derelict,* a prostitute into a *strumpet.* For him, an autopsy was *the legal necropsy* and he wrote mean-spirited captions under photos: *This is the miserable construction worker; Here we find the despicable ranch hand.* The first time Johnny tried to interview him on the phone, Rangel took an immediate dislike to him. He imagined him as crippled, fat, squat, and greasy-faced. And he didn't get the reporter's sense of humor, which seemed to require that someone else be humiliated.

Rangel read this article quickly, because he already knew what it would say: *Efforts in vain, murderer on the loose, defenseless public, incredibly slow, disgraceful investigation, police incompetence.* Incompetence? He said to himself, Fuck him! I'd like to see him in my shoes, the piece-of-shit reporter. The article was cut off abruptly: *Continued on page 28.* He set the main section of the paper aside and looked through the rest until he found, in the section with the horoscopes and comics *(Continued from page 1)*: *because we can't expect anything from this system. A lead could stare them in the face, and they wouldn't even notice it.*

Fucking jerk! The column was an attack on his boss, but for a second Rangel took it personally. Of course. Johnny was in complicity with the mayor.

He was brooding unhappily, about to close the paper, when he noticed an unusual headline on the opposite page: UFO'S IN PARACUÁN. Damn, what's this about? Above the head, there was a note in italics explaining that, thanks to an agreement with the AP, *El Mercurio* finally had access to the most interesting column to come out in the last few years, straight from the ranks of the FBI: ALL ABOUT UFO's by Professor Cormac McCormick. Oh, man, what's up with this?

In today's installment, the daring investigator was reporting on the strange case in the town of Yuca in Wyoming, where Martians were believed to be taking possession of the bodies of earthlings. They arrived at nighttime, witnesses said, hid their ship, and entered houses. They took over their hosts' minds and bodies. The only thing that stopped them was the presence of a mineral called Mobdolite. The professor quoted a woman named Stark: "They have Bob."

Mobdolite, thought Rangel, that stone is going to sell like hotcakes.

He threw the newspaper onto the desk next to him and walked to the end of the hallway to get some coffee. He thought he saw

someone watching him from behind the window. Ah, *cabrón,*
who's that? He was so tired that his own reflection surprised him:
long hair, a Sergeant Pepper mustache, thick sideburns, and a
white shirt—always a white shirt—brown boots with white stitch-
ing, and blue jeans. Why didn't I recognize myself, maybe because
I don't have on my dark glasses? Someone needs to tell the chief
to buy a new coffeemaker. This one doesn't work; it spews the
coffee out of the pot.

Whenever the conditions allowed for it, Rangel wore his dark
glasses, to hide the fact that he had one brown eye and one green
one. One for each side of reality, like Mr. Torsvan had told him.

Once he was at his desk, he picked up El Travolta's report on
the body found in El Palmar and read it through quickly. Then he
reviewed his own notes: A fracture of the pelvis . . . legs separated
from the body with a serrated object . . . white fuzz . . . a cigarette.
All of a sudden, he said to himself, What a coincidence, the other
girl also died on the seventeenth! But he didn't find this detail important and filed the random fact deep in his subconscious.

If he didn't solve this problem soon, the reporters were going
to get even more aggressive. Why I am doing this? I shouldn't be
here, he said to himself, my back hurts. As usually happened at
this hour, his body began to mirror his tension. The proof came
when he tried to pick up a pencil and it slipped through his fingers. Whenever he was under extreme pressure, unavoidably, his
hands would sweat for hours, and a moment would come when
they would start to bleed. He couldn't stop it, not even by taking
a tranquilizer or wrapping his hands in a handkerchief. First, his
hands would start to itch all over; a few hours later, he would have
to dry the sweat off his hands every few minutes, and then soon
he wouldn't be able to feel the texture of things. The worst came
after that, because he couldn't touch things that were very hot or

cold without pain, he was unable to touch certain things at all, and even something as simple as reading became complicated: to drink coffee he had to wrap the mug in a handkerchief, to read he would wet the tips of his fingers with saliva. A moment would come when his hands would finally dry out, but this false sense of relief just told him he was in the eye of the hurricane. If his worrying continued, from that point on, there was no cream or oil that could prevent the arrival of cracks and slits, and when his hands dried out completely, they started to bleed: sometimes at his fingertips, sometimes in the middle of his palm.

The last time his hands bled was in September, when he was investigating a bank robbery, a suspicious attack on the governor's own bank. A really wild case that caused me a lot of problems, he thought, and he rubbed his eyes. *What am I doing here? I'm not trained for this, what they need is a real expert in sex crimes, not a dozen people making it all up.* As had happened before, Rangel told himself it was time to throw in the towel and do something else for a living. Even though he was hearing good things about his work, the way he tracked down criminals, Rangel knew it was all based on misinformation: he didn't have an infallible sense of intuition, he wasn't particularly cunning, and he didn't know anything about martial arts. It had been more than a year since he'd been in an actual fight. The truth was he was a musician, or at least he thought so; how had he allowed things to go this far? And if El Travolta hadn't been able to solve the case, how was he going to do it?

4

It was his uncle's fault he got to this point. When no one would give him a hand, when even people who said they were his closest friends turned their back on him, the only one who provided him with a way to make a living was his uncle, Miguel Rivera, whom the family had practically disowned. Rangel had called him to ask for work and his uncle arranged for them to meet: "Of course, Vicente, come over tomorrow and we'll talk." He met him at his desk next to the chief's office. He drank a cola drink, as he talked with a guy who was about twenty-three years old and a woman in her forties.

"Young people, I'd like to introduce you to my nephew, Vicente Rangel. Nephew, this is Lolita and this is Joaquín Taboada, a promising young man in the investigative unit."

The woman turned out to be the chief's secretary. At the time, she was thinner and sexier. The second guy was tall and chubby; he wasn't particularly well-built but one punch from those hands would be enough to knock anybody to the ground. Rangel's first impression was of a violent, insecure fat guy. Before he could come to a final conclusion, his uncle called him to one side and they went to the restaurant at the corner, Klein's, a legendary eatery.

"It's the best there is around here."

They ordered two coffees that ended up being watered down.

"I read in the newspaper that things were going well for you with your band," his uncle said. "You're not going to play anymore?"

Rangel explained in very general terms that he had fought with the band leader, he was going through a transitional period, and he wanted to stop playing for a while.

"That's a shame," his uncle said. "I think you have real skill." Without another comment, he offered him a job.

"Doing what?"

"The same thing as me, Vicente."

"Well, thanks a lot, but I was thinking I'd look for office work."

"No, no, no, we already have an accountant, and one is enough. Come with me and I'll show you how to work."

"But I don't think police work is my calling."

"That's the same thing I said thirty-seven years ago. Look, Vicente: you're not going to find anybody here who dreamed about being a police officer; we all got here some other way. You'll start tomorrow morning, early. I'll see you at six right here."

And that's how Rangel became a police officer. The first few weeks were incredible. His uncle had him look through the files on terrorists and bank robbers, so he would recognize them if he ran into them on the street, and let him read the latest folder they had sent him from Mexico City with the stamp reading STATE DE-PARTMENT, a report about a group called the September 23rd Terrorist League, and at the bottom it mentioned the names of two people in the port suspected of belonging to the group. No shit, he said to himself, I never thought I'd jump from the art scene to the crime scene.

For the next three weeks, Rangel went with his uncle on all his assignments. He made arrests, inquiries, followed up on crime reports, and started to get to know the city. Since he was the type of person who had never left the bars and music stores, he had to change his ways. People told him their problems and Rangel listened to them, went inside houses that had seemed impenetrable, and talked with people he never thought he would meet. All without having to be violent, because that was his uncle's style. He told him, "There's one golden rule, nephew, and it's this: If you're going to pull out your gun, it's because you're going to use it." His uncle acted like he went everywhere unarmed, but Vicente noticed that he carried a .38 caliber, sometimes stuck in his belt, other times in his shoulder holster.

The first days were the most dangerous. As that universe was completely foreign to him, several times he was on the edge of causing an accident and even someone's death, because he didn't know how to react yet. One Monday, after the weekly meeting with the chief, his uncle asked him to go with him to the Coralillo to make an arrest.

"*Ay, cabrón,*" Rangel answered, "I've never been there, they say it's really dangerous."

"It's not so bad, it was worse at the end of the forties, after World War Two; then, you really did have to watch out for the unsavory types that came in from overseas: Turks, Chinese, Koreans, you'd even run into Italian mafiosos."

"Listen, uncle, I'm not armed."

"Don't worry, we're going to arrest the Petrolera thief."

"What do you mean?"

"The jerk who's robbing from the neighborhood where the oil workers live, don't tell me you haven't heard about it."

"And who is it?"

"I'm not a hundred percent sure, but I've got a hunch."

"And are we going to go to the Coralillo because of a hunch?"

"Nephew," his uncle said to him, "in this job, you've got to go on your intuition. If you wait to find conclusive proof, or if you think they'll just turn in the guy who did it, you should look for another line of work. To stay alive you have to use your intuition." And since he saw that Rangel was interested, he added, "There are times when you just know, without anyone having to tell you. You're deep in the worst case ever, you have no idea how to tackle it, and suddenly, *boom!* You hear a voice saying, *Over here, cabrón, there's no other way.* You have to drop whatever you're doing and follow it wherever it leads you. It might seem strange, but your intuition is never wrong. Now you're going to see the proof."

As they got closer to the Colonia Coralillo, Rangel's nerves came back and he began to feel his hands itching. "Listen, Uncle, they say the last police officer to go in that neighborhood almost left feet first."

"No. You don't say? And what else do they say?"

"They say like twenty people attacked him, and when they were about to let him go one of them cut him with a knife, and the bastard ran out of there with his intestines in his hands."

"And they're right," said his uncle, and he lifted up his shirt. He had a scar that ran the length of his stomach. "Damn, what a stupid nephew I have! You got everything you know secondhand."

They left the last paved alleyway behind and drove down a steep gravel gully. There weren't a lot of cars around. When he saw his uncle's furrowed brow, Rangel knew that despite his jokes, the idea of wandering around this area made his relative nervous. As soon as the vehicle appeared, the people moved away from them distrustfully and it was obvious they were being watched from behind the curtains of the buildings.

As he turned a corner, his uncle said, "OK, now for real. Keep your eyes peeled."

"Is there going to be shooting?"

"No way, don't get ahead of yourself; we won't have any problem. The Coralillo is a crucial area in this line of work; they know me, and it's about time I presented you to the bigwigs around here."

They parked in front of a butcher's shop and his uncle got out of the car with a huge smile on his face.

"Juanito!" He waved to a man in his fifties wearing a bloody apron, cutting steaks behind the counter.

"How you doin', boss? What can I do for you? You come for some round steak?"

"No," said his uncle, "I actually came for your assistant there."

Rangel turned to look at the guy he was talking about, a rough-looking man who was taller and thicker than his uncle and him combined. The giant didn't bat an eyelid. He had an ax in his right arm, resting on the cutting board, and on each side of him there was a big segment of beef ribs, recently broken into pieces. Does my uncle really think he's going to arrest him? Don Miguel at seventy years old and Vicente at twenty-four, even working together, couldn't subdue this gorilla. If he could split cow ribs into pieces with one single blow, how could my uncle think we could catch him?

The owner must have known his uncle for a long time, because he came out from behind the counter with the knife in his hand and walked over to the old man to turn the heat up on him.

"Hold on, let me see here." He made like he was examining him. "You're fatter and older. And your partner here doesn't look so tough. You should have brought a different lackey, because this one isn't going to last long against my assistant."

His uncle just stood there, exposing himself completely to the butcher's knife like he was hanging out with friends.

"Not so fast. They call him *Jackie Chan,* just so you have an idea. Besides, he's not my lackey, he's my nephew."

"Ah," said the butcher, studying his face. "Nice to meet you."

Rangel nodded.

"So, what then? You going to tell your assistant there to get in the car?"

"He's all grown up; you tell him. Or tell Jackie Chan to get him. Let's see if he can handle him."

The giant stared at him. Damn, thought Rangel, is he for real? And he looked at the giant with the ax in his hand. He hadn't moved since they got there, but Rangel knew he was sizing them up. He'd just need a little push to jump over the counter and attack them both.

"What do you say?" his uncle asked the giant. "You wanna mess around with my nephew?"

But the giant didn't answer.

"Well," said the owner, "he doesn't want to go. You'll have to carry him, lieutenant, but I don't think you could. He moves washing machines for fun in his spare time."

"That's why I came to see you, Gaptooth." His uncle got in the butcher's face, and the butcher did the same, like two bulls sizing each other up. "I'm not going to take him with me, just as long as you give the stuff back. Why are you breaking into my friends' houses?"

Gaptooth opened his huge mouth and smiled broadly, and Rangel understood where the nickname came from.

"Damn, I can't believe you, boss! Every time you come around here it turns out you're trying to help out your friends."

"It's not my fault I have so many friends. You already know how I work. You probably just don't like my car. You want me to come back here in La Julia?"

"No, that truck's damned ugly and it doesn't have air-conditioning." "Don't worry about it, just imagine you're in a sauna."

"And what will my neighbors say?"

"That you went on vacation up north."

The Nagual Prison was up north, built on a hill of the same name.

Gaptooth laughed again, but he didn't say anything, and Rangel noticed that the giant was discreetly trying to slip out the back door. Rangel's uncle also noticed and shot a look at Vicente.

They were standing right in front of the butchers, and Gaptooth hadn't put his sharp knife down. All he has to do is lift up his hand to cut my uncle's guts out again, he thought. But even though he was at a disadvantage, his uncle was the one who accelerated the situation. Without moving an inch, without deflecting his body despite the danger he was facing, he broke the tension with an impatient remark.

"Look, Gaptooth, you know I was always straight with you. It's not in your interest to lose this relationship. The ones coming into power aren't as patient as I am."

The butcher considered his options. Finally, he nodded.

"All right, Shorty, tell the lieutenant here where you put those things you found in the trash."

The giant had a deep voice. "At Teobaldo's shop."

"With the Spaniard?"

"Yep, there."

"Ah, goddamn Teobaldo. When did you take him the stuff?"

"Just yesterday."

"He already paid you?"

"No."

"Good. That way you don't have to give him the money back. Let him know we're on our way over there."

*   *   *

Half an hour later, Rangel helped his uncle put a television, a sound system, and a jewelry case in the trunk. The owner of the place, a Spaniard with Moorish roots, spit a lot and cussed them out.

"I wonder if this is all of it. At least this much is going back where it came from. And don't take any more stuff that's been lost, Teobaldo, because I'll lock you up. This is the last time I give you a warning, dumb-ass. The next time I'm locking you up for good."

They made a U-turn and went back the same way they came. The car could hardly climb the gravel incline with the additional weight, the wheels were spinning.

As he accelerated with great care, his uncle spat out, "And all this fucking work so they can say we stole whatever's still missing."

Maybe his uncle wouldn't do it, but any of the other officers would, Rangel thought.

He was appointed to the force a month later, since the chief owed some favors to his uncle. Soon, he started to receive his check every two weeks, much to the surprise of the lackeys who had been waiting for theirs for months. It wasn't a lot of money, but for other people it was a lot, and that tiny step that was so difficult for Rangel to take, because he thought he was lowering himself, debasing the image that he had of himself, incited a lot of envy among those who worked with him. An example: because of his criminal record, Chávez could never have a stable job and be a normal police officer. According to him, he'd clarified what happened when he stabbed two people—"It was self-defense"— but Chief García didn't care about that: Chávez was sentenced to being a lackey his entire life, being paid out of the others' salaries, living at the expense of El Travolta, his partner, who became even more famous with every arrest Chávez made. Chávez took the risks, El Travolta took the credit.

Rangel went and bought some shoes and a pair of pants with the first pesos he got. He trashed his Hawaiian shirts and the pastel-colored suit he had used as a guitarist. A musician had died and a police officer was born.

His days were long. Wake up and iron a shirt, do a few crunches, exercises for the arms, abs, and legs—so as not to end up with his uncle's potbelly and his smoker's cough—then he'd take a quick shower and head out to take the first *águila* (taxis in the port were called *águilas,* or eagles, because of the union emblem that identified them). He never could beat his uncle to the breakfast spot. No matter how early he woke up, by the time Rangel sat down in the Jewish guy's place, Don Miguel Rivera had already finished his gigantic plate of *chilaquiles* with beans, *salsa roja,* or *verde;* orange juice; and a sweet dark *café de olla.* Then they'd go over the cases one by one. Rangel gave him a report from the day before. If no one was visibly eavesdropping on them, his uncle would entrust him with one or two interesting things that were about to happen: apprehensions, rewards, the interception of a gringo shrimper in Mexican federal waters. Then they would leave to clock in and organize themselves for the day. Or days plural. Two days were never the same.

As soon as the work routine seemed normal to him, Rangel noticed that the dark depression that had afflicted him began to disappear, though not completely. It would always come back like a chronic sickness, and he would have to scare it away each time.

He got a semi-used Chevy Nova a year later. He bought it from a coworker who came from the border. He left the nasty downtown room he rented and went to live on the other side of the river, in what he called his mansion: an old wooden house he stumbled upon one day while chasing a suspect. It was one of those old houses that exist in many ports, a house built at the beginning of the century in a New Orleans style. There was a large living room, a kitchen, a small dining area, and two bedrooms in the back. The high ceilings cooled off the inside, and it was a delight to sit on the huge terrace looking out on the river. The mansion belonged to a ranch foreman, and the owner was an elderly woman who charged him a symbolic amount to live there. Behind his house, the cornfields began. Between his house and the dock, there was an eternally muddy path, preventing anyone from coming around to bother him. The houses closest to him belonged to two families of fishermen, and they were located a good distance in front, by the river's edge. The only sound to be heard was the occasional whistle of departing ferries. After living in a noisy room in the city's historic downtown near the docks, he got to know something like calm those first afternoons he spent in his mansion, when he would listen to music on the terrace, lying in his hammock with a drink in his hand, looking at the indigo sky and the lights reflected on the river.

Soon, he noticed that once a month El Chicote walked by certain desks to hand out checks with a PETRÓLEOS MEXICANOS stamp on them. He also realized that on the fifteenth of every month a guy in an ostentatious suit who looked like an accountant would walk by and leave them tips, courtesy of millionaire John Williams, owner of the local Cola Drinks bottler. And as if this weren't enough, the chief had a monthly meeting in his office with a guy wearing expensive plaid suits, who, it was said, was the owner of three motels and a gasoline station. After meeting with these people, the chief would always seem to be in a better mood and he'd call a few guys into his office, where he'd hand out some bills in envelopes with the logos of several different government institutions. Then he understood why Chávez and El Travolta spent more money and dressed better than he could, despite making the same. When he asked his uncle how he tolerated all that, his uncle cleared his throat and took a minute before answering.

"Look, Vicente"—he swallowed his saliva—"this is a very complicated job. I'm not saying you shouldn't do your job, but what I mean to say is that sometimes you can't . . . or you shouldn't . . . and if you do, you run into a lot of problems. Your good intentions ricochet back in your face, like you were shooting at a wall."

One of those afternoons when the guy in the plaid suit came to visit, Chief García sent for him.

"Rangel," he said, "this is Congressman Tobias Wolffer. Yesterday someone threatened to kidnap his daughter, and I want to help him, because the poor guy's busy helping the Professors' Union. I'm going to ask you to drop whatever you're doing"—the last few days Rangel hadn't been doing anything—"turn over your cases to someone else, no matter how many there are, and tomorrow, starting at seven A.M. you're going to be on watch at the lawyer's house, on the lookout for any suspicious activity."

Then he spoke to the congressman.

"Rangel is one of our most qualified officers. He was the one who solved the kidnapping in Tantoyuca, Veracruz."

The chief was exaggerating things, but Rangel wasn't about to contradict him in front of a benefactor. The chief would often play the role of protector of souls for the people who came to ask him for favors. Normally, the visitors weren't looking for spiritual help, since Chief García was no saint; rather, among his many other duties, he always represented the only legal means to hire a bodyguard. Rangel asked himself why he had called him, since normally the chief turned to El Travolta, Fatwolf, or Cruz Treviño, who'd earned his trust. Him, on the other hand, they respected, but they didn't involve him in many things, because he was Miguel Rivera's nephew. Usually, they saw his uncle as an island set apart from the rest; he did his work well, but without rubbing shoulders with the others, and he didn't normally skim a little off the top when he solved his cases, unlike the rest of them.

Since Rangel was already an experienced officer, he asked himself what Congressman Wolffer's secret was. When he tried to look him in the eye, Don Tobias looked away from him. No, Rangel said to himself, no one's threatened this guy. If he wants a police officer to keep watch at his house, it must be for other reasons; maybe he wants someone to keep an eye on his wife. He probably thinks she's cheating on him.

The next day, he was at his post at ten minutes to seven. The *licenciado* was waiting for him.

"The last few days, my daughter's been trying to ditch school. I want you to watch the entrances, and as soon as school's out bring her home."

He gave him the keys to a light-blue luxury van and sent for his daughter, a dark-skinned girl who was in sixth grade at a private school run by nuns. She was wearing a thin sweater, even though winter was ending, and it was obvious that she was sweating.

"Do you want me to turn on the air?"

The girl didn't answer. Where her left sleeve ended, the girl had a huge bruise, as if someone had ruthlessly squeezed her arm. There was a similar mark near her neck—and then Rangel understood the sweater and her long hair, down in this heat. Child abuse; no wonder she didn't like her dad. Nothing's going to happen, he told her, but the little girl stayed quiet, looking out the window.

He kept on with that job for eight days. Until Friday the following week when the congressman asked, "She doesn't give you a lot of trouble, does she? The little brat."

Rangel answered, "No, but she must have fallen down, because she has some strange marks on her arms. Do you want me to take her to a doctor?" The congressman turned red. "They already looked at her," he said, "you don't need to. That's all for today."

The worst thing that ever happened to him was his uncle's death. He thought about quitting. He was left up in the air, without anyone to support him at headquarters, and immediately the other officers set about making his life impossible, above all El Travolta and Chávez, until one afternoon he got into a fistfight with Wong. Even though Wong planted a right hook in his face, Rangel was agile enough to dodge the following punch and give him an impeccable kick. That was enough for them to stop messing with him.

What he regretted most was that his uncle had died suddenly, before he'd finished teaching Rangel the job. That was why he thought about submitting his resignation. Or he'd just stop going. He felt really nervous: he was just a musician faking at being a police officer, he hadn't finished his training period, and his teacher, the only trustworthy officer, had died. That's why, every time he found himself in a complicated situation, he asked himself: Would my uncle have done it this way? And it seemed like he could hear a voice giving him advice: *The surprise factor, look for the surprise factor, nephew. The person, the most important thing is the person; learn to get inside his skin.* Or his most memorable advice: *The first impression is the most important, don't forget that, nephew: who got you this job anyway?* The reason why he was doing well in the job was that the majority of the other officers focused their attention on a small, set group of people, but he always stepped out of the box and looked farther afield.

They got a call from El Travolta around midnight. Rangel knew because he noticed Cruz Treviño covered the phone receiver and lowered his voice.

"Where were you, man? They found another girl. You remember El Palmar? And you remember who's in charge? Well, hurry up, the chief's been asking for you since four o'clock. . . . No, *cabrón,* I'm not joking. You're gonna see I'm not joking soon. . . . Yeah. . . . Well, that's what you think, but if I were you I'd already be walking in the door."

El Travolta showed up in the hallway a half hour later. Fatwolf stopped him before he walked in the glass door and updated him as to what was going on. Rangel was talking to Lolita, watching as El Travolta said nothing, not a word; he just stared at him, his straight hair covering his forehead. Cruz Treviño looked at Vicente and told him, "Now it's on, man. Now you started something."

Lolita turned toward the hallway, saw the two fat guys talking— oh, God, goddamnit—and walked toward the chief's office, her heels clicking on the floor. El Travolta whispered something, like looking for an explanation, and Fatwolf tilted his chin at Rangel.

Taboada kicked a metal file cabinet that tumbled down the hallway toward the detective; Fatwolf tried to grab him by an arm but El Travolta was quicker. Rangel snatched up the only blunt object at hand, the heavy phone receiver, and stood up. When the fat guy passed in front of the chief's door, García called him from inside his office: "Taboada!" But the fat guy walked straight ahead toward Rangel.

If Cruz Treviño thought he could just look the other way and let the fight happen, he realized he was wrong as soon as he saw the chief stick his head out. Even though he would have liked to see Rangel beat up, he had to stop El Travolta, but with his bad luck, when he did he got popped in his left eye. Despite that, Cruz—who had to win some points to make up for past mistakes—grabbed hold of El Travolta by his arm and stopped him. As they were tussling, the chief yelled, "Taboada!"

Lolita was biting her nails with a look of terror on her face. Finally, Cruz Treviño pacified El Travolta.

"They're talking to you, man!"

And he didn't let go until El Travolta settled down and went into the chief's office.

They yelled at each other for ten minutes. Rangel listened as their bellowing echoed through the office. The chief was giving him the scolding of a lifetime. "What's going on in your head? Who do you think you are? The next time you mess up like this, you'll be locked up for a month, understand?" Then they lowered their voices.

No one knew what they said, but the fat guy came out quietly and didn't look for a fight with Rangel. He just sat down next to Cruz Treviño and faked like he was reading the autopsy report. Every now and then he'd raise his eyes, look toward Vicente, and send him all the bad vibes he could. He was only there for about half an hour, because he couldn't work, as drunk as he was, and he only left when Lolita handed him a sealed envelope from the chief.

Then, when Rangel thought it was all over, El Travolta stood up and said to him, "You better watch out, *cabrón*. I'm gonna get you."

Rangel stayed quiet, completely quiet, and when he saw the man was leaving, he said to himself, Well, there's nothing I could do about this one, it was fate.

* * *

His hands were stinging as he left headquarters. What the fuck, he thought, why do I have to go through this again? I thought it was under control. He left the office exhausted and went straight to his house, more to change his clothes than to sleep. After much difficulty, he was able to park at the dock, next to the ferry ramp. He peered through the fog but couldn't make out the ferry. Whatever, he thought, it must be on the other side, so he walked over to Las Lupitas, the only place open at that hour. There, under three dim lightbulbs, a fisherman was talking with two transvestites and the owners of Las Lupitas. When they saw Rangel coming, the fisherman stood up. "Shit, it's that same damn guy again."

The man tried to run away, but Rangel grabbed him by the arm and took him over by the river. It was El Lobina, a fisherman with a criminal record, a bad guy. Rangel had been looking for him because he was selling marijuana, but he was waiting for the chance to arrest him on a more important charge. When El Lobina tried to get free, Rangel punched him in the back.

"Ah . . . *cabrón*. You throw a heavy punch."

When Rangel was tired, he acted arbitrarily; why should he explain himself to a despicable character like El Lobina?

As they were walking, the fisherman shouted, "Hold on, wait, my sandal—my sandal came off! My sandal!" But since the officer didn't stop, he shouted to the trannies, "Keep it for me!"

Once at the river, the fisherman started his boat's motor. "What, the ferry left you again?"

But Rangel didn't respond. The fisherman looked at him defiantly— fucking cop—and ferried him to the other side of the river.

"There you go, boss."

Rangel whispered something incomprehensible and stumbled off to his house. He took a quick shower with cold water, and took out a shirt and a pair of pants from the closet. As he was picking his clothes, the faint light in the living room illuminated the armchair, where he made out a bottle of whiskey that still had a little bit in it, just a swig, and he said to himself, Anyway, I'm already here, and I need to get some shut-eye. So after getting dressed he lay back in the armchair, just for a second, with the whiskey in his hand and Stan Getz in the CD player. . . .

He heard the sound of a trumpet. That's strange, he thought, I know how to play the guitar, but in the dream he was playing the trumpet, it was a really soft jazz, the best of Stan Getz. Rangel was the first trumpet in the ensemble; he was doing whatever he wanted with the music, and the others followed him without a problem. A great group, João Gilberto and Astrud and António Carlos Jobim play so well. *Kick Getz out!* he suggested. *Now I'm gonna do a solo that'll blow their minds,* and in the dream he stood up and blew really hard, and the gorgeous Astrud watched him with complete admiration. Of course, Rangel thought. She's going to leave her boyfriend to come with me. He was going to play the final note when he heard his uncle's voice: *What are you doing, nephew?* And he played a note off-key. Aw, man, I wanted to try it again, and, aw, man, it was worse: the trumpet didn't make a sound; inside there was just a dark black hole and his uncle next to him, it seemed like his uncle was standing in the living room wearing his perpetual white shirt and his shoulder holster. *What are you doing? You're falling asleep. Aren't you going to work?* His eyes shot open with a start: Ah, *cabrón.* It was 5:15. I'm just barely going to make it.

Part II

5

García arranged to meet them at the Restaurant Flamingos. It was a pink-colored place behind the bus station. The chief preferred to have his meetings there, because it had air-conditioning, the waitresses didn't bother them, and they had enough coffee. Taking advantage of its being open twenty-four hours a day, the officers got there between six and seven in the morning, went to the most discreet corner—the table all the way at the back—and Cruz Treviño or Fatwolf took care of clearing out the nearby tables if the people didn't leave as soon as they saw them arrive.

They were all there: the Professor, Wong, the Bedouin, the Evangelist, Crazyshot, Fatwolf, Cruz Treviño, El Travolta, and Chávez. No one bothered them there, but on that day, March 18, 1977, at six in the morning, as they headed to their usual corner, Rangel noticed that a large number of reporters with notepads, tape recorders, and even a TV camera were seated at the tables closest to them. Now what? he said to himself. What are they giving away now? He recognized three local journalists and one who was from Tampico, but he had never seen the others before. There were two, four, six, eight, ten, twelve. They must be from Monterrey or Mexico City, or maybe from San Luis Potosí. One of them, a guy who looked more awake than the others, elbowed his photographer when he recognized Rangel: Get a picture of that guy. Which guy? The one with his hair done like the Beatles.

Oh, shit, what's up with these guys? he thought; why are they pointing at me? Rangel was completely drained; he'd only slept half an hour the whole night. He needed to drink some coffee fast. He was about to sit down when he heard Crazyshot say *"Mamacita"* and saw he was talking about La Chilanga, who, out of character, had retired her normal baggy Che T-shirt and was wearing bell-bottoms and a half-open denim blouse. Rangel, who'd never seen her dressed like that before, suddenly didn't feel so tired anymore; he shamelessly studied the cut of her clothing, which highlighted her tiny waist, and focused on the way her blouse accentuated the shape of her breasts. He was looking for an excuse to get a closer look when he noticed that next to her was a tall young man wearing expensive clothes and poofy, long hair like the Jackson Five. Just a sec, he said to himself, who's that guy? Jackson Five grabbed La Chilanga by the arm and led her to the reporters' table. The detective was wondering what kind of relationship she might have with the long-haired guy, when he saw the chief come in. Instantly he knew something had happened, since Lolita was two steps behind him, her high heels clicking.

As soon as the detectives saw the older man, they fell silent. Rangel felt a stiflingly hot wave of air blow into the room. Aw, man, he said to himself, he's in a bad mood. The chief looked around at everyone and sighed with frustration.

"No reporters and no *madrinas,"* he said, and most of the crowd left.

Since four or five stragglers had stayed, Fatwolf stood up, dripping with greasy sweat, and got rid of them, pushing them out. He was a really quiet guy. He was always sweating, weighed four hundred pounds, and was five feet nine inches tall. There was just one tuft of black hair on the middle of his head, which he tried to slick back. When he didn't like something, he didn't waste time explaining himself; he made himself understood with his fists. When they saw him coming, the rest of the reporters stood up and went into the street. How weird, Rangel said to himself, I wonder how they found out the meeting was here. As La Chilanga left, the detectives focused their eyes on her, and more than one of them stretched out his neck to see her leave.

"Jerks, *cabrones,* fascists," she said, "we have a right to information."

When the young woman was gone, Rangel noticed the chief looking at El Travolta, who took a while to realize it. Finally, the fat guy gestured to Chávez: you'd better go, bro.

The weasel left, but he was upset. His presence had been tolerated at headquarters for the last month, and no one mentioned the fact that he had a criminal record. How strange, thought Rangel, Chávez had been trying to get some recognition for a long time. In the last few days, he'd even heard a rumor that they were going to name him a detective with a badge and everything, but the chief's attitude made it clear he was going to stay in purgatory a while longer. Nothing you can do about it, thought Rangel, it goes with the territory, my friend.

The chief took the seat farthest away so they couldn't surprise him from behind, an old habit he'd acquired after spending thirty years on the force and watching a lot of action movies. At a normal meeting, the chief asked each one of them what cases they were working on and what kind of progress they'd managed. He gave some advice, set deadlines for solving cases, and assigned new investigations—from coordinating the investigation of an assault or a violent death to simply sitting in the car and keeping watch on the entrance to the oil refinery or the Cola Drinks plant—and received the corresponding shows of appreciation. Very rarely would he redirect a line of investigation, and the meetings were normally calm. But that day, March 18, was not a normal meeting.

What is it then? Rangel asked himself. First, it occurred to him that the chief was angry about the newspaper's criticism of police "ineptness." But that couldn't be; the chief had heard worse things and wasn't ruffled before. Maybe he got in a fight with Torres Sabinas? Ever since Licenciado Daniel Torres Sabinas had become mayor of the port, the chief argued with him on a weekly basis. Torres was a young politician, an enemy of Governor Pepe Topete, and he didn't get along well with the chief. A rumor was going around that they'd set him up as mayor because of his friendship with President Echavarreta. Who knows, he said to himself, Torres Sabinas probably asked him for a report last night and they got pissed again. The chief has never been very diplomatic.

The waitress served eight coffees and a cola drink. As soon as she had left, the chief showed them a color photo: Colegio Froebel, Group 2A. A girl between seven and ten years old, white skin, black hair, dressed in a school uniform.

"This," he roared, "is a little girl named Lucía Hernández Campillo. She disappeared January fifteenth, and her mother came and reported it. Who took her statement?"

Rangel looked at Wong, but he deflected responsibility by showing his palms: You can search me, I don't know what you're talking about. Then he looked at the other officers; no one showed any sign of reacting. The chief was irritated, and the silence continued until El Travolta lifted his meaty right hand.

"Oh, you. Why didn't you follow up on it?"

The ones who had been in his position before knew that was a rhetorical question; there was no answer. There were only two reasons why a report wasn't provided to the chief: negligence or complicity, and both reasons merited punishment.

"Why didn't you investigate it? Was it intentional?"

"No, sir. I had a lot of work to take care of, and it got lost on my desk."

The old man shook his head. "Two months," he said to El Travolta, "and you didn't even bring it to my attention. I had to find out from the governor's assistant at three in the morning."

The chief was talking about the governor's right-hand man, Mr. Juan José Churruca, a disreputable man, part of the PRI ruling party mafia, a real snake among snakes. They called him Urraca—magpie—because of his hooked nose and his love of money. Now What does Churruca have to do with all this? Rangel said to himself. The photo flew toward El Travolta.

"Get in touch with the parents today. I'll expect a report at two."

"Yes, sir."

El Travolta leaned over a little, and Rangel noticed he was losing his hair. He almost felt bad for him. Meanwhile, the chief lit his first Raleigh of the day with a disposable lighter. He took a drag and puffed out a thin cloud of dense white smoke that curled around him like a wraith. When the cloud had risen enough, he spoke.

"Is anyone else investigating cases of dead girls I don't know about?"

The chief looked at them one by one, but no one answered. He waited a prudent amount of time, insistently tapping his cigarette to knock off the ash.

"Lolita, hand out the folders."

As the officers opened the folders, a murmur spread among them. Rangel was dying to see what was inside, but the supply ran out before reaching him, so he leaned over toward the Evangelist and asked what it was about. The Evangelist opened his file and acted like he was reading it out loud.

"The end of the world is near. Repent and believe in the Gospels."

"Stop fucking around, idiot." Rangel snatched the folder away from him. Ever since he became a Jehovah's Witness, the Evangelist was unbearable. He didn't understand why he couldn't talk about religion with the guys at work.

Behind a photocopy of the report Rangel had written, there was a magazine of the same size with yellow letters and a modern design.

"This," the chief explained, "arrived at the governor's personal airplane half an hour ago. It's the magazine *Proceso*. We're in it."

When a nationally circulated newspaper or magazine criticized something going on in the state, it was normal for the governor to send his people out to buy all the copies to be distributed in the area. That way, the issues that criticized his administration never reached the public.

The contents said, Page 30: "Due to police ineptitude, lunatic's crimes multiply." Before Rangel could find page thirty, the Professor whistled and said to him, "Damnit, Rangel, you're getting famous."

The magazine had used the photo of Rangel and Dr. Ridaura taken by La Chilanga from the window of the bar just as the detective pointed inside the bathroom stalls. The article was signed by the editorial staff "with reporting from Johnny Guerrero." Fucking Johnny, he thought, he's building his career at my expense.

He was still looking over the picture when the chief showed them the front page of *La Noticia:* GRISLY DISCOVERY DOWNTOWN. They had used the same photo as *Proceso* and five more shots of the bathroom, with Vicente Rangel in three of them. Holy shit, he thought, now they really screwed me. Just then he noticed a menacing look on El Travolta's face. The fucking *cabrón* was dying of envy. El Travolta loved getting his picture taken. In Rangel's opinion, the police should always go unnoticed. If it were up to him, there'd be no press conferences or news bulletins, nothing at all. Like his uncle had said, detectives should be invisible.

"But this isn't the worst of it," the chief went on. "According to Churruca, reporters from *¡Alarma Roja!* are on their way."

¡Alarma Roja! was the most widely sold weekly tabloid in the whole country. It had headlines like MACHETE RIGHT IN HIS FACE; HE ATTACKED HIS OWN MOTHER; RESPECTED GRANDMOTHER DISTRIBUTES MARIJUANA. The Ministry of the Interior had closed the paper down several times, but the editor would change the name or the design, and the tabloid would circulate again.

As they looked through the papers in the folders, Chief García took a long drag off his cigarette and blew out a cloud of smoke even more dense than the previous one.

"If one of you is leaking information, you won't have the pleasure of working here much longer. When I find out who it is, you'll have to leave the state, but first you'll head to the cell for a while." The cell was an underground concrete chamber where they interrogated the most stubborn prisoners, a tiny room in the headquarters basement with leaking pipes and no electricity or ventilation. "I'm the only one authorized to speak to the press. I want that to be very clear. I don't want any more leaks. Understand?" He watched them one by one, as he played with his coffee cup. "OK, men, what do we know for sure?"

He went to take another sip, but the cup was empty.

Because he'd coordinated the investigation, Vicente was in charge of reviewing the facts instead of El Travolta. Everyone was used to El Travolta's ambiguous way of speaking, so Rangel surprised them with a succinct, elegant, well-organized reconstruction. He quickly reviewed what had been accomplished, laid out the loose ends, and pointed out the contradictions. Unlike El Travolta, who didn't pay much attention to material evidence, Rangel had found new leads: as he was searching the area behind the bar, he had found a Raleigh cigarette butt. Later, when he compared it to the trash found in El Palmar, he found a second one. Both were bitten around the filter, in a way that revealed the mark of a long sharp canine tooth. "If we add to this the fact that on both occasions the killer used a hunting knife," he explained, "this allows us to conclude that it is the same individual."

After finishing his presentation, Vicente examined his coworkers' faces and decided they were nervous. Ever since they started to work in the port, experience had taught them to solve their cases according to a set of established steps, which included all kinds of abuses. As El Travolta would say, "The best police officer is the most arbitrary." When he was facing violent thieves, drunken sailors, or guerrilla fighters, what rules could he follow? The easiest thing to do was to locate a subject and arrest him, even if there was no proof: that's why the police had the option of preventive imprisonment. If the suspect ended up being innocent, he'd be given an apology and that was that. When a poor guy was killed, they'd get together one by one with each person who had last seen him alive, and El Travolta would interrogate the one who'd had issues with the deceased. When money disappeared from a company, they got their hands on the accountant or the person entrusted with the money: one or another of them was always the guilty party. If someone kidnapped a businessman, which happened once or twice a year, they'd interview the relatives and servants, concentrating on the one who had a criminal record. If none of that worked, they'd go to the docks or to the slums at the outskirts of the city, like the much feared Coralillo, where all the state's lowlifes hid, and get in touch with the snitches or the established criminals. But in the Jackal case, they had no leads, and they didn't know where to start.

"The little girl went to Public School Number Five, around the corner from the Bar León," Rangel went on. "That means he caught her in the street and killed her in a separate location, and instead of leaving her at the scene of the crime, he took her to the bar. We haven't been able to figure out why he needed to put her body there and whether or not he was trying to incriminate the bar manager. There's no motive and no witnesses; that's what we have."

There was a murmur of general restlessness.

The Professor interrupted. "Chief, I'd like to add something."

"Keep it brief." They called him the Professor for his tendency to pontificate.

"I spoke with Dr. Gasca, the psychiatrist. She was struck by the fact that, on the one hand, the killer could act with such brutality and then that he could cover up his tracks so perfectly, like we were dealing with two different people. From one angle, he seems to be a lunatic, but from another he's a very calculating guy."

"He's right," Crazyshot said. "This doesn't fit together. It could be a group of people."

"Hell, yeah," said El Travolta. "Otherwise there's no way to explain how the killer could have left her in the bar."

"For now, let's focus on the evidence we've got, the serrated knife and the cigarette," the chief said.

"The fact is that after attacking he disappears from the port for prolonged periods. It's probably a sailor," said El Travolta, "or a traveling agent."

"Could be. We can't rule anything out. And you? Did you find anything?" The chief asked the Evangelist. He had gone the whole night without sleep, immersed in the files of neighboring cities, studying the fingerprints found in the bar.

"I didn't find anything, sir. None of them had a record."

"What else?" He went back to the Professor.

"Dr. Gasca showed me a report from the LA police department. According to her, this type of"—he checked his notes—"*schizoid* is affected by the lunar cycle. They're really calm for part of the month, while the moon is hidden, and start getting more active again when the moon reappears; the level of criminality increases close to twenty percent when the moon is full. The evidence makes it clear that the proximity of the moon influences the tides, women, people with nervous temperaments, and, above all, the mentally ill."

The chief fidgeted in his seat.

"When's the full moon?"

"Day after tomorrow."

The chief's stomach groaned loudly. Every time he found himself in a delicate situation, the old man's belly spoke for him.

"OK," he nodded. "Starting today, we're going to set up surveillance at the schools, the same system we followed with the insurance company. I want you to be there at the times when school starts and lets out, between eight and nine, and one and two. Lolita has the list that'll tell you your assignments. One important thing: when you get to the schools, introduce yourselves to the principals. I need them to see you, because the Parents' Association is getting really upset. Any questions?"

They hadn't dealt with one delicate matter. Rangel tried to lean on Wong, but he acted like he didn't notice. I've got no other choice, he thought. I'm the one who's in charge.

"Chief . . ."

"Yes?"

"Do we need to call Jack Williams in?"

The chief stared at him. "Don't screw around on this one. I already spoke with him, and he doesn't have any information."

"And all the time he spent in the bathroom, sir?"

"I dealt with it, Rangel. Don't try to teach me how to do my job."

In the silence that followed, the sound of fierce gurgling erupted from the chief's stomach. Lolita took the opportunity to pass him the latest edition of *El Mercurio,* and the chief remembered.

"Oh, yeah, one more thing."

A paid insert announced that an anonymous donor was offering twenty-five thousand dollars to whoever assisted in the apprehension of the murderer.

"Twenty-five thousand dollars! The guy who gets the Jackal is gonna be swimming in dough."

"Twenty-five thousand dollars," said Crazyshot.

"That's a lotta cash," Wong whispered.

"So now there's no excuse. Get out in the street and follow the rules. Anything else?"

"Could you help us out with our gas?" Wong had an eight-cylinder.

"There's no money for that. Rangel, you have anything else to add?"

"No."

"He's keeping it to himself," El Travolta joked.

"Like Serpico," shot back Cruz Treviño.

"What time you got?" The chief asked Lolita.

"Six forty-five."

Putting out his cigarette, he gave the instructions for the day.

"From now on, we're going to set up forty-eight hours on duty with twelve hours off: Jarquiel and Salim will start it off." He pointed to the Professor and the Bedouin. "For the rest of you, it's your chance to investigate while the tracks are fresh. Jarquiel and Salim, go and visit our friends at the psychiatric hospital." The chief was referring to sex offenders. "Talk to the doctors, the guards, the nurses. Find out if anyone was released or has been stealing controlled substances: anything that could lead us to the psychopath. When you're done, go see Dr. Gasca and ask her to get us a profile of the killer. Cruz, check out alibis for the merchants in the area, from the jewelry dealers to the street vendors. Start off with a small perimeter, no more than two blocks, and then expand it. I'm interested in everything: people selling snow cones and popsicles, mailmen—I want you to interview everybody, even the Bible sellers. Get Mena and José to help." That was Fatwolf and Crazyshot. "Taboada and Rangel, check out the crime reports, and you, Wong, you're going to make me a list of the regulars at the Bar León. I want you to compare what you find out with Jarquiel's list. That'll be it."

Cruz Treviño raised his hand, and Rangel and Taboada glanced at each other.

"Sir, who's going to be in charge of the investigation?"

The chief couldn't hide his bad mood. "The guy who's in charge of sexual crimes, who else? Hurry up. I want you in the office at three o'clock. Lolita?"

"Yes, sir?"

"If the reporters are still there, have them come in. As far as you guys are concerned, this meeting's over, so get a move on. I want results."

6

After the announcement of the reward, everyone ran out to look for suspects. Everyone except Rangel. He was disappointed by the investigation and didn't know what to think.

He parked next to a food stand selling *tacos de barbacoa*, hidden behind a mass of customers. While he was there, in front of a Jesuit school, he noticed that the Parents' Association had organized a group to supervise as students entered the Instituto Cultural de Paracuán. Half a dozen adults in neon-yellow shirts were stopping traffic and helping kids cross the avenue. Looking at a metallic-blue pickup truck, he recognized Mr. Guillén, a businessman who had become very popular because of his idea to offer "humanitarian credit." Rangel had bought a record player from him on an easy monthly payment plan. Mr. Guillén stopped his truck, let out his seven kids, and watched them cross the avenue. As he waved to someone he knew, Mr. Guillén lifted his jacket and showed off a pistol stuck in his belt.

"What's up Mr. Guillén, you hunting?"

"Just to be safe. He better not show up around here, because I'll get justice myself."

"Oh, Dad," his daughter Paloma chided as she said good-bye.

Ah, what a drag, Rangel said to himself, we're going to have to organize a campaign to disarm the city; we can't have so many guys running around packing guns.

Nothing out of the ordinary happened in the half hour the parent watch group was on duty, except for a Cola Drinks truck, going too fast, that almost ran over the people in charge of stopping traffic. The parents spoke to the driver with as much courtesy as they could muster as they made him stop; once the row of students had crossed the street they let him go as they showered him with insults. Goddamn drivers, Rangel thought, screw them. He had thought it would be impossible to watch all the girls who arrived alone, but the whole city had come together to support them. When a girl traveled alone, the buses or taxis stopped right in front of the door to her building, even if they were stopping traffic, and carefully let out their precious cargo. A yellow bus parked in front of the school, a few feet away from Vicente, and let out twenty tiny little girls, the majority of them carrying metal lunchboxes.

Rangel watched one girl with big eyes, who must have done her hair by herself because she had one ponytail higher than the other, but smoothed down with a lot of gel. Another boy about five years old had pulled his pants up to his armpits and was showing his friends how he could reach over his shoulder and stick his hand into his back pocket.

When the bell rang at 8:00 on the dot, a few students were still running up, and an orange Caribe just managed to slip through as they were closing the gates. The driver, Dr. Solares Téllez, a well-known pediatrician with a bushy mustache, let his three kids out: "Hurry up now, I don't know why you kids like to get here late. Run, run, you're gonna get in trouble." The Jesuits told the kids to get into rows in front of their classrooms. Another day of strict discipline was beginning. Rangel was just about to leave when he noticed a shadowy figure pointing a video camera at him from behind some curtains on the second floor. Goddamnit, they're filming me, he said to himself, and got out of his car to investigate. When he lifted up his badge toward the window, the video camera pointed in another direction and a hand waved to him. False alarm, he thought; it must be a teacher.

Rangel's lack of sleep from the night before was starting to affect him. It made sense to get some breakfast before going to work, so he headed to the Jewish guy's restaurant two blocks away from police headquarters. There was a newsstand right in the doorway to Klein's, and he stopped to look at an issue of *Notitas Musicales* with Rigo Tovar on the cover. The headline said, TRI-UMPHANT TOUR FOR SINGER AND LAS JAIBAS DEL VALLE. Judging by the cover, Rigo had grown his hair out long in the last few months and was wearing electric-colored shirts.

"Hey, hey! Wait up!"

The person yelling was the owner of Klein's, Don Isaac in person. Rangel turned just in time to see the shape of a man turning the corner. Because of his lack of sleep, he didn't react quickly.

"Did he steal something?"

"No, what could he steal? He already paid. But the guy was in such a hurry, he left his change."

The old man showed him a twenty peso bill, then shrugged and stuffed it into his pocket.

How strange, thought Vicente, that guy was flying out of here. At the table where the guy was sitting was a copy of *El Mercurio* with the photos La Chilanga had taken of him. Fuck, he thought, mulling it over; then it dawned on him. Was that guy trying to avoid me? He stood up to investigate, but when he got to the corner, two buses were pulling away in opposite directions. Whoever it was had a lot of luck. He probably had a criminal record.

There wasn't anyone in Klein's at that hour, except for the manager and the waiter, who was mopping, leaving a strong pine disinfectant smell behind him.

"I saw you in *El Mercurio,*" said the waiter, but Rangel wasn't in the mood to talk.

They brought him some *chilaquiles rojos,* which he didn't even touch; the image of the dead girl was haunting him. Goddamnit, he said to himself, this fucking case is causing me a shitload of problems. If I had known, I never would've gotten involved. In less than twelve hours, he'd fought with El Travolta and El Chaneque, photographers had taken tons of pictures of him, and the burning feeling in his hands was back.

As they served him a cola drink, Rangel had to admit he was bewildered. The chief had never acted like that before; he even got nervous when Rangel suggested they call Junior in. And he couldn't explain why he would have put El Travolta in charge of the investigation. Fucking chief, he thought, I bet they already bought him out. If he wants us to play stupid, that's up to him, but I'm going to investigate other things. The burglary at the electric company, for example. During the four years he'd spent in the port, Rangel had heard all the rumors about Jack Williams, and he wanted to get his statement. Like all spoiled brats, Williams was used to mistreating people and had an infinitely large ego. They said he organized private bacchanals, that he had orgies at his house in the country, that he handed out all kinds of stuff, from morphine to caffeine-aspirin combos, that he took all kinds of drugs.

When Rangel touched the cola bottle, he felt a burning pain in his hands and he thought about putting cream on, since no one was nearby. Cream? His uncle would have asked. You putting cream on? Goddamnit, Vicente are you a fag now or what? Rangel took the medicine out of his pant pocket and put it on anyway. The medicine worked so well that he took another squirt, spread it around on his palms, and enjoyed the cream's soothing effect.

The owner of Klein's turned on the ceiling fans and a cool breeze swept through the restaurant. Man, he said to himself, if only I could sleep a little while. But he had to get back to work if he wanted to get his check on Friday. I hope I don't run into El Travolta. Just thinking about him spurred on another wave of itching, and he thought about putting on more cream, but the doctor had warned him about overdoing it: Don't use too much, he told him, or the medicine will wind up being worse than the disease.

He was about to put on a third layer anyway when he thought he saw a ghost. There, by the front door, he spotted La Chilanga's blue eyes, half-open blouse, and large rounded breasts headed toward him. Rangel imagined a lot of things as the woman came in: he imagined that he was with her, embracing her on a beach like Burt Lancaster in *From Here to Eternity* or with her hair braided, like Bo Derek in *10,* and suddenly he got nervous because the girl wasn't just looking back at him, she was walking right at him.

"Mr. Rangel?" She looked confused. "You wanted to see me?"

"I'm sorry?" Vicente was surprised.

"Oh . . . then it wasn't you?" The girl bit her tongue, and then asked, "Did you see the pictures?" It was obvious she was changing the topic.

Rangel nodded. "Yeah, I saw them. They're gonna fire me because of you."

"What? You looked good in them! They even picked those pictures up in Mexico City!"

"Well, yeah, like I was saying. We're not allowed to talk to the press."

La Chilanga smiled, and Rangel looked her over without saying a word. Even though he couldn't be sure, he thought that even though the words were hostile, a current of friendliness ran underneath them, an almost tangible charge that floated in the air.

The detective and the girl would have exchanged looks for several minutes more, but someone interrupted them.

"What's up, boss? We made you famous; you were in *Proceso.*"

And Rangel noticed that Jackson Five was behind her, looking at him derisively. This guy, he thought, where'd he come from?

Seeing his obvious surprise, La Chilanga introduced them. "Mr. Vicente Rangel, I'd like you to meet my colleague, John Guerrero."

"Nice to meet you, lieutenant. Mariana says you're the only honest officer on the force."

"Oh," Rangel said, "so you're Johnny Guerrero." And he pulled his hand back. "From Chihuahua, right?"

"Yeah, from Chihuahua, that's right." He didn't see the tongue-lashing coming.

"Don't you have any sense of professional ethics? Why are you putting all our business on the streets? How can we arrest the murderer with you telling everyone about our investigations?"

"People have a right to information," the journalist smiled.

"Of course they do," Rangel replied, "as long as the information doesn't damage society at large."

"That's a fascist argument," Johnny said.

"Not at all," said Rangel, "not at all. I'd like to see you two in my place; every time you publish something, the chances of us catching this killer go down."

"Well, *I'm sorry,*" said the reporter, "but instead of getting angry, you should work with us. Mariana says you're the only honorable officer on the force. What did you think of being in *Proceso?* Mariana was the one who made the contact."

Even though he wasn't the most informed guy, Rangel knew that *Proceso* was one of the few media outlets, or maybe the only one, that criticized the corruption in Mexico. Johnny took advan-

tage of Rangel's momentary doubt to ask, "Can we take a seat?"
And they sat down with him.

Rangel thought about leaving, but right then he saw the girl
smiling at him for the second time. She had a pretty smile and
golden tanned skin. Besides, the girl was leaning against the table,
and her breasts were squeezed into a more rounded shape, her
cleavage about to explode.

He was focused on these noble thoughts when Mr. Klein interrupted him. "What would you like to order?"

La Chilanga barely looked at the menu.

"I'd like a fruit cocktail, or—what time is it? We can eat lunch
right now. You don't have soy, spinach, wheat germ?"

"No, miss. We have beans, meat, and tortillas. The special of
the day is *chilaquiles con cecina.*"

"Do you have anything with no meat? A salad?"

"I have a ceviche, if you'd like that."

"Is it the same one from last month? That fish was really tough,
man, it seemed like you shot it or something," Johnny said. "That
must be why it wouldn't come apart."

"So, you don't have any salads?"

"No, we don't," and Isaac Klein stormed off.

Johnny gave the girl a hard time. "What's going on, girl?
You've been here a month and you still haven't figured this out?
I don't know what the most important words are to this tribe,
but nobody can mess with their food. Criticize whatever you want:
their government, the weather, the potholes, the lack of movie
theaters, the tar on the beach, how ugly the city is. Right, but not
the food. Don't even think about criticizing what they eat. In this
town, turning down a bowl of pozole or a plate of *zacahuil,* even
if it's the umpteenth time they've offered it, can get you in big
trouble. I've known families that stopped talking to each other

over an enchilada. The people here tolerate all the local nastiness: bad weather, mosquitoes, the government, but when one of them comes to eat, what they want is delicious food, and plenty of it, and if possible in huge portions. Strong flavors and a generous serving. How is the manager not going to get upset when you ask him for an alfalfa salad? You insulted him in the core of his being, his way of understanding the world. Right, lieutenant?"

What an asshole, Vicente thought, and he didn't say a word. Safe behind his dark glasses, he preferred to admire the girl in front of him.

"Look, Johnny," La Chilanga interrupted him. "There go the guys from *¡Alarma!*"

The two men swung around just in time to see a van with the logo of the most insidious newspaper in the country drive by. "Damn," said Rangel, "*¡Alarma!* is in town!"

"Did you know they pay their witnesses?" Johnny asked. "They give a hundred dollars for each solid piece of information to get people to spill everything about their tragedies. What happened, when, how, where. And details."

"A hundred bucks for every piece of information?" The girl leaned forward on the table.

"They've got that kind of money. They sell a million papers a week. What do you think?" Johnny said to the detective. "Come on, boss, do your town a favor and work with the objective press. My colleague here is Julio Scherer's niece and published in *Proceso.*"

"Hey, I don't think so. What are you insinuating? They publish me because my pictures are good, not because of who I'm related to." Her eyes were shimmering.

Right then, Rangel felt a knee leaning against his own, and when he looked at the girl, he noticed that she was looking at him, too. *Ah, caray,* is she doing that on purpose? Johnny tried to make conversation, but Rangel gave one-word answers, staring at the girl, whose smile was getting bigger and bigger. The situation was starting to improve when the journalist stood up.

"Let's go, Mariana, this isn't the guy. They stood you up."

Then he got it all. No shit, he thought, they came to meet with their informant.

"Who were you going to meet with?" he asked them.

"We can't tell you, it's a trade secret," Johnny replied.

"You don't know?" he asked the girl.

Before he could push her, Johnny burst out, "I'm really sorry, but a reporter doesn't reveal his sources."

There was no way to get them to say anything. Since Vicente was still staring at the girl, she said to him, "Man, look here: we're trying to do activist journalism, work that produces a social consciousness. Didn't you see the pictures from Vietnam, from My Lai? The photograph is a weapon of social struggle."

She said she was part of the Revolutionary Dissident Group of Reporters "Vamos Cuba"; McLuhan this, that, and the other; that the photograph had a social function; that we have to raise the people's consciousness so the public learns about the people's poverty and capitalist exploitation.

"You're the right-hand man of the capitalists," said Johnny.

"What the hell," Rangel joked, "I'm not the Federal Security Administration." He wanted to point out to the girl that he was just working as a police officer while he found himself, that this job was temporary, he didn't take it seriously, but instead of saying it, he just repeated, "What the hell," and walked away, steaming.

As he was leaving, he looked at the girl, totally disappointed. Damnit, girl, I was gonna take you to the beach.

7

The first thing Rangel did was to start looking for his main suspect. He began in a neighborhood where all the streets are named after trees: pine, olive, cedar, oak; the next one had streets named after gemstones: lapis lazuli, amethyst, topaz, diamond; and in the third all the streets were named for flowers: rose, iris, hyacinth. Rangel, who lived on the highway to Paracuán, crossed all these streets until he came upon a large wall and then he turned onto a street named after orange blossoms.

There was a mansion on the biggest block in the best part of the Buenavista neighborhood, right next door to the golf course and the lagoon. The owner could go in and out of his house without his neighbors seeing; there were two entrances for the car, one on each side of the mansion.

Rangel parked under a huge avocado tree, with no particular idea about what he expected to find, and he focused on reading his magazine, *Proceso*. On the high white wall, a young man was painting over a recent graffiti scrawl that shouted in bright red letters, ARREST THE JACKAL. The young guy looked at Rangel out of the corner of his eye, and when he was finished, he gathered up his things and went in through a side gate. A minute later, the door opened and an incredibly tall white guy, dressed in a suit and tie, walked over to mess with him.

"Hello, could I see some identification?"

Man, Rangel thought, this sure is a classy bodyguard. The guy was a foreigner, with thick muscles and a haircut that reminded him of American army soldiers.

"What?"

"Your driver's license. Some ID."

"Why?"

"You're on private property."

Rangel looked at the wall. "As far as I know, the street belongs to everyone."

"Not here. Show me your ID." He spoke in Spanish with a heavy Texas accent.

"Where are you from?"

"That's none of your business."

"Oh, American? Why don't you show me your papers? Do you have your F-three visa, or are you working illegally?"

The gringo glared at him. "Look, I don't wanna fight. You better get a move on." And then, in English, he added, "Have a nice day."

Vicente spat out the window. Fucking asshole, like he was the law or something. Before turning the corner, he saw the bodyguard writing down his license plate number, and he beeped his horn at him five times.

Ever since his uncle Lieutenant Rivera died, Rangel didn't have a good relationship with any of the guys on the force: he went into the office, did what he had to do, and talked as little as he could with his coworkers. But that Tuesday, as soon as he clocked in, he looked so tired that El Chicote asked him, "Hey, Rangel, who do you work with? I'm going to get you an assistant, you need a *madrina* so you can get more work done."

"Whatever, Chicote. The chief kicked Chávez out of the

meeting this morning, said he didn't want outsiders working in the office."

"Yeah, but no one's going to find out; besides, you need one; you look really beat up. How long's it been since you had a good night's sleep? At least two days?"

Rangel said he didn't need anybody, but he got someone anyway. A half hour later, El Chicote told him they were looking for him on the first floor. To his surprise, it turned out to be the same guy—in his forties in a plaid shirt and coke-bottle glasses—who was at headquarters the day before, when they called him from the Bar León. He introduced himself as Jorge Romero. "They call me the Blind Man—the Blind Man—because I'm trustworthy: I don't see anything, I don't know anything. If you wanna give a suspect a few shocks, I'm your man. I've done it before with Chávez."

"What? You helped Chávez interrogate suspects?"

"Yes."

"And you're a specialist in administering electric shocks?"

"Well, yeah," said the Blind Man.

Rangel had the feeling he was just trying to impress him. Obviously he needed this job and would do anything, even lie. Certainly Chávez never needed anybody's help to do his interrogations.

Rangel explained he was looking for an assistant. Deep down, he still thought his time as a policeman was a temporary thing while he did some soul-searching. Besides, his recent self-esteem problems were strong evidence that hiring a lackey would send him down the path to complete corruption.

The man with coke-bottle glasses was disappointed by the rejection and spent several hours on the first floor, helping El Chicote with the mop, looking for little jobs, running errands for the officers. At 10:30, when Rangel went down for his notes, he noticed his Chevy Nova, normally covered in a layer of dust, had returned to its original white color.

"At your service, sir," said a voice behind him, and he saw the Blind Man, a rag in his hand, cleaning another car.

"Fuck," Rangel said, and gave him five pesos.

"Thanks a lot, boss, and just so you know: whatever you need, I'm here to help."

Rangel acted like he didn't hear him and started the car fast. There's no way around it, he thought. If I act nice, I'm going to get stuck with him. He already got five pesos out of me.

The rest of the morning, he talked with teachers, neighbors, security guards, and old ladies. Ever since *El Mercurio* published the news about the reward, the police just couldn't keep up. As soon as they hung up one call, another came in, and they spent all day listening to both real and made-up stories of people reporting on a neighbor, a relative, an employee, or even their own boss. Rangel even got one call from a hysterical woman who swore she'd seen a huge creature, half-man half-wolf, running around at night, stalking the docks and the market: "It's the *naguales,*" she said. "As soon as they arrest all those witches, the Jackal will disappear."

But Rangel wasn't a therapist. He said, "Good-bye, ma'am," and hung up. Witches, he said to himself, that's all I need, goddamn stupid people, this is too fucking much already. Ever since he was little, he'd heard everyone has a double, a *nagual,* in the mountains, and this double takes the form of an animal. Whatever happens to the animal happens to its human counterpart. Some of his friends joked that his *nagual* was an eagle or a panther, and people said the state governor, thanks to a witch's help, had several *naguales* at the same time. Fucking lies, he thought, these people don't have enough to do. I wonder what my *nagual* is.

"Has anyone seen Mr. Taboada?" Lolita had the mayor on hold, Mr. Torres Sabinas himself.

"I saw him," said Romero. "He was going into the Rose Garden."

How strange, Rangel thought. What's El Travolta doing in the city's priciest restaurant? And why would he meet with Torres Sabinas?

"Did you see yourself yet?"

El Chicote was handing him the evening edition of *El Mercurio,* but since he was frowning so much, he decided to just leave.

As if the morning edition hadn't been irritating enough, the evening paper recycled La Chilanga's photos all over again. Fuck, he said to himself, goddamn traitorous bitch, this is just too much. When he finished the last of his cigarettes, Rangel crumbled up the pack and flung it out the window.

"Another pack?" It was the Blind Man, fishing for a few coins.

Rangel sighed. "Raleighs . . . no, better get me Faros," and he handed him a bill worth very little.

Fuck, he thought, now I've lost ten pesos. He told himself Romero had to be really hard up to put up with this humiliation. El Chicote told him he had a wife and three kids. But I'm not giving him anything else, Rangel said to himself. If I'm nice, I'll never get rid of him.

He picked up the copy of *El Mercurio* and looked for a distraction, but he couldn't find McCormick's column. Why am I going around in circles? He remembered Julia Concepción González's body. Every time he read through the report, he got the feeling that he was forgetting an important bit of information, but he couldn't put his finger on what it was.

Looking for inspiration, he stood up and walked into the hallway; once there, he looked over an old bookshelf. It didn't offer very many options: a law book, a highway map, a copy of the *Gulag Archipelago*— who knows how it got there—*Jaws,* a couple of *National Geographics* that had pictures of the port, six Oil Workers' Union brochures, and *Treatise on Criminology* by Dr. Quiroz Cuarón. Dr. Quiroz was his uncle's greatest teacher and an internationally renowned expert. He caught and studied some of the most sought-after criminals in the world and knew exactly how the mind of the killer worked. He taught classes in Scotland Yard. He was so famous that even Alfred Hitchcock hired him as a consultant while filming *Psycho.* If my uncle were still alive, Rangel said to himself, I'd get in touch with him.

Rangel was immersed in deep thought when the most unstable person on the force came in: Luis Calatrava aka the Wizard. In charge of the old checkpoint on the way out of the port, he just barely passed as a police officer. Long-haired and with a thick beard and ratty clothes, he only put on his uniform when he had to show up in the office. The chief had gotten tired of suggesting he should cut his hair; the guy just wouldn't obey.

Now he stopped to say hello. "What's up, Rangel? I haven't seen you lately."

Ever since they assigned him to that awful job, the Wizard lived right at the checkpoint and spent the whole day sitting there, watching the cars. It was rare to see him in the city. It was about a forty-minute ride from the checkpoint to headquarters, but the Wizard preferred to show up for his paycheck out of the blue, once every month or so, when a couple of pay periods had passed. At his boring job, there wasn't much to do or anywhere to spend money. Ever since Rangel could remember, the Wizard spent all his time listening to the radio, reading, and watching the people driving by. Once every twenty-four hours, he chose a victim. He'd signal for the person to stop and he'd confiscate their newspaper, just so he'd know what was going on in the world. Rangel remembered the first time he saw him, as he was on his way to the port to look for work. The ratty-haired guy signaled for him to stop and pointed at *La Noticia:* Would you give me your newspaper, *carnal?* There's nothing to do here. Rangel gave him the newspaper and didn't see him again until later, when they turned out to be coworkers.

In theory, the presence of the Wizard was meant to discourage drug dealers and other smugglers. Since Paracuán is at the crossroads of three states and close to the river and the sea, the route should have been an ideal one for trafficking in illegal goods. The reality was that it was almost always the same nondescript ranchers passing by, and there wasn't much to do. They assigned the Wizard to that post because he was irritable and impossible to deal with, a kind of never-ending punishment. Calatrava didn't have a car, but all he had to do was ask for a ride to the dock and then take a bus from there to the center of town; despite that, he preferred to live as an exile—he said he was studying physics—and not visit the city. Just so he didn't have to see him, the chief assented to Lolita taking his reports over the phone. Ever since Rangel went to live in the house facing the river, it was inevitable that he'd run into Calatrava at least once a day. El Chicote said that Calatrava lived off what he fished from the river: crabs, shrimp, and even sea bass. All of which he caught without even leaving the office, with a few fishing lines he hung from bars in the window.

"Well?" the Wizard asked him. "When are we gonna drink some beers?"

"One of these days," Vicente said to him, and let him walk by.

One night when Vicente was in a good mood and didn't have anything else to do, he bought a six-pack at the Negro's gas station and went to give it to his neighbor.

"I don't drink alone," the Wizard said. "Do me the honor of staying."

They finished off the six-pack of Tecates and drank the last of a questionable bottle of *aguardiente* that the Wizard bought by the liter. The next day, Rangel had one of the worst hangovers of his life. He didn't go back for months, but the night of conversation helped him to keep up a good relationship with the Wizard, who every once in a while left messages for him at headquarters. Looks like they're shipping drugs in a green truck, license plate 332 TBLB or I've got a hunch the owner of a white Ram is a pimp, license plate 470 XEX. Sometimes the Wizard would ask him to pick up some alcohol, soap, or toothpaste for him; Rangel even had to lend him money once.

"Aw, shit, what're you writing down on there?"

"I've got a logbook."

The Wizard kept an excessively bizarre diary in a book with a green cover, in which Rangel had seen him writing. That Tuesday, when they ran into each other in the office, the Wizard reminded him it was lunchtime.

"What's up, Rangel? Wanna get a beer?"

"I wish, man. I've got a lot of work to do."

"Well, then, what do you think? When are you gonna come by?"

"Yeah, well, another day; soon."

"Friday?"

"Could be. I'll look for you."

Just then, Lolita showed up and interrupted them.

"Mr. Rangel, Mrs. Hernández is on the line."

"Who is it?"

"The mother of the girl who disappeared, the one from Colegio Froebel."

"No, goddamnit," Rangel said. "Tell her to get in touch with Officer Taboada. He's in charge."

"I already told her that, but she insisted on speaking with you."

"Tell Wong to pick it up."

Lolita came back a minute later. "He says he can't right now."

She turned toward his desk at the back of the room, where the Chinese guy was giving him the finger: Fucking Rangel, whaddaya think I am, an idiot or what? That's Taboada's job, man.

The clock read ten o'clock on the dot. Rangel said to himself, If this woman keeps calling, I'm going to have a very long day.

At one o'clock, a guy selling guayaberas came into the headquarters. Cruz Treviño bought one from him, Crazyshot bought another, and, before he left, the salesman left two more on El Travolta's desk.

"You wouldn't want to buy one, would you, sir?"

"No, thanks."

"You can spread out the payments."

"Some other time."

"It's not a shirt, it's a way of showing your support for the president of the country."

Ever since President Echevarreta made guayaberas fashionable, all the government employees were wearing them. Not only that, they also put photos of him on their desks, as if Echevarreta were a saint handing out miracles, able to deliver them from evil. Just then, Lolita stuck her head into the hall. Since he didn't get along with the girl, the guayabera seller waved good-bye and walked out with his things.

"Oh, you're over here? I called your extension but they didn't answer. Mrs. Hernández is looking for you on line one. It's the fourth time today."

What a fucking pain, he thought; this lady just doesn't get it.

"Tell her I'm not in the office, that I'll be back tomorrow."

The girl nodded angrily and added loudly so everyone could hear her: "And Licenciado Barbosa on line two."

It seemed like everyone who was there—Wong, the Professor, the Bedouin —lifted up their heads to look when they heard that name. Oh, shit, Don Agustín Barbosa was the mayor of Ciudad Madera, one of the leading opposition mayors. Those were the days when going against the will of the establishment was practically impossible. Barbosa, who, thanks to his renown as a lawyer and independent businessman had beaten out the establishment candidate and won the elections, was not viewed kindly by the chief. Rangel had seen him twice, both times while he was with his uncle, and they had a cordial relationship. How strange, he thought, why's Barbosa looking for me? And since the secretary was waiting for an answer, he said, "Thanks, Lolita. Forward the call to my desk."

The Bedouin shook his head in disapproval. A minute later, Lolita connected him with the mayor of Ciudad Madera's office.

"Don Agustín just left," his secretary said. "He said you should catch up with him at his restaurant. It's very important."

OK, he said, I guess I'm going to the Excelsior.

8

He took Calle Juárez to Avenida Hidalgo and waited at the intersection for the red light that always refused to change. There was a Cola Drinks billboard that Rangel tried not to look at, and another for the Oil Workers' Union. The second billboard consisted of a picture of the refinery with a union boss saying, "Honesty first." When the cars coming from Las Lomas crossed the street, the left turn light came on and a Cola Drinks truck headed the other way almost ran into his car. The Cola Drinks logo was just inches from his face. Their drivers do whatever they damn well please, he said to himself, like the road was all theirs. One day they're gonna end up killing somebody. Gotta do something about that. Then the light finally turned green and he accelerated the car.

He passed by the National Professors' Union office and parked in front of the Excelsior. As he got out of his car, he saw two crabs crossing the road. It was normal to see them picking through the garbage dumps, since the ocean wasn't far away. Rangel walked across the sand covering the asphalt and into the restaurant.

The air-conditioning hurt his throat. Damn, he said to himself, why do they turn it up so high? Besides the cold, one of the things that stood out in the Excelsior was the interior decorating. Extravagant objects hung from the walls, and behind the bar an amateur had done his best to paint the palm trees at the beach, the cargo cranes at the port, and the pine forest: some limp cornstalks, a pasture and a few cows. Rangel wouldn't have gotten hung up on the picture were it not for the eyes of a tiger shining in the middle of the forest.

The voice of the waitress caught him off guard. "Good afternoon, just one person?"

Blinded by the fierce light outside, he couldn't see her, even though he strained.

"No, I'm here to talk to Don Agustín Barbosa."

"In what capacity?"

"As mayor."

"But it's not time yet—"

"He asked me to come."

"Please take a seat, he'll be right with you."

Rangel sat down at a table away from the others, under a huge, impeccably preserved swordfish. There was a ship's anchor behind the bar and a row of crabs, also dried out, with their claws at the ready. As he waited, he flipped through a copy of *La Noticia*. On his way through the region, the leader of the National Professors' Union, Arturo Rojo López, had taken the opportunity to criticize Daniel Torres Sabinas and Don Agustín Barbosa: THE CHILDREN AREN'T SAFE. Don Agustín came out to receive him in a shirt with its sleeves rolled up.

"What's up, Rangel, thanks for coming. Have they taken your order already?" And he called the waitress without waiting for an answer. "What do you want to drink? Vodka, whiskey? Natalia, bring us one of those bottles that came in yesterday."

The waitress, a tall brown-skinned girl with unruly hair, smiled and walked away with a sway in her step. Her curves were highlighted by her tight skirt, and Rangel, who had quite a few months of involuntarily celibacy under his belt, couldn't keep himself from admiring the girl's figure.

"She looks good, huh?" the mayor asked him. "As soon as I find a new hostess, these assholes go and get her pregnant." He pointed to one of the regulars. "I'm going to set up a marriage agency."

"How's the budget going?"

"Bad."

. "And respect for the government?"

"The same, you know how it is. The governor doesn't send me the funds and what they give me just isn't enough. But we gotta keep pushing, there's no other way."

Rangel smiled a little. Don Agustín had been mayor for the Partido Revolutionario Institucional, and was a respected mayor, according to the rumors, a man straight out of the business elite, but two months into his term the governor kicked him out on a whim. Three years later, Don Agustín ran as a candidate for the same position, but representing the left. He won impeccably, thanks to all the work he did. And since he didn't belong to the official party, they took forever to authorize his expenditures each budget period. He always had to come up with a creative way to get financing; he even lent the government money from his own funds. Even before getting into politics, Don Agustín had two gas stations, a hotel, and the Excelsior restaurant, which he ran in his free time, like a favorite toy. One of his anecdotes had become famous.

Two representatives from the gringo consulate went to talk to him at his office in City Hall. They worked out the issue they were concerned about, and at the end of the meeting they asked Don Agustín's assistant where the best place to eat was. The assistant recommended the Excelsior, and they headed over. Because that day they were missing a few waiters, Don Agustín himself was forced to work the tables, bussing plates, and taking orders. They saw him and were nudging each other, until the older one asked him, "Excuse me, aren't you the mayor of Madera?"

"Yeah," he told them, "but just in the mornings. The governor hasn't sent me any funds and what they pay me doesn't cut it, so I have to work two jobs."

As the waitress leaned over to serve their drinks, Rangel made out the girl's long neck. The sunlight glinted off the silky golden fuzz on her neck.

"Thanks, Natalia, that's all. And you, Rangel, don't get distracted on me," he joked.

"You're the boss."

"I read in *El Mercurio* that you're taking on the investigation into the girls again. Your uncle would be proud of you. It's long past time you got Taboada out of the way."

"I'm not getting him out of the way. Yesterday I had to investigate because I was on duty."

"What? No way, Rangel, don't say that! You know just as well as I do that you're more qualified than Taboada. As long as he's in charge, the investigation's not going anywhere. Your uncle always thought you would take his place. He said you had a natural instinct for solving these things."

"I'm not so sure," he responded, and he scratched his hands.

"Can I take your order?" The girl was back.

"How about some nice fresh braised sea bass? We got a few fillets this big." Don Agustín gestured to show how large they were.

"I have to get back to the office."

"You better stay. Natalia! Take this man's order."

Rangel said no, but he could do with a beer, and the girl smiled. Damn, thought Rangel, she has green eyes, like my ex.

"Twenty-five thousand dollars, what do you think? They're going to give twenty-five thousand dollars to the guy who nabs the Jackal. With that money, you could start over wherever you wanted to. You could buy a house here in Madera, or in the United States. You wouldn't want to come live here in Madera?"

"Why are you asking me?"

"Because I know about a couple of spacious, comfortable houses, built by the government, that they're about to sell to people who worked with my administration. With all due respect, Rangel, my people think you're going to catch this guy. But there's one thing you haven't thought of. Once you've arrested him, how are you going to turn him in?"

Rangel leaned back in his chair. Where was this guy going with all this?

"I want to make a deal with you. When you find out who did all this, because everybody's convinced you're going to catch him, don't take him to Chief García. Bring him to me and Sergeant Fernández."

Rangel smiled. "Look, Don Agustín: first, I'm not looking for the killer, I'm in charge of smuggling and kidnappings, not homicides, and second, what would I possibly get from turning him in here in Madera?"

A huge smile lit up Mr. Barbosa's face. "That we'll actually try the case here. The rumor is going around that your boss is protecting some bigshot." And Agustín pointed at the cola bottle that was starting to sweat. "The girl they found in the Bar León was originally from Madera, even though she lived in Paracuán. Last night I went to see the parents and I stayed with them until one in the morning. They asked me to intervene, because they said when they reported what happened to your boss he turned his back on them. Catching this guy would be a big achievement for the opposition. The kidnapping occurred in Madera, but the murder took place in Paracuán," continued the mayor, "and that makes things a little complicated. As you can imagine, I don't have access to the fingerprints, for example, and your boss refused to send me a copy of the case file. He said he needed to prevent information leaks. Can you believe that? The old man shut the door in my face, but I know the governor's the one giving the orders. If you turn over the killer to me, you'll keep the reward, all of it, and you'll get a promotion, because as soon as you quit your job with the old man, I'll hire you and give you a raise. We need an assistant police chief."

Rangel stayed quiet, thinking. Because of the rivalry between the two mayors, it was in Don Agustín Barbosa's interest to solve the murder before Chief García. Vicente wasn't a traitor, but, on the other hand he was fed up with El Travolta. Shit, what would my uncle have said? At the far end of the bar, next to the cash register, the girl was peering at Rangel curiously. For a minute, he imagined the life a guy like him could lead in Ciudad Madera, with a girl like that and twenty-five thousand dollars in his bank account. He saw himself dressed in new shirts with huge collars, unbuttoned to the waist, drinking in this place, listening to Elton John and holding the girl close. . . . The rosy dream evaporated in the air as soon as he pictured his old coworkers retaliating against him. He wished his uncle were still around to give him some advice.

9

Get one thing straight: as long as you're in this business, you're not going to have any friends. You heard right: not one friend. Everyone who gets close to you is going to ask for something or want to use you for something. You can't trust anybody. A police officer doesn't have friends when he's doing his job; a police officer only has enemies. The trick is to learn how to avoid them.

Don't tell anybody where you live and never open your door in one fell swoop, just in case they're messing with you. If you eat out for lunch, look for a seat where they can't surprise you (the doors, keep an eye on the doors), and if you have to be next to a window, close the curtain or lower the light, so they won't be able to shoot at you from outside.

Don't drink too much, don't take drugs, don't go into a dark place unarmed, don't make deals with people from that world (the criminal world, I mean, but don't make deals with your coworkers, either, just in case one day they get sick of you and want to get rid of you), and like the *santeros* say, put a glass of water next to your bed every night and pray to Saint Judas Martyr; just in case your soul gets thirsty, you don't want it to head off looking for a drink and never come back.

One day, years ago, Rangel and his uncle had just got back from making an arrest, when Lolita called them aside.

"Lieutenant, a man came to look for you. It was an older gentleman, about eighty years old. He left you a book."

His uncle's face lit up. "Look at that, what good news!"

Don Miguel smiled big and showed the book to Rangel. It was a copy of *The Treasure of the Sierra Madre*, dedicated *To my good friend, Don Miguel Rivera*. And it was signed *T,* just like that, all alone on the page, like a cross.

"A man about eighty years old, leather jacket and a straw hat?"

"Yeah. He said he was staying in the same place as always."

The old man nodded his head and went to make a phone call. Twenty minutes later he asked his nephew, "You got a lot of work right now?"

"The usual."

"Drop what you're doing and meet me at the bar in the Hotel Inglaterra at two."

At two o'clock on the dot, Rangel met his uncle at one of the tables in the middle of the bar. A man with graying hair was at his side, a straw-colored hat on the seat next to him.

"Vicente," his uncle said, "I'd like to introduce Mr. Traven Torsvan, a writer."

They ate lunch at a restaurant on the riverbank: a few giant shrimp; an oyster, octopus and ceviche cocktail; little cheese tortillas; and the house specialty: crabs à la Frank (crab meat with cheese and a magnificent olive oil). During the lunch, Mr. Torsvan took out a copy of *The Death Ship* and signed it for Rangel.

"You don't see the waiter, do you?"

"No."

"He hasn't been paying any attention to us. If you see him, wave him over."

But the waiter was nowhere to be seen.

"Where do you live?"

"On the other side of the river. Near the dock."

"Near the Williams hacienda?"

"Right next door, in the foreman's house."

"And you know what they say about that house? I'll tell you the story while we wait to order."

As you know, the Williams family came from Germany, escaping from the First World War. They settled all along the coast and their largest property, their hacienda, started here in Paracuán and extended all the way to the Cerro del Nagual: as far as the eye can see. The oldest son, who was a bum, a drinker, and a womanizer, went to live in Haiti. When his father died, he returned to run the hacienda. He did it for a month, but soon his employees started to die. An animal was eating them in the forest, a tiger. It was hunting them down. It was so strong it could carry a man in his jaws and eat him up in a tree where no one could stop him. Bullets didn't affect him, even if the rifle had been blessed.

One of the few men who survived an encounter with the tiger spread the rumor that the animal looked like the young Mr. Williams and even had his same eyes. After that point, no one wanted to go near the hacienda. It seemed that the employees killed were those who had worked closest to Mr. Williams in the past few weeks. Some people said it was the ghost of the old man, that his son had cast a spell on him and forced him to wander around like a lost soul. Others thought it was the son himself. In any case, the animal was going to eat them one by one. They tried to kill it with silver-tipped bullets, but no marksman could shoot it; the tiger was always too quick for them. The ones who wanted to leave and go somewhere else found themselves locked in by huge iron fences and guards preventing their escape: they had signed a contract, and they had to work on the ranch until the end of the year.

Soon they realized the animal attacked on a schedule, once every thirty days. It attacked once and then relaxed for three weeks. Each time it made it's monthly kill, the survivors would breathe easier; they had another three weeks to live.

Five months later, it was the turn of the poorest family on the ranch. Mr. Williams went to visit them and said one of them was to go into the depths of the forest to guard the harvest. The oldest brother excused himself, because he had four children; the second brother did the same, because his wife was expecting twins; and the third, who was said to be incredibly brave, was terrified and burst into tears. Then the youngest in the family asked for them to let him go. He was named Jacinto and he was fifteen years old; everyone loved the boy. Perfect, said Mr. Williams, and he left.

When Mr. Williams's niece found out, the girl, who had been Jacinto's playmate, went to see the boy and gave him a packet with a word of advice. The boy didn't doubt the girl's sincerity, but he asked himself, What if the others got the same advice? Unlike his friends, he didn't take a rifle with him into the jungle, just a few chickens and the girl's packet. When night fell, he made a fire and started to make an exquisite dinner. When it was so dark he couldn't see beyond the fire, he heard something close by, stepping on some twigs. He stood up, grasping a picture of the Virgin Mary. And the tiger showed up. Just as people said, the animal was huge and horrific, more than six feet long. It had claws the size of knives instead of hands. It's tail was as thick as an elephant's trunk, and it had long whiskers. Its hair was blond with black stripes. It's eyes were green. And it smiled, its tongue hanging out of its mouth. The animal came up and said, "Good evening, may I sit down?"

"Of course," said Jacinto, "please take a seat, sir."

"Whatever you're cooking smells great. What is it?"

"Chicken with boiled cabbage."

"Ah, sauerkraut. And those bottles you're chilling, what are they?"

"Riesling wine."

"Riesling wine from Germany! It's been a long time since I ate sauerkraut and drank Riesling wine. And it's my favorite dish. Are you going to ask me to eat with you?"

"Yes, sir. All of this is for you."

"OK," the tiger said, "but don't think I'm going to spare your life. I'll eat the sauerkraut and the chickens, and afterward I'll have you for dinner as well."

"As you wish, sir." And Jacinto rushed to pour the wine.

After taking the first bite, the tiger said something had hurt; maybe there was a stone in the food. "It must have been a chicken bone," said Jacinto, and the animal took another bite, licking its whiskers. After finishing the first chicken, the beast asked Jacinto for the second. Then it ate the third and the fourth. The fifth one was eaten directly from the pot. As the beast ate, Jacinto served the first, the second, and finally the third bottle of wine. As it drank, the animal was getting happier and happier, and it roared in between bites. When Jacinto served the second bottle, it was talking to itself and singing in German. When he poured the third bottle, the animal scratched his arm. When it had finished the last chicken, it threw the pot and shouted, "The appetizers were good, but now it's time for dinner!" The animal stood up and, taking its first step toward Jacinto, slipped and fell. Jacinto took advantage of the animal's being drunk to escape.

Everyone was surprised to see Jacinto come back. And they were even more surprised to see the young Mr. Williams fall ill that same day. First, they said, "He woke up with a headache."

And then: "He's sick; he ate something that made him sick." The foreman, another German, went to ask Jacinto if he had run into an animal in the forest. Jacinto said no. "Are you sure you didn't see anything?" Jacinto was positive.

The second day, the foreman went to ask if he hadn't seen a tiger or something like that. "And you didn't notice if that animal hurt itself somehow?"

"No," said Jacinto, "I didn't see anything."

The third day, Mr. Williams died. The doctor who examined him said there were five silver bullets in his body. "One perfectly hidden in each chicken," said Jacinto.

From then on, the workers didn't have any other problems. Jacinto married the old man's niece and they founded a soda company, Cola Drinks. That's why the Williamses are dark-skinned with light-colored eyes.

"Ah," Mr. Torsvan concluded, "finally the waiter is here. What are you going to have?"

After lunch they drank a bottle of whiskey, then coffee.

"Why don't you take us to visit your mansion, Vicente?" his uncle suggested. "You can see the dock from there. Besides, it's not far from here."

They bought a bottle of cognac and Mr. Torsvan handed a cigar to each of them. Since the old men wanted to see the ships, Rangel set them up in rocking chairs on the terrace, so they would be able to talk at ease. The breeze coming off the river scared away the mosquitoes and made the heat more bearable.

The sun descended slowly in the sky, lighting up the other side of the river. Don Miguel Rivera was happy. "In the twenties, you could see javelinas and deer drinking from the river. Do you remember?" he asked the German. "You lived around here."

"Yes," he replied.

"You had to kick them to scare them away."

Ah, Uncle Miguel, Vicente thought to himself. He'd never seen him so happy. Obviously he was happy to run into his buddy.

Half an hour later, Don Miguel Rivera poured the last glass and confessed, "Vicente, I'm thinking of retiring."

"Really? Why?"

"It's about that time."

"No way. What are you talking about?"

"Wait a second, let me speak. As I was saying to you, I've been in this job forty years, and the other day I really started to think."

He was referring to something that had happened recently. Eight days before, while they were chasing a thief on the docks, Rangel had noticed that his uncle was short of breath, so he parked the patrol car and let the suspect go. "It's over," the old man said. "You had that asshole."

"Don't worry, Uncle, your health is the most important thing." And they went to see Dr. Ridaura.

"It's been forty years. Besides, I hadn't told you, but there's a killer on my tracks."

"What!" Rangel shouted. "You should have told me, *tío*. Tell me now, and I'll go look for him."

"They call him *the silent killer*. And when that killer's after you, there's no reason to take any risks."

"No, don't get ahead of yourself, *tío*. We'll look for him and put him in his fucking place. Besides, if you retire, I retire, too. What am I going to do by myself?"

"If you like it, keep at it. I think you're made for this. How long have you been working, a year?"

"A year and a half."

"That's right. When I retire, I'm going to leave my pistol to you, to help keep you out of trouble."

"Yeah, but don't say that. You've got a long time till retirement."

"We'll see."

"The first ones your uncle arrested," said Mr. Torsvan, "were Cain and Abel."

"Look, skipper, you can't say anything; you've got ten years on me."

"That's why you should show some respect."

"If you're so respectable, why don't you write anymore?"

"Of course I'm writing. I just finished a novel for children. It's the story of a woodcutter who gets lost in the jungle. A run-in with God, the devil, and death."

"It's all fairy tales. Why don't you write something more realistic, something more serious, more worthy of you? That story about the woodcutter has been told a thousand times!"

"You want a serious story? Vicente, I'll tell you the story of a police officer who let a guy with no papers go in the thirties."

Rangel thought, What are they talking about?

"You know, your uncle knew who B. Traven was and didn't turn him in. All around the world, the press would have paid to find out who Traven really was. Even though your uncle knew, he let him go. A long time after that, when Dr. Quiroz Cuarón discovered Traven's identity, he boasted about being the best detective in the world. I had to tell him: But you aren't, Dr. Quiroz. The first one to find out was Don Miguel Rivera in the port of Paracuán, more than thirty years ago."

"More than forty," said his uncle.

"Who's telling this story, you or me?"

"Well, if you're going to tell that one again, you'll have to forgive me but I'm going to go lie down. Will that hammock hold me, Vicente?"

"Yeah, go right ahead."

His uncle stood up. "Excuse me, skipper," he put his hand on the older man's shoulder. "This officer is retiring from circulation."

"Go and relax, you deserve it at your age."

His uncle laughed loudly and patted his friend on the shoulder, then headed off to the hammock.

Torsvan sang a few verses in a foreign tongue, which made Rangel's ears perk up. "Excuse me, sir, where are you from? Are you German?"

"What? You don't understand me when I speak Spanish? Is my pronunciation that bad?"

"Of course not, your Spanish is very good."

"Then I'm Mexican."

And since he could see Rangel was surprised, he told his story.

"I came to Tampico in 1929. I got here in the cargo ship *Alabama,* with no money and no papers. They had kicked me out of three countries. I was in the Alps, between France, Belgium, and Holland. At that moment, they were kicking me out of Belgium, so I considered my options. If I went to Holland, the sentence for traveling without papers was six months in a nasty prison, sharing a cell with a lot of shady characters with bad food and the chill of the cold at night. That was the punishment in Holland. In Belgium, it was eight months, but I knew the Belgian police were looking to give me a good beating if I went back to cross the border again. If I waited for my escort to leave and went back to Belgium, most likely they'd still be waiting for me, and before locking me up for six months with only bread and water, they'd torture me: those border guards were a mean lot. If I returned to France, they would sentence me to ten months in jail, but I'd be well fed, with decent food and a blanket. So I went to France. After they kicked me out of Spain, I went to Portugal and then to Mexico, as I already told you. I lived between Tampico and Paracuán, and then in Acapulco and Chiapas.

"I met your uncle in 'twenty-nine. I was able to avoid deportation that year. Someone who wanted to do me harm reported me as illegally in the country. The average cop would have taken advantage of the situation, but your uncle came to interrogate me, understood my case, and didn't bother me again. Curious, no? I've only told the story of this part of my life twice, and both times Lieutenant Rivera was present. I'd say the circle is closing, wouldn't you?

"Imagine it's 1928, a little before the Great Depression. Imagine a young German playwright—handsome, strong, intelligent— and imagine an actor. Do you know who Peter Lorre is? No? It's not really important, but he was of his best friends. The playwright is becoming very popular. At that point in his life they are mounting his third production in Germany, and people wait in long lines to get in to see it. Offers from producers rain down; he has to push actresses away, everyone wants to work with him. His girlfriend is one of the most well-known blondes of the stage. They swore their eternal love for each other, and he's thinking of writing a drama so she can play the lead.

"One day at the end of the play they tell him a producer wants to meet him. Usually, the playwright would not have seen him, since those matters were his agent's responsibility, but the playwright was about to have a birthday and thought it was a joke by the owner of the theater. So he received the visitor in his girlfriend's dressing room, and instead of the ostentatious millionaire he was used to dealing with, he found three men dressed with a marked simplicity; they hadn't polished their shoes and one of them had a suit with patches on it. From the start of the conversation, the playwright behaved as if he were playing a role, and that was his error; it's enough to fake your belief in something to make that something become reality.

"The playwright asked in an exaggerated tone: 'What can I do for you, gentlemen?'

"'Mr. Torsvan, I presume? A pleasure. We are Misters Le Rouge, Le Jaune, and Le Noir.'

"'I guess they're fake names.' The playwright was pleased with the apparent joke.

"The one who seemed the most together says to him, 'they told us to come and see your work and we weren't disappointed. We enjoyed it quite a bit, and we'd like to make you an offer.'

"The playwright appreciates the kind words but doesn't know how to respond. These guys want to hire him? How are they going to pay him? Do they really not know how much he charges? They ask him if he thinks the same way as the play's main character and he explains to them that the author always identifies with his characters, but that in this play in particular, his favorite character is indeed the young idealistic lawyer who defends the poor. The playwright notices them nudging each other, and they decide to continue. They ask him very intelligent questions about the background of his stories, very honest questions like simple people ask.

"With his interest piqued, he asks them what their offer is all about. They look at one another, and one of them sticks his hand in his suit jacket and hands him a paper. When he unrolls it, he notices the poster is printed in red ink, with a hammer and sickle. They were members of the German Communist Party, which at the time was underground. They defended the workers, organized resistance groups, and wanted to build unions, and that was why their lives were in danger.

"'You haven't realized it, but your plays have a lot in common with our struggle. We want to hire you to write a play for us.'

'Yes, the other visitor added, your new play could change a lot of lives.'

"'Change lives? That's not my project,' the playwright argued. 'I'm looking for other things. Besides, a writer requires a certain comfortable environment to write peacefully.' He thought this was going to scare them off, but one of them, wearing worn-out shoes, stepped forward and offered him an envelope. The playwright opened it and looked through its contents. 'Ha, you must be joking. I'm very sorry, but it's too little. I spend this in a weekend!'

"'What for some is very little, for others represents a lot of work,' they told him. 'Thirty of our most dedicated comrades worked extra hours for months to collect that money. It represents the sweat and toil of three dozen workers.'

"The playwright stutters. He says he already has deals for his next two plays and he doesn't have time to write on request, but they insist. They tell him that his play is going to be important, it's going to change many people's lives, and he has to write it. To clear up any doubt, they invite him to attend one of their clandestine gatherings. When? Right now. Always looking for new subjects, he accepts the invitation and leaves the envelope on his girlfriend's dressing table, hidden behind a number of actors' photos and bottles of makeup.

"OK, so as not to draw the story out, he ends up accepting. What he sees in the meetings moves him and reveals a part of the world he didn't know about until then. Inconceivable stories for a civilized country, incredible injustice, regions of suffering he should have known about. So he drops everything and sets to work on that play, he helps mount the production, and he even participates in the rehearsals. A week before the opening, there's an important meeting. The playwright attends the meeting with his actors, but they're attacked by the police and many are shot. They take him for dead and throw him in the truck with the other bodies. He saves himself from being killed, because he jumps out of the truck as soon as it starts up.

"He crosses the border into France; he's illegal in five countries in Europe. Finally, he's able to board a ship in Portugal and get to the United States, but they don't let him in. He takes the cargo ship *Alabama* and gets off in the Gulf of Mexico.

"He gets to a town, Tampico: What a town! Afterward he moves to Paracuán. He sends a letter to his girlfriend using a false name. He tells her what happened and asks for her help. With the money he earned on the ship, he rents a little room on the docks and waits, but the money disappears quickly. He has to do any and every job just to make it as an illegal. He becomes a stevedore on the docks, a delivery man in the market, a worker in the oil wells. A hard, hard life! He lives in horrible rooming houses, on flea-ridden cots, sharing a room with twenty other people. When there's no work, he begs for money from foreigners. He ends up fighting over a cigarette butt with other bums.

"Every Friday, he goes to check the mail to see if he got a letter. There is no response for months. Once, he gets a contract to work in the most remote of the oil wells. He has to work fourteen hours under the relentless sun, in a place where tigers are heard roaring at night. He's there for two months. He loses more than twenty pounds.

"When he gets back from the oil well, they tell him he got a telegram from the United States. The playwright almost tears up the envelope, he's so excited. The letter is from his girlfriend, who was able to leave the country and is living in New York. She doesn't give any address. If you are alive, she writes, send a letter to this post box. A week later, she sends him a money order for two hundred dollars (a fortune for someone who doesn't have a cent) and asks him to wait for her in Tampico at the Hotel Inglaterra.

"He goes to the barber shop, buys a new outfit, lives in a cheap but more respectable hostel than the ones he used previously, and a week before his girlfriend arrives, he moves to the designated hotel. The white room seems huge and empty to him. He knows that everything is OK, but as the days pass, he is overtaken with doubt: *Why didn't she tell me to meet her at the border? Why didn't she tell me to meet her in New York? Why couldn't she drop everything and come look for me?*

"When she finally arrives, the playwright goes to meet her at the docks. They hug for a long time, and she tells him that he can't go back to Germany. Officially he is said to be dead, but the police are waiting to kill him. They read his Communist play and know he supported the organization. 'This has to be very clear,' she says, 'you can't go back. They know you're alive. They're looking for you to kill you.'

"He tells her he doesn't care; the best thing is that she has found him and finally they are going to be together again. 'Oh, Torsvan,' the girl explains, 'I have to tell you something,' and she pulls loose from his arms. While he was in jail in France, she met a movie director, a Mr. Lang, and they were married. 'Understand, we thought you were dead. I'm at the prime of my life, it was a huge opportunity. We don't have a future together. The best thing would be for you to stay in this country and forget about me.' He doesn't respond, but goes out onto the balcony for a cigarette, watching the ships take up their anchors and set out from the docks. He stays there for a long time, even though she calls for him from inside. He realizes the Communists were right; his play changed at least one life—his own.

"He decides to turn his life around. Back inside, he asks his girlfriend, 'And the money? Were you able to take out my savings?'"

"'I'm sorry, Torsvan. They canceled your accounts; the only thing I could recover was this. Do you want me to lend you money? No? Then take this.' And she hands him the envelope he left in her dressing room, the envelope from the three Communists. What a paradox! He, who used to spend that amount in a weekend, is now forced to make it last for a while.

"When she leaves, he decides to grow his own food. In all, he lives for a year on the money from the envelope. He buys the basics to hunt and plant crops and he goes to the country, between Tampico and Paracuán. He rents half the fields from an Indian. He lives in a wood hut, where there are scorpions as big as his hand. Every morning, he takes an insect out of his shoes. To get water, he has to walk almost two miles. He writes a novel living like that—really, autobiography disguised as fiction—in which he tells the story of his escape from Germany. Then he writes two others about his experiences in the jungle. There comes a time when he decides to do something with them, and, using a pseudonym, he sends them to his former theatrical agent. He knows he's playing with fire and this could cost him his life, but despite it all he signs with his mother's maiden name, that almost no one knows, and instead of his first name he uses the single letter B. Inventing that initial, he thinks it through like this: until they killed me, I lived on the A side of my life; now I'm on the B side.

"His agent responds with an enthusiastic letter, saying that he likes the books but that he only works with plays, but B. Traven insists: They have spoken very highly of you; they say you are an honest person. The agent doesn't promise anything but tells him he will try.

"A year and half later, the writer receives another telegram. He has a contract for his first novel. A year later, it's a bestseller in Europe. He sells a hundred thousand copies in the United States. There's an offer to make a movie out of the third novel; they want John Huston to direct. He gets mountains of letters, and the most frequent comment is: Your novel has changed my life. At that moment, the author says, I don't understand anything anymore, and he moves to Mexico City."

Mr. Torsvan doesn't say another word. Rangel takes the chance to ask, "Do you think a person like me could find his path again?"

To respond, the writer takes out an old gold coin, a heavy little German mark shimmering in the afternoon light.

"Are we, each of us, just one person or are we inhabited by a multitude?"

And he handed him the coin. Rangel took another sip from his drink. It was a splendid afternoon, and his uncle was missing it! So he decided to wake him.

"*Tío,*" he said.

But Miguel Rivera Gonzáles didn't answer. He had died in his sleep, after smoking a cigar and drinking half a bottle with his friends.

Since they didn't know what to do, they called Dr. Ridaura, who came and took his pulse and placed a mirror under his nose, but it didn't steam up.

"The silent killer," she said, and since the others gave no sign of understanding, she added, "That's what they call high blood pressure. It kills quickly and leaves no trace. One day you're healthy and the next day, *bam!* Believe me, I'm so sorry. He was a good person."

They buried him on Friday afternoon. In attendance were Mr. Torsvan, the mayor at the time, all his police coworkers, from the night watchman to the chief, and, a little removed from the crowd, two dozen residents of the Colonia Coralillo.

Three days later, still grieving, Rangel had to go to the wreck of a place where his uncle lived to gather up his personal effects. His ex-wife kept the money in his bank account, which she was supposed to distribute to the kids, and Rangel took away the rest. He kept a picture of his uncle and Mr. Torsvan and some other people. If Rangel had had some knowledge of the movie world, he would have known that those individuals were Humphrey Bogart and John Huston, and that the picture was taken during the filming of *The Treasure of the Sierra Madre* in the port of Tampico . . . but Rangel wasn't an educated guy.

To his surprise, he found four records: Los Panchos' *15 Hits*, *Supersonico* by Ray Conniff, Vivaldi's *Four Seasons*, and Frank Sinatra's "Somethin' Stupid": his uncle was eclectic. Without saying a word, he piled up the suits, the ties, the white shirts, the shoes, and the jackets that he was going to throw out. He only kept two things: the thirty-eight caliber Colt and the shoulder holster.

10

The police department was a hundred years old in the year of the El Chacal case, and for twenty-nine of those years, Chief García had been in charge. The first case anyone remembered happened in the second half of the nineteenth century: the murder of a wealthy rancher in his own mansion. Since at that time there was no police force, the port's mayor decided to hire two notorious but very respected bounty hunters to find the people responsible: Mr. Mariano Vela and Mr. Aurelio Santos, also known as Vela and Santos. Beginning in the thirties, Miguel Rivera was on their trail. He was the real brains of the office, the real director of the department for four long decades. Chief García was more like a politician than a detective. Even if he didn't share his predecessors' talents, there was no doubt he was born to lead and to stand up to pressure. Staying in his position for so long had been due in large part to his alliances with the governors and to his knack for identifying good agents, who ended up taking on all the weight of the investigations. That's what happened with Miguel Rivera and then with Wong, the Evangelist, Taboada—El Travolta, who in reality only worked as a team with El Chaneque—and, of course, with Vicente Rangel.

This last one was drawing spirals on a blank paper when a pack of Faros fell onto his desk.

"Sorry for being late, but I had to go all the way to the avenue.

Do you need anything else?"

There was no one in sight. The rest of his colleagues had gone to lunch, so Rangel motioned for Romero to keep the change and offered him a cigarette.

"Did you see Taboada eating?"

"Of course I did: he was in the Rose Garden, talking with Professor Edelmiro."

"Edelmiro Morales?"

"Yeah."

"Are you sure?"

"Why would I be wrong?"

Professor Edelmiro was the leader of the Professors' Union for the entire region.

"Who else was with him? Cruz?"

"Mr. Cruz, no. Some other people I don't know, and Mr. Chávez."

"All right," said Rangel, "get me a cup of coffee."

It seemed strange to him that El Travolta would be seen with Professor Edelmiro. He rolled this news around in his head for a few minutes. Then he reviewed his notes from the Bar León, until he had his first hunch. Hmm, he said to himself, before I make any moves, I have to find more evidence. If I want to arrest that guy, I've got to come around the back way, so he doesn't have a chance to retaliate. He wanted to light a cigarette, but the lighter slipped out of his grip: Fuck. His hands were all chapped and he was losing feeling. If he kept up like this, they were gonna start bleeding again.

At 4:30, he saw Chief García come back and then go into his office. Lolita went in, too, her heels clicking behind him. "Sir, they called from City Hall—" And she closed the door.

Still worried about the possibility that the suspect would complain to the chief, Rangel stood up and looked out the window toward the docks. Twenty minutes later he saw El Travolta pull up. The fat guy parked his patrol car and took out a handcuffed man, a person he knew. No shit, he said to himself. Taboada had arrested the Prophet. The Prophet was an ice-cream vendor who waited for his clients in front of schools, like everyone in his line of business. Fucking Taboada, now I know what you're trying to do. And he stood up. From that moment on, things between Rangel and El Travolta were headed on the wrong track.

On El Chicote's battery-powered radio, an announcer gave the weather: "Button up if you're going outside, my friends. The weather's cloudy and getting cloudier, with the possibility of rain tonight. You know how the city gets before a storm: the fog comes in, no visibility at all, hot as hell, and you gotta turn on the fans just to breathe. If you gotta drive your car and you don't have air-conditioning, bring along an oxygen tank. . . . You are listening to *La Cotorra,* and next up is Rigo Tovar and Las Jaibas del Valle." Fuck, Rangel said to himself and switched the station.

As he was walking in front of the chief's office, García called him in.

"Rangel, come here a minute."

He showed him a reddish paper. It was a flyer printed on newsprint, with the logo of Cola Drinks.

"Salim found them blowing around in the street."

The headline said, A KILLER AMONG US. The flyer reproduced the photo of Karla Cevallos's body, taken from *El Mercurio,* and on one side there was an image of a smiling John Williams Jr., with a wineglass in his hand, at a party with friends. For the flyer's author, there was no doubt that the murderer was young Williams. It even called him Jack the Ripper. The article said: *The same day that the second girl was violently killed, Mr. Jack Williams, Jr. was seen in the Bar León. The officers let him leave and Chief García didn't mention his name in the press conference. How do you explain that?* The flyer reasoned it through: *For the murderer to go unpunished, he has to be extremely powerful; Jack Williams is such a man and he was at the scene of the crime, so he must be the guilty one. Everyone knows El Junior has exotic habits, and the police don't go after him for anything. How long are they going to protect the Jackal?* At the end, the flyer suggested it was even possible that the Jackal was dissolving his victims at the family-owned bottling plant. More than one person had found strange things floating in their cola.

"Do you have something to do with this?" The chief stared at him for an eternity. His look could have taken X-rays, but Rangel didn't move a hair. "I'm asking you a question."

"You know I don't."

He was sure the chief thought he was responsible. That's what I get for asking around to find out if the chief was meeting with Jack Williams. He watched as his boss tore up the reddish paper and threw it in the trash can.

"Don't get mixed up in this one, Rangel."

When he got back to his desk, El Travolta was getting up.

"What's happening, Taboada?" Fatwolf asked him. "How'd it go?"

"Fucking great."

El Chicote and the other officers turned to look.

"You got him?"

But El Travolta didn't answer. He sat down at his desk and typed with two fingers, while he smoked a cigarette. Then he called El Chaneque on the phone and he brought him the Prophet. The prisoner had a black eye and his shirt was torn.

"Fucking Taboada: that's him?" Fatwolf gloated.

"He already confessed."

Everyone was consumed with excitement about the reward, except Vicente Rangel. Fatwolf slapped Taboada on the back, El Chicote congratulated him loudly and immediately followed up saying that an officer about to write a report would probably want a cup of coffee. Taboada agreed and motioned to Romero, who ran out, hurrying, to get the drinks.

"What do you think?" Wong asked, and tossed Rangel the papers.

Rangel picked up the document and read the first page. Taboada whined, "Fuck, that's none of your damn business." And when Vicente stood up, he stared at him.

Rangel walked over to a file cabinet, pulled out a notebook, and checked a list of crossed-out names. After a minute, he lifted up his head and concluded, "This isn't the one."

"What?"

"I said this isn't the one. It's not possible."

El Travolta moved toward his desk. "Who the fuck made you the motherfucking judge and jury?"

El Chaneque stood next to Rangel's desk and stuck his hand in his pocket. The people working at nearby desks stood up discreetly. On another occasion, Rangel had seen Chávez pull out brass knuckles from that pocket, and even though he was dying to take him on, he realized the best idea was to avoid this fight. He was in a really bad spot, stuck between the desk and the wall, with the fat guy in front and El Chaneque behind, so he adopted a more conciliatory tone.

"Look, Taboada, calm down a little. I'm just saying this isn't the one."

"Prove it."

Rangel noticed out of the corner of his eye that Chief García had entered the room, behind Taboada's back, so he was emboldened a little and showed the fat guy the list of prisoners from the month before.

"Is this your signature?"

Taboada didn't answer.

"This is your signature. This *vato* was sleeping in a cell from the thirteenth to the twenty-first. You yourself picked him up for being drunk. He can't be the murderer."

El Travolta trembled with anger. When he started to add something, he saw the chief's icy stare.

"Taboada," said the chief, "I want to talk to you."

Now he'd really fucked it up, Rangel thought. El Travolta left without looking at Vicente. The rest of their colleagues toiled conscientiously on their paperwork. Only El Chaneque stared at him resentfully.

Vicente decided to respond. "What the hell? What do you want, asshole?"

But El Chaneque just stared at him and went back to the main entrance.

When El Travolta came out from his discussion with the chief, Romero offered him the coffee—"Here you go, chief"—but the fat guy hit the tray and the liquid spilled out onto the *madrina*'s clothes. As Romero dried himself off, El Chicote said to him, "Don't take it the wrong way, Blind Man; they're just joking. Jokes are a fact of life around here."

Rangel went down to supervise the release of El Profeta and ran into Wong.

"What you did was right. Cruz and I are going to get a drink at the Cherokee, if you want to come."

"Thanks, but I don't think so. I've got a lot to do."

*   *   *

He took people's crime reports on the phone until 10:30 at night. There arrived a moment when the entire city seemed suspect to him, and he was thinking along those lines when in walked Congressman Tobías Wolffer. "Good afternoon," said the politician. Rangel saw him go into the office of Chief García and realized that the majority of his coworkers were almost salivating, waiting for the next money delivery. To everyone's surprise, the expensively dressed congressman pointed to him, before leaving, and the chief called him into his office. When Rangel went in, the chief was facing away from him.

"The congressman left this for you. He said you did a really good job with his family. Keep it up, Vicente. Don't get distracted by the bullshit."

There was an overstuffed envelope on the desk, an envelope with the logo of the Professors' Union. The congressman was an advisor of theirs. The chief offered him the package and Rangel left without saying anything. Once at his desk, he saw that it was a considerable amount. He left a third of the money in the envelope and put the rest in his pockets. Wolffer was repugnant to him, but nothing could be done about it.

When it was eleven, he decided he couldn't take it anymore. Since his shift had ended hours before, he announced he was leaving and went down to look for his car. As he made his way through the first floor, he ran into the Blind Man, who was coming out of the bathroom with the stain on his shirt. Rangel got his attention and threw him the envelope.

"For the coffees," he said to him, making sure no one else could hear, and left before the Blind Man was able to respond. His gofer stood there, like an abused dog who couldn't understand kindness.

El Chicote was in the parking lot. Rangel wanted to give him a piece of his mind: Why'd you do that? How could you do that? Why ruin all the time he put into the investigation?

"What's the deal, Chicote?" Rangel asked. "Were you in on it, too? How much were they going to give you?"

El Chicote was stunned. He didn't say another word. The Blind Man came up to him, holding the envelope's contents tightly, and said, "Jokes. Jokes are a fact of life at headquarters."

11

Rangel turned on the car radio and heard the sound of mysterious drumbeats. It was the voice of Rubén Blades: "The roar of the roiling sea / the waves break at the horizon / the blue-green of the great Caribe glistens / in the majesty of the setting sun." Since he stopped playing and dedicated himself to his current work, Rangel's only pastime was listening to music, certain music that helped him disconnect from everything: Rubén Blades, Willie Colón, Ray Barretto, Benny Moré, disco music, soul, Aretha Franklin, the sappy songs by Marvin Gaye, blues, Eric Clapton, the rhythms of Creedence, the harmonies of the Beatles, but no *corridos* or Rigo Tovar, even if they were in style. He had lived without a record player ever since that ill-fated Sunday when he decided to kick it to pieces because it reminded him of a certain person. He didn't get another one until he saw the sales at Mr. Guillén's store, but he hardly ever used it. Now his time for daily leisure activities consisted of the songs that he listened to in his Chevy Nova, while going to or coming from the office. But something must really be going wrong, the policeman reasoned, when even his last refuge had become unbearable. The Panamanian's lyrics had taken on another dimension:

> The shark goes out looking
> the shark never sleeps
> the shark out on the prowl
> the shark a bad omen.

Holy shit, thought Rangel, this case is really getting to me.

Anyone else would have gone home and focused on his own life, but Rangel was a good and decent police officer and felt obligated to arrest the person who was guilty. Against the advice of his uncle, he was becoming obsessed with these girls who'd been killed. *Look, Vicente, you have to toughen up so your work doesn't affect you so much. Get a thicker skin; listen to what I'm telling you and don't dick around. You gotta understand you can't get involved in your cases and keep your objectivity. When you make a job into a personal issue, your blind spot grows, you can't see clearly, and that can get really dangerous. You have to work from outside, like it's someone else who's dealing with all this stuff.*

The fog is getting thicker, Vicente thought; as far as he could see, the street was empty. It looks like a ghost town, he said to himself. Whenever there's fog, it's always the same; everyone runs to their houses to escape the heat. It's what I should do myself. He was exhausted. The only thing he wanted to do was roll into bed and sleep eight hours. Get rid of his worries, forget the pain in his hands, the fight with El Travolta, the accumulated tension. But sometimes we make tiny decisions that change our lives, without even noticing it. Just when Rubén Blades sang,

And the horizon swallows up the sun
and the volatile sea begins to calm
you can hear the mermaids' lullabies
captivating the sky with their song,

Rangel turned to the right, looking for a way out.

When he got to the corner of Ejército and Aduana, he saw the outrageous neon lights at the Cherokee Music Disco, a second-rate club that was going from bad to worse. He said, Oh, shit, and parked. He had enough money to down a few drinks, even to leave with a bar girl, and still be able to eat like a king the following day at breakfast at Klein's. Besides, today was a show day. Every Tuesday, starting at eleven, the Cherokee Music Disco attracted a good number of hookers, and there was a show where they danced in bathing suits. Rangel decided he wasn't going to take one home, but he thought he should distract himself for a few hours, send his brain on vacation, forget about the case for a while.

It was past eleven. Before turning off the car, he heard some more Rubén Blades lyrics:

The stars are shining in the night
the moon rests in the silence
only the shark is still on the prowl.

He was just getting out of his vehicle when two kids ran up to him: "I'll take care of it, man" and "You want it washed, chief?" Rangel shook his head and headed to the club.

El Watusi and Juan Pachanga were guarding the main entrance to the Cherokee. El Watusi was a black man from Jalapa, almost six and a half feet tall, who had previously been a fisherman. Juan Pachanga was the administrator, always a little tipsy, a few whiskeys above sea level. Since they knew Rangel by sight, they let him go in without searching him, like they should have done. For sure, they can see how tired I am, thought Rangel. A sign was hanging off his face that said: DON'T BOTHER ME.

He pushed aside a beaded curtain and waited a second while he got used to the contradictions of the place. Even though there was one of those mirror balls spinning nonstop at the center of the dance floor, the music was a salsa by Roberto Roena: "You're loco-loco . . . and I'm chill." The decoration was leftover from the prior owner, Freaky Villarreal, a disco music aficionado who went bankrupt and had to sell the business. Another person bought the club and salsa pushed the Village People aside.

The bar had started to liven up. Four bar girls danced on the floor, and their mistress, Madam Kalalú, was mingling with the regulars, leaning on the bar in a wispy red dress, with her customary cigar in her mouth. As soon as she saw him, she sent him two bar girls, who went to give him the traditional welcome. As soon as someone came into the Cherokee, one or more of these scantily dressed women would rush to stroke him suggestively a little, so the new guy would buy them a drink. The ones who hugged the detective now, wrapping themselves around him like a pair of boa constrictors, were very disappointed, because Rangel sent them away with an ugly gesture. He had walked over to the bar when he heard someone talking to him.

"Jackie Chan!"

It took him a minute to recognize the butcher from the Colonia Coralillo, the black man he had almost arrested with his uncle. He didn't seem to have any hard feelings and raised his glass to toast him. He was at a nearby table with two other guys and three bar girls. As he remembered the circumstances of their last meeting, Rangel moved his head discreetly to say hello and continued on his way. Two steps from the bar, he heard someone else shout his name—"Rangel!"—and saw that the Evangelist was motioning to him from another table close by. Rangel accepted the fact that the solitude he longed for was not possible and went to sit with his colleagues.

Wong and Cruz Treviño were with the Evangelist. A bar girl was comforting Cruz. There was a half-empty Bacardi bottle in the middle of the table, about the size of an elephant's foot. Since the Evangelist had a Coke in front of him, Rangel assumed that the rum was flowing through Cruz Treviño's six-foot, three-hundred-pound frame. Cruz hadn't even seen him come in. The Evangelist offered his hand, and Rangel did the same.

"What's up, John One Four?" Every time they saw each other, Rangel rebaptized the Evangelist with a verse from the Bible. "I thought you didn't drink. Aren't you condemning yourself?"

"Of course not. I'm just taking care of this sinner, making sure he doesn't get himself killed." The Evangelist pointed to his partner, who was trying to explain something to the bar girl.

"Hey, man."

Rangel said hello to Cruz Treviño, whose head swayed until his eyes focused on the musician; then he extended a huge hand, with a lot of effort, and finally crashed it into Vicente's palm. Then Cruz Treviño pointed at him with the other hand and said a few words under his breath. Rangel didn't understand a thing. Even though his relationship with the giant was passable, Rangel always kept a certain distance to avoid problems. Just like El Travolta, Cruz Treviño had some kind of teenage problem, always about to explode. That was his personality. He'd get red with anger at the slightest affront.

"What'd he say?" the Evangelist asked him. "I didn't get it."

"He's fed up with his boss," the bar girl mumbled, so drunk she swayed back and forth. She was a fake redhead in a green sequined dress. "He says he's a fucking asshole."

The giant nodded his head in agreement.

"Who knows what's going on?" shouted Wong. You had to scream to be heard in that club. "They're saying the Federal Safety Administration is going to come."

Rangel felt a shiver make its way up his spine; the FSA was the Mexican president's personal police force. The last time agents from the Federal Safety Administration had visited the port was in 1971, during the repression of the student movement. That was the year Rangel got to the port, but people told him that his uncle had had to do everything he could to stay clear of their abuse. They called a student who witnessed the massacre to make a statement, and as soon as he sat down, one of the agents, a deaf mute, stood up and punched him in the eye. *There's no need to hit him*, Lieutenant Rivera had said, *the young man came of his own volition*. They let the student go, but things were really tense for months, and people thought the government agents would retaliate.

"Get yourself a Coke," the Evangelist told him, "it's the only nonalcoholic drink in the bar."

Rangel was still deep in thought, and since he didn't respond, the Evangelist took a cup that looked clean, poured the petroleum-colored liquid, and offered it to Rangel, but before the drink reached its destination, Cruz Treviño grabbed it from him, dumped its contents on the floor, and filled it up halfway with rum. Then he handed it over to the new guy with an animalistic roughness.

"No, compadre, what's wrong with you? Our friend wasn't going to drink, I don't want any craziness," the Evangelist protested, but the giant lifted a finger and pointed at Rangel, as if to say it was an order. "Fine, fine," said the Evangelist, and whispered to Vicente, "Let him have his way; he's already bent out of shape."

At that moment, the song ended and they heard a screeching noise that nearly burst their eardrums. Then a voice started to test the sound equipment with a tap on the microphone and the traditional "Testing . . . one, two, three . . . testing." There was one last screech and the DJ announced to the *elegant clientele* that the Cherokee Music Machine was pleased to present that night's show: a contest between the elegant ladies of the Mulatto Dancing Club, direct from our sister republic of Chihuahua, here to entertain you with a few classy melodies. They put on "El Bodeguero," and the dance floor filled up with artificial smoke. In the darkness, a half dozen girls did their best to reach the dance floor without being pinched.

"They're spring chickens," said the bar girl, and since Rangel didn't respond, she added, "I already saw them, they're not professionals. They don't know how to move their hips, and they don't show their breasts."

As soon as the girls came out on the dance floor, the policeman noticed something was wrong. There were six presentable young ladies, wearing tight outfits. There were two artificial blondes, two long-haired dark-skinned girls, a black, and a Chinese. They didn't look like conventional hookers; the oldest one was about twenty-five years old and the fattest one weighed about 130 very-well-distributed pounds. In terms of their clothes, they looked straight out of an Olivia Newton-John movie.

"Sinners," said the Evangelist.

Just like the announcer had said, the girls fanned out on the aerodynamic dance floor and started doing a supersonic dance. Rangel thought that the choreography was too structured for a show in a place like this. They didn't move in a sexy or provocative way, and so, as they always did when something reeked of culture, the distinguished clientele of the Cherokee started to yawn. Insults would follow quickly.

One of the dancers lifted her hands and arched her back as she fell to her knees on the dance floor. Her gesture would have had better luck in a TV program, not on this well-used floor, designed for dancing to Jackson Five songs. Up until that moment, Rangel didn't understand what was going on: It's modern dance, he thought; they're modern dancers. As he realized this, he imagined what would come next: the humiliation of the dancers and widespread booing. Poor girls, he said to himself, that's what's gonna happen.

Rangel took the glass the giant offered him, added two ice cubes, and drank half. He put the glass back on the table. Let's see, he said to himself: the chief doesn't want to mess with Jack Williams. Instead of assigning me to the case, he orders me to take crime reports and gives the case to El Travolta. Then he chews me out like I had anything to do with those fucking flyers; Congressman Wolffer shows up in his office, and he gives me a huge tip. If Uncle Miguel were sitting here, with his customary white shirt and shoulder holster, he would have snorted and leaned toward him: *Ah, you're so stupid, Vicente. Did they only hire you because you knew somebody? Look at the facts; that's where you'll find the answers, if you know how to think it through.*

The salsa was still rattling the speakers, and a second girl moved a few steps forward to meet the first girl. She fell to her knees and lifted up her hands.

"Fucking bitches, what are you smoking?" screamed the bar girl.

Cruz Treviño finished off his drink suddenly and the redhead prepared him another one. Rangel asked himself why the chief was trying to distract him. It seemed unthinkable that the old man would protect the murderer, not because of professional ethics but because that kind of thing is always found out, and there was still a chance of his being removed from his post. That's not the answer, he decided. The chief wasn't stupid; he wasn't going to risk his job. In his opinion, it could only be due to one or two reasons, Rangel decided; either someone very powerful had ordered him to freeze the investigation or—more likely—he was trying to get the reward for himself.

In the distance, Rangel made out a person in a white shirt and glasses who was doing his best to get around El Watusi and Juan Pachanga. It's over, Rangel thought, here comes this idiot. The character finally got to the dance floor, looked around, and came to sit down with him: it was the Blind Man, the guy who wanted to be his gofer.

"Hey, boss, I just came to say thanks for the envelope."

"Don't call me boss."

"Call me master, for so I am. John thirteen, verse thirteen," said the Evangelist.

"Sit down. And you, fucking fanatic, go evangelize the neighborhoods on the North Side."

"Do you want a drink?" the bar girl asked. "Cruz is paying."

Rangel thought about leaving, but he heard a sudden pattering on the roof, growing louder. A violent rain shower had started, like a creature with a thousand fists slamming into the corrugated sheet metal. Fuck, he said to himself, I can't leave now.

"What?" He had to scream at the Blind Man.

"I asked if you're interested in getting the reward, Mr. Rangel. It's four years' salary. Four years! Imagine everything you could buy with that money."

Rangel didn't answer. To the left of the bar girl, Wong nodded off on the table.

When the dancers passed by, Rangel, already loosened up by the drink, decided they looked pretty good. The majority looked better when they weren't fooling around with that modern stuff. Damn, I'm already drunk, he said to himself, fucking cheap rum. Why am I drinking this stuff?

One of the dancers at the bar walked up and came on to him, and since his anger was starting to diminish, he let himself play a little with her. Rangel brandished his evil side: even though he saw how much she wanted to have a drink, he didn't invite her to sit down.

"Come on, get me a drink. I have to support my dad and my seven little brothers and sisters."

"Damn, why that many? Are you Snow White's daughter?"

"Come on. If you don't get me a drink, I'm going to have to go to that table, where that guy is waving at me. But I'd rather stay here with you."

And the girl leaned forward, grazing Vicente's arm with her breasts as if by mistake. Then she stretched out her arms and pretended to dance, shaking her shoulders frenetically.

"What's up, *mi rey?* Deal or no deal?"

"Sorry, no deal." And he regretted it as soon as he sent her away.

Even though the majority of the girls were really good-looking and had voluptuous figures, Rangel wasn't interested in the blonde or the Chinese girl or the redhead. He was only interested in a thin girl with short black hair in braids who was smoking at the bar with some girlfriends. Goddamn, he said to himself, that one's really hot. The girl had a long, thin nose and white skin. He was admiring her legs when the girl noticed that he was watching her. She shot him a sharp look, like a cat discovering a rat, and Rangel lowered his eyes. Fucking bitch, for sure she's trying to figure out how much she can get out of me. All of 'em are whores, total whores, just like the bloodsucker next to me.

As soon as the dancers got to the bar, the men closed in to buy them drinks. A really fat guy took the redhead by the hand. Two guys fought over the Chinese girl. In less than ten minutes, three assholes moved in close, one by one, and took the ones who were left. Only the girl with the little braids off to the side rejected two admirers. How strange, Rangel thought, she must be charging a lot. Meanwhile, her girlfriends, legs crossed, kept on talking at the bar. Rangel was serving himself another drink when he noticed that the girl with the little braids was staring at him. Is she looking at me? He even looked behind him, but no one was there. What an idiot, he said to himself, I'm leaning against a column. Rangel turned red for the first time in a long time and the girl started laughing. Fucking bitch, I'm gonna make you pay for that.

Rangel served himself another drink and the girl with the little braids came over to his table.

"Excuse me, aren't you Rigo's guitarist?"

"Huh?" Rangel was shocked.

"With Rigo Tovar. Didn't you play with him?"

"I don't know who you're talking about."

"You were the guitarist, the one from Las Jaibas del Valle."

"No, you've got me mixed up."

"Don't lie! Tell me it was you."

"Why do you want to know?"

"I was in his fan club."

"Really? Rigo Tovar had a fan club?" Rangel was flattered, but he didn't want to admit it was him. "Yeah, they say the guitarist was good."

"No way! He was the best! Who knows why he retired?"

"All right, well, thanks. The guitarist would be happy to hear that."

The girl sat down on the chair next to him, subtly pushed by the redhead. "So, really, are you him or not?"

She had huge blue eyes that stood out when she laughed. They must be contact lenses, he said to himself, everything here is fake. He was about to make his getaway, but the girl moved in closer to him. Damn, Vicente said to himself. For a moment, the girl's laughter reminded him of someone else. Suddenly, it was as if something from the woman who was *not* there reappeared in the face of the dancer who was, only diluted and changed. Instead of paying attention to the girl, which is what he should have done, Rangel remembered other days and other nights, from more than six years ago, when he was a musician and lived with his lady, Yesenia, the one with the perfect curly black hair, his girlfriend since high school, the most beautiful girl ever, famous in musical circles for her angelic smile.

And he thought of other afternoons with Yesenia by his side, as he tried to write the arrangements for the group leader. *Look, Rigo, what do you think of this deal?* The tune's far out, brother, what's it about? *It's the story of a mermaid, or really about a guy who falls for a mermaid.* Ah, damn, don't go getting all cultural on me, Rangel. Are there mermaids in your pueblo? *Don't be a jerkoff, Rigo, that's why you're not hitting it big. You're never gonna take any risks?* In Vicente's opinion, Rigo was getting stubborn and overbearing. If he didn't come up with the idea for a song, that meant the deal wasn't worth anything. He was becoming a star and he didn't accept anyone else's point of view. I've got to watch out, brother, a lot of people want to put an end to my career. Rangel insisted for a few days, but Rigo wouldn't give in. The song was almost finished, especially the music. Then, one night, after a concert, Rigo and his group, Las Jaibas del Valle, went to a bar to finish getting wasted. Rigo, his fans, and his agent were on one side of the place. Yesenia, the keyboardist, and Rangel, stroking his guitar, were on the other side. All of a sudden, Rigo, who was already pretty drunk, lifted up his head and looked toward the back of the club, like he was scanning for smoke signals, and as his fans drank the last drops from the vodka bottle, he stood up real slow, with his drink and everything and walked over to Vicente. What's up, Chente? Is that song yours? *It's the one I told you about, friggin Rigo, the one about the mermaid, I'm just wrapping up the lyrics.* It sounds good, Vicente. Let's see, who's got some paper?

They worked on the song for the rest of the night. Rangel played, Rigo nodded his head in agreement or shook it to say no, but always very authoritatively, and between the two of them, they put the song together. There was a moment when the song finally straightened out and Rigo burst out: That's it, we're done, we've got it. But one line was missing— Damn, Vicente, we just need that one fucking line—and Rangel, by this time very inspired, suggested they go back to the original idea: *It doesn't make sense for them to have normal kids, Rigo; if they're gonna procreate, it'd be better if they had mermaids.* Wait, wait, what do you mean? *Okay, look: Where it says: We had six little angels, tra la la, tra la la, it'd be better as: We had a little mermaid.* Damn, Vicente! That's really good, lemme see: what next? *As the fruit of our love.* No shit, Vicente, that's really corny; that's like fifth-grade stuff. *Oh, all right, what, you're really high-class now?* Go on, go on, don't slow down. *OK: We had a little mermaid.* And what else? *Like a year after being married.* You're doing well, Vicente, and then what? *With the face of a little angel, but the tail of a fish.* Damn, man, now you broke the record, *pinche* Vicente; we've got a new songwriter.

The euphoria was gone three days later, when, after getting back from touring around Montemorelos, Vicente opened the door to his apartment and caught her wrapped in the singer's arms, her hot pants thrown in the corner of the room. Fucking assholes: you, *cabrón,* I thought you were my friend; you ain't shit. And you, fucking bitch, you're really faithful, huh? What about you being totally open and honest and all that bullshit? What a joke! Go fuck yourselves, I don't want anything to do with this band; I'm out of the group. And don't even try to play that song.

The girl's eyes reminded him of Yesenia. Rangel, the only person in the world who hated Rigo Tovar's biggest hit, looked intensely at the girl and said, "No, I'm not him."

She covered her face with both hands and pulled her cheeks down, like someone putting on a fake mustache; then she turned around and walked away. The Blind Man watched her, his mouth hanging open.

"She was really into it. Why'd you let her go, boss?"

"Because I don't have enough money."

The Blind Man grabbed the envelope he had in his pants as if his tip was in danger and said, "But that girl is one of the ones that doesn't charge. . . . But it doesn't matter, when we get the Jackal, you're gonna have thirty of them."

Rangel pushed his drink away, fucking worthless Bacardi, and the Blind Man's words reverberated in his head for the rest of the night.

It's four years worth of pay, boss.

Four years.

Imagine what you could do with four years' pay.

You could buy a house.

You could even retire.

Two drinks later, when they asked him what was going on, Rangel was able to murmur, "The Chief supports El Travolta more than me."

"Fucking idiot," the Blind Man said to him. "Even though the Chief doesn't want to face it, everyone says you're the good one and you're gonna get him. Why don't we work together, boss? Two heads think better than one."

Rangel just looked at him and didn't say no, but he didn't say yes either. Damn, he thought, what a messed-up situation. All I wanted was to relax.

Celia Cruz sang "El Berimbau," and Cruz Treviño fell asleep on the table. After everybody was nodding off, Rangel waved to the fan with the little braids. Hey, you, you want a drink? The girl said yes and he prepared her a gigantic Cuba libre that never ran out, and they drank it the rest of the night. Damn, this woman is so supportive. He looked at the girl and then at the vampire on the rum label; another drink and another look at the girl. One more drink and the girl started to look irresistible.

His vision blurred and the next thing he saw was an immense, grassy plain, somewhere in the country. He was asking himself where he was when suddenly he saw the silhouette of a mountain, perhaps the Cerro del Nagual, and he realized that an old-fashioned UFO was floating at the summit, one of those interplanetary space ships in black-and-white movies that looked like two soup bowls stuck together. Then he realized he was standing on the peak of the mountain. There were a lot of journalists all around him, the ones he had run into that morning, and six TV cameras. An announcer said, *We are witnessing the first contact between a human being and the people of Mars. Mr. Vicente Rangel, police officer from the port, has been chosen to receive this great honor, this grand distinction.* And there was a round of applause.

Deeply moved, Rangel watched as the Martian ship descended. Judging by its dimensions, he reasoned that it was the mother ship, landing and opening its double doors. The king of the Martians came out on a long bridge, joined by ten ministers and a legion of secretaries. These women were straight out of a Mexican science-fiction movie: they were wearing silver miniskirts, sixties-style beehive hairdos, and long fake eyelashes. One of them, a long-legged good-looking blonde, placed a medal on Rangel and he began to whisper softly, *Thank you so much, but I do not deserve this. There are many more competent people.*

Nevertheless, the King of the Martians made it clear that Rangel was his choice and he is allowed one wish: Ask for whatever you want. *Whatever?* That's right: whatever you request will be provided.

Suddenly, the king of the Martians looked just like Chabuelo, a television personality, and Rangel thought he was on a game show. And Rangel asked himself, *What should I ask for, an all-expense-paid trip to Hawaii? A new car, a washing machine, a CD player?* He was aware that it was a once-in-a-lifetime opportunity, but the professional part of his subconscious took over before he could stop it: *the murderer, ask who the murderer is.*

Your time is up, the Martian said. Let's see what's behind curtain number one, the prize the contestant did not select. Wow! The audience grumbled. A millionaire's mansion, with a huge car out front and three servants: a blonde, a redhead, and a brunette, all ready and at your service. Rangel heard applause, a round of applause, and the game show host continued. Let's go to the second curtain, what's behind the second curtain? Jimi Hendrix's guitar, the guitar that Jimi Hendrix played, and next to it . . . the secret to immortality! Mr. Vicente Rangel González just turned down the secret to eternal life. But don't lose hope, there's still one more chance to redeem yourself. What do we have behind curtain number three, please? The last servant removed the curtain and the announcer said: A monkey. A spooky monkey.

Inside, under a powerful spotlight, a baboon was sitting on a stool. Oh, my God, what an ugly monkey! The baboon was dark gray and he had a terrible look on his face, almost human. When it realized that Rangel was looking at him, the primate reprimanded him: What do you want, dude?

Frightened, Rangel apologized: *I don't know what's going on, I'm here for the contest.* The baboon seemed to get upset: What contest? What a stupid nephew! *Uncle Miguel? Is that you?* Yeah, it's me. *And what are you doing here?* Working, I'm still a detective, but now I'm an undercover agent, I investigate dreams, and you, what do you do now, nephew? *I'm tracking two murders, a guy who kills young girls.* A little girl murderer . . . that's unbelievable! And do you have any evidence? *A little, but it hasn't helped any.* That's too bad, Uncle Miguel said, too bad. Sometimes you win, sometimes you lose. *Listen, Uncle Miguel, what if you help me?* Nooo, I'm really sorry but I can't, why should I drop my work just to help with yours? Besides, if I don't charge, I don't work. *But before, you would always help me.* Yeah, but now you're all grown up, and there's nothing in it for me. *Uncle, the years have made you really egotistical, you only think about money.* Do you or don't you want to solve the case? *Yes.* Well then, shut up and watch.

The baboon climbed down from the stool and walked over to a door in the back. For starters, you need to get out of this building. Don't dawdle. Before Rangel could react, he ordered: look, there's the guy you've been looking for, and he pointed to the other side of a window. A scary-looking man carrying a French poodle was outside. He was wearing a wide leather duty belt, loaded with sharp tools, and when he saw a young girl pass by, he offered her the French poodle. No, he thought, don't take it, but it was too late. Rangel wanted to stop him from attacking her, but the door was locked with a key, and when he looked out the window again, they were no longer there. He asked himself where they could have gone to, and the next thing he saw was an enormous curtain, a yellow curtain, ruffling in the wind. He couldn't explain why he was so afraid. But the wind lifted the curtain and he saw the girl's feet, submerged in a puddle of blood. . . .

He woke up, stamping his feet violently, and for a minute he confused the curtain in his dream for the real curtain. *Ooof*—he opened his eyes—*at least I'm in my own house.* There was a ceiling fan, and everything was fine, except that he didn't have any ceiling fans.

"Oh, shit, where am I?" he said out loud.

"We're in the Motel Costa Brava," a voice answered. "What happened to you? As soon as you got here, you started snoring," the girl with the braids complained.

As the image of the room came into focus, the detective concluded with growing amazement: The French poodle! *The fuzz,* he thought, *we have to analyze the fuzz.*

Part III

12

When he called Dr. Ridaura, she thought he was kidding. "Are you sure?"

Rangel explained that he was serious and said that running the test was urgent.

The old woman didn't like the idea of getting up so early in the morning, but because she was dealing with him, she replied very kindly. "Call me in half an hour."

Before the time was up, the specialist called headquarters.

"It was complicated, but it was worth it. You're half right. I have your results here, but first, tell me how it occurred to you to do this."

"Another time," he apologized, "we have to hurry."

"OK, I have to admit that I forgot the principle of Poe's 'The Purloined Letter': when you want to hide something, leave it in plain sight. There they were, but since they provoked my allergies, I overlooked them. Do you remember how I was sneezing at the crime scene?"

"What are they?"

"I'm getting to that. I don't understand how it didn't occur to me, but anyway, I checked the material that we recovered from under the nails and indeed I found two samples of animal origin."

"White in color?" Rangel inquired.

Dr. Ridaura was stunned. "You already knew? Well, yes, a grayish white. And you want to know something? They are also under the nails of Karla Cevallos. You were right so far. But you were wrong about one thing: They're not dog hairs. It's sheep wool. A very young white lamb."

"Are you sure?"

"Either I'm sure or Ridaura's not my name. That guy attracts the girls with a little lamb."

"Thank you so much, Doctor. And listen, don't mention this to anyone. It's very important."

"OK. Congratulations, Rangel. I'm going to be following this to see what happens."

He confirmed that no one had heard him, but his nervousness was unjustified. The Professor and the Bedouin had gone to sleep in their respective cars at 4:30, and El Chicote was snoring on the first floor.

He went down to get some coffee. When he heard him moving around, El Chicote half woke up.

"Are you going to want some more? I'll make it right now."

"You're really on top of things, *cabrón*."

"It'll be ready in a second. If you want to, go back to sleep," he suggested. "If something comes up, I'll wake you."

Sure, thought Rangel, even though you can't even handle your own business. As he waited for the coffee, he heard the new edition of *El Mercurio* arrive and went outside to get it. Let's see what's new, he thought. The first page grabbed his attention: SIERRA DE OCAMPO ON FIRE. DROUGHT CAUSES CONCERN IN PORT. But it was two other headlines that bothered him: NO TRACE OF THE JACKAL and WORK OF JOURNALISTS OBSTRUCTED. Holy shit, it was La Chilanga. There was a photo of the chief on the cover, promising an intense manhunt and an arrest. On one side, the weather report contradicted him with a certain ill will: *Only light winds and isolated rainfall in the region.* And the satellite image did in fact show a persistent cloudiness parked over the metro area. Farther down, Johnny Guerrero's column said: NEW POLICE ERRORS: SECRET SERVICE STILL HAS NO LEADS ON SADISTIC MURDERER. He said to himself: Let's see what this idiot wrote about, and to his surprise, Johnny told the story of El Profeta. Goddamn, *cabrón,* this shit is serious. The columnist told everything about Taboada's failure in exacting detail, but he was careful not to identify the agents. "According to our sources, a good detective who has been working on the case is about to quit due to internal pressures." Rangel realized he was turning pale. Shit, he thought, now they really are going to fuck with me; fucking dumb-ass reporter, this is gonna make my life impossible. They're gonna think I'm ratting them out. Goddamnit, somebody's got me in their sights. He didn't want to think about what El Travolta would do. Holy shit, he said to himself, if I'm in the office, I'm gonna be in trouble.

A rooster crowed somewhere in the neighborhood, and Rangel considered working with Agustín Barbosa. What am I gonna do with my life? He didn't have a lot of options; he hadn't even finished college. At his worst moments, he imagined himself dealing with the humiliation of going to ask for work from the Williams family. No fucking chance of that. Besides, the Federal Highway Patrol was the only thing left after the Secret Service, and there weren't many positions in the city. Whatever, he thought, I'm gonna end up in a fucking checkpoint, just like the Wizard. He thought over Barbosa's offer and concluded that his coworkers would never let him work for the opposition. They'd make his life impossible. He decided that if he was fired, he wouldn't apply to the Federal Police. The pay was so bad he'd have to end up corrupt.

It had been a crazy night and he couldn't take it anymore. The sun would come up in a few minutes and he had a pounding headache. For a minute, he thought about going back home, but there was no time, so he cleared off his desk and tried to get some sleep.

Vicente thought about his childhood and his brief professional career in music. The year he learned to play bass. The Beatles, Pink Floyd, Clapton. His first gigs, touring with Rigo Tovar. But as always happened when he remembered his life in the band, he ended up thinking about his first girlfriend and his friend's betrayal. At that moment, the needle of his memory, accustomed to protecting him from his past, skipped on the LP album of his life, and the next thing he saw was the place where he was right then. He was a police officer pursuing a murderer. He didn't like his job but he couldn't leave it: he didn't know how to do anything else.

That's what he was thinking about that day, Wednesday the nineteenth of March, at six in the morning, when Chief García came in dressed in a suit and tie. Rangel barely had time to stand up.

"Is there anything new?"

Vicente presented his findings. As he spoke, the chief watched him and nodded.

"It's about time. Have you distributed this information?"

"Not yet."

"I'd like you to personally advise the other officers. This is very good information. I can't have it wasted in the papers."

He thought the chief would reprimand him, but he did not seem to be upset. It was obvious he hadn't read *El Mercurio*.

"And Taboada?"

"He hasn't come in." He was the only officer on watch, Rangel explained; the others were sleeping in their cars. He didn't want to talk badly about his colleagues, but he had to tell the chief the truth.

Chief García shook his head with disgust and thought about the situation. "Rangel, I need your help: bring a notebook so you can take notes. We leave in ten minutes."

"Yes, sir. Where are we going?"

"To a meeting. You drive." And he threw him the keys to his personal patrol car.

Vicente opened up the bottom drawer of his desk and took out a jar of gel, a razor, toothpaste, and dug around until he found his Odorono deodorant. Five minutes later, he emerged from the bathroom, his hair combed and with an acceptable shave.

He started the chief's car—it was always a pleasure to drive that patrol car—and pulled up at the entrance. The chief was waiting for him.

"Where are we headed, sir?"

"To the palace."

He was referring to City Hall. They were going to see the Mayor Torres Sabinas.

Passing through Parque Hidalgo, he saw the fog was starting to clear. The birds were screeching in the cypress trees and a large orange cloud was moving closer to the city. For a moment, the fog seemed to dissipate.

At the stoplight in front of the cathedral, they had to wait for a garbage truck to move. As they were waiting, the old man commented, "Churruca called me again. He wants this case resolved in two days."

Poor guy, he thought. The chance of García's staying in his job was worse than ever, and, in a gesture of friendship, he made an offer. "Sir, would you like me to help interrogate Jack Williams?"

The old man responded by looking at him. Everything he wanted to say was understood in that one look. "Don't pressure me, Rangel, don't pressure me."

As soon as they turned onto the Avenida del Puerto, Rangel saw that the doorman was waiting to open the gate. There were already six cars there.

Rangel parked next to Torres Sabinas's minivan, and they walked up the wide staircase. On the second floor, they ran into six bodyguards, who moved to one side to allow them to pass; one of them was the gringo security guard who had questioned him at John Williams's mansion. Shit, what is he doing here?

The chief walked on one side of the guards, who greeted him with their customary phrase, "At your command, Chief." As was the norm, he responded to their greeting with a slight head movement.

In the main assembly room, a handful of people were arranged around a rectangular table. Seeing them arrive, Licenciado Daniel Torres Sabinas went to welcome them.

"Anything new?"

"We have evidence, but we can't announce it at the press conference."

"Why?"

"There have been too many leaks. We can't allow ourselves to lose track of this one."

"OK. Here, just between us, tell me what it is."

The chief took him off to one side.

Rangel saw that the mayor was nodding. "Very well, very well." He looked over at Rangel. "It's a shame we can't announce it, the reporters are going to think we woke up this morning with empty hands. . . . Well," and he spoke to the chief, "proceed as instructed."

As the rest of the people said hello to the chief, Rangel identified the men assembled. Damn, he thought, this meeting is serious. Besides the mayor of Paracuán and his chief of staff, there was also the chief of the municipal police of Tampico, the director of the Federal Highway Patrol for the state, the coordinator of security services for the Oil Workers' Union, the director of intelligence for the eighth military regiment, and a representative of the federal government. At the end of the table, two people Rangel didn't know were having a conversation: a young man in a plaid shirt and a bald man with a dour look on his face. Rangel remembered that the young man in the plaid shirt was the president of the Parents' Association, Mr. Chow Pangtay. He didn't have time to identify the bald man because at that moment the door between the hall and the mayor's office opened and Rangel thought that he was dreaming.

Mr. John Williams and his lawyer, Carrizo, sat down at the end of the table, to the right of the mayor. Everyone stood up to welcome the men, who were wearing suits, tie bars, and cuff links. It's not possible, he said to himself. What was he doing here? Since he had been on night watch the last few days, Rangel would have heard about anyone who was detained, or even any rumor of an arrest, but nothing of that sort had happened. He assumed that working straight for the last two days without sleeping had begun to affect his sense of reality. The following half hour he had to make a huge effort just to stay awake. Everything seemed to be far away, blurry, like a thick fog. He drank two cups of coffee, one after another, but the liquid only filled him with apprehension.

The dark hall had velvet curtains and there was a green covering on the table. When everyone had a cup of coffee in front of him, the mayor ordered the secretary to leave. If you all agree, he said to them, we're going to get started; I'm not going to do introductions because you already know each other. He directed himself to the millionaire and his companion. "John, Ricardo, thanks for coming." Then he summarized the situation and suggested that they should all work as a team to resolve the emergency. He avoided mentioning the fact that a group of Texans wanted to invest a large quantity of money in the fiestas the following month, but the Jackal was scaring them away.

"One of the priorities of my government is the purveyance of justice," he said. "That's why John and a representative of the Parents' Association are here—so that they can work with us on what we decide today." Next he reiterated that in the port there were seven schools, two private and five public. The private schools had already hired private security, he said, which left the public schools and their three thousand students. "We have two plainclothes officers in each one, and to placate the parents, we have a uniformed officer at the main entrance, but it's not enough. The schools have a lot of exit doors, and at opening and closing times, everything becomes a complete chaos, impossible to control."

Mr. Chow replied that that wasn't any kind of excuse. The association was exasperated, they couldn't understand how it was possible that the murderer had struck again. Mayor Torres Sabinas replied that they already had a firm lead, and Chief García trusted that they could get results in the next few days. The Chief enumerated the few clues and at the end he focused on the cigarette butts: "He smokes Raleighs and bites on the filter." Rangel saw that Mr. Williams, hearing that, leaned forward on the table and listened attentively. "We consulted with two dentists," the chief continued, "and both of them were of the opinion that the mark corresponds to an upper canine. This is the first firm lead we have, and it must be handled with a lot of care: if the murderer finds out, we run the risk of putting him on alert."

"Could we distribute that inside the schools?" asked Mr. Chow.

"I'd prefer you didn't. The best idea would be to tell the security guards in private, one by one, in order to avoid leaking the information. Imagine, with this knowledge, our agents will be more prepared and will protect our schools even more efficiently. But if this gets to the press, we'll lose a golden opportunity."

At this point, the bald guy whispered something into Mr. Chow's ear; Chow nodded and asked to speak.

"Mr. Mayor, with all due respect, that's not good enough. Those of us who have school-age daughters can't wait for the government to handle this. We want a serious investigation, done by professionals."

He proposed that they ask for help from the feds, but the mayor didn't agree. The last time they asked for help from the Federal Safety Administration, he said, was in the sixties. They took over a month to show up and, when they did, they complicated a situation that was already resolved and filed away. We all know what happened as a result. Several people looked at the director of the Federal Highway Patrol; he was sweating profusely. He had had a really bad time of it nine years ago. The bald guy passed a note to Mr. Chow, and he nodded. When the mayor finished speaking, Chow commented that the Parents' Association was completely outraged because of what was going on, and the Professors' Union wanted to intervene. If the government did not respond, he said, there would be a general strike.

The comment was a direct threat to Daniel Torres Sabinas. The Professors' Union was not only one of the most powerful in Tamaulipas, but its leader, Professor Edelmiro Morales—whom El Travolta had met with the day before—was one of his personal enemies. During his campaign, the union had opposed him fiercely and mobilized its thousands of members; only the intervention of the governor was able to hold it back. On the Monday before, during an official function, Arturo Rojo López, head of the National Professors' Union expressed his opposition to what was going on in the port.

Visibly upset, Torres Sabinas commented that he had only taken office in January, and he was met by a police force with few members, badly paid and without professional preparation. "One of the crime-scene experts didn't even know how to do a gunpowder residue test, that test—what's it called—?"

"A sodium rhodizonate test," the chief prompted.

"That one," the licenciado said, "and they had to ask the chemist, Orihuela, to do it. As if that weren't enough," he added, "the papers have been on my back ever since all this started. Colonel Balseca and Mr. Nader come every week and offer me advertising packages: buying ads to keep them from discussing the issue in the newspapers, but since there's no money for that and I don't want to go into debt, they attack me. The same with the Parents' Association," he said resentfully.

Mr. Chow said that the reporters always exaggerate whatever someone says. "That columnist—Guerrero? He interviewed me about security in the schools and put words in my mouth."

Torres Sabinas gracefully asked if the military intelligence had any leads. The director said no: only rumors, no real substance. More than one person looked at Mr. Williams.

The bald guy asked for permission to speak. Torres introduced him as Padre Fritz Tschanz, a Jesuit priest. The Society of Jesus had brought him from Ciudad Juárez, where he was assistant director of a school, to work on student security at the Instituto Cultural de Paracuán. The Jesuit summarized the measures the institute had put in place. As Rangel suspected, the Jesuit revealed that, since the day before, two modern Beta video cameras, strategically located, were filming everyone who came through the institute's entrance. "You'd be surprised by the number of well-known people who are around there"—he looked at John Williams —"people who have no children enrolled in the institute." The chief asked for a copy of the tapes and the Jesuit promised to hand them over, to the embarrassment of all those present. Then he admitted that the newspapers' sensationalism was contributing to an increase in the sense of worry, and he proposed asking the bishop to help calm the public, so that the climate of fear and panic wouldn't grow. The Society could convince His Excellency to publish an open letter in all the newspapers, in which he would criticize the journalistic excesses and call for calm.

"Sir," said the mayor, "that would be very good. . . . John, would you like to add anything?"

As a response, the businessman's lawyer, Licenciado Carrizo, said that the Grupo Industrial Gamma, and Mr. Williams in particular, had their reasons for being upset with the local government, but they had come to make a proposal.

"The Grupo Industrial Gamma would like to make a donation in order to find the guilty party as soon as possible. We will donate another twenty-five thousand dollars that, added to our previous contribution, makes a total of a fifty-thousand-dollar reward. We think this second sum is difficult to refuse and could attract more people to share information with the police."

"Thank you, John," Torres Sabinas said to Mr. Williams. "I expected no less from you."

"Yes." The businessman pointed with his finger at the mayor. "But in exchange I'm going to ask you for a favor."

The millionaire was famous for making drastic decisions during his bouts of anger, like firing his most faithful employee without a second thought or threatening congressmen in public places. In the port, people said he had ordered Colonel Balseca, the owner of *La Noticia,* to stop publishing editorials against his son or he would remove all his advertising.

"I'm listening."

"I want you to stop pursuing my son. Monday night, a black minivan was circling around the main entrance to my house, and yesterday a Chevy Nova was parked in front of my door. Here are the license plate numbers."

Rangel said to himself: It's all over. His dismissal seemed to be imminent. The director of security at Pemex smiled.

"Were you following Mr. Jack Williams?" asked the mayor. "Could you explain why, Chief?"

"Yes, sir," the old man didn't even hesitate. He had seen more than five mayors parade by while he was in his position. "We do not doubt Mr. Williams's innocence, but we are worried about his safety. As the rumors have increased, we've decided to provide protection for Licenciado Williams so as to avoid any attack against him."

Rangel looked at the chief with concern. The millionaire was irritated; he didn't expect this.

"I appreciate it, but the private security I've hired is quite enough. My bodyguards were trained in Tel Aviv."

"The police will not follow him anymore," promised the mayor, and hurried to continue. "By the way, would you like to share what you mentioned to me in my office?"

"I told you that the only mistake my son made was to listen to me. If he was present in that goddamn bar it was because the daughters of a Texan business partner were visiting, and I asked him to take them out on the town. Is that clear?"

"Case closed," the mayor said, and noticing that Williams's lawyer was looking at his watch, he added, "From now on, sirs, we need to work as a team."

Then they focused on what would be the next steps in the following days. They would order the schools' principals to only use one exit door for the duration of the crisis in order to redouble their surveillance. The teachers should lend additional support with increased vigilance, and if the governor authorized the budget, they would add another unit of undercover security for each building, so they could monitor the area around the schools. The search would go more quickly, the chief complained, if we had a bigger budget.

When things seemed to settle down, the bald guy said something in Chow's ear. Chow insisted that a completely professional investigation was in order, and Torres Sabinas asked what he meant by that.

"You could hire consultants."

"Yes," the mayor responded, "but who?"

With a look, Rangel asked for Chief García's permission. The chief indicated that he could speak, so he gave his opinion. "Why not invite Dr. Quiroz Cuarón?"

Hearing that name, the head of security at Pemex and the head of military intelligence looked at each other for a second. The first to react was the Jesuit.

"Wow. Dr. Quiroz Cuarón, a man of his stature. . . . Well, he would be ideal, but is he still alive?"

"Dr. Quiroz Cuarón!" the director of police in Tampico blurted out. And he got really excited. "Oh, goddamn, goddamn, is he really still alive? He must be, like, ninety years old. I don't think he'd do it, but it would be great. Dr. Quiroz Cuarón is an institution."

"Let's see, sirs, we are working against the clock. Who is this doctor?" the mayor asked.

"The best detective there is in the country. One of the best in the world."

"*Time* magazine called him 'The Mexican Sherlock Holmes.'"

"Wow, hot shit," said the federal government representative.

The head of military intelligence reviewed the facts.

"He identified the man who killed Leon Trotsky. He arrested Enrico Sampietro, who worked for Al Capone, and disarmed the new uprising of La Causa de la Fe. And, above all, he tracked down El Pelón Sobera and the Tacubaya strangler. He's a legend."

"And how much would he charge for his services?"

Military Intelligence explained.

"The doctor doesn't charge. If the case is of interest to him, he takes it on and pays all his expenses himself. That gives him independence."

"Well, a person like that would be ideal."

"Besides, he's from here," the Pemex rep said.

"The doctor wasn't born in the port," interrupted the chief. "He was raised in Tampico, but he's from Jiménez, Chihuahua. He has only bad memories of that place."

"Have you met him?" the mayor asked.

"One time," he nodded. "One time, around 1940," and Rangel understood that the doctor and the chief didn't have a good relationship.

"It's not a bad idea, but we have to make sure that he's alive."

"From what I know, he retired in 'sixty-eight."

"Do you have any way to get in touch with him?" Torres Sabinas was looking at Vicente.

"Maybe."

"OK, then, you contact him. If he's interested, ask him to come as soon as possible."

Rangel watched the millionaire. He looked really uncomfortable, as though the meeting had gone in a direction that he didn't like.

Once in the car, the chief asked him, "How many years have you been doing this?"

"Four and a half, almost five."

"I've got thirty," said the old man. "If your uncle were here, he'd tell you that to find a criminal you don't always go in a straight line. You have to spiral in, with a strategy. Find the leads. You get it?"

"Yes, sir."

"When was the last time you slept?"

"Three days ago."

"You were nodding off in the meeting. Take the afternoon off and come pick me up tomorrow at seven."

"Thank you, sir."

"And another thing: before you head out, ask Lolita for the doctor's information. Invite him on my behalf and offer him a hotel room and a plane ticket."

They found his information in an old yellowed address book with brittle paper. She found him under his first name: Alfonso Quiroz Cuarón, 54 Río Mixcoac, México, D.F. I can't believe it, Vicente said to himself. Years ago, when Vicente had been a member of Las Jaibas del Valle, their headquarters in D.F. was a house at 27 Río Mixcoac, in a discreet, spacious apartment. Who knows, I may have even run into Dr. Quiroz on the street and know him by sight.

Lolita made the call for him, but the phone rang without luck. He tried again five minutes later and the voice of an older man answered.

"Yes?"

"Dr. Quiroz Cuarón?"

"Wrong number." And he hung up.

Vicente thought it strange and called back.

"Have I reached the home of Dr. Quiroz Cuarón?"

"He doesn't live here. Wrong number." And he hung up.

He was going to try again when El Chicote reminded him that the chief was waiting for a summary of the meeting. Vicente put two blank sheets of paper into the typewriter and typed out the conclusions from the meeting for a few minutes. He stapled the report and handed it to El Chicote for him to copy and distribute. At nine, he went out to get *gorditas en salsa verde* for breakfast. He drank a soda—no gas, no color—returned to his desk, and put the call through again. It was answered on the third ring.

"Dr. Quiroz Cuarón?"

A firm voice answered, a voice used to giving commands. "Yes. Talk to me."

13

Instead of going home, Vicente went to get a cup of coffee at El Visir, a well-known café in front of the Plaza de Armas. An idea had obsessed him all morning. He checked his wallet discreetly to make sure that he had enough money for what he would need to buy. At exactly twelve noon, he headed to the historic center of the city. He was circling around *El Mercurio* when finally, on the umpteenth pass, he recognized the photographer coming out. Perfect, he said to himself, and drove over to her.

La Chilanga was walking unhurriedly along the Avenida Central. She looked odd without her usual camera slung over her shoulder; she didn't even have her backpack with all the equipment she needed for her job. Rangel pulled up to the curb.

"Want a ride?"

Much later, Marianna turned over in bed and started to talk. "Johnny Guerrero says that Fidel betrayed Che Guevara; can you believe it? He says he sent Che into the Sierra Maestra hoping he wouldn't come back and, since he had the power, he didn't give him enough reinforcements, because it wasn't to his benefit to bring him back. What are the Cubans going to do without Che, the lion, the warrior always out front, the brain for everybody? Who knows if Fidel can recover from the loss? Do you think he'll try again in Bolivia?"

Rangel turned on the radio. He wanted to find English rock to cheer the girl up, and it wasn't till then that he realized they had substituted Freaky's show for one with *música tropical*: *This is for you, Benny Moré, and next: Chico Che y la Crisis!* Goddamnit, he said to himself. No shit, I didn't even notice when this station went downhill.

"Hey, Mariana, are you Mr. Sherer's niece?"

"Johnny made that up."

A thunderclap signaled a coming storm.

"No hard feelings?" the young woman asked.

"Everything's fine."

"Good." She got out of the bed, her hips swaying.

Rangel couldn't get over how strange it was that all this had happened so quickly and easily. If he weren't so hurt by what Yesenia did to him, he told himself, he could even marry a woman like this. . . .

At six in the evening, the girl said she was hungry, and Vicente proposed going to La Rivera to eat seafood. As they took a quick shower, Vicente asked if they'd see each other after dinner.

"I'm supposed to get together with a girlfriend," she explained, "but I'll try."

"I'd love to see you," the detective insisted.

They didn't have to wait for the ferry take them over, and they crossed the street with their arms around each other. They were going toward the Chevy Nova when a horn began honking repeatedly; someone was trying to get Vicente's attention. From the other side of the avenue, a white pickup was coming over to him. It was Práxedes, the accountant. His uncle had introduced them several years ago.

"Get in," Rangel said to the girl, and he held out the keys to his car. The girl took them without asking for an explanation, and

Rangel cautiously went over to say hello to the accountant through his window.

According to what Práxedes himself had said, because of his high status and his criminal record, they were always trying to pin crimes on him, but he was innocent. Rangel didn't know exactly how he made his living, but he knew it bordered on the illegal. Today he seemed to be in a hurry.

"*Quiubo,* Práxedes."

"*Quiubo, cabrón*. Who'd you get in a fight with?"

"Aw, shit, what do you mean, who'd I get in a fight with?"

"Some asshole on the docks. He was looking for someone to kill you."

Fuck, thought Rangel. "He asked you?"

"Yeah."

"I guess you didn't accept."

"What do you think?"

"Who was it?"

"I didn't know him."

"Goddamnit, Práxedes!"

"I swear I've never seen him before."

"Could it be one of the guys from work?"

"No, it was a short guy. I think he was there for somebody else."

"Was it Chávez?"

"No, I know Chávez. The guy who came to see me looked indigenous."

"Are you sure?"

"Yeah."

He thought about it a minute. "All right, thanks."

"Put a double lock on your door. If they keep asking around, someone's gonna take the job."

"Let me know," he told him, and hit the side of the truck two times, saying good-bye. The accountant left immediately.

"Who was that?" Mariana asked. The fun and games were over.

"Someone I know. Where should I take you?"

"Drop me off downtown. If I leave my girlfriend early and want to go back to your house, how do I get in?"

"Here. I have another set in the office." Rangel gave her his keys, and a huge smile lit up the girl's face.

Before going back to his house, he stopped at Parcero's store and asked for a thirty-eight-caliber bullets. It was time to take out the big guns. Afterward he went to the Modelo Superstore, where he bought food for two people, a bottle of whiskey, and a six-pack of beer.

He crossed the river in a *colectivo* boat and locked himself in so no one else could enter. Despite the pressure he was under, his time with La Chilanga had relaxed him. But then he remembered the accountant's warning and considered the danger again. *Damn,* he said to himself. I'll probably have to move. He didn't have neighbors or anyone to ask for help in case he needed it, because there were no telephone lines on his side of the river. Anyone could force open the front door; it was only locked on the inside with a symbolic lock and, as if that weren't enough, the windows were made out of plastic sheeting, which was simple enough to cut through. Come to think of it, it's a miracle they haven't gotten me yet.

He should move somewhere else, but it would be a shame to go. He loved that place. On one side of him, there was a mango tree, delicious fruits that woke him up when they fell on the roof. A cooling breeze came off the river and scared away the mosquitoes. On the other hand, if he left any food outside the refrigerator, pests would immediately devour it. He once bought a poison powder to stop a plague of army ants that were threatening to invade. Another time he killed a tarantula as big as his hand. What can you do? he thought to himself. Soon, once he had time to think it through more calmly, he'd have to decide if it was time for him to move. But before then, I'm going to get this motherfucker and throw him in jail.

The rest of the afternoon he oiled and checked out his uncle's pistol. After that, he took out his shoulder holster and tried it on: he didn't remember it fit him so big.

At night, before going to bed, he split a melon in two pieces and absentmindedly left half of it above the sink in the kitchen, right next to the window. Vicente was completely worn out, but he couldn't fall asleep. The conversation with Práxedes might have put him on edge. Every time he was about to drift off, some nearby noise would wake him up, noises that he couldn't identify. What the fuck was that? It wasn't the sound of a mango falling or the rumbling of the water heater, it was something different and repetitive, almost like Chinese water torture. As soon as he was about to get to sleep, there would be a new sound that he couldn't identify, and on more than one occasion he thought he saw a person standing up next to his bed. The umpteenth time he woke up, his nerves destroyed, he went out to look for where the noise was coming from, furious, his twenty-two in hand. He wasn't prepared for what he found.

Outside the window in the kitchen was a family of raccoons, two big ones and five babies. The biggest had been able to cut through the plastic sheeting and reach in his window. Between his hands—because they were hands—was the other half of the melon.

When the raccoon saw Rangel, he let out an amusing little scream, and the babies crowded around the mother. The detective recoiled and observed their handiwork. One by one, the five babies headed into the forest, preceded by their mother. When the father understood that Rangel wasn't going to follow, he stood up on two legs and sniffed in his direction. He's thanking me, Rangel thought. Then he dragged the part of the melon that was his with one hand, like a person would do, and disappeared into the brush.

The policeman settled down on the terrace and drank two beers, one after another, with the lights out. A cool breeze started at eleven at night. I'm never leaving. If those motherfuckers want to come, let them come. I'll be waiting.

14

On Thursday, the twentieth of March, at seven in the morning, Rangel parked his Chevy Nova in front of the chief's house. The chief's wife, Doña Dolores Rosas de García, asked him to wait in the living room, where he found the latest edition of *El Mercurio*: NO TRACE OF THE HERNÁNDEZ GIRL. FALSE LEADS MULTIPLY. The article added that, according to rumors, a brave officer in the Paracuán police force, a detective who had contributed several revealing pieces of evidence in the Jackal case, was about to quit "because his investigation was being stymied." Guerrero not only summarized the previous day's meeting at City Hall but also quoted the leader of the Professors' Union, who took the opportunity to bash Mr. Barbosa from the state capital: PROFESSOR EDELMIRO CRITICIZES THE GOVERNMENT OF MADERA. Goddamnit, he said to himself, who told Johnny Guerrero about that meeting? And poor Barbosa, they've really got it in for him.

Then, since no one had come to get him, he skipped to page thirteen:

CONFERENCE ABOUT UFOS PROVOKES UPROAR: This evening, in the city of Searchlight, Nevada, researcher Cormac McCormick will read an excerpt from his forthcoming book, *The Truth about UFOs*. The popular columnist's editors assure us that the book, fruit of more than twenty years of work, will be the most important in his field, as is clear from the interest shown in McCormick's articles. They also confirmed that important revelations will be made during his talk.

"Oh, Rangel, come on in." The chief was out of the shower, recently shaved, and smelling of aftershave lotion. "I'll be with you in a minute."

"Don't be rude," he heard his wife's voice.

As a response, the chief grunted. "Did you already eat breakfast?"

"Yes, sir."

"Come drink a cup of coffee. Do you take milk?"

"Please," he said to the chief's wife.

"You can't go out without your breakfast." She was referring to the chief. "You're not twenty years old anymore."

"Right."

As the chief spread butter on his bread, the telephone rang in the kitchen. Doña Dolores answered the call and passed it to her husband.

"Churruca."

Even though he could have used the phone that his wife offered him, the old man went to take the call in the living room.

Rangel and Doña Dolores listened without blinking.

"What happened, Juan José? Yes . . . yes, the doctor is coming to the port, but it wasn't his idea; we sent for him. . . . No, why would there be problems? He's independent, but I know him very well. He was my teacher years ago. . . . No, it's impossible to cancel: I'm about to pick him up at the airport. . . . Huh? Repeat that again." The chief had put both hands on his stomach. As the conversation progressed, his discomfort worsened. Soon he was forced to rock forward and backward with his belly in his hands, as if he were cradling an infant. "Tell him I'm at his service. . . . Whatever he wants. . . . Oh, very well. . . . Affirmative."

After hanging up, the old man stayed seated a few seconds, swallowing the last sharp pain. The whole time, his stomach's grumbling was as loud as his voice had been.

"*Mijo,* do you feel all right?"

"Rangel, take me to headquarters," the old man answered. "I'm going to the state capital. I have a hearing in two hours."

"You can't drive anywhere on your own," his wife insisted. "Remember what the gastroenterologist told you." She spoke to Vicente. "You can't take him?"

"Of course I can. Whatever you say."

"No," said the chief, "Salim will take me. You go pick up Dr. Quiroz Cuarón and take care of him. Explain that I was called away. Lolita has all the allowances for the hotel and meals. If he needs something else, let her know. Remember, the doctor's very particular. I'm leaving him under your care."

"Of course, sir."

"Let's go. Before hitting the road, I need to go by the office for some papers."

"Do you know what time you'll be back?" his wife asked.

"I have no idea."

The old man slammed the door shut. He hadn't even tasted his coffee.

Fifteen minutes later, the Bedouin bounded down the main stairs of police headquarters, eager to serve as chauffeur. A few feet away, the chief was getting ready for his trip to the state capital.

"That motherfucker Churruca, he could have let me know yesterday. . . . Taboada hasn't come in yet?"

"No, sir," El Chicote responded.

"That lazy fat-ass, who does he think he is?"

As he was going out the door, Lolita caught up to García and told him he had a call from his wife: "She says it's an emergency." The chief reluctantly headed back and ordered them to forward the call to the first telephone he found. The chief's mood was getting worse, if that was possible; he shouted into the phone. "What? Are you sure?" A few seconds later, he said, "And what did you tell him?" He listened in silence. "Well, it seems like complete idiocy to me. How do you come up with these things, woman?" He hung up and asked the secretary, "He's already here, right?"

"He's waiting for you in his office."

"Well, go entertain him, Lolita. You know no one can go in if I'm not there already."

As the secretary went up, the chief gestured to Rangel to follow him into the hallway. "Rangel, besides what I already asked you to do, I need you to take care of another equally important item of business. One which requires complete discretion."

This was disconcerting to Vicente, because even though the chief was giving him signs that he had begun to trust him since he got involved in the investigation of the girls, it was obvious that he preferred to work with El Travolta or Cruz Treviño.

"It's a very delicate matter."

He explained that his son-in-law, who was the state attorney general, had wanted to do an audit on him since Christmas. He was sending an agent who pretended to be on a different assignment but in reality meant to do him harm. The agent had put one over on them; as soon as the chief left for the office, he appeared at the chief's home and began to investigate. Since Doña Dolores didn't suspect anything, she not only gave him information about certain activities "which could be misunderstood," but she also sent him directly to the office. Immediately, Rangel thought about the envelopes that came in every month from grateful politicians and businesspeople, and the special assignments that Chief García took on for those individuals. The chief asked him to keep the visitor occupied for a while, preferably outside the office.

"We can't bribe him or scare him and, what's more, we can't mistreat him because of one reason: he's my nephew. Since it's an assignment that requires tact, I'd like you to take care of this one."

Shit, thought Rangel, how am I going to manage with two visitors?

"Oh, I almost forgot! His alibi is that he came to write an article. Play along and do everything he asks unless it goes against my instructions."

"Yes, sir."

"Let's go on up. I'll introduce you."

As they approached the chief's office, Rangel noticed that a young man was sitting on the edge of the desk, reading a comic book with a psychedelic cover: *L'Incal* by Moebius and Jodorowsky. That's the agent he's so scared of? Rangel guessed he was sixteen years old, seventeen at most.

"Rangel," the chief said, "this is Rodrigo Montoya, my nephew." The boy stood up to say hello. He was a young guy with long hair, dark glasses, an easy generous smile, and a mustache that in reality was just the intention of having a mustache; it grew down around the corners of his mouth and onto his cheeks. He shook hands with unexpected enthusiasm, and the chief made his apologies and left.

Shit, Rangel said to himself, what do I do now? As if the problem with the girls weren't enough, now he was in charge of the doctor *and* had to deal with this youngster: a pain in the neck. He asked the visitor to wait for him a minute and ran to talk with the Blind Man, who was mopping a hallway.

"Romero, leave that be and come give me a hand."

"Whatever you say, boss."

15

He was supposed to arrive on the first flight, but he couldn't be found anywhere. Dr. Quiroz Cuarón, the most famous detective in Latin America, couldn't be one of the guys in cowboy hats with *piteado* boots and jeans or one of the oil workers in dark sunglasses or one of the bronze-tanned businesspeople in short sleeves waiting to claim their baggage.

From the moment Dr. Quiroz Cuarón agreed to assist them, Chief García's office was stirred with unusual energy. They had let Torres Sabinas know, so that he would authorize the expenses, and Lolita had reserved a plane ticket for the first flight in on Thursday. The doctor was to arrive around eight o'clock. He had to go through the neighboring city of Tampico, a few minutes north of Paracuán.

When there were only a half dozen travelers left in the reception area, Vicente noticed an elderly man drinking a cup of coffee at a bar nearby. The elderly man waved him over.

"Are you Lieutenant Rivera's nephew?"

"I was on the first flight," he said, "it's strange you didn't see me arrive." He was wearing a double-breasted blue suit and an impeccable white shirt, and he smelled of lotion from six feet away. He was carrying a small leather suitcase and a medium-sized wooden trunk with labels from a recent trip through Portugal and Turkey. "Careful with that. The contents are very fragile."

He must have been about seventy years old, but he didn't look it. Rangel noticed he wasn't carrying a gun, and he asked himself if he might be accustomed to having bodyguards, like some very important officials. He carried a book in his hand: *The Psychology of Crime* by David Abrahamsen.

As they went outside to the car, a wave of heat assaulted them. Rangel explained the chief's reasons for not being able to welcome him, and he thanked him for agreeing to come. The doctor nodded. "Poor García, those idiots are always ordering him around." After he settled down inside the patrol car, he didn't say another word.

The city seemed to be a huge mirage. It was hot, and the air coming through the windows did nothing to cool them down. As they got onto the main avenue, by the Hotel Posada del Rey, they passed a considerable crowd waiting for the bus. The detective glanced briefly in the rearview mirror: they were carrying picket signs. When they came to the Beneficencia Española, they ran into another large group. They must be members of the PRI, he thought, marching in support of President Echavarreta.

As they passed in front of the normal school, they saw a third crowd, which was getting ready to march with a loudspeaker and signs. As he turned down a steep street, he strained to hear what they were saying. Where the street ended, they could see the Río Pánico and its loading and unloading area.

They went in through the back door and walked up to the second floor, where the doctor settled into the chief's office.

"To start," said the specialist, "I'd like to read the report."

Lolita handed him a photocopy. As soon as Rangel was sure that the secretary was attending to the visitor, he ran to see what the chief's nephew was doing. He found Romero reading the

Treatise on Criminology by Dr. Quiroz Cuarón in an armchair next to the coffeemaker.

"What's up, Vicente? What time does the conference start?"

"I'll let you know. Don't go anywhere."

"Don't worry, I've got everything I need right here."

Rangel had promised to invite Rodrigo to the meetings with the doctor, as long as he didn't insist on going to the airport.

"All right," the nephew had said. "In the meantime, I'm gonna get ready, I'm gonna read his complete works."

As he turned away, Rangel wrinkled his nose. For a moment, just for a moment, he could swear he smelled a sickly-sweet smell around the kid, a smell he had gotten a whiff of before, during previous investigations, a tobacco scent . . . or *Cannabis indica*. But no, that's not possible, he told himself, it's the chief's nephew—and we're at police headquarters.

"I'll wait here," said the boy, and concentrated on his reading.

When he got back, Quiroz Cuarón's suitcase and trunk were on one side of the table, but he couldn't see the criminologist anywhere.

"And the doctor?"

The secretary motioned toward the door at the end of the hallway, and Rangel went to look for the expert.

He was quite active for someone over seventy years old. As Rangel was checking in with the nephew, the doctor had underlined the first few pages of the photocopies. Rangel hurried to review them. The doctor had made notes with a color pencil. On first impression, the inscriptions seemed to trace out a diagram—or, rather, a drawing of an equation. Sometimes he crossed out a line with an X, sometimes he put a check next to a sentence or marked it with a square root sign. And in one place he had drawn a circle around a word, with a line from it down to the bottom of the page, where he had written a number of indecipherable symbols, of which Rangel could only recognize the question marks. He had drawn a map by hand of the city's principal avenues, indicating the two schools and the locations where they found the two bodies with arrows. He doesn't waste any time, Rangel said to himself, and went to look for him in Ramírez's office.

As soon as he entered, a smell like the chemicals used to clean pools filled his nose. The tiny size of the cubicle, ten by sixteen feet, was evidence of the chief's lack of interest in the analysis of evidence. Ramírez moved around very nervously as he pulled together the materials requested by Quiroz Cuarón. The doctor asked if he could examine the evidence collected around the bodies. The forensic expert held out a plastic bag, sealed with Scotch tape.

"How large was the perimeter you studied?"

"About six feet, at the most ten feet, doctor."

The old man poured the contents out onto a white sheet of paper and began to separate them with tweezers. There was grass, cigarette butts, wads of gum, popsicle wrappers, bags with leftover fried food, and other wrappers from candy sold in front of schools. For a few minutes, the doctor worked in silence. When he lifted his head, he acknowledged Rangel.

"This is complete chaos. We have to hurry, I don't have a lot of time. Two days, at the most. I can't be here any longer."

Before Rangel could respond, loud noises rose up from the street, growing louder by the second. Rangel looked out the window at a violent crowd carrying picket signs.

"What's going on?"

"It's a protest, doctor. Going by the signs, the Professors' Union must have organized it."

According to *El Mercurio,* there were two thousand people, all demanding quick justice. They were asking for Chief García and the mayor of Madera to be dismissed from office. They alleged they were conspiring with the killer. From the second story, Rangel looked at the variety of inflammatory signs that made reference to Barbosa and to Chief García.

The doctor shook his head. "Same as always. It's already started. Rangel, take me to the crime scenes."

Rangel drove Dr. Quiroz Cuarón to the Colegio Angloamericano where Karla Cevallos had studied. They turned at the corner so the doctor could examine the entrances without getting out of the car. Afterward they went to see El Palmar. When they pulled up to the lagoon, they noticed two groups of teenagers were getting ready to go waterskiing. Rangel asked him if he wanted to check out the islet, and the doctor said yes. In the Regatta Club, they gave them a boat and a driver. Once they got close to the island, the doctor jumped out with an agility unexpected for his age, and a huge crow appeared in the reeds. The old man scared it off by throwing a rock at it and shook his head. As quickly as he could, Rangel crossed through the police line, which was marked with four branches, and answered the doctor's questions as well as he could. The doctor asked for very specific details about the conditions in which they found the body. Rangel responded acceptably, thanks to his having read El Travolta's report.

"What did they find here?"

When they were investigating on the islet, Rangel explained, the only thing they found was a footprint in the mud. The doctor stressed that the remains of both victims were found in plastic trash bags. He asked if the two girls were from the same social class, and Rangel explained the first girl went to a private school and was middle class, while the second girl was the daughter of Pemex workers. The specialist commented that the islet was not the ideal place to hide a dead body.

"It's very close to where they rent the boats. . . . The killer ran the risk of being discovered because so many people pass by here. I guess you've already interviewed the security guard at the club, but we should enlarge the perimeter of the crime scene to the entire shore of the lagoon and interview the fishermen one by one. Most likely, he didn't rent a boat at the Regatta Club. Probably, he started far away. But in that case, why would he want to leave the body here where he risked being discovered?"

Immediately, they went to Public School Number Five and the old man asked him to drive around the block, without getting out of the car. Afterward, they headed to the Bar León, where Rangel parked in such a way that he was able to show the doctor the entryway to the alley, where the killer would have had to enter to drop off the girl's body. The doctor didn't want to get out of the car.

"I know this area. It's not necessary." He wrote something down in his tiny notebook. "OK, I'm done for the day."

When Rangel went to drop him off at the hotel, the doctor asked, "Can you take me to Tampico? I have to make two visits."

They went to the old railroad station, and the doctor got out. "I have a strange tradition," he explained.

They walked to the old manager's offices and the doctor looked at the inside through a dusty window. There was a rusted metal desk and a chair thrown on the ground. Ever since they had closed this train station, trash and spiderwebs had taken over. Rangel knew the visit was very important for Dr. Quiroz Cuarón. The rumor was that his father had been killed in that office sixty years before. One of his employees got in an argument with him and shot him in the back. The doctor was fourteen years old when it happened. An uncle went to pick up the boy from school and explained that someone had assaulted his father. The doctor said he had never been able to forget the impression caused by the visit to his first crime scene, seeing his father's desk covered with blood and his papers strewn everywhere.

"I remember as if it were yesterday. It was a cloudy day. Even before my uncle arrived to pick me up from school, I had a feeling that something was wrong. Imagine: you get to your father's office and suddenly he isn't there. In that moment, my career began."

The doctor broke off a branch from a tree with his foot and kicked it toward the street. It made Rangel think about a gardener accustomed to stubbornly clearing weeds and dead leaves from the same land.

"Now, the cemetery in Paracuán. Let's go see your uncle."

They stopped in front of the gray headstone. Ivy was starting to grow over it. *Damn,* Rangel said to himself, *it's obvious I've totally neglected my duties, I should come here more often.*

The inscription was simple:

MIGUEL RIVERA GONZÁLEZ
1900—1975
DETECTIVE
YOUR RELATIVES AND FRIENDS REMEMBER YOU

The widow had insisted on inlaying a black-and-white photo of his uncle in a suit and tie, standing with one boot on the bumper of a Ford.

"Look at that!" the old man exclaimed. "I was sure I'd never see your uncle again, and now there he is, just like I remember him."

The photo must have been from the fifties. In the picture, Rivera looked thin but his expression was friendly.

"So what do you think, Miguel? Are you going to help us solve this case?"

The doctor didn't notice, but a wind gust rustled the ivy.

A moment later the doctor asked, "Is the bar at the Hotel Inglaterra still there?" he asked.

16

They were looking out over the lagoon in Paracuán. At the far end of the immense sheet of water, they could see the horizon and the hills of Nagual. From there, they could make out El Palmar, the area where they found the first girl, but they weren't talking about that. The chords of a melodic organ were coming out of the bar, where a musician was playing a song by Julio Iglesias: *I love, I love, I love.* . . . Every now and then, they smelled a slight odor of disinfectant, and the wind scared away the mosquitoes. Three *gringas* were going in and out of the pool, enjoying themselves. Meanwhile, the doctor finished his fish *à la veracruzana,* put down his utensils, and looked around for the waiter, but couldn't find him anywhere.

"My parents' house was in front of the lighthouse in Tampico, near the jetties. Where do you live, Vicente?"

"Here, in Paracuán. On the other side of the river."

"What part?"

"Near the ferry landing."

"Near the old hacienda?"

"Next to it," he said, "in the house that used to be the foreman's."

"You know what they say about the hacienda, right? You have to be brave to live there."

"I don't believe in that stuff."

The girls exploded laughing and made Rangel shudder. When they had quieted down, the doctor asked, "I don't see the waiter anywhere. Could you order me a cognac?"

Rangel went to the *palapa* and returned with the drink. Then he said he was going to make a call, and the doctor nodded. Not soon after, the doctor fell asleep.

The sound of a heavy person diving clumsily into the water woke him up. Someone got the girls all wet, how inconsiderate, he thought. The doctor saw the blurry silhouette of the diver swimming around at the bottom of the pool. *That's insane,* he said to himself, *he's been down there too long.* As if he had heard him, the man came up for air and started to breathe. The detective said to himself that the man moved with incredible agility despite being so large, and as he said that, lightning struck: *I know that guy.* He wanted to stand up, but his body felt remarkably heavy—it must be the cognac—but I do know him. What's he doing here on the Gulf of Mexico?

From where he was sitting, the doctor saw that the swimmer was crossing a strip of light reflected in the water. He said to himself that he would wait until the guy got out of the water to confirm his impression, and he watched him swimming from one end to the other, from one side to the other, like a huge frog. The repetitive motion of the swimmer was hypnotic, and the doctor closed his eyes again.

He remembered a long-ago afternoon when he was five years old. His parents swam in the lagoon in Paracuán while he played onshore with one of his favorite toys, which he hadn't remembered in years. My blue bike, he said to himself, I never think about it anymore; visiting the port reactivated my memory. He watched out of the corner of his eye as his parents floated in the water, his father holding his mother in his arms, as she smiled timidly. He was thinking how much he would have liked to hear his mother's voice, when one of the three *gringas* let out a shrill scream and the doctor stirred in his seat. He was afraid that the same anxiety as always was about to overtake him. Lately, as soon as he got to sleep, he would dream about a man dressed in black, who seemed to laugh at him, a guy he hadn't seen in his whole life. He told himself that the dreams were a puzzle with one question: How close am I to dying? He told himself he should think about that.

A meaty hand came out of the pool and grabbed the staircase. Then another hand, and a really fat man emerged. The doctor asked himself who it was, but no matter how much he thought about it, he couldn't figure it out, the same grogginess that prevented him from getting up also kept him from remembering. The man put on his sandals, wrapped himself in a white bathrobe, and covered his neck with a little towel. All of a sudden, the girls were not to be heard. The man came over to him. Because of the glare coming off the pool, the doctor couldn't be sure it was the same person, but he looked very similar.

The man, red as a shrimp, leaned over to say hello. Dr. Quiroz Cuarón? What a surprise! What a pleasure, it's been so long! He recognized the face of the film director, but the name escaped him: *When was the last time? Eleven, twelve years ago?* A little more, Doctor, we saw each other in 'fifty-nine, through my agent. *And your wife, Sir Alfred?* She's fine, resting in our room.

The two men were silent until the swimmer clarified. I'd like to tell you something, Doctor. I am so sorry for what happened between us. *Listen, Sir Alfred*—No, no, let me say this: When you criticized the script for *Psycho,* I got really upset, because the evaluation got into my producer's hands, because of a mistake by my agent, and they wanted to cancel the project. But you were right to say the story didn't hold up to a logical analysis, that it wasn't believable. And because of all that, I decided to rewrite it, with better results, I let myself believe. *I'm really sorry*—Don't say that, Doctor, the misunderstanding was caused by my agent— you know how meddlesome agents can be—don't worry about it. By the way, I never knew if you saw the film. *Yes, I saw it in Mexico City*. And did you think it was believable?

The doctor laughed and said to him, "*Sir Alfred, tell your detractors that if you were concerned about believability, you would make documentaries*. The swimmer smiled. And you, doctor? *What are you referring to, Sir Alfred? I don't understand*. Sir, how are you going to catch the killer? You're not too old for this yet?

"Excuse me?"

The doctor shifted in his seat. Vicente was leaning over him. "It's five-thirty. We need to get going."

17

At the request of Don Daniel Torres Sabinas, the meeting took place Thursday afternoon in the assembly room at City Hall. Torres Sabinas introduced the specialists and left him with the agents, as he couldn't stay for the meeting. Over by the door, Vicente confirmed that a majority of his colleagues were in attendance. Besides the policeman from Paracuán, there were a dozen other officers from Tampico and Ciudad Madera in attendance, all willing to cooperate in the investigation. El Travolta and Cruz Treviño were talking quietly. Chief García's nephew said hello. When the meeting was about to start, Rangel noticed that one of Torres Sabinas's secretaries was calling him, waving him over urgently.

"Sir, are you Vicente Rangel?" The girl asked.

"Yes."

"You have a call. This way, please."

She led him to the large offices near the main entrance. As they walked down the hallway, they ran into the Professor, coming toward them with a taciturn expression. When he recognized Rangel, he called him over, and said quietly, "Someone killed Calatrava. They put a bullet through his neck."

"What?" Rangel stopped. "Are you sure?"

The Professor nodded. "They took him out at the checkpoint. The ambulance already went for him."

"Sir," the secretary interrupted them. "Your call is long distance. It's very urgent."

He went up to the first floor, where a new surprise awaited him: the person calling was Chief García, from the state capital.

"Rangel? I'm glad I found you."

It may have been caused by the distance, but the chief's voice sounded old and tired. He was calling to send his regards to the doctor, but he didn't want to interrupt the meeting; he'd already heard what happened to Calatrava.

"Lolita told me a few minutes ago. Wong's handling it."

"Sir, I'd like your permission to take part in the investigation—"

"Don't get distracted." The old man was unequivocal. "Wong is already on top of it. You worry about the doctor and the girls."

"Taboada is with him."

"Rangel, this is an order. Is that understood?"

"Yes, sir."

"Does the doctor need anything?"

"No, everything is fine."

"Remember, he's very sensitive. If something upsets him or makes him distrustful, he'll leave and slam the door on his way out. My nephew isn't giving you any problems, is he?"

"Not really." He was still being watched by the Blind Man. "He just went into the meeting."

"No, get him out of there. You don't know what he's capable of! Get him out immediately."

"I'll do it right now, sir."

They said good-bye. Rangel made another call, this time to *El Mercurio,* and spoke briefly to Mariana in the editorial room. When he hung up, Rangel noticed that Cruz Treviño had been listening to his conversation.

"What do you want, Treviño?"

His coworker looked at him with contempt. "We know you're talking to Barbosa. You going to Ciudad Madera, man?"

"You're a complete jackass."

Rangel pushed past his coworker and went back to the room. Cruz Treviño followed two steps behind.

When he entered the conference room, he signaled to the Blind Man.

"I'm leaving the doctor with you," he ordered. "I'll be back in a half hour. You keep the patrol car and give me the keys to my car."

And he went out to look for the Chevy Nova.

Getting to the checkpoint took him a few minutes. As he was parking, he noticed that Wong was already at the Wizard's post.

"What's up, Rangel? You're going off with Barbosa?"

Rangel was fed up and ignored the question. "What have you found?"

Wong, aware of Vicente and Calatrava's friendship, gave him an update.

"Look." He showed him the holes in the exterior of the checkpoint. "Nine bullet holes, and Calatrava hadn't even pulled out his gun."

"A machine gun?"

"It's gotta be. I'd say an Uzi. Another two bullets hit on the inside of the checkpoint. The body was lying inside, but it was visible from the highway."

It was impossible not to notice the blood.

"A driver headed to the refinery reported it. Everything's in order."

Holy shit, Rangel thought, he probably stopped some driver to ask for the paper, and the guy had a record. Maybe the driver thought he was in trouble and took Calatrava out.

"Look, here's another." Wong pointed at a piece of metal on the ground. "The shooter didn't even get out of his car. He called him, or Calatrava came up to him; the guy pulled out the gun and shot him. On my first count, I got seven bullet wounds between the left leg and arm, like he was trying to cover up. One pierced his neck."

"How big's an Uzi?"

"They're small, not too heavy, made by the Israelis. Some are as small as a clothes iron."

With Vicente's help, the officer was able to open a closet.

"Hell-o," said Wong, "no wonder he didn't have a TV."

He was holding up a piece of newspaper full of marijuana. Rangel said nothing but followed the trail of blood with his eyes.

"They shot him over there." Wong pointed to the highway. "The killer got away. Calatrava dragged himself to the desk and picked up the phone, but he couldn't speak—he had a bullet in his neck— and he stayed right there on the ground. Poor fuck. He ran off to his meeting with infinity."

"Yeah," said Rangel. "Poor *cabrón*."

When the jugular's cut, the only way to stop the hemorrhaging is to strangle the person.

"What did you see?"

"It's just that he didn't come back to finish him off."

As Wong looked through the late officer's personal effects, Rangel lifted up the previous Monday's copy of *El Mercurio* and found a green notebook: Calatrava's diary. The front said: UN-SOLVED MYSTERIES, and the inside was divided into two columns. In the first, there were a series of notes along the lines of: "Every new moon, green lights are seen floating toward the mountains." "A dove who loses a baby returns every day to the same spot for four months." "The cat activity picks up at dawn." Dreams were recounted in a very thoughtful way: "I dreamed that my father was sad and dejected. In the dream my father was like a small child who had to be consoled. When one consoles someone in dreams who has shrunk in size, who is being consoled in reality, that part of our consciousness is afraid of disappearing. Identity is like a wave, in which crests will rise at times, then be submerged and then disappear." One note attracted his attention: "There are times when one dreams of monsters or deformed dwarves that refuse to leave a room or a vehicle in motion and even come back furious after we've made them go. These dreams announce pain, what is left of a great pain or the remains of a stubborn sickness that will soon be destroyed or forgotten."

Pure poetry, Rangel said to himself; this information is useless. I don't know what the hell he was doing here, no reason to include this in my report. Luckily, there was a second column, where the writer didn't beat around the bush so much, where he found what he was looking for. As he well knew, Calatrava took note of the day and time when certain suspicious vehicles passed through the checkpoint: "Tuesday, March 4, 11 PM: White Volkswagen Brazilia, possible electrical appliance contraband, license plate XEX 726." "Wednesday 5, 2 PM: Yellow Renault 12 Routier, XEX 153, the owner passes by here toward Madera." The last note was written the Tuesday before, the day the girl died in the Bar León. With a certain apprehension, Rangel read the following: "Tuesday, March 18, 11:30. The black van again." Ah, *caray,* Rangel thought about it a second and rapidly reviewed the preceding pages. The black van appeared previously on two dates: January 15 and February 17. "Official plates," Calatrava had written. Rangel thought this over and everything fell into place: the strange arrangement of the bodies, the grim coincidences, the Wizard's death. Ah, *cabrón,* he concluded: the white fur, the hunting knife, the clues that the subject passed by here on the days of the murders; the Wizard discovered the killer and they knocked him off. It's more transparent than water.

Rangel closed the diary as he heard Wong's footsteps.

"Ready to go?" Wong asked. "We've got to lock this place up."

Heading down the Avenida del Puerto, Rangel saw Public School Number Five and decided to stop. In the last few months, they had added two stories and a new exterior, with an ultramodern seventies design. He lowered his speed and parked on the side of the road, on the gravel street, in front of the director's house. *Slow down,* the voice of his uncle said. *Slow down, Vicente. Think with that big head of yours, before you dive right in. El Travolta is going to be mad; he's going to kick your ass if he finds out what you're up to. What have I told you all these years? Patience, nephew, move as if you aren't up to anything.* And seeing Vicente wasn't frightened, he added, *I'm just saying that if you get out of the car you won't be able to go back in. Are you sure we're relatives? Damn, what a stupid nephew I have! Seems like they must have adopted you.*

Well, Vicente said to himself, we're already here. He got out, slammed the car door, and knocked at the house with authority. A woman's face looked out the window.

"Who is it?"

"Police, ma'am. You called for us."

"Mr. Vicente Rangel?"

Though he thought it strange that they were looking for him specifically, Vicente nodded.

A skinny, impressively beautiful woman opened the door. Her hair was short and very black; she had the prettiest nose that Rangel had seen in his life. He estimated she was thirty years old. Mrs. Dorotea Hernández looked like a statue. When Rangel arrived, she was drinking linden blossom tea in an armchair in the living room. A copy of *La Noticia* was spread out on the table, with a short interview they had done with her: MOTHER OF DISAPPEARED GIRL STILL HAS HOPE and DENIES DAUGHTER WAS MURDERED, PREFERS KIDNAPPING THEORY. It would soon be three months since her daughter's disappearance.

A group of children were playing happily on the other side of the windows in the back. The majority of the boys were playing soccer. The girls were jumping rope.

"My husband is the principal of this school," explained the woman. "I want to ask you not to let him know about our conversation. He did not agree with my being interviewed in the newspapers."

"I wouldn't have called them, either. It seems like a mistake."

"What could I do?" she said. "The officer in charge of the case never gave me any information."

"Who was it?"

"Mr. Joaquín Taboada."

Oh, yeah, he remembered: they chewed him out in the meeting for that, goddamn irresponsible fat ass.

"I'm at you service, ma'am. Why did you send for me?"

"Take this."

She handed over half a dozen photos to him, in which Lucía Hernández Campillo played, clapped, or had her birthday. In the last one, a framed photo, the girl was wearing a school uniform. Her bangs hung in front of her huge eyes and she smiled innocently. First in her elementary school, Group 1A. She looked like her mother.

"Do you think she's alive?"

Rangel knew that when a minor disappears, the possibility of finding the child alive after the first seventy-two hours is radically diminished. But he didn't have the heart to say this.

"Could she possibly be hiding in someone's house, like with friends or family?"

"Impossible. Lucía is a very obedient girl. Besides, she's only seven years old. She still depends on me for so many things."

"Did you already check the hospitals? The one in Paracuán? In Tampico? In Ciudad Madera?" And since he saw that the woman was nodding, he added, "Did you already go to the morgue?"

"I even went to see the El Palmar girl, thinking it might have been my daughter. What they did to her was horrible." And he was blinded by the sun coming through the window.

It was obvious she was keeping quiet about something. If I don't put some pressure on her, I'll leave empty-handed.

"Ma'am," he said, "I don't have much time. I have to investigate other reports."

"I think she was kidnapped."

"Do you suspect anyone in particular?"

The woman nodded and sipped at her tea. Rangel noticed her hands were shaking.

"Four months ago, when they started to rebuild the school, my husband introduced me to the donors and the architects, very powerful people. Two days later, one of them came to the house when he knew my husband wouldn't be here." She swallowed. "This despicable man wanted me to go with him to his ranch. I grabbed that vase and told him I would hit him with it if he didn't leave, but it didn't work. He stalked me the whole week. He would park outside, he had bodyguards—he always had a bodyguard—and they would come and knock on the door. Since I wouldn't open the door, he'd leave me obscene letters. This continued until I stuck my head out the window and told him I was going to tell my husband. Then he told me he would get his revenge, and my daughter was gone the following week."

"Do you have proof? It's a very serious accusation."

She offered him a paper with letterhead on it. "This is the last letter he wrote me. I threw the other ones away."

Rangel examined the paper. "This is a photocopy."

"Would you please read it?"

As soon as he finished it, he felt his throat dry out, his tongue sticking to the roof of his mouth. Goddamm it, I need water, a glass of water. Even so, he found the strength to say, "The letter speaks for itself. Tell me something," said Vicente. "Does anyone else know about this?"

"Officer Taboada. I told him a month ago and he hasn't done anything. He kept the original copy of the letter."

"Joaquín Taboada?"

Rangel felt his knees buckle. He was facing the worst moral dilemma of his career. From that moment on, he would have to think twice before each step forward.

Before he started his car, he thought over what Mrs. Dorotea had said to him. El Travolta, who would have thought it? Through the rearview mirror, the three gigantic flames from the oil refinery seemed to shine brighter than ever.

When Rangel got back, the office was full of unusual activity. Cruz Treviño and his coworkers watched him distrustfully.

"And the doctor?"

"He left."

"Excuse me?"

"The meeting ended and he left without telling anybody."

"Fucking asshole," added the Evangelist.

Rangel said to himself: That's really strange. He decided to go look for him at the hotel.

The chief's nephew opened the door, naked. There was a redhead on the bed. *And the doctor?* Um, he was here, but not anymore. *Yes, I know that, but what happened? Where did he go?* I wouldn't be able to say. It's really complicated. *And how did you get here?* I'm not sure. . . . *Shit,* said Rangel, *what a fucking disaster.*

At the front desk, they told him the doctor had paid his bill and left. *How could you have let him pay? He was the city's guest!* Well, yes, but he insisted. Rangel went outside and kicked the tires on his Chevy. In one second, everything had fallen apart. And it was just the beginning.

Part IV

18

Testimony of Rodrigo Montoya, Undercover Agent

Of course I know Paracuán. That's where the biggest criminal case of my career started. It was when I was helping my uncle out, before I found my destiny and was shot off into infinity.

I was at the ripe old age of twenty-two . . . or it could be a little less, because at the time I was still looking for myself, and I was going to say, I only found myself because of my uncle. He was the chief of police in Paracuán, a tropical port that had problems with smuggling and drug dealers. Like Juan Gabriel said, *Pero, ¿qué necesidad?* Why does it have to be this way? The first time I found out about this crap was at a Christmas dinner. My uncle was never really into all these family things, but his wife, who's my mom's sister, made him spend the holidays with us. So we're all stuffed in there, all the relatives together. I decided I wasn't going down to eat dinner because all that stuff is such a drag, especially because they wanted me to put on a suit and tie, so I locked myself up in my room. I should probably be clearer: I didn't live with my parents anymore, I lived in the Distrito Federal, and I only went back to see them at Christmas or for Holy Week. That night I was thinking I'd just pretend I went to sleep early, but since

I had to go to the dinner, I took a hit from La Clandestina, a special pipe that doesn't leave any smell in the air, put a couple drops in my eyes, and went downstairs, prepared to deal with my folks. I was especially sensitive, you can probably imagine, so I went and sat down on the carpet in the living room, ready to listen to it all.

My dad took advantage of the fact that my uncle had gone off on one of his long, never-ending tangents and asked him to tell the story about the Chinese mafia, a shoot-out in the port that was so insane it made the papers. And wham! My uncle told a story he never would've told if he were sober. Even though his wife and kids tried to shut him up, he started to tell them the story: they had to take on about two hundred Orientals. And the asshole said it like it was funny, like if he was saying how many ants he had stepped on, just cracking up. Everything started when two agents that patrolled the Laguna del Carpintero detained a very respected old man from the Oriental community. If the rumors about the patrolmen were true, they probably stopped him because they didn't like him or because he refused to give them a bribe; but of course, my uncle didn't say that. He hadn't drunk *that* much. The problem was the old man turned out to be a respected martial arts professor at the Instituto Kong, a respected older man who knew all the Chinese in the port by name, so a sizable portion of the Oriental community organized a protest outside the police headquarters, from seven in the morning till noon. Since they didn't release him, the situation got more and more tense, and my uncle ordered them to keep on fucking with them until they left. But two police officers who passed by there decided to start yelling at a Chinese girl and flirting with her. Their catcalling got louder and louder, and her boyfriend came out to defend her. Despite what the elders recommended, the boyfriend challenged the policemen to a fight right there, in front of everyone. Since the officer thought he looked skinny, he said why not and took off his shirt: an inexcusable mistake, because the skinny guy sucker-punched him like a boxing champion. He kicked him twice and broke his face in, and each time the officer tried to get up, the Chinese guy sat him back down with another punch. He didn't even sweat when the officer tried to hit him with his belt. The bad thing is that in the meantime the officer's partner called for backup from the department. In a few minutes, all the available officers in the area had closed the avenue on both sides. Arrogant and cocky, they stepped out of their cars with rifles in their hands and the standard-issue semiautomatic pistols clipped to the front of their pants. They wanted to grab the guy, but the community made a barrier, and since they wouldn't let them get through, they started to massacre them in the middle of the street, as the Orientals retreated toward the entrance to the police headquarters. At first, the older men called for order, but when they saw that the cops had no code of honor, and that they were beating the young men with their nightsticks, the elders got into the fight, too. So the police fired off smoke grenades and under cover of all the chaos, they started to shoot. The Chinese didn't know where all the bullets were coming from and they ran toward the police headquarters and started to go in through the door and the windows. You know how the cops are, always waiting for a chance to shoot, so just imagine, as soon as they saw people running in they thought the worst and *boom*! They reacted according to the logic of "Shoot first, ask questions later." I was transfixed by my uncle's story, among other reasons, because I couldn't take my eyes off him. I imagined everything he was saying in complete detail, so that instead of everything happening over there in the port, the Chinese were actually coming into *my* house, through the windows with Ninja swords, Bruce Lee style. The hit I took from the pipe had knocked me out. The truth was, my uncle wasn't the best conversationalist, and even less so when drunk, but that night he was the only one who could tell the story of what happened in the police department, and he had us all listening—until my dad said to my uncle, "Oh, yeah? Well, in your public statements you said something else," and my uncle turned white in the face. It even killed his buzz.

But me, I just said to him, Right on, and started to sketch out a plan. I knew right then what I was going to do for my final project at the Ibero. As we were carving the turkey, I was thinking about how to find my place in the world, and more than anything else I was thinking about New Journalism. I'd found out about it on a recent trip to New York, and I remember a talk that Monsiváis gave at a conference at college about how all of us communicologists had to get busy, and then all of a sudden it hit me. There was a lot of movement at the table, the cups of red wine and whiskey came and went, but I was completely calm, because I saw the truth. With each slice of turkey my mom cut, certain dark clouds that had prevented my growth as a human being simply disappeared, each slice she took off the turkey was like another obstacle she took out of my path, and suddenly I saw my future so clearly it scared me. That night, I decided I would be an undercover agent working on behalf of the New Journalism. I was going to write a book about Paracuán. So as soon as I could, I went to the port to look for my research subject. I got there on the first morning bus, took a taxi to my aunt's house, and said hi to her. *What's up, Tía? I just got here, didn't my mom let you know?* Of course no one had called, but that was part of the plan. In a few minutes, I had her convinced that we had talked about it at the New Year's dinner and that her husband had said yes. My aunt made a face like she was going to get upset with her husband for not telling her anything, then she went into the living room and called his office on the phone. Her husband hadn't gotten there yet, so while we killed time, she made me breakfast: scrambled eggs, orange juice, and coffee. I took the opportunity to get up to speed on the news from the port in the last few days, and she told me that her husband was really worried about a problem with a drug dealer that had just shown up on the radar screen. Like always, my aunt started complaining about the newspapers, about how the reporters were always twisting everything around, especially that Johnny Guerrero. Of course, I thought, if they only read Tom Wolfe. . . . There was a busy signal at police headquarters, and my aunt recommended I go look for my uncle in his office, so as not to lose time. I left the house, walking with my own special style—laid back but steady, cool and calm, no problems—and I took a cab downtown.

Are you familiar with the police headquarters in Paracuán? It's that old white building, just two floors, that's right off the plaza. I got there in a few minutes. I was a very efficient agent. I have an incredible ease with directions; they could drop me off in the middle of the Kalahari, and I would always find my way home.

The secretary told me that the chief was about to head out to the state capital, but that she would try to reach him, and since I was his nephew I could wait for him in his office. There wasn't that much to see, and the majority of the drawers were locked, so I started to spy through the window. But all of a sudden I felt really worried, out of place, uncomfortable, like my uncle's office was full of bad vibes or like the place was sliced through by all kinds of dark energy currents—just like what happens in *The Exorcist* when Max von Sydow goes into the girl's house for the first time. Who knows what kind of stuff was going through there, but the officers looked like they were used to it and didn't even notice. But I did. And every time some officer stuck his head in looking for the boss, they'd give me some weird look, like I was a suspect or they didn't like how I looked. Since I have never been able to deal with pressure, I waited until the coast was clear and then took a toke off my pipe. I needed to have everything in good working order; I didn't know what I was up against. Intelligent men like us need to have an open mind, a heightened sensibility, and a body ready to react.

Since no one arrived, I opened my backpack and started to read a Moebius comic. I was totally getting into one of the characters, DogHead, when my uncle came in with one of his detectives. It was Rangel, the biggest badass in the secret service. The first impression I had was that the character from the comic had come alive and that Rangel also had a dog's head and the look of a canine: sharp teeth, rabid, ferocious. But a Super Agent of New Journalism can't get carried away by his impressions. I said, Good to meet you, man! And I shook his hand.

Rangel was well-known as my uncle's best officer, a goddamn bloodhound. He was a decent man, an honest and determined officer, so he didn't get along well with his coworkers. As soon as he came in, Rangel puckered up his nose and sniffed at the air. I thought, He caught me. I know he was going to ask me what I was smoking, but right then my uncle explained to me that I had come at a bad time, because the governor had given him an ultimatum: he had to arrest a murderer in forty-eight hours, and, as if that weren't enough, he also had to go to a meeting in the state capital. Oh, shit, I thought, a murderer? That could be a great idea for my final project at college, the subject for my book. A crazy man who killed three girls, my uncle explained. Three titles came into my head: *M, The Vampire of Düsseldorf,* and, of course, Hitchcock's *Psycho.*

I was too young for Woodstock and too little for Avándaro, I said to myself. The Beatles split up, Janis Joplin died, they killed

Che, Bob Marley disappeared. The only utopia left is New Journalism, and I'm going to focus on that.

I convinced my uncle to let me stay, and he asked Rangel to be my escort. The bad part is that they sent me off to shave and to get a hair cut. Yeah, man, just like that. I was wearing bell-bottoms, an open shirt showing half my chest, several necklaces, and I had sideburns and an afro. Rangel and another agent they called the Blind Man told me that if I didn't want to be noticed, I'd have to change my look. You're in the secret police, god-damnit, not in the Atayde Brothers Circus. I was really into my look, and I hated the idea. Even so, I understood that I was now an agent in the service of New Journalism, so I went to a barber and—snip, snip, snip—I said good-bye to all of it.

While I was getting my hair cut, the Blind Man was messing with me. As soon as I was done, I said I'd like a Colt Cobra .38 or, if possible, a .357 Magnum. What's up? You guys aren't gonna give me a gun? The officer didn't say anything. He was a decent guy but just real serious.

So I looked in the mirror: shaved, hair cut, and with no chains hanging from my neck, I looked like a different person. And I asked myself if the port was ready for a detective like yours truly.

From the beginning, I showed a remarkable talent for doing this kind of work. I found relationships between concepts that other people weren't aware of. If I had stayed in the port, and above all after my conversation with Dr. Quiroz Cuarón, criminology would've evolved millions of years in a matter of minutes. I would have developed a way to detect murderers before they decided to kill their victims, like in that Lars von Trier movie, *The Element of Crime*.

But just as I was starting my mission, I realized that Rangel was trying to shake me; the Blind Man insisted that I go for a walk with him; Vicente was going to the airport to pick up a specialist who had come to teach a course for the officers. Can I go? No, man, there's no reason for you to go. You'd get bored. What's the course about? Criminology, with Dr. Quiroz Cuarón. Dr. Quiroz Cuarón, the great detective? Hey, I said, now that's what I'm talking about! Dr. Cuarón was a leading figure on an international level. *Time* magazine referred to him as "the Mexican Sherlock Holmes," because he had captured literally hundreds of criminals, beginning in the forties: feared murderers like the lunatic Higinio Sobera de la Flor, who killed on a whim, picking his victims at random, or Gregorio Cárdenas, the Tacubaya Strangler. He also apprehended Shelly Hernández, the most wanted con man in Venezuela, a real chameleon of a man, and Enrico Sampietro, an amazing counterfeiter who worked for Al Capone and decided to establish himself in Mexico. Sampietro was so good, he could counterfeit himself. In addition to a lot of other police units, Interpol and the FBI were after him, but the only one who was able to bag him was Dr. Quiroz Cuarón. As if this weren't enough, the doctor also had the honor of clearing up the true identity of Jacques Mornard, the man who killed Leon Trotsky. Do I wanna see him? Damn yes, I told him, sure as hell I do.

OK. The Blind Man scratched his head. We'll let you go to the meeting, but you have to keep quiet. If you don't, I'll send you back where you came from. Whoa, I said, no way, but I accepted. I was the epitome of an irreproachable agent.

Even though I considered myself more prepared than most to take advantage of this course, above all because I was already an undercover agent in the service of New Journalism, I was willing to keep my mouth shut, and I went. I had hardly sat down when Rangel stuck his head in and called for me. He said that I could not attend the meeting, because my presence would bother the agents. He explained to mc that none of the police officers had finished middle school, and they would be inhibited if a young man like me, with such advanced education and of such obvious cultural stature, were to ask intelligent and elaborate questions. If you want to meet the doctor, I'll introduce you later. In the meantime, he wanted me to go with the Blind Man to patrol the tourist area on the docks to help him to look for a supposed drug dealer, but since I had already made that trip in reverse when I was looking for stuff to smoke in my pipe, I refused: I was risking the chance that one of my hookups would say hi to me or, even worse, that he'd think I was ratting on him. Besides, this guy trying to keep me from entering the course was violating my fundamental human rights. Obviously, a Super Agent like me couldn't be duped that easily, so I told him sure and I asked the Blind Man to wait for me in the street, but as soon as I could, I went right back and went into the meeting. Of course, before I did, I took not one but two tokes off my pipe, just to be ready for whatever.

Listening to Dr. Quiroz Cuarón's talk in that condition was an amazing experience. At first, for obvious reasons, it was hard for me to understand what he was saying on a syntactical level, but I did something better: spurred on by the initial effect of the pipe, I was able to meander between the doctor's words, in the space that he left between one word and another, and begin to dive down deep into their meaning. The detective seemed like an ancient Oriental musician who had come to delight us with his lute. Each time the doctor spoke, his words were like the strumming of its strings. Those interwoven sounds glided through the air, like wisps of smoke filling up the room. My consciousness dove through the spaces, literally submerging itself in different spots, in order to discover hidden associations. It was a good talk: refined, fluid, with the consistency of water.

To begin, the doctor drew an incomprehensible equation on the board. Gentlemen, he said, you all know that in order to solve a murder you have to answer the seven golden questions of the criminal equation: what happened, where, when, how, who, why, and with what instrument? In the case of the two girls, we are faced with a crime with no apparent motive, with no witnesses or leads, and that after a certain period of time was repeated with identical violence on another individual. I had read in some magazine that the doctor was attempting to develop a formula to study serial murderers and, if possible, to catch them: a mathematical equation. So I took note of it.

I had to try really hard, but for a long time I could only latch onto incomplete ideas: "We are facing a creature who lives in the borderlands between insanity and sanity. . . . Despite erasing his tracks impeccably, the butchering of the bodies had an obviously offensive meaning and he carried it out irrationally. . . .

"Despite having been able to hide successfully, every killer leaves almost imperceptible evidence behind, which can lead us to him. Even the most impeccable killer commits unconscious mistakes that expose him, small oversights that reveal his identity. These combine to form the killer's *signature* and they are the first variable of my equation.

"Imagine a solitary being that appears to lead a normal life. He is normally quiet and shuns the spotlight. He prefers to stay away from the world and avoids talking about himself, because, what could he say? That he has fantasies in which he tortures his acquaintances to get revenge on them? He lives alone or with some relative who takes care of the practical things.

"He only studied through middle school, if that. He has never had any kind of relationship as a couple and is sexually frustrated.

"He can't bear people humiliating him. Generally, he has brain damage in the frontal lobe, which is where moral feelings are located, as is our capacity for recognizing other people as individuals. That damage could have been inflicted at birth or as a child, causing him never to be able to identify his victims as people, but rather as animated dolls he can manipulate at will.

"Psychopaths like the one we are looking for begin with their fantasies, then they commit sadistic acts against animals, and finally they attack people. When they assault, they feel neither mercy nor pity. For the killer, his victims are less than human, with no right to live. As he attacks them, he considers himself the master of the other person's body. Before killing, he normally feels very anxious. He kills in order to avoid that uneasiness. Afterward he relaxes, his mood improves and he can even sleep without remorse.

"In order to resolve these cases, you must put yourself in the shoes of the guilty person and reason like him. You must think like the murderer, this is the right way, but it's also the riskiest. Unfortunately, not everyone can do it."

When I noticed it, the doctor's face was a few inches from my own. I had to make a huge effort to understand his questions; those sentences came from so far away that they produced a kind of echo.

"Let's see, Mr.—"

"Montoya."

"Mr. Montoya, very well. Tell me, what do these faces have in common?"

He paused and showed the girls' pictures, Karla Cevallos and Julia Concepción González, taken in front of their respective classrooms. One was dressed like a rich girl; the other was wearing a modest public school uniform.

"What do you see here? At first glance, there would seem to be no connection between the two of them: they live in two different parts of the city."

He took the pictures of the two girls and covered the background so that only their faces were visible. Then he covered their uniforms and the González girl's braids. The result was alarming: they looked alike, the two girls looked the same!

"Impressive," said Dr. Ridaura, who was in the room.

"There is a logic to all this. This subject chooses his victims; the Tacubaya Strangler acted the same way. He chooses girls who seem to be around ten years old, no more than about three feet high, white skin, black hair, a straight nose, and braids. This is the type of victim he prefers. In his strange way of thinking, he wants to punish them. He deceives them as he attracts them and then kills them with a serrated knife."

I agreed with him: Right on, I said, and I gave him the thumbs-up sign. He was quite the expert.

Then the doctor looked at his watch and picked up the pictures. "When a homicide like this occurs, it affects us all. Society clamors for quick justice. Justice in a case like this must be backed up by a responsible and scientific investigation. Men, go and do your duty."

When the session ended, the lackey signaled to me and then came over. "Rangel had to leave," he said. "He ordered us to take the doctor wherever he wants."

"Right on," I said, "that's awesome! Spending time with one of the best detectives in the world is a huge privilege."

The Blind Man drove toward the richest neighborhoods in the city and passed in front of a mansion that occupied the longest block, a mansion with incredibly white walls.

"What are we doing here?" asked the doctor.

"I thought you'd be interested to know where the main suspect lives," said the Blind Man.

"Look," answered the detective, "I have asked for no such thing. The only thing I want is to be returned to my hotel."

It was obvious that he couldn't stand talking to the Blind Man, who you could tell from a mile away was a fan of his.

So we took the old man back, and on the way the Blind Man was so angry that I decided to keep quiet. We dropped the doctor off and before I realized it, the Blind Man had returned to the main suspect's house. There were a lot of cars parked on the nearby blocks.

"It looks like there's a party," he said. "A lot of security, too." There were two bodyguards at each entrance. "Just think," he said, "while the people are scared to death, the guy inside there is having a party."

"What's his name?" I asked.

"Who, the suspect? Williams, John Williams, some people call him Jack."

As the Blind Man drove, I said to myself: Williams, John Williams, I know that name. "Hey, Romero," I asked, "is John Williams a tall guy, Jewish, like twenty years old? Because I know him. Is that who you're talking about?" Romero looked at me, shocked by the news, and I explained to him that the summer before I had met Jack at boarding school in New York, and the two of us had gone partying. We were drunk for three days, but who knows if he remembered me; they were some hectic days, if you know what I mean.

At that moment, our patrol car stopped in front of the main entrance. "What's up, Romero, why are you stopping?"

"I have no idea," said the Blind Man, "the engine stopped."

"Well, start it up, idiot."

"I'm trying," he said, "but the engine isn't starting." An incredibly tall bodyguard was watching us distrustfully. He elbowed his buddies and they stared at us, too, just watching to see what would happen. A minute later, they came up to us, accompanied by a gringo more than six feet tall, who looked like a soldier.

"Damn," said the Blind Man, "now we're fucked, first they're gonna beat us up, then they're gonna report us to the chief. What am I gonna tell Rangel?"

The situation was making me nervous. I wanted to take a hit from my pipe, but the bodyguard was already on his way. So I leaned back in the seat and came up with a foolproof plan.

When the guard stuck his head in through the window, I said, "Good evening, I've come to the party."

"What is your name, sir?"

"Rodrigo Montoya."

"I'm going to check the list."

"I won't be there," I explained, "I'm just back from a trip; tell Jack I showed up unexpectedly."

"Wait," he said, and took out a walkie-talkie.

The guard had a response in a few minutes; he looked me over again and said I could go in.

"That's it, dude," I said to Romero, "I'll tell you later how it went." The Blind Man couldn't believe my luck. He grabbed my arm and said, "Find out if that asshole is right- or left-handed. The most important thing is the weapon; look for the murder weapon. Don't forget: it has to be a serrated knife. If you find it, we're halfway there." It was clear to me that I was on a special mission.

I had to be really tough to head straight into the belly of the beast, but, no problem, I said to myself, I'm a warrior, I can handle this.

As soon as I got out of the car, the car started. "What a coincidence," the Blind Man said.

"It's not a coincidence," I said, "it's a cosmic sign, I'm used to it." I was now carrying the weight of the investigation on my shoulders.

There was a huge blow-out party, the kind that make history. Jack came up to welcome me. "What's happening, Rodrigo? What're you doing here in the port?"

"I'm on vacation," I said; I wasn't going to reveal my mission just like that. And we drank a few whiskeys, in memory of our time together in New York.

Jack asked me what I'd been doing the last couple months, and I told him about studying in the Ibero, about the art house theaters I was going to—films by Fellini and Antonioni—and about how my vision of things was evolving. "Listen," he insisted, "what's missing in this port is a person like you, with your experience and your knowledge of art. Why don't you stick around and work here? My dad wants to invest in a cultural project, he wants to fund a kind of museum and expo center, I think because he wants to get around paying taxes, you know? It would be awesome if you were the director." In short, he insisted that I accept. I said to myself that I could stay on in Paracuán; in any case, my dad's businesses were never really interesting to me, but being twenty years old and directing a cultural center, that sure did seem like a cool job. Although, of course, a warrior like me couldn't succumb to temptation just like that. I thought for a second that Jack knew why I was crashing his party and was trying to bribe me, but he wasn't going to get off that easy. I was going to identify the perpetrator.

From where we were standing, I could see the kitchen, and I said to him, "I'll be right back. I was planning to look for the serrated knife, but Jack grabbed me by the arm.

"Come with me, I want to introduce you to some girls," and he dragged me off to the actual party.

In this mixed-up world, if you don't get trashed, you get smashed. When Carlos Castaneda figured out the enemies of a man of knowledge, he forgot to mention alcohol and women. Jack introduced me to three girls. "Where are you from?" I asked.

The blonde said, "From California."

"That's Carolina—Iowa—and this is Claudette," said Jack, motioning to the redhead. "She's from Canada." The three of them were out of this world.

The mansion had two visible buildings; the bigger one was the main house and the smaller one was the guest house. Between them, there was a huge garden and in the center of the garden they had set up a dance floor with lights and everything. The girls and the other guests were gathered around the drinks, talking. The guys responsible for putting on the CDs were none other than the legendary Freaky Villarreal and René Sánchez Galindo, both total experts. They played soul, blues, and disco and the place was getting hot.

Jack wanted to dance but he didn't; at heart, he was a shy guy. "Do you know how to dance to this?" he asked.

"For sure," I said, "it's totally easy: you point one hand down, then up into the sky, and you move your hips. What's the deal, dude? Tough guys don't dance, or what?" Jack was upset because his girl had broken up with him, the prettiest *güerita* in the port. "They say that I'm the Jackal; that goddamn rumor is messing up my life."

I was an upstanding agent, but I also had feelings, and I said that it was really wrong for her to break up with him so quick.

That's when I had a revelation, a real vision that hit me all of a sudden: these folks were going to die without ever having lived, life was going to fuck them up, just like my family does to the Christmas turkey, slice by slice, and they were going to die without finding out why or for what they had come into the world. It was enough just to see how they were all standing there, staring at the empty dance floor. I was overcome by an overwhelming sense of sadness.

Right then, they put on "Bring It On Home," but nobody had it in them to dance, the people were fired up, shaking their feet, there were even a few people moving in their seats, but nobody would start dancing. Then they put on "I Can't Leave You Alone" by George McRae, and I realized that my mission on earth was something more dangerous than writing a thesis. I said to myself, This is a dangerous mission, but someone's gotta do it. It takes a real warrior to deal with this situation.

I went out to the center of the dance floor and started to dance in a ritualistic kind of way; I don't know if you understand that. They shouted at me; "What's wrong with you, dude? You're acting stupid," but I told myself, *Who cares?* I just danced, totally focused on that song; I showed them how it's done. I danced like it was my last night on earth; like I'd had to travel all around the country to figure out that stuff about the turkey. I danced with my whole body, and suddenly what do you think happened? Everybody started to get up and dance with me; not one or two or three girls, everybody in there stood up all of a sudden, they joined me, and we danced like the primitive cavemen must have danced in the caverns in Altamira; the girls would come up in front of me, one by one, then they'd move on and leave their place to the next girl; I was so moved watching them, I had tears in my eyes, but I didn't miss a disco beat, one hand down, one hand raised, pointing up into the infinite sky. *Can't leave you! No! Can't leave you alone. Can't leave you! No! Can't leave you alone.*

And then, can you dig it? The prettiest girl in the party came up and stopped in front of me, that incredible redhead, goddamn, I mean really incredible, the redhead from Canada; I guessed she was like seventeen years old but I wasn't really sure. The girl came and smiled at me like no one had ever smiled at me before, and the volume of the music went down a little, enough for me to ask her, "What's up, girl, where'd you come from?" And her eyes sparkled. I moved closer, it was an intuition, bro, the first intuition of my life, and I moved closer.

We were in the middle of that when El Freaky decided to put on a slow song, and everybody booed. Everyone fled the dance floor and the girl signaled to me to follow her. Like I already said, there were guest rooms, and she took me in that direction. She gave me a long, wet kiss, as we held each other just inside the door; then she went into the room.

Damn, I said to myself, what do I do now? I knew I had to investigate the case, that I had a really important mission, but what could I do? I tried to resist with all my strength, I even grabbed the doorframe, but she kept calling me and I just said over and over again: No, I shouldn't, I'm a warrior, not just the puppet of my desires. My brain controls my body, not my pelvis. So she did something I didn't expect: she started to take off her clothes without looking at me and walked toward the bed.

From my point of view, I saw her walk away from me, showing me her back, as she tied up her hair. When she got beside the bed, she turned—she had the most delicious breasts—and smiled. So I closed the door and pulled the curtains shut. As I took off my clothes, I understood that I wasn't going to be the one to resolve this case, because already my consciousness was being submerged in nirvana, and my identity and my name were dissolving into infinity. That was the last of the undercover agent.

19

Report of Dr. Alfonso Quiroz Cuarón, Detective

We were drinking coffee when the phone rang. My sister Consuelo answered and then hung up. It was another case, she told me, they want your help with another case, but you need to rest; remember what the doctor said. And it was the truth, the cardiologist said I needed to take a vacation, preferably at sea level. As soon as Consuelo left, I asked myself if it wasn't time to retire, and the dusk light seemed to confirm my fears. It would be a pity to stop now, I told myself; at this rate I'll soon have enough material to finish the book, and to do that I'll need more cases. I was telling myself this when I looked out at the street and oh, what a surprise! There he was: the man in black, as I'd taken to calling him.

Of all the guys who have followed me, this one is the least discreet. Who knows who's monitoring me now? I've been followed by the Chinese Mafia, the Russians, the Germans, the Czechs, Batista's police, a certain faction of the CIA, that French guy with the knife, and three dozen fellow detectives; it's part of the job. I must have done something, I thought, to make this boy stand there outside. In my head, I went over the cases I was working on: the bank fraud, the counterfeit stamps, the businessman's disappearance, but none of them seemed important enough to justify the sentry out there.

It could be the government, I said to myself. Since I quit, the president has been keeping close tabs on me. When he or one of his friends is interested in a case I have, one or more agents from the Federal Safety Administration take shifts to follow me, agents that sometimes I myself trained. Of them all, the easiest to notice is this stubborn young man who spends hours in front of my house. He peers inside, making no attempt to conceal his interest, wait-ing for the moment that I head out into the street. Well, now he's fucked, I said to myself, it's going to start raining and I have no plans to leave the house.

I was looking outside when another phone call came in. A voice that I seemed to recognize identified himself as a police of-ficer from Paracuán, Tamaulipas: Vicente Rangel, at your service. The voice reminded me of someone and I couldn't remember who. Paracuán, Tamaulipas? I asked, "Does Miguel Rivera still work there?" He was my uncle, said the young man, he was my uncle, but he passed away. "How is that possible? When did he die?" The young man said: Three years ago. "That's a shame," I said. "I had a lot of feeling for Miguel Rivera." Yeah, he's really missed, the young man said to me, we could really use his expe-rience right about now—and I understood that the young man's voice sounded familiar because he had the same voice as Miguel: a firm, friendly voice. "Believe me, I'm very sorry," I told him, "your uncle was an amazing individual . . . how can I help you?" Quite the opposite of what I'd expected, Miguel Rivera's nephew had not only inherited his uncle's kind voice, but also his voca-tion, and he had read my books. He was calling on behalf of the mayor of Paracuán, who wanted me to assist his agents in the course of an investigation. Rangel summarized the case: two little girls dead, both killed in the same excessively violent way, two murders without witnesses or leads. "Don't get your hopes up," I told him. "When dealing with a perfect crime, the only way to find the perpetrator is if someone calls in a tip. Look for someone else because I'm already retired." It's important, he said to me. "I know it's important, but a man my age simply doesn't have the same strength." Rangel insisted and I said to him, "Look, I'll think about it. Call me back in one hour."

Two voices battled in my head. One told me: Don't do this, Alfonso, you have to relax, and the other insisted: You have a responsibility, damnit, do it for Miguel Rivera, your friend, who helped you so much. A guy who murders girls, I thought. From what I've heard, the case reminds me of what happened in Mexico City with Gregorio Cárdenas, the guy who strangled women. The case in the port would be a difficult one to solve. Although, on the other hand, if organized well, it would undoubtedly be a leap forward for criminology. I could even prove the system I propose in my book, the criminal equation. Why not? I said to myself. I know the port and I could find the perpetrator. If all goes well, I will contribute something and also confirm my theories; besides, Consuelo can't get upset: I'm just following my doctor's advice, I'm going to the beach. Little by little, that line of thought won out in my head, so when the officer called again, I accepted and prepared my bags to travel that afternoon. I only insisted on one condition, the same one as always since I retired: that I would investigate at my own expense, independently, and that I would continue the investigation to its full extent, without considering the interests that might be affected. Rangel accepted and I set out on my trip.

I reviewed the notes from my book in process, *The Criminal Equation,* without a doubt my most important work since I wrote the *Treatise on Criminology*; I packed three shirts and left out the back door in order to evade detection by the lookout. I'm more than seventy years old, but I can still avoid the watchmen if I set out to do so. Over the years, I've developed a flawless technique.

Nothing notable happened during the flight, but when I got to headquarters, Rangel left me in the care of a suspicious character who couldn't have been on good terms with the law: you could smell his criminal history a mile away. "Dr. Quiroz Cuarón? I recognized you from the photo at the end of your book; it'll be quite an honor to work with the Mexican Sherlock Holmes." I replied that Sherlock Holmes was a fraud, a simple literary invention, not a real police officer. I've never seen anyone resolve a case like Sherlock Holmes, without doing scientific work. As soon as I could, I called Rangel aside and asked him, Is that your lackey? He sighed—*Yes, he's my assistant*—so I told him that assistants like that one give you more problems then they solve. Your uncle never had assistants, he always worked alone or in a team with other policemen like him. *I'd love that!* The young guy said, *but the way things are now, I can't trust my coworkers. At least I know that this guy'll support me for money.*

I said to myself that if Vicente couldn't trust his own colleagues, things were worse than I thought. Rangel needed help, but I wasn't sure I could support him. It's been years since crime became completely transparent to me. . . . There are a small number of story lines about criminals and detectives, and I've seen each one of them so many times, in all their variations, that I can recognize them immediately. I suppose that's the advantage of experience. Just by seeing a situation, I can predict how it'll end; that's why it's so hard to keep hope alive.

The way I see it, everything went downhill starting with President Miguel Alemán. The bureaucrats were only looking out for their own advancement, there was endless fraud. The idealists like us who started out during the time of Lázaro Cárdenas, people like me, who were looking for justice, we had a tough time just getting our jobs done. It was so much work to find that counterfeiter in Tampico! And to find the guy who killed Trotsky! The way I see it, everything started to come apart when Alemán was president, things got worse with López Mateos, and ended up completely rotten when Echavarreta came to power. We moved from knives to pistols, then to machine guns, then to kidnappings and massacres. I remember when I quit: Look, I told the president, I don't have anything to do here, I'm leaving and I'm taking my team. We left en masse: Carrillo, Segovia, Lobo, yours truly. We couldn't keep on like that.

That's why, when I heard Vicente, I thought I'd just head back home immediately, but in the end he was Miguel Rivera's nephew and he was asking for my help: an idealist in a sea of corruption. If I accepted the assignment, it was in memory of his irreproachable uncle.

I studied all the evidence that they had. Even though I was tired, I examined all the circumstances of the crimes one by one and visited the crime scenes. It was true, there was no concrete evidence, just one or two inferences that could be made. As I ate lunch with Vicente, it occurred to me to try out my equation. I asked the young man who he thought, out of all the powerful people in the port, had certain characteristics that could predispose them to committing sexual crimes. Who frequented certain places, who was famous for certain excesses, who among them had a criminal history of sexual offenses with a minor? Occasionally, Rangel mentioned an interesting idea and I noted it down in my list. As I made my notes, Vicente got more and more aggravated, because he didn't understand my system. He was disturbed by the fate of the little girls, and he wanted to do something quickly. Vicente was a good person, but if I tried to explain my theory about the criminal equation, we would lose precious time, and I was starting to feel tired, so I said to him: Look, Vicente, I'm going to look over the information and later I'll explain my conclusions; right now, I just want to relax. I was planning to review the possible explanations in light of the system that I myself invented.

He stood up to make some calls and said to me, Sometimes I don't know why we're in this, if everything is going against us. Perk up, I said. Sometimes the isolated actions of an individual can change the society at large. That's what I said to him, and I still regret it. Enthusiasm can provoke delusions.

The rest of the afternoon, I was mad at myself for being so short with Vicente. I went to give my talk, and I realized Rangel wasn't there. I should have given him some advice, I told myself, after all, he *is* Miguel Rivera's nephew. I even wrote a long list of tips that I was planning to give him, I really didn't rest at all, writing that list of pointers, but when the talk was over, despite what I had expected, his gofer the Blind Man was the one who came to pick me up. And Vicente? I asked. Vicente had to go out, he replied; he went to investigate the death of a colleague. How strange, I said to myself. Doctor, the man asked me, what do you want to do now?

I asked him to take me back to my hotel. I had to think. So I took out my notebook and started to insert the concrete data about the crime into the abstract structure of my equation. I had it all ready, but I was missing names, profiles.

I went up to my room and tried to sleep. Half an hour later, the phone rang and the Blind Man asked me if I could join him in the bar: New evidence had been uncovered. I had to go down, even though interacting with the Blind Man bothered me. We sat at an out-of-the-way table and I didn't let him speak until after the bartender had left. So, what's the evidence? I asked. I wanted to tell you some things I didn't tell you in front of Rangel because he doesn't like rumors. So, what is it? I took sips off my caipirinha as the Blind Man explained the dark side of the port, stories in which several of the most powerful men of Paracuán played a role, but no concrete leads. At two o'clock, I looked at my watch and took my leave. How awful, I said to myself, a city so small with such murky depths. What the Blind Man had told me put me in a bad mood, as always happens when I'm about to solve a case. I went to my room and felt like something strange was going on.

When I looked at the wood grain in the door, the lines started to quiver and shake, like an army of ants were moving them little by little. I saw blue spots sparkling in front of my eyes and I thought, They drugged me; there was poison in that drink. I staggered over to my bed, opened my suitcase, and got out a first-aid kit I always carry with me. I drank an antidote as if it were water and waited. It took forever to recover my breath. Damn, I said to myself, if the poison had taken effect when I was downstairs, I wouldn't have been able to come up.

I was beat. I should have called an ambulance but I didn't have enough strength, so I stayed in bed. The situation is more complicated than it seems, I thought. Someone does not want me to work on this case and is sending me very clear messages. No matter how much I tried, I couldn't remember a moment when the Blind Man touched my glass, so I decided that the poison came from the bartender. Or perhaps they were conspiring against me; I can't trust anyone in this city, I said to myself.

I took out my pistol and prepared to wait: the first person to open the door was going to find quite a surprise.

The windows were open. They looked out over the patio on the inside of the hotel; not exactly the best idea in terms of security. I should have got up and closed them, but I was exhausted. As I slowly got my strength back, I kept pondering the situation, lying on my back in bed. The names of the suspects began to parade through my mind. On one side were the suspects' names that Rangel's man had mentioned to me; on the other was the equation I came up with to identify murderers. The different possibilities clashed with each other, but suddenly, before I could even finish the process, I knew who the murderer was, it was as clear as day. My intuition, which never fails me in these cases, slipped in the name of a person that the Blind Man mentioned in passing, without knowing that he was related to the case. Wow, I said to myself, the equation does work. Among the suspects, there was only one person who could have killed those girls and gone unpunished. Memory might get worse with age but the system just gets better. I have to publish that book; the equation works!

At that moment, I was able to sit up on the bed. I had to see a doctor soon, but I said to myself—how naive I am—that the crisis had come to an end. I was standing up to close the curtains when I realized that the man in black was spying on me from the interior patio. It's not possible! It was not possible that he was there, staring at my room. I don't know how they found me, I said to myself, but the investigation is in danger. It's never been a good thing to be close to the Federal Safety Administration.

I went out into the street with my pistol in my hand, covered by my suitcoat, and hailed a taxi. Take me to the airport, I told him, take me to the airport immediately. I thought of calling Rangel from Mexico City, finishing the investigation there, informing the independent press, but I had to hurry to move faster than the people following me.

I barely made the first plane of the day. In Mexico City, with all my stuff and my suitcases, I hailed another taxi to Balderas and climbed the three flights of stairs, gasping for air. I went to the Ministry of the Interior and went directly into the main office.

"Dr. Quiroz Cuarón, in person," said the personal assistant to the minister, a conniving, impertinent young man who was smiling for no reason; "it's an honor to have you here." Thank you, I said, but time is of the essence, I must speak with Gutiérrez. "He's on vacation," he said, "he left for the Gulf of Mexico." To the Gulf? I just came from there. "You can tell us all about it, Doctor, but before you do that"—and he took out a document—"the Minister would like you to sign this statement supporting the president in the incident of October second." How presumptuous, I thought, I was already familiar with the document and had refused to sign it. I didn't come about that, I told him. I came to report injustice. What you people want to do is a crime, if you don't stop now, I'll report you to the president. "Doctor," he said without dropping his smile, "there's no use insisting, the president isn't going to listen to you. Don't waste your time." I understood that he was serious. Look, I told him, tell the president that he does not have my support, I'll never sign that paper—and I left, slamming the door. I had broken with the government once and for all.

When I got to my house, I felt I was about to explode. I called and called but no one answered in the president's office. The last secretary who answered the phone, a rude and offensive woman, made such a sarcastic remark that I hung the phone up violently. On few occasions had I felt as irritated as I did that morning. It was hot, and I was sweating. I should relax, I said to myself, I'm stressed out; the heat from the Gulf has followed me here. When I moved to take off my shoes, I saw that my left arm was trembling. Argh, I said to myself, this time I've overdone it. I breathed in deeply, but it was too late, soon the pain was intolerable and I lay down to relax. I couldn't feel my arm below my shoulder and I knew I was in trouble, I'd brought on another heart attack. Suddenly, *boom!* It reached my chest. The pain increased minute by minute, it was like giving birth. I couldn't beat it, until I said to myself, Enough already, Alfonso; you've overcome bigger challenges in your life, don't give up. Deal with the pain. That's what I told myself, only instead of resisting I relaxed my body, as if the pain were a river and I was swimming in the middle of it, and I lost consciousness as I floated in its current.

I woke up the next morning. The sun shone through the window and everything seemed incredibly real. I called my sister. Consuelo, I'm exhausted, and I told her what had happened. But I was so tired I couldn't be sure if I actually called her on the phone or if I had just imagined that I did it. Nothing happened the rest of the day. I had no strength to move. Luckily, there was a bottle of water on the bedside table, and that allowed me to survive.

The next day, my sister and her children came to see me, but I was so tired I couldn't get up to open the door. I shouted to them: Use your key! I'd given them a copy before, and they were able to come in. As soon as they saw me, they said we had to call a doctor. No, no, I said to them, I'm not so bad off, I just need to rest, but they didn't listen to me. Consuelo stayed by my side and I slept like a log. Once, my sister stood up and said to me, "Alfonso, I love you a lot, and I was angry with you when you left for that port, but I understand you had to do it, your vocation is stronger than your body." Consuelo, I told her, you're my sister and I love you, too. There's no need to apologize, just the opposite; you've always been very kind to me. But now it's midnight and I'm very tired. I need to sleep.

The next morning, I woke up before her and her children. I felt like new. I even put on my shoes without feeling out of breath. Rest, I said to myself, I needed the rest. From here on, I'll rest every weekend.

I wanted to surprise everyone by going out to get the newspaper, so I headed to the door and opened it. How strange, I thought, the paper isn't here. I thought about going to buy one myself at the corner and I headed that way, but then I saw the kiosk wasn't there. And not only that: there wasn't anyone in the street. The largest city in the world was suddenly empty. Where was everyone? I thought. Is there another protest? Or is it really early? As for the kiosk, they must have moved it somewhere else. So many things happened in two days! That's what I told myself and I headed to Avenida Insurgentes, where there's another kiosk. Only when I turned the corner, I saw the same guy as always: the man in black. This is too much, I thought, this is just too much, and I went up and confronted him.

Look, I told him, I'm fed up with your following me. Why are you doing this? He didn't respond. Who do you work for? The young man stayed quiet and took off his dark glasses. Up close, it was obvious he was very young, you know, with long hair like those singers from Liverpool. Why are you following me? I persisted. The young man smiled. "Because you're dead, Doctor." What? Me, dead? What are you talking about? And he showed me the death certificate: On said day at said time Dr. Alfonso Quiroz Cuarón passed away at his house at 54 Río Mixcoac. "You died in your bed, after coming back from the port." Are you sure? "Very sure, I've been keeping an eye on you for the past few days, but you have been very clever and I haven't been able to reach you. You've even been able to live your last few days three times."

For a minute, I thought it was a trap set by Echavarreta and the Federal Safety Administration, but the young man's calm demeanor gave the impression of being beyond question. So, what am I doing here? "I suppose you wanted to solve that case, you've been very busy." Oh, yeah, I said, the girls. I almost forgot. "It happens when you're old, don't worry."

All of a sudden, I realized what I was doing was utterly ridiculous—me, one of the most brilliant minds of my generation —and my legs gave way. I feel bad, I said, I think I'm having another heart attack. The young man took me by the arm. "The stars, Doctor, look at the stars." Even though it was a gorgeous day, I could see the stars as never before; I could see the constellations and the planets —Mercury, Venus, Mars—and all of a sudden the pain dissipated.

"It's over?" Yes, it is, he said. It was very simple; in the end, it was very simple, I feel much better. He looked at me and smiled; he was actually wearing white. I understood intuitively that I should have kept quiet, but I said to him: There's one thing that worries me, it's about the case. "There's no time anymore, Doctor: it's time to go." That's a shame, I said, I had it all solved. . . . At the very least, wouldn't you like to know my explanation? Two minutes, just give me two minutes, and you'll know what really happened. And I explained the whole case, detailing the system I had developed over the years, the foolproof criminal equation. When I was done, the young man gave me his opinion. "Impressive," he said, "a little bit like Sherlock Holmes."

Sherlock Holmes was a fraud, I said, a huge fraud. I lost it like I always do when I hear that name, but that time I didn't have the sense of conviction, as if a gigantic hole had opened up in the middle of my sentence and all the resentment had just flowed out. And then I understood that the mystery, the real mystery, was just beginning for me.

20

Back at headquarters, Rangel picked up the evening edition of *El Mercurio*: COLUMNIST CORMAC MCCORMICK DISAPPEARS.

Tuesday night, the renowned FBI investigator Cormac McCormick disappeared under mysterious circumstances. The author of *All About UFOs,* the famous column reprinted in more than a hundred and fifty newspapers in the United States, was headed from Mojave, California, to Searchlight, Nevada, where he was to give a talk on UFOs (Unidentified Flying Objects). The writer's vehicle was found abandoned on the highway in Death Valley. Prior to his disappearance, the investigator spent the weekend in a Las Vegas hotel, where he won a considerable amount of money that was found undisturbed inside the car. There was no sign of theft or violence, no evidence or blood. But around the vehicle, a curious circular track was found, a meter wide and with a diameter of twenty meters. The grass around it appeared to be charred. The detectives in charge of the case were baffled—

He had thought things couldn't get any worse. Then the phone rang again, the secretary answered, and, suddenly frightened, she covered her mouth with her hand.

"Mr. Rangel?"

"What's wrong?"

"They just found two more girls, near the train tracks."

José Torres loved his three daughters, especially the youngest, Daniela. He had named her after an actress with green eyes from the *telenovelas*. The girl's eyes were brown, but to please the mother, everyone said that they were green at first, as if the actress's name had changed them for the better. Ever since the first *telenovela* in Mexico, an actress's popularity was measured by the number of girls baptized with her name.

She'd woken up sad that morning, because of a dream she had, and didn't want to go to school, but her parents dressed her and sent her on her way. Since they lived in a neighborhood with no electricity or paved streets, the girl had to walk through a small wooded area with mango and avocado trees to get to Public School Number Seven.

She was very small, her father thought. She looked so pretty with her hair wet and combed, just after her bath. She always wanted a metal lunchbox, like her classmates had, but José Torres never could buy it for her: I'm sorry, *mija,* but the most important thing is to have enough to eat, and he handed her her breakfast wrapped in a plastic bag.

The girl waved good-bye. It was the last time he saw her.

A group of Boy Scouts was responsible for finding the body: Augusto Cruz, Jesús Cárdenas, Carlos Síerra, and Martín Solares. Not one of them was more than seven years old. The first thing that was strange about the chaotic statement they gave was that they had no reason to be there, because their group, Number 7, was based out of the other end of the city. It all started when they tried to skip class and see *The Exorcist* at the Cinemas del Bosque, but—they'd never skipped class before—they took a bus headed in the wrong direction and when they got off, they were caught in a thunderstorm, so they sought shelter in an abandoned building. Later, one of them wanted to explore the second floor and he found the body.

The address was for an abandoned building on the outskirts of the city. The Evangelist's car was in the street, and there was an ambulance next to it. Rangel jumped the barrier restricting access to the crime scene. Crazyshot tried to stop him.

"Hold on, man, you can't go in."

"Why?" He tried to push his way through, but his coworker got in his way.

"Chief's orders. Taboada's in charge."

"Fuck Taboada." And he pushed his coworker out of the way. Cruz Treviño made such a small effort to hold him back that Rangel realized the giant really wanted him to take the case, so he wouldn't have the responsibility. Fucking jerks. All of them just want to get off the hook, and here I go like a complete idiot.

He walked to the first floor, and immediately the awful smell hit him, like he was entering a tiger's den. Damn, he said to himself, this is the place, no doubt about it. His legs almost gave way when he passed the stairs and walked into the foul-smelling hallway; it was impossible to breathe and he started to cough. The Evangelist ran out of the room, covering his nose with a handkerchief and didn't stop till he made it to the window. Then he started vomiting.

"Watch out, *cabrón*!" they shouted at him from below.

Rangel deeply wanted someone else to take the job from him, but he found himself on his own again, so, summoning all his strength, he covered his mouth with his handkerchief and walked through a door that seemed to lead to another world.

The scene of the crime was so overwhelming that while he was in the room, he couldn't think. He could only ponder the insanity that was behind it all, trying to imagine what kind of person could do something like this. His hands weren't even sweating anymore, they were literally cracking open, but he didn't realize it at that moment. He realized he was covered with cold sweat when Dr. Ridaura came into the room.

"Oh, finally, you're here. If you thought this was it, follow me; I'll show you some more."

The old woman went back down the hallway and, completely exasperated, opened one door after another.

"Look."

There was blood splattered on the floor in each of the rooms. "Holy Mother of God," said Rangel. The building had a parking area inside it, so the killer was able to go in and out without being seen. Of course, he thought, that fucking pig, he killed all of them right here. I'm in the killer's den.

The doctor sneezed and angrily blew her nose.

"And that's the least of it. You know what's the strangest part, Vicente? That girl who's lying on the ground has been dead for two months. There's evidence that the maniac came back and attacked her several times."

"Two months?"

"At least. Look: advanced state of decomposition, cadaver fauna; the skin comes off like a glove. It's awful, I don't understand how no one found her sooner. But right now, the most important thing is that this guy's got to be caught and brought to justice."

The doctor picked up the clothing with a metal wire. The sound of the flies buzzing was unbearable, and Rangel couldn't take it anymore. And right then, he said to himself, the clothes, the clothes. Vicente was able to decode the strange arrangement of the bodies.

In the three plastic bags he had examined so far, the killer had covered the girls' remains with strips of their school uniform. First, he put the girls into the bags and then he added the uniform. Was he trying to cover them? Exactly, he thought, covering them up is his calling card, as Dr. Cuarón would say. Holy shit, that's it, why would he possibly want to cover them up? And he said to himself silently: To identify himself. Horrified, completely stupefied, Rangel looked over the first layer of clothing, a white shirt with bloodstains. Using tweezers, he spread it out, and his amazement multiplied infinitely when he recognized that, if he squinted, the shape of the stains seemed to spell out three block letters.

He went to his car, took out the two girls' files and reviewed the black-and-white photos: three letters, damn it, it was obvious. On the front of both shirts he recognized similar markings. It wasn't hard, because they were the initials of one of the most powerful political associations in Mexico, which was especially powerful in the area. Cigarettes bitten on one side, white wool from a sheep, a hunting knife, three letters. . . . Holy shit, he thought, it's crystal clear. He saw *El Mercurio* out of the corner of his eye and the hair on his arms stood on end. That day, they had published the perpetrator's photo; he was at an official event, practically in the place of honor, receiving applause from the public.

Holy shit, he thought, holy shit, this is about to blow up. They had to take Mrs. Hernández seriously. Covering his face with his hands, he considered the possibility of telling Wong and the Professor, but if the fucking idiots didn't support me before, he thought, they sure as hell won't do it now. He mentally ticked through the rest of the officers on the force and concluded that he had his reasons not to trust any of them, just like none of them trusted him. Ever since the rumor about his quitting had made the rounds, they had even more reason to buddy up to Taboada and stop working with him. Shit, he said to himself, what do I do now?

When Taboada pulled up, he was surprised to find Rangel parked there.

"And what the hell are you doing here? Weren't you going off with Barbosa, you fucking asshole?"

Surprising everyone, Rangel headed right at him, more than willing to break his face in, and he walked so purposefully that even El Travolta took a step back.

Now you've gone and done it, fucking fat-ass, Rangel thought. El Travolta was about to jump on top of him when Wong and the Bedouin held him back. Not now, *cabrón,* not here. A little calmed down and without the look of fear in his eyes, El Travolta puffed his chest out like normal.

"You're gonna pay, asshole."

"Bring it on, man."

And he turned around slowly, giving the fat guy a chance to go after him, but he didn't try it. Taboada's a fucking idiot.

He pulled his car out, tires squealing. If I could've, I would've quit right that fucking second. If Taboada wants to get mixed up in all this violence, let him, let him get in the mud and stay there, like the pig he is. I've had enough.

He wasn't able to calm himself down until he got to the avenue, but as he headed down the boulevard in Tres Colonias, he had no more doubts about what he had to do.

After making his decision, it took him two minutes to put together his plan. He needed someone desperate who'd be willing to help him. And since he couldn't trust anyone, he called the only investigator with that profile.

21

Testimony of Jorge Romero, AKA the Blind Man

Not like it was anything new, but they started to assign me to follow up on the most fucked-up calls; they sent me to the Colonia Coralillo. You know what they say about that neighborhood: One time a cop went in there and they diced him up alive. I asked the boss, Why don't you go? It's really far; you've got a car and I don't. "You don't really want to be part of the secret police, do you?" he said. Yeah, I do. "OK, then, go. And don't be late coming back." So I went.

I had a fake reporter's ID and, depending on the situation, I wasn't sure if I'd say I was a cop or not. I had a fake badge in one pocket, and in the other I had a mini–tape recorder that my cousin lent me so I'd be more convincing. When I headed into that part of town, I remembered they'd assault you for a watch or your glasses, so I thought I'd better keep it in my pocket. Just then, the taxi driver turned around at the traffic circle instead of going in. What's up? What's the problem? Why're you stoppin' here? "It's union orders; they're really worked up today about the girls who got killed. One of 'em was from here." And what do I do now? "Sorry, that's not my problem."

As soon as I went in, I wouldn't have anywhere to hide. The neighborhood's calmed down a little now, but you can't even imagine what the Coralillo was like in the seventies. None of the streets were paved; it was just a dusty pit where everybody went to throw their junk. No drinking water or electricity, not even a sewage system. Malaria, diphtheria, polio . . . the river was so dirty there were dead burros floating in it. The government never went there except to arrest somebody. A few months before I went in, a mob lynched a cop from Ciudad Madera. The guy went in, chasing some robbers, and he left in an ambulance, with his ribs broken. That's why I was trembling. But the only thing I could think to do was to go in a straight line, never pass by the same place twice and entrust myself to the Virgen María.

And that's how I did it, cussing the whole goddamn way. The first person who made a report lived in a house in front of a pharmacy called La Perla, an old termite-ridden wooden place. In front, there were like twenty kids fighting over a bike with training wheels. A skinny kid was hitting another kid when I came up.

"Hey, kids." All of them stopped playing except for the one whose turn it was to be on the bike. "Is Mrs. Mariscal here?"

"Why you wanna see her?" A kid in a striped shirt asked. The other ones were curious, too, and they surrounded me.

"She asked for me to come. I'm a reporter with *El Mercurio*."

"From *El Mercurio*?" the one in the striped shirt asked. "My mom didn't talk to no reporter. She called the cops. That's why my dad sent her to the hospital."

I had to swallow my spit. The kids started shouting that I was a cop and that they were going to tell Juan's dad. Luckily there were no adults around. I was trying to come up with something to say to interrupt them when I took a step backward and tripped on a bike wheel, almost breaking it. El Flaco, the skinny one, shouted,

"Fucking cop! Don't let him go!" And they all came at me at once. They started kicking me, throwing rocks, hitting me, whatever they could do. El Flaco held my legs together while the others grabbed my hands. I was still thinking, *Aww, what sweet kids,* and I wanted to get free without making noise, but one of them hurled a stone that hit me right in my left eye. No more Mister Nice Guy, I thought, and I got really mad and started to hand out knuckle sandwiches. Take that you, fucking kids, *güegüenches,* you cocksuckers. Little by little they started to let go, but El Flaco was holding onto my pants really tight, and when I looked down I saw he was about to bite my stomach, the little bastard, so I gave him a good loud slap.

All of them turned to look, and when the kid saw he was at the center of attention, he started to cry. Typical. Then he shouted, "Now you did it, asshole! I'm gonna get my dad's gun."

Gun? What the fuck? I thought and ran to take cover in the little store on the corner. Since the kids were right at my heels, I took out the only pesos I had, put them on the counter, and shouted, "This is on me!" And I emptied a jar full of candy and gum into my hands.

The kids surrounded me like piranhas and I offered them the candy. That got their attention and they stopped shouting. It didn't stop one of them from yelling, "Fucking cop," and another from smearing mud on my shirt, but as soon as the first one grabbed a piece of candy, the others did, too.

"My mom told you to get all this?" asked the kid in the striped shirt.

"Sure she did." I assured him.

Then the little devil showed what he was really made of. "My mom always buys us Chaparritas."

After I bought a case of those little bottles of soda, the kids finally quieted down. I was just starting to breathe normally, when

El Flaco showed up, carrying a plastic bag. He seemed surprised by our little party.

"What's happenin'?" he asked the one in stripes.

"Nothin', this dude got us some Chaparritas." He was talking with his mouth half full of candy.

"And you, buddy, you don't want anything?" I cut him off.

El Flaco looked at me distrustfully until the one in the striped shirt egged him on.

"Right on, get some chips."

Still worked up, El Flaco watched me in silence, but he couldn't resist the feast.

"OK," he said, "I want some chips." And before I could order them, he added, "The big bag. And I want salsa and peanuts on them, too."

The guy behind the counter said, "You don't have enough. And you owe me ten pesos for the Chaparritas."

I had to give him the tape recorder for two bags of chips and a box of grape Chaparritas.

El Flaco, like a real vulture, was still mumbling. "We should go get El Chucho and the Ostrich, so this pig can get stuff for them, too."

Just to follow up, I called the kid in the striped shirt over away from the other kids—as far away as I could, since two kids followed him over. "Hey, bro, what'd your mom call us for?"

He answered with his mouth full. "She thinks the Jackal is my Tío Abundis."

"Your Uncle Abundis?" I gave him my last piece of gum. "Abundio Mariscal?"

"Yeah." He took the gum. "That's why my dad hit her, 'cause she reported my uncle to the cops. He hit her so bad he sent her to the hospital."

"Oh, yeah?"

"Yep. I'da done the same thing." He was a really tough kid.

I knew who Abundio Mariscal was. He was a lowlife with a repair shop that used all stolen parts. He was from Tamuín, and he was missing an arm. There was no way he could be the Jackal, because, according to the medical examiner, the killer had to be ambidextrous to inflict the wounds.

"Right," I said.

"I'm gonna want another Chaparrita," said one of his body-guards.

"No problem," I promised. "Just lemme go to the bank," and I started to walk away.

El Flaco threatened me. "Don't go too far, copper. We're watching you."

I left them there, focused on stuffing themselves silly.

I didn't get anything from the next three houses: a teenager with a big imagination who wanted to be a police officer, a woman getting beaten by her husband, and an old woman who'd come to her own conclusions about life. I'd promised to visit Mrs. Dorotea Hernández, the mother of one of the victims, but I was already fed up. I just wanted to get out of there and relax. I was about to leave, but I thought, well, I'm already here, and if I don't go, this old lady might just cause me problems at headquarters, besides it's the only thing Rangel specifically assigned me to do.

Around that time, Mrs. Dorotea Hernández had appeared in the papers, talking bad about the police and saying we didn't know how to do our job. The woman was really annoying. We were all fed up with her statements in the press, most of all for having led the protest. Her daughter disappeared on January 15, but no one helped her and the case got lost in the shuffle. If some-one had paid attention to her, we could have avoided the whole problem. Maybe I'd still be working in the secret police. But it didn't happen like that. Then the second girl disappeared, the woman called the office every day and now no one even took her calls. Rangel had assigned me to ask her if she knew where Mr. So-and-So's ranch was, so I went. I was getting more and more nervous by the minute, because, after leaving the last interview, the same people who had called the police could spread the rumor that a cop was walking around the *colonia*. Besides, every time I left a house, I'd always run into El Flaco's gang, El Flaco riding the bike with the training wheels. When I left the old lady's house, I saw the kid waiting for me under a mango tree, like a bad omen. Then he ran toward me and introduced me to a big group of future gang members, not one of whom trusted me.

"You buying?" El Flaco asked.

"Sorry, bro," I told him, "I don't have a dime. I'm gonna have to walk back home." Despite its being the truth, I didn't convince him.

"Whaddaya mean? You don't have any more cash?"

"Are you deaf? What don't you understand?" I said it so rudely his friends made fun of him.

Then the kid really did get mad. "You fucking cop! Now you're really in for it."

Go to hell, I thought, and I headed off to Mrs. Dorotea's house, at the end of the market, next to Public School Number Five. The majority of the gang members dispersed, but El Flaco followed me at a distance, pedaling his bike with two bodyguards behind him. I had made him look bad in front of his friends, since they had to leave without their chips.

"Now I'm not telling you nothing!" he yelled at me.

But I didn't stop. If I could get to the market without any problems, I'd be safe, or at least that's what I thought. The idea was to avoid one of the busiest streets, the one by the dock.

So I'm heading that way with El Flaco grumbling behind me. As soon as I made it out of the market, I breathed deep and started to run. I lost them at the Danny candy store. It was tough to get through because it was payday and the market was packed, full of women running their errands and transvestites, prostitutes, dockworkers, and the normal customers. I went out a side door and saw no sign of the kids. I got to Mrs. Dorotea's house around noon; the sun was beaming down hard, and as soon as I saw her I knew this was it. I questioned her relentlessly, until suddenly she confessed. Oh, shit, I said to myself, I got him. But I would've preferred it wasn't him, because the guy was such a pain. The news made such an impression, I got really quiet, and she turned pale.

"Did I do something wrong?"

"Yes," I said to her. "You should have said something before."

And she started to cry. I was already way beyond thinking about right or wrong, and I ordered her not to tell anybody what she told me, and we'd see if I could still help her. Don't tell anybody at all, I insisted. At that moment, I was only thinking about the reward: I couldn't believe it; I had found a needle in a haystack, a four-leaf clover. The money would be mine soon, twenty-four hours at the latest. I couldn't hear what the woman was saying to me anymore, I was in another dimension and a voice was saying to me: "The reward, *cabrón,* go get the reward." The woman didn't know how to get to the person's ranch, but she gave me the number of someone who did.

When I went out into the street, El Flaco and his dad were

waiting for me. His dad was a crazy-looking black guy, with the face of a boxer. He looked mad as hell.

"Cop!" El Negro yelled. "Fucking cop!"

I acted like he was talking to somebody else and turned my head, like he wasn't talking about me, and went up the street that leads to the plaza. I heard the kid's voice, saying, "That's him, dad, that's him!" and I heard the father's steps, following me—"Officer!" he yelled at me—but I didn't turn around.

Fucking Rangel, I thought, I never should've agreed to come here without a pistol; he should've lent me his. All I needed was to get killed just when I'd found the murderer. Then El Negro shouted, "You're not even a real man! You just mess with little kids!" And I heard him spit. I noticed El Negro was giving instructions to two people who ran off toward the market, and I felt the sweat pouring down my back. I thought, Oh, God, they're gonna block the street off; they're gonna kill me like a rat. I walked faster. The alley sloped up really steep, and I thought I was going to pass out. El Negro kept on shouting, but I didn't turn around. Then I noticed that people were moving out of my way, like I was in trouble. I figured he must've been pointing a gun at me. For sure, they got him a gun. Since I saw there was a group of guys waiting for me at the end of the street, I turned off toward the customs house. As I walked by the *tortas de la barda* shops, El Negro's steps sounded so close to me, they might have been my own. I almost passed out from the fear alone, but I made it to the train station. Then I saw that the kids were back, "Negro, Negro, here he is!" And I didn't have any doubt. I said to myself, Fuck. Now they did get him a gun. I turned left onto a street that looked busier, but it didn't help me at all, because the people jumped off to one side if I got close to them. Some of them even looked at me like a person condemned to death who still doesn't know his fate, and I said to myself: Oh, God, they're going to execute me. And I didn't want to look back, because I figured El Negro wouldn't shoot me in the back—or maybe he would; I mean, I was in the Coralillo. Nobody likes the police here. Then I knew very clearly that a crowd of people had gathered behind me, ready to see me die, like they were at the Roman circus, and right then a guy coming in the opposite direction ducked down as I came up next to him, like he was trying to duck something and I felt the first shot hit my back, hard and compact, and it made my whole body shake. I remember I thought: Oh, shit! That was it. My back was wet and dripping: Oh, God, oh, God, they got me! I couldn't breathe and my nose was running, but I didn't stop: Holy Mary Mother of God, Holy Mother of God! Get me out of here! When I got to the top of the hill, tears started to pour out of me, and I took the second hit, boom, and that was when I said, Ave María Purísima, I made it this far! But something strange was happening to the people, because instead of shouting or getting scared, they were laughing at me! All of a sudden, my legs gave way as I felt a soft, juicy substance slithering down my neck. I reached back, and my hand came away covered with yellow pulp: papaya. El Negro had thrown papayas at me! "Hey, officer!" he shouted, "I don't think you'll come back here no more!" Everyone was laughing wildly, and my nose wouldn't stop running. I went up Calle Héroes de Nacozari, cleaned off the pulp, and didn't stop until I got to police headquarters. I could breathe again. I was humiliated and dirty, and I had lost my tape recorder. But I was alive and I knew who the murderer was.

22

They arranged to meet at the Tiberius Bar at six in the evening. The Blind Man had ordered tequila, enchiladas, bread, and a *queso fresco*. As soon as he got there, Vicente asked, "Did you find what I asked for?"

The Blind Man handed him an envelope from Congressman Wolffer, the envelope with the bribe, which had an official seal. "You got lucky. I was about to throw it out."

"And did you go see Mrs. Hernández?"

The Blind Man showed him the letter with the threats.

"This is it," he said. "But first, we have to negotiate my percentage."

He told him about his interview with Mrs. Hernández. He was so happy he didn't even mention the attack in the market. As soon as he finished, Rangel noticed his hands were sweaty.

"Do you have the map?" That afternoon, he had asked for a map of the state highways.

"Here it is. What I don't understand is why such an influential person is hiding out there in the middle of nowhere."

"Why do you think?" asked Rangel, pointing to a path on the map. "It's a perfect location, if he feels threatened by the law in Mexico, he can just walk across the border into Texas. They've got it all figured out. That's why we have to show up there at dawn, before they can get away. Did you find out how to get there?"

"Yeah, we just take this highway."

"No way, Romero, that whole stretch is full of drug dealers. I don't want problems with anybody. Imagine if we crossed a poppy field or if they pointed an AK-47 at you. Look for somebody who knows that area real well. Or what? You don't wanna take half anymore?"

The Blind Man mentioned that Mrs. Hernández gave him the number of a guy that worked on a ranch close by there.

"Go talk to him, but watch out, man. Careful with what you say or you could fuck up the whole thing."

They looked over the highway map. The Blind Man added up the miles and said the hideout was at least six hours from the port. "I'll drive there and you drive back. We bring him in and divide the reward." Then he asked, "Have you ever dealt with such a big shot before?"

"Do you want out?"

"No, I just wanted to know if maybe we're setting our sights a little high."

"If you want out, there's still time."

"No way," said the Blind Man. "No way."

Rangel handed him the keys to the Chevy Nova. "Get it ready for the trip." In the meantime, he'd go rest a few hours, since he hadn't slept at all.

"Do you want me to take you boss?"

"No, I'll go by myself; you focus on what I told you to do. Hey, Romero, would you really use electric shocks on a suspect?"

The Blind Man seemed to think it over. "Well, yeah . . . as long as my wife was working that day."

"What does your wife have to do with this?"

"I'll explain later. If I don't hurry, I won't see any money."

"OK, but like I said: not a word to anybody."

The Blind Man left there right at nine o'clock. He had to go to the mechanic's house to find him, force him to open up his shop, and check out the Chevy Nova. The mechanic checked the timing, topped off the oil, adjusted the belts, and rigged it so it would get more speed. The Blind Man went to fill up the gas tank an hour later, made sure the tire pressure was right for the highway, and got into the car, but before he went to pick up his partner, he went to Flamingos, the only place that was open on the avenue. Inside, there were just the usual regulars: taxi drivers, truckers, and journalists leaving work. Johnny Guerrero was one of them; he seemed really worked up and was having dinner with a secretary from the paper. Romero went straight to him and motioned for him to follow. They met in the men's bathroom.

"What do you got?" Johnny asked. "Why so mysterious?"

"I've got something really—and I mean *really*—good, Johnny, but you've gotta double my cut."

"Like what?"

"Like we've got the Jackal."

The reporter rolled his eyes. "You got here too late, my friend. I already know the guy who arrested him and I even interviewed him."

The Blind Man's face turned white and he felt his mouth dry out. "Who was it?"

"What do you mean who? Your friend, the fat guy."

"El Travolta? Not a chance. That idiot can't even piss straight. Remember what happened with El Profeta?"

"I already told you: the perpetrator is in jail, he confessed, and they're gonna give him his sentence the day after tomorrow. Sorry, amigo, I have to leave because my little friend is waiting for me."

"Wait a second, *cabrón*. According to El Travolta, who's the Jackal?"

"A Jehovah's Witness: he drives a truck. He works for Mr. Juan Alviso. They have him in solitary right now, because the governor's coming the day after tomorrow and they don't want the news to come out till then."

"Is his name René Luz de Dios López?"

"Yes, that's him."

The *madrina* sighed with relief. Then he explained to Johnny that René Luz de Dios couldn't have been the perpetrator, among other reasons because he wasn't in the city when the first killing took place, he had alibis for second one, and it was more than obvious that El Travolta had been looking for a scapegoat for days.

"Hold on, hold on, what are you trying to say?" Johnny asked as he lathered his hands.

"I'll give you an exclusive tomorrow. And if I were you, I'd get rid of that interview."

Johnny Guerrero burst out laughing. "Fucking Romero. If what you're saying is true, you're the one they're gonna get rid of. They'll dump your body out there by the Texas Curve."

He was talking about a part of the highway that was practically deserted, where certain criminals went to unload their rivals. Since the area was full of coyotes and there wasn't a lot of traffic, the bodies were unrecognizable by the time they were found.

He left the bathroom shaking his hands. The Blind Man understood that he didn't have a hookup with Johnny anymore. But that doesn't matter, he thought, the reward will be enough to get out of here and start again somewhere else. He dreamed about setting himself up in Guadalajara.

"OK," he yelled, "I'm going with the competition!"

And he left in a bad mood. He didn't notice when the person in the last stall flushed the toilet, stood up mad as hell, and left through the door that was always half open. It was El Travolta.

At the same time, Rangel went by *El Mercurio* to look for his girl. He asked for her in the lobby and she came out a minute later. She was smiling, her hair was slicked down and tied back. A half hour later, they were walking into the house.

"If you want to go get something, now's the time. I don't know if we'll be able to come back later."

"Just like that? I can go with what I have on; I don't have any problem with that. But when Johnny sees that I don't come back, he's going to be angry as hell. This place you're going to is close to the border?"

"Yeah."

"Be really careful. They say weird things happen up there, like there's an alien base. Here, take this. It's my Mobdolite lucky charm."

It was a wide flat rock like a paperweight, hanging off a strip of leather. The stone slipped, fell off, and rolled in Rangel's direction.

"Look, it wants to go with you." She was pleased. "It likes you."

In exchange, Rangel gave her Mr. Torsvan's German coin. The girl looked it over carefully, and told Vicente he shouldn't part with it just then.

When she was asleep, Rangel went out on the terrace and looked up at the red clouds in the sky. They seemed to be warning him: holy shit, this could be the last time you're here. The hum of the Río Pánico and the sound of the ferry whistle floated through the trees. Over there, on the other side of the current, was Luis Carlos Calatrava's checkpoint, where he was killed by a gun. How strange it was to think that he wouldn't ever see the

Wizard again; he found it hard to believe that such a loyal ally had actually died. Fuck, I'm all alone. He was meditating on that until he realized he was falling asleep, and he got comfortable in the deck chair, ignoring Práxedes' advice. I'm taking a big risk, he thought, I should go inside. He meant to go in, but he was feeling heavier and heavier by the second and he fell asleep right at the moment he was going to get up.

Five Black Minutes

23

Rangel heard something moving by the trash can, but he thought it must be the raccoons. His uncle's presence, sitting somewhere on the terrace, was what really alarmed him: Careful, *cabrón,* I can't help you if you're not paying attention. There was something there outside, and he told himself he had to look into it. The noise grew louder and he remembered Práxedes' warning: Don't get distracted, Rangel, put a double lock on the door. But he had slept so little the last few nights he couldn't wake up completely. . . . He was startled out of his sleepiness when he heard the sound of the trash cans falling to the ground. What's up, man, what's going on? He made a monumental effort to stand up and walk to the door. As soon as he walked down the stairs, his feet sunk into a disgusting, muddy sludge. So nasty, he thought, they don't take care of this land. He was taking his feet out of the mud when he saw the tracks of an animal with long nails, without a doubt a jaguar. Ay, *cabrón.* He thought that it wasn't possible, it'd been years since a jaguar was seen in the area, but he was contradicted by the rustling sound coming from the corn fields. Oh shit, he thought, I think I saw something, and he understood the predator was on his tail. It's not possible, he thought, it can't be. He moved up as quietly as he could, and was able to make out the hindquarters of an animal moving into the field. Oh, man, he thought, the jaguar's more than six feet long. As a public safety officer, his responsibility was to trap it, but he wasn't a hunter, he was a policeman. A worrisome purring told him he had no time for doubts. He was squinting to look past the trash, just as a flash of yellow at his left caught his eye. When he saw the feline in all its grandeur, his hair stood on end. Fuck, he said to himself, what am I doing? And as he touched his belt, he realized he'd forgotten his gun. What an idiot, he thought, I left it on the deck chair. Violent breathing made it clear the animal was coming back. He looked on the ground but he found nothing with which to defend himself. As if he understood his advantage, the animal purred with delight, and the sound of the corn crunching under the animal's paws came ever closer. Holy shit, Rangel thought, holy shit. He instinctively ran to the abandoned hacienda, it was the only thing he could do, run like that, sideways, without turning completely, so the jaguar couldn't attack him from behind. He went into the building's central patio and hid in the first room he found open. Unfortunately, it was an empty room with rickety doors that didn't close completely. When he had the first door half-closed, he saw the jaguar's hide through the cracks, and he knew he was trapped. Then he understood that the animal had driven him there to devour him at his leisure. It was playing with me, he thought, like everyone does, and he tried to prevent it from entering, but the animal stood up on his hind legs and pushed on the door. He tried to push back with his body even though he knew it was useless because the jaguar was stronger than he was. The weight was wearing him down but he was unable to keep the jaguar out; the door collapsed and they fell to the ground. As the jaguar dug his claws into his shoulders and brought his snout up to his face, it looked like the animal was smiling. He was amazed to see that the animal had huge, sharp fangs, but his lips and the shape of his mouth were human. He heard him say: "That's why they call us wild animals, because of the way we leave our victims." And that was it.

He woke up just as he was about to fall out of bed, with his legs tangled up in the blanket. He had both hands up in the air, like he was fighting against an invisible enemy. Oh damn, I don't even remember how I got here. Didn't I fall asleep outside? He felt the other side of the bed, and was pleased the girl had spent the night.

Rangel tried to get up without making any noise, but the girl still said, "Mobdolite, take the Mobdolite."

So he took the stone the girl was handing him and put it in his shirt. She curled up again and went back to sleep.

He looked at his watch. It was two-thirty, if he didn't hurry, he wasn't going to make it. He splashed some water on his face and, before he put on his windbreaker, he stuck his .22 in the waist of his pants. When he was about to leave, his nightmare came rushing back to him, so he went to the chest of drawers in his living room and took out a .38 Colt and his shoulder holster.

Ever since his uncle died, he hadn't had a chance to use it. He just took it out once a month to clean it and oil it, and he didn't store it with the safety on so that the spring wouldn't loosen, but that night he seemed to hear his uncle's voice: You're going to need the big guns, Vicente, these guys are traitors. He put five bullets in, made sure he had backup cartridges, and put his jacket on top. The stress had caused him a lot of pain in his neck. By force of habit, he was going to leave the door open, but he remembered what Práxedes had warned and he went back to lock it. It was safer for the girl.

He walked through the corn fields on the shore; the corn wasn't as lush as it was in his dream. He had walked through there so many times that he didn't even hear the crickets chirping and he didn't avoid the black, sticky mud in the path. It was a cold night, the fog was thick all around, and as he felt the night's coldness, he thought his throat hurt. Shit, he said to himself, the fog's come in.

He took the muddy path that ran alongside the edge of the river, through the thick fog. When he didn't find the ferry on the shore, he assumed it must be on the other side. There was no one on watch at the dock, just empty boats. Well, if I have to, he said to himself, and went to kick the shack's door. A fifty-something fisherman came out in his shirt and underwear. Again? he asked. What time is it anyway? Rangel didn't say anything, and the fisherman added: What can we do about it? The law's the law. Let me go get my sandals.

When they were halfway across the river, they passed by the ferry on its way back. What time are you coming back, *cabrón*? And Rangel had to move to the side so that the force of the wave didn't tip them over. The boat rocked so much that Rangel, who wasn't as used to all that movement, could barely stay on his wooden seat. When one of the waves hit, he almost went flying, because the bow lifted up so high it almost launched him up into the air. When he fell back down on the deck, he saw that the fisherman, holding onto the motor with no problem, was looking at him with an amused expression on his face. El Lobina hates me, he thought, if he had his way, I'd already be drowned at the bottom of the river.

When they got to the other side, he was able to make out the sign on the shore: "Welcome to Paracuán, home of the Oil Workers' Union." As he expected, his assistant hadn't arrived yet, and Rangel used the time to rub his eyes.

A black butterfly landed at his feet. The kind of butterfly that people think is a premonition or an omen of death. Rangel felt a tightening sensation in his chest, because he wanted to know what time it was, and the batteries in his watch had gone dead. Oh man, he said to himself, what if I don't make it back? What if they kill me? Who's going to let my girl out? The world seemed very menacing and he saw dark omens all around him.

He asked himself why his lackey hadn't come yet. They had to travel under cover of dark if they wanted to surprise them; they had decided what they were going to do and were aware of the consequences. As far as I'm concerned, I've made my decision and I'm not going to go back on it now. He sauntered from one end of the dock to the other, enveloped in the wetness of the fog, and he started to sweat. His throat started to hurt.

He had the suspect's photo in his right pants pocket, but he didn't want to look it over. Ever since he tore it out of the newspaper, the image had intrigued him. The first time he saw it, he felt a shiver go up his spine. It was like someone who could see the totality of his life had given him a key that he didn't know how to interpret: "Take this photo. Who does it remind you of?"

When he crossed his arms, the butt of his gun poked him and he asked himself what the person he was about to detain was like. A calculating killer, a savage lunatic, a misfit locked up inside himself? Would it be dangerous to take him away in the back seat of the car? Oh shit, he said to himself, I hadn't thought about that. Crazyshot has my handcuffs, what am I going to tie him with? I don't think I can lock him in the trunk.

The sound of the Rubén Blades song "Tiburón" wafted over to him from a faraway boat. Hidden deep inside the murky blackness, the ferry horn sounded, and the lights of a car shone in the officer's direction. His lackey quickly located him.

"All set?"

"Everything's ready, boss: gas, engine, oil, water, breaks, air, and coffee."

Right as he was getting into the car, he felt strangely apprehensive about leaving the girl and he looked toward his house, but the fog had swallowed it up.

24

Testimony of Sidronio Garza, Ranch Foreman

I remember it like it was yesterday. The Blind Man asked me how to get there and I told him. I worked right next to that ranch my whole life; how could I forget?

From San Juan Río Muerto, I told him, you take Highway 180 toward Victoria. You can't go through Aldama, because the Río Colorado flooded around Siluma and they closed the road, so at the crossroads in Estación Manuel you have to head toward González. Once you've crossed the Arroyo del Cojo and the Cerro del Nagual, you'll see a dirt road that goes to Gómez Farías: take it, because the others are all closed. When you see a sign that says Ciudad Victoria, you go straight through there, and at the next intersection you head for San Fernando. Don't take the old highway, because you'd end up in the part that's flooded out. This highway I'm telling you about crosses the Río Purificación, which feeds into the Río Colorado and passes by the Padilla Reservoir. From there to San Fernando, it's easy.

About twenty minutes after San Fernando, you take the road toward Matamoros; if you see a sign that says Valle Verde, don't even think about going that way. Instead, take the road that goes

Martín Solares

through Arroyo del Tigre; you turn fifteen minutes into it, when you see a sign that says Paso Culebrón.

From there on, everything gets really complicated; there's a lot of curves. You're going to see a road that goes toward the checkpoints, but don't take it, keep on straight and you'll go through Las Ánimas, La Venada, El Refugio, and Ojos de Miel; you just go straight through till you get to a ranch called La Gloria. Once you're there, at the very end of Paso Culebrón, you'll find a dirt road with a row of mango trees alongside it. There's a rusted tractor that's falling apart, and about thirty feet past that is the ranch you're looking for. You have to go through two gates before getting to the house. Watch out for the security guys, El Chuy and Don Cipriano. Don't let your guard down with El Chuy, he's kinda crazy; he's always got his rifle and he watches out for Cipriano, who's an asshole. You better not get there at night, because if people aren't allowed to go in there in the daytime, who knows how they'll react at night. What did you lose over there, if I may ask? You don't know who owns that place? OK, OK, I'm just asking.

25

They paid at the Federal Highways and Bridges tollbooth, and a sign bid them farewell on behalf of the city: HASTA LUEGO, AMIGOS TURISTAS.

They left behind the stretch of places to eat lunch: buildings with palm roofs, surrounded by eighteen-wheelers and cattle trucks, where only truck drivers ate. They saw a hot-sheets motel that had no doors, just an insufficient number of plastic curtains, through which it was possible to see dozens of bodies making love in plain sight; a little later the first shacks appeared, along with banana fields planted in rows, boarded-up beer stores, dark houses with no outside lighting, a gas station abandoned before being finished, a restaurant with no one inside except an old man and a teenage girl, who remained standing, bored, leaning against the doorframe. . . .

Plastic tanks to store water, orange groves hidden by invading plants, so extremely overgrown they covered the tree entirely, and above them, the wind rustling the palm trees, truly majestic giants. . . .

A flattened red-necked vulture with black feathers on the side of the road; a pack of wild dogs fighting over the remains of a sheep run over by a car. . . .

A sad little stream full of leaves and fallen tree trunks, a row of weeping willows with their branches covered in moss. . . .

An abandoned gravel mine, a moonscape with no plants or trees, a bulldozer with its shovel stuck in the ground and, next to it, two tow trucks and two dump trucks, motionless, turned off, waiting. . . .

Two advertisements for Cola Drinks; when they passed the third, Romero clicked his tongue, opened the Thermos he kept in his lap, and gulped from it anxiously.

A sign announced the next highway crossing: Matamoros to the right, Valle Verde to the left. They saw the cemetery next to the road, an abundance of small crosses, painted in pastel colors, and, farther along, the Paso Culebrón sign. The highway became a dirt road and it wasn't long before they saw the sign for Arroyo del Tigre and the fresh-water springs.

A thick fog bank that appeared out of nowhere took them by surprise. A little later, the car's bumper hit the base of a hill and the fog became incredibly thick. They passed through three consecutive gates, made of wood and barbed wire, that Romero got out and pushed open. He didn't close them, just in case there wasn't time to open them on the way back.

When they got to the top of the hill, they saw the stump that had the name of the owners on it. This is it, said Vicente, and he took the safety off the Colt. Following Rangel, his companion took out an automatic pistol and lodged it between his legs; the wheels of the car turned ever so slowly.

"Seems like it's a hundred degrees," said the Blind Man, and Rangel nodded.

The fog would clear up every few seconds and they could briefly make out the road. The fog was like a grimy white sheet rolling over them. They saw a horse grazing and Romero lowered the high beams. It took Rangel a minute to make out the little wooden houses at the other end of the hill.

"Shit," said his lackey. "We're fucked."

Three dogs barked at them from the top of the incline. They hadn't counted on that.

"Now what do we do?" the Blind Man asked.

"Improvise. There's no other way."

Romero turned on the lights, and, escorted by the three animals, drove the car toward the ranch. There was a tire swing hanging from the only tree they could see. Behind it were two shacks; a guy with a small rifle ran out of the first one. "Hold up, hold up!"

Romero didn't see him and was just barely able to brake. The shadow got into firing position behind the tree. At the same time, a brawny older guy stuck his head out of the second shack.

The guy with the rifle blinded Romero with a flashlight and he lost his cool. "Turn that off!"

"What do you want?" a voice screamed.

Romero couldn't see anything. The dogs' growling intensified beside him. "Turn that flashlight off, goddamnit!"

Rangel intervened before Romero messed everything up. "Police!"

For a few seconds, all they could hear was the deafening buzzing of the cicadas. The light from the flashlight reflected off Romero's glasses.

Rangel noticed the man waiting in the door of the hut, lit by the headlights, talking to someone inside the shack. Rangel made out the shape of a girl or a woman squatting down through the Ocote pine branches that formed the wall of the shack. She went up to the man and handed him a gun.

"What do you want?" the guy with the flashlight repeated.

Romero moved to pick up his pistol, but Rangel stopped him. He didn't want to die like a deer on the run.

"I came to talk to Don Cipriano."

The man with the rifle pointed the flashlight on the ground. Rangel was able to make out a young man, about thirty years old, with a mustache and mutton-chop sideburns, pointing a small machine gun at them. Because of the rush, the guard only had on his boots and his pants.

Rangel recognized the gun and knew that if they started shooting, he and his partner wouldn't have a chance.

"Put that away, Chuy," said Vicente. "Your boss sent us."

Judging by the silence, the ranch hand was doubtful. Then the other guy shouted at them without moving. "What are you looking for?"

And Rangel answered, "We came for the shipment."

The guy in the shack gestured to the younger guy, and, to get some time, asked, "Chuy, what's the man saying?"

"I don't understand him. Who the hell knows."

The man in the hut came over to them—Rangel saw he was hiding a pistol in the small of his back—walking up to the right side of the car. He stopped as the detective tried to get out.

"Let's see. Show me something in writing."

As he lifted himself up to take out his wallet, Rangel kept one hand on his Colt. But the guy didn't try anything, just struggled to read the document.

"Vicente Rangel González, Secret Service. . . . Why didn't the boss come?"

"He sent you this, a bonus."

Rangel handed over the envelope from Congressman Wolffer, with the government seal and the rest of the bribe. Don Cipriano counted it and put the package in his pocket, while the second man kept his gun pointed at Romero.

"Well, now," Vicente joked, "tell the lady here to put the toy away. She seems real anxious."

Rangel thought the one with the machine gun was going to go after him, but he just snorted and spit in the grass.

"You taking the truck?" the older man asked.

"What?"

"Are you gonna go back in that wreck or you gonna take the boss's truck?" Don Cipriano pointed at a black truck parked behind the house.

Rangel turned on the high beams and saw the official logo: the same three letters he had seen on the girls' bodies.

"It wouldn't hurt to have Chuy follow us out," Vicente explained. "We'd appreciate the support. We have to be at the airport in a few hours, because the boss needs to move the shipment. What do you think?"

"Yeah, sure," said Cipriano. "Just one thing: why'd you guys come?"

"To deliver you from evil," Romero said, and he patted his pistol suggestively.

The ranch hand didn't look convinced but he gave in anyway. "Okay, Chuy, give our friend a hand here."

Rangel calmly got out of the car. The dogs immediately went for his legs, but Cipriano yelled and they stopped. Fucking coyotes, Rangel thought. The mud had made their fur bristle.

"And why so early?"

"He has to take a plane to Matamoros. We'll just have to wake him up."

"He never sleeps, right, Chuy?"

"Is he here in the house?"

"No, they'll take you to him. But your partner stays here."

"Why?"

"What do you need him for? Is he your wife?"

Romero grumbled under his breath but didn't respond to the insults. Chuy put the machine gun under his arm.

"Is that an Uzi?" Rangel asked.

"What do you think?"

"That gun's only allowed in the army."

"What, you gonna take it from me? Guess who gave it to me?"

Don Cipriano intervened. "You'll have to take the horse to get him." And he motioned to an enclosure where two horses were grazing.

They went up to two dark-colored mares, who snorted at them as they approached. Chuy jumped up on a horse and Rangel did the same.

"Come on," the ranch hand said.

The mare tried to bolt and knock him off, but the detective tightened his grip as well as he could. As soon as he had the chance, he stuck his gun in the front part of his pants: I can't trust El Chuy, this guy just rubs me the wrong way.

When they left the enclosure, he saw a corral where sheep were sleeping. Of course, he said to himself, that asshole used animals from his brother's ranch to lure the girls to him. He got them from here.

The two of them rode until the hill descended into a small creek bed. They crossed a forest of tamarind trees. Once in a clearing, fingers of far-off lightning seemingly illuminated the sky, drawing lines across it and surprising the men. The vegetation grew denser, and Rangel heard a bird screech. El Chuy slowed his horse, and they came to an even bigger clearing.

There was a house made of concrete and three shacks around it. The concrete house was built where the forest began. In case of danger, Rangel said to himself, you only had to run out the back door.

"Is he in the house?"

"No," said Chuy, "over here."

They stopped in front of the smallest and most miserable shack. The noises coming from the forest ceased for an instant and then continued.

The walls were made of Ocote pine branches. The gaps in between them had once been filled with clay; now you could make out the forest on the other side of the shack without much difficulty. A hammock creaked inside.

Without losing sight of the ranch hand, Rangel moved closer. His heart was beating so hard that he thought he was going to have a heart attack.

"Mr. Morales!" he shouted.

"Be careful, amigo," El Chuy reprimanded him, "don't talk to him like that. Don't you know who he is?"

Rangel thought he was being very considerate of the man who had killed so many girls, so he got off his horse and walked inside the hut. The ranch hand was horrified. Immediately, the creaking stopped. As he got closer, a group of flies buzzing warned him to be careful. What the fuck is this? He immediately recognized the same stench from the abandoned building. It doesn't matter now, Rangel said, it was already God's will. He lifted up the swaying fabric covering the doorway and went into the shack.

He had to blink so his eyes would adjust to the lack of light. Three empty cans of cola led his eyes to the hammock, where a body was wrapped up in a blanket. Rangel told him he'd come to look for him, and the man got out of the netting.

He was the spitting image of his brother: a small thin man with blond hair, no more than a hundred and thirty pounds or so, with lank, greasy hair. When he was close enough to him, Rangel asked, "Clemente Morales?"

The man nodded.

"You killed the girls?" he asked him quietly.

The man sighed, as if a weight had been lifted off his shoulders. "It was me."

"What was the first girl's name?"

"Lucía Hernández Campillo."

"Where did you kill them?"

"In a school over by the train tracks."

"Shut up and let's go. Don't say a word. You don't have the right to speak."

And that was it.

Once they were back at the ranch, they loaded the suspect into the Chevy Nova and said good-bye to Cipriano.

"Let's go, Chuy, hurry up, you have to escort us."

The ranch hand got into the black truck and followed the Chevy Nova to the first wooden gate. Once there, the Chevy stopped so Rangel could get out to relieve himself.

"Goddamnit," said El Chuy, "weren't you in a big hurry before?" And he got out to shut the gate.

When he got back to his car, Rangel jammed his Colt .38 into El Chuy's kidneys.

"What the fuck? What's up?"

"What's your full name?"

"Jesús Nicodemo."

"Jesús Nicodemo, don't resist. You're under arrest for the murder of Luis Carlos Calatrava."

He tied his hands together behind his back with a cable and put him into the backseat of the Chevy.

A few minutes later, Don Cipriano finished counting the money inside the shack and listened intently.

"What happened?" The woman could have been his daughter.

"Shut up!"

The sound of the car on the road faded away. The man listened closely, and when the sound was completely gone, he ran out onto the hill. As soon as he saw the truck parked, he snapped his fingers at the woman.

"María! Get me my boots."

"Where are you going?"

"To the gas station, to call the boss."

"Why?"

"They took El Chuy and left the truck!"

26

This is the Jackal? Rangel thought. The guy who killed the little girls? On first impression, the man looked like he couldn't kill a fly. He was thin, with blond hair and blue eyes that were about as expressive as a wall. No one would look twice if they saw him on the street. His name was Clemente Morales and he worked for his twin brother, Edelmiro, supervising the union's work. As the older brother became the leader of all the teachers in the whole state and built schools, his twin spent his time killing the female students.

In the last year, Professor Edelmiro Morales had built four schools to consolidate his power. The buildings were impractical, with inadequate light and ventilation, designed irrationally, completely illogically, with no emergency exits. Professor Edelmiro had a strategy: when they were done with the construction, they noticed there was no budget for their maintenance, which wasn't really serious, because they'd already paid the builder. A few of them closed after a few months. The remains of these schools can be seen throughout the city.

The mother of the Hernández girl had reported that while they were expanding the public school behind her house, Morales saw her and became obsessed. When her husband wasn't at home, the man would try to seduce her; because she always rejected him, the man had promised to get his revenge in the most hurtful way possible. Eight days later her daughter disappeared, and out of fear she didn't report it: she knew Edelmiro Morales was extremely powerful.

The day of his arrest, the Jackal rode along in silence. Sometimes he closed his eyes, sometimes he looked at the floor of the patrol car. He yawned once: he had a crooked canine tooth. As for El Chuy, he stared at the scenery. "Don't get distracted, Romero," Rangel said to his partner. "Even though they're handcuffed, anything could happen with two guys like this." That's why Romero pointed his pistol at them and didn't take his eyes off them, especially the Jackal. If he could have just one wish granted to him, Romero would've asked to know what the guy was thinking. There was a moment when the Jackal seemed to be smiling, so the Blind Man pointed the gun at him and demanded, "What're you laughing about?" The Jackal, surprised, continued to stare out the front of the car. "Don't pressure him; you don't want him to get nervous," Rangel said.

"If he tries anything," said Romero, "I'll belt him one and throw him in the trunk."

He didn't have to. The guy in the backseat got very, very calm.

Each one of them made their own plans. We're gonna get a shitload of money, the Blind Man said, even after dividing the reward up between us. As for Rangel, he was going to leave the state and start somewhere else. Maybe in Mexico City, maybe on the border. . . . Maybe he'd ask for work from Dr. Quiroz Cuarón, that is, if he could get in touch with him. For his part, Romero was going to buy a present for his wife and his girls; that is, after he paid six months of back rent. He'd take his wife to Acapulco on vacation and he could open a business, maybe a lunch place.

"Hey, Romero," said Vicente, "what does your wife have to do with you using electric shock on suspects?"

"Thing is, when my old lady doesn't go to work, I send her out to take a walk. Then I take her clothes iron, plug in the cord, and, damn, anybody'll confess. I sit the suspect down in a full tub with just his underwear on, and I graze his wet knees with the tip of the cord. I say, *You like 110 volts? 'Cause you can also get 220.*"

"Holy shit." Vicente shook his head. "Just tell me one thing: is this gonna be in the papers?"

"Why do you ask?"

"'Cause you're the snitch, Romero. You went to Klein's last Monday. You had a date with some reporters you thought you could get some money from, and you ran out when you saw me walk in."

The lackey looked straight ahead. "Swear you won't tell the other guys; they'd come after me. I've gotta make a living somehow. I don't make anything at the station, even though they fuck with me all the time."

Rangel turned on the radio. They were playing that Pink Floyd album, the one with the clock ticktock sounds and a woman yelling like she's scared: *Dark Side of the Moon*. By free association, he remembered the German who gave him the coin as a present. Soon he'd be able to go looking for the B-side of his life, he told himself. He who started out a musician and ended up a cop.

Romero noticed a billboard on the side of the highway that advertised a luxury auto dealer: THERE'S A FORD IN YOUR FUTURE. He took out a pen from the glove compartment and scribbled down the phone number on a paper: 31539.

"What do you want that for?"

"You never know."

The one time they stopped was near González to fill up on

gas. As he was paying at the cash register, Rangel saw the front page of the paper and his smile faded fast.

ARRESTED FOR DRUG TRAFFICKING. The picture was of Agustín Barbosa, Ciudad Madera's mayor.

Fucking A, he thought, fucking A. And he showed the paper to Romero.

"Hmm," Romero sighed. "What're we gonna do with these guys? There's no way we can take 'em back. What do we do?"

"The only choice," he said, "is to try to turn him in to Chief García. We've gotta take that risk."

They called García from a pay phone, even though it was three in the morning. Doña Dolores answered. "My husband hasn't come back from the capital; he should be here any minute." Vicente explained that they had the Jackal under arrest and he'd confessed. The woman asked who it was and Rangel told her, summing up his investigation: the cigar and the wool, the report, the stains on the girls' shirts, the circumstances of the man's arrest, and the spontaneous confession. Doña Dolores understood.

"Go turn him in at headquarters. I'll tell my husband to meet you there."

27

They locked him up at 3:00 and let him go at 3:05. Romero was still talking but Rangel wasn't listening anymore. He had seen something in his rearview mirror and an alarm went off.

Romero noticed Vicente's restlessness. "What's going on, Rangel? What did you see?"

"Look at that black car, the Grand Marquis. Do you want me to point at it? In violation of all safety recommendations, even in violation of all common sense suggestions, the *madrina* turned around toward the back part of the car. You're such an idiot! What do you think you're doing, Romero? Don't be so obvious, jackass! But his *madrina* didn't move, he just kept staring. Are they official plates? I can't tell. Then sit down, man. Speed up, his lackey said to him; let's see if they follow us. This is too much, Rangel thought, now Romero is giving me orders. He sped through a red light, making a pickup screech to a halt, and took the street that went to headquarters. He was about to chew his lackey out but, looking behind him, said instead, "He ran the light, too; there's no doubt he's following us. Do you know them?" Rangel asked. I've never seen him before. Rangel took out his Colt and put it between his legs. "There's no problem," Romero said, "we're almost at headquarters. They wouldn't dare attack with all those cops around."

They parked in front of the main entrance to headquarters. The Grand Marquis stopped six feet away. "Watch out," remarked Rangel, "be on guard, Romero, anything can happen."

A bum was headed toward them but they motioned decisively for him to get lost. The beggar got the picture that something was about to happen and stopped with his leg in the air, turned around, and went back where he came from, as fast as he could. When he was gone, Rangel flicked on his hazard lights and put the car in first, just in case they had to gun it out of there. But the black car didn't move: the engine was still on.

"I don't like this at all," Romero said. "What is it? What do they want? You know them?" El Chuy shook his head. When he looked at the Jackal in the rearview mirror, Rangel noticed he was trembling.

The officers didn't move. They watched the car and they didn't budge. The black Grand Marquis still had its engine on, the radiator was roaring. Rangel checked out the main entrance. There wasn't a single cop to be seen, not even El Chicote dozing off at his post. Where were they? He noticed a red glow light up behind the black car's tinted windshield and thought, *He's smoking, whoever it is, he's smoking.*

An orange Caribe two-door, loaded up with suitcases, parked behind the Grand Marquis and the patrol car and started to honk at them. It was a family: a man, his wife, and their kids. They must be going to the bus station. Since the cars were blocking the street, the man honked his horn. Then the Grand Marquis pulled over to the curb a few centimeters and turned on its hazard lights, two small, elegant, yellow lights that emerged from the headlights. Then, demonstrating the ostentatious features of the fancy car, the lights moved from one side of the bumper to the other. The driver of the Caribe ran out of patience and passed the two cars. As he passed by the patrol car, he shouted, "Idiots!" And kept driving.

Rangel finally saw movement on the first floor. He parked about ten feet from the door and told Romero, "OK, partner, turn those guys in."

"And what are you gonna do?"

"I'll cover you."

"And if you don't come back, can I keep your half?"

Rangel smiled—there was something suicidal in that smile—and answered, "It's my gift to you."

Romero took his automatic pistol and pointed it into the backseat. "Look," he said to them, "the first one to do something stupid gets blown away." But he didn't have to say it, because both of them were scared to death and got out peacefully.

"Move it, move it," he spurred them on.

Once at the door, he had to kick it for someone to open up. A tall, incredibly brawny guy he'd never seen before opened it. He was wearing a black suit and tie.

"Oh, fuck, where's El Chicote?"

"On vacation. What do you need him for?"

This rubbed Romero the wrong way. "I'm a special agent," he informed him. "I arrested this guy."

"What did he do?"

"He's the Jackal."

"Oh, the one who killed the girls?"

"Yeah, the Jackal."

"You don't say?" The man gestured with his hand and two huge, gorilla-looking guys came up from behind him. "Gutiérrez, the Jackal just got here. What do you think?"

"That's great. We have to congratulate this man. Come in, come in. Leave him with us."

"And who are you?"

"Mr. Fernández, Mr. Gutiérrez, Mr. Barrios."

"The Jackal, awesome! Was it hard for you to find him?" another one asked.

"Listen, who the hell do you think you are?" asked Romero. "You have to start the process. Why don't you advise the chief?"

They burst out laughing. "The chief doesn't work here anymore. We're in charge now."

Gutiérrez took the prisoners by their arms and escorted them toward the door.

"Listen, *cabrón*! What are you doing?" Romero asked indignantly.

Calm down, they insisted. Romero looked around but couldn't find one familiar face. He went to the desk and tried to make a phone call, but they had cut the line. "OK, *pendejos,* what the hell's going on? This is the Jackal! Arrest him, he'll get away!" The Blind Man thought he was going crazy. You're not going to do anything? I'm not going anywhere. Fernández, what about you? No, me either. By then, the third man was leading El Chuy and the Jackal to the door. He motioned to the black Grand Marquis and the prisoners left the headquarters. These motherfuckers are gonna let him go just so they can grab them and get the reward for themselves, Romero thought. The guys in Paracuán had done this to him once before, when he was just starting out. So he walked toward the Jackal, but Officer Gutiérrez pulled him by the arm. "Look, buddy, these are my instructions, if you don't like it, talk to the boss."

"To the boss? Who's the boss, if I might ask?" And right then, he saw El Travolta walking down the stairs with no shame or guilt.

"Hey, Joaquín, what's going on?"

El Travolta took out one of the chief's cigars from his pocket. "What happened was you got confused, jackass, and now the man has to go free."

"No fucking way," Romero said. "He just confessed and we've got proof. It's an open-and-shut case."

"Look, Romero." El Travolta perforated the bottom of the cigar with a needle. "If you know what's good for you, you'll leave now, before I get upset. Things are changing. We don't need people like you anymore."

One of the three gorillas offered him a light, and Romero could see his badge: Federal Safety Administration. Then he understood everything and he started to sweat.

Edelmiro Morales, the head of the Professors' Union had asked for help from President Echavarreta; that's why the guys from the Feds were there. That's why Morales come out against Don Agustín Barbosa the last few days: since he knew Barbosa would charge his brother, so he decided to oust him, which meant that the president of Mexico was on his side. That's why they didn't want to hire Dr. Quiroz Cuarón and why they rebuked Chief García when he asked Cuarón to investigate. The thing was so big he hadn't seen it. He was so focused on getting his fifty thousand dollars, he didn't see what was right in front of his face.

Right then, someone pushed him from behind: it was Fatwolf, with El Chicote. While one guy distracted him, the other took his pistol. Holy shit, he thought.

"What's up, Romero? How much they pay you for each article?"

"Fucking traitor. Asshole. Who woulda thought? Ass kisser."

Well, he said to himself, you have to recognize when your luck's run out. Ten minutes ago, I was a millionaire; now the only choice is to run. So he said to them, "Excuse me. I'll be right back."

"Where are you going?"

"Right there, to the corner."

"Hold on, it's dangerous to go out at this hour. We need to talk," added Fatwolf.

Romero, sweating, walked toward the door and watched out of the corner of his eye as the men followed him. Before he could pull the door handle, El Chicote reached out to stop him.

"Just a second, hold on. Your buddies are talking to you, *cabrón*."

"Goddamnit, Chicote," he begged, "let me go." El Chicote had known him for years, he had helped him get the job in the first place, but he didn't let him go. "What's wrong with you, Chicote? What's the deal? Why won't you let me go? What's wrong with you? What did I do?"

"Look, Romero, I'm just following orders. I don't know what's on your conscience." Romero noticed there wasn't any security at the door to the parking lot, so he ran that way. He was halfway there when a voice shouted at him, "Romero!" But he didn't stop. He was opening the back door when a hand grabbed him roughly by the shoulders and turned him around. It was El Travolta, with Gutiérrez. "I'm talking to you, *cabrón*." By that time, the other agents had him surrounded. While Taboada grabbed him by the belt, Gutiérrez stood behind him. Romero lifted up his hands to try to stop them, but when he saw Gutiérrez smile, he knew no human force could save him. He tried to make himself small and dodge the punches, but the fat guy pounded him so hard he dropped to the ground, and their kicks started to rain down on him.

* * *

They locked him in the concrete room and the four of them beat him. "Let's see who protects you now, rat. This is what happens to guys who sing: they end up with no tongue." He was hit from one side, near his temple, and the last thing he saw was a black lightning flash that expanded. . . . He didn't know how long it lasted. The next thing he knew, he was sprawled out on the ground, and they were putting a piece of metal in his mouth. They were knocking his teeth out; they pulled the last ones out with pliers. He regained consciousness because he could feel they were poking his eye. "No, not my eyes, no."

"Shut up, bitch." It was the two guys from the Feds. "They call him the Blind Man, right? But he's not blind, looks like he's got two eyes to me, what do you think?"

"Yep, two eyes. But they call him the Blind Man, let's give 'em a reason." And they pulled out his left eye. He could do nothing to prevent it, because they'd tied his hands together with a wire.

He woke up because someone was shouting, "That's horrible! Stop!" And he saw the mayor come in.

Licenciado Daniel Torres Sabinas saw Romero crumpled up on the floor; the blood horrified him. Two shadowy figures were reasoning with him.

"Think it through. The president has sent word that it would be shame to waste all the money that's been allocated," said a voice. "And cancel the June fiestas? Do you know they approved two and a half million dollars to organize your carnival? Imagine all the investment that would disappear, the unemployment you could fight, your plans for modernizing the port. Are you going to let someone else take that money? Are you going to leave, right when they just authorized your budget? Do it for the city, licenciado; the president will find a way to thank you. If you govern for the sake of one person, you govern for the benefit of all."

"And this man?"

"Don't worry, we'll take care of him."

Torres Sabinas looked at Romero one last time. Then he turned toward the shadowy figures and made them understand that he accepted.

Son of a fucking bitch, Romero thought. Everybody's come to agreement: the government agrees, the president agrees, they made their agreement over the girls' dead bodies. As happens everywhere, the city grew up around its tombs.

He heard them saying, "There's the Texas Curve, behind that hill," and they were laughing at him. "Listen, Romero, the ride's over." The federal agents reeked of alcohol; the one who was closest to him was drinking straight from the bottle. "You want your eye?" asked the other one. "Here it is," and he threw it in the river. "Now go look for it, dumb ass, with a pound of lead to help you dive deeper. Get up, you son of a bitch." As they were crossing the bridge, he said to himself, It's now or never, see you later, boys, thanks for the ride. He jumped from the moving car, and fell badly on the road. The truck stopped, braking suddenly, but by then the Blind Man was rolling toward the river. He tumbled down the hillside and fell into the water, the current sweeping him away immediately. He heard bullets buzzing around him; at least one of the agents emptied his gun.

Some fishermen pulled him out around where the river flows into the lagoon. The bones in his face were splintered and he had a broken thighbone. The *curandero* who took care of him told him his jaw would never heal completely and he'd be lucky just to live. But that was nothing in comparison to what happened to Vicente Rangel. This is how the city rewards its honorable citizens.

28

Vicente was watching the Grand Marquis when two guys waved to him. They were coming from the parking lot of the headquarters and each was wearing a suit and tie.

"Vicente Rangel González?"

"Yes."

The taller one put out his cigarette.

"Miguel Miyazaki, from the Federal Safety Administration. We were waiting for you. Let's go for a ride."

"I have to finish up here."

"With the guy you arrested? Don't worry about it, they'll take care of him. You come with us. Or what? You don't wanna talk?"

"D-d-d-don't t-t-be a coward," the second officer stuttered. Rangel offered them the keys.

"No, you drive, we don't know the port. Let's go to the dock. They say you live in a really cool house. Right? Take us to see it."

Miyazaki sat down on his right and the stutterer got in the back. As Vicente drove, Miyazaki noticed the bulge of the .38.

"Allow me," he said, and reached out his hand.

Rangel thought about it a second but ended up handing over his gun to the man.

Oh, nephew—he could almost hear his uncle's voice—*you never lend guns or women.*

Miyazaki found six cartridges in the barrel, and as soon as he closed it, he pointed it at Rangel's temple. Vicente looked at him out of the corner of his eye, and the man lowered the pistol.

"Look, Manuel: a thirty-eight Colt, like the old ones." And he handed it to the stutterer, who looked it over with real delight. "Manuel loves the Colts."

"It was my uncle's."

"It used to be," the stutterer replied from the backseat.

Miyazaki backed him up with a mocking laugh.

Five minutes later, as they approached the last stoplight, Miyazaki said, "Stop. Don't run the light. We don't want to do anything illegal, do we?"

Rangel braked under the huge Cola Drinks sign. The woman on the billboard seemed to be laughing at him, as if she were singing a victory song. From this perspective, she had long sharp canines and was smiling at Vicente.

When they got to the dock, the sun was setting over the Pánico. The last rays of light were shining on the other side of the river.

"Stop there." Miyazaki pointed to an abandoned lot, and the three of them got out.

A dense cloud of smoke wafted from the other side of the river. A furious wind ripped through the corn fields on shore and Rangel understood.

They had burned down his house. There were only a few smoking logs left, which the firefighters were doing their best to put out. Farther away, sitting on a patrol car, El Chaneque was poking the sand with a stick. And El Albino, always the same El Albino, stuck on rewind, froze when he recognized Rangel.

"That was your house? Look, my friend, there was nothing we could do."

The stutterer was rubbing his arms, as if he was trying to heat them up. He'd stopped stuttering. "A tragedy, right? A fucking crazy-ass tragedy. The forensic guys already came for her."

Rangel grabbed the stutterer by his lapels and head-butted him in the face. This was what the agent was expecting; he pulled out the .38 and fired, but the gun jammed.

"That's to be expected," said Lieutenant Miguel Rivera. "That's normal. The gun doesn't work anymore; it broke twenty years ago."

Before Rangel could react, Miyazaki put his own gun to his temple. "Calm down, Rangel, don't make this any harder."

As they were crossing the river, he felt a hard object on the seat and found Mr. Torsvan's German coin. The girl must have slipped it into his pants at some point the night before. When they were halfway across the bridge, he asked himself, *How many sides, cabrón, how many sides?* and he threw the coin into the river. Then he gripped the steering wheel tightly, very tightly with his hand.

BOOK THREE

THE SPIRAL

1

Joaquín Taboada woke up earlier than usual on the first morning of the month. He had a dream that his predecessor, Chief García, was standing at the foot of his bed. The problem was that Chief García had died twenty years ago.

As soon as he recognized his old boss, Taboada tried to avoid looking at him. He pretended to look somewhere else; he turned over in his bed, but he couldn't avoid him. The old man, who looked kind of like a Greek oracle, pointed a heavy finger at him.

"Your time is up, it's over. They're going to do to you what you did to me."

As he was calming himself down, Taboada had the impression that part of the anxiety that was tormenting him in the dream was also biting his leg in real life. It was the crafty French poodle who insisted on sleeping in the bed.

As soon as he was able to bring his heartbeat down, he tried to wake Zuleima, the bar girl with the cosmetically enhanced breasts, but she didn't respond. Zuleima had painted her nails neon green and was sleeping next to a bottle of Valium. The detective lifted up and let go of one of her arms and it dropped like a log. This bitch, he said to himself, she's popping pills again. There was a cycle to his relationships: it started at the whorehouse or with a table dance, then to his bed, where they ended up sleeping, and from there back onto the street. His father was right, he said to himself. In the end prostitutes end up making your life miserable.

Taboada kicked the dog and went to relieve himself in the bathroom. His reflection in the mirror made him even more worried. His cheeks were sagging, he was rapidly losing his hair, and his gut hung out over the waistband of his underwear. I'm fucked, he thought. Ever since I turned fifty, everything's gone from bad to worse. He told himself that the best thing to do was to get dressed and eat breakfast. That's it, he told himself, get something in your stomach. Unfortunately, the only thing in the refrigerator was a bottle of spoiled milk and what was left of a pizza, now hard as cardboard. I have to talk to Zuleima, he said. If it keeps on like this, I'm gonna have to tell her to leave me the fuck alone.

The sound of a *cumbia* from the street convinced him it was better to wake up, so he put a cup of water in the microwave to make some instant coffee. As the machine began its downward count, he went over the scraps of his dream in his head. The source of his anxiety wasn't the chief. No, I'm over that; a guy like me doesn't worry about that kind of stuff. He can rot in hell. No, it's not that, it's something else, but what? For years, he had dreamed about snails, disgusting snails that climbed up the palms of his hands. But eventually the snails disappeared, and then he started making deals with Norris Torres, the governor. Since then, not a thing, he felt like he was immune to it all: a little power changes you a little bit, but complete power corrupts you completely. So, with no remorse about the past, he thought about his dreams. The microwave had started to beep just when he concluded that one of the shadowy figures with the chief was Vicente Rangel.

2

There's a moment in every man's life when he begins to turn to stone. In the case of Chief Taboada, this development began twenty-five years ago, when he took the reins of the police force in Paracuán. He remembered an afternoon in 1977 when they still called him El Travolta. He was going back to the office to write the report of an uneventful day when Cruz Treviño stopped him at the main entrance. It seemed like he was waiting for him.

"You heard what's going on in Madera?" Treviño asked. "They're gonna fuck Barbosa over. They made him quit."

"That's fucking great," Taboada responded. "As far as I'm concerned, they *should* fuck him over, fucking communist asshole. I don't know how they ever let him be mayor."

"Wait, wait, it's not just that," Cruz remarked. "We've also got an inspection."

"Oh, man. The chief know about it?"

"The chief isn't back yet, he's still in the capital."

"And what's he doing there?"

"I was gonna ask you the same thing, man. What? You don't have a clean conscience?"

El Chicote interrupted them. "Mr. Taboada, they're looking for you up there."

They'd turned the chief's office upside down. Six guys were digging through Chief García's papers, and Lolita was with them, handing over files. An incredibly tall guy tried to keep El Travolta out but El Travolta tried to push his way in. The rest of the agents noticed the tussle and pulled their guns. Lolita barely had time to interrupt.

"That's him, that's Mr. Taboada."

"Relax, relax," ordered a dark-skinned guy wearing a suit and tie, who looked like he had more authority than the others.

"Oh, Mr. Joaquín Taboada." A heavy-set man about fifty years old, with a double chin and wearing dark sunglasses, walked over to him. "We wanted to speak with you, sir."

El Travolta smiled.

"Licenciado Pedro García González has some problems in the state capital. That's why the president asked us to come look over the books and make an assessment. If we have to pay off a debt, we'll pay it; if there's an account open, we'll close it and that's it."

"May I ask who you are?"

The badge said FSA: Federal Safety Administration, the personal police force of President Echavarreta. And above it, in italics, José Carlos Durazo, Managing Director. Taboada had heard of him over the years: Durazo, the scourge of the cellblock. One of the most violent people in the country.

"Nice to meet you."

Durazo put his arm around El Travolta's shoulders, like they were old friends. "Come with me; let's walk. Walking is good for the knees, isn't it? How old are you, buddy?"

"Twenty-nine."

"Twenty-nine years old. You're very young, very young. If you just clear up a few questions I have, you're going to be young *and* very lucky."

El Travolta didn't know what was going on. He got the drift though, that's for sure. This large man had to be extremely powerful, just going by how submissive his assistants were.

"Tell me, Javier."

"Joaquín."

"Tell me, Joaquín, do you think you're prepared to lead this office?"

"What about Chief García?"

"Don't you worry about that. The chief just turned in his resignation. It's better that way, right? He was already very old, he was sixty-five, and what we need around here is a changing of the guards, don't you think?"

The impact of this news made El Travolta stop, but Agent Durazo took him by the neck and they continued on down the hallway.

"Look, Javier—"

"Joaquín."

"Look, Joaquín, people much more important than you or I would like for you to take over the chief's office. People very high up. I don't know if you understand."

Taboada's jaw dropped. The dark-skinned guy, who had been following them, broke the silence. "He probably had other plans, Licenciado."

"Of course, he probably had other plans. But the people who sent me want him to be the one to do us this favor and accept. What would you do in his place, Negro?"

"No question about it, Licenciado, I'd take it. It's a favor for a favor," said El Negro.

"That's it. A favor for a favor. What do you think, Joaquín . . . or Javier, either one, right? Doing favors is good for a friendship, right?"

Taboada swallowed saliva before he answered. "Yes, Licenciado."

"That's it! Good work, boy, you're the person I'm looking for. Now we need to talk about serious matters. I'd like to know about your deductive abilities. In your opinion, who killed the girls?"

Taboada took a step back. Oh, he said to himself, that's why these guys are here; I got it now. He thought about it for a minute.

"Up until a few hours ago, I was sure it was a guy named René Luz de Dios López."

"René Luz, good. Bring me that guy if you think it was him."

"No, hold on, sir."

"No, you hold on. If you think it was him, that works for us."

"The thing is there's no proof—"

"Oh, well, Javier. . . . Look, buddy, in this job you have to learn to trust in your intuition and in your deductive abilities. Right, Moreno?"

"Yes, Licenciado. A favor for a favor."

"That's it: a favor for a favor. Bring me René Luz and we'll talk some more. Got it, buddy?"

By then, they had made it back to the chief's office. Durazo patted Taboada on the back and ended that part of the conversation.

"So," Durazo said to Lolita. "There's nothing to drink around here? Go get some bottles and some ice, I can't deal with this heat. We should make a toast to our colleague's future. We've got a long night ahead of us, and we're just getting started."

That night, once they were drunk, they celebrated El Travolta's good luck, so young and so lucky, for sure they had a lot to talk about. "Just one thing, once they've promoted you, don't forget about all of us." "No, of course not!" "'Cause we're coming back, buddy, we're gonna come back so you can take us to the beach with some girls. You know girls, right?" "Yes, sir." "Oh, that's good news, I expected no less from you." Once they'd finished off the second bottle, one of the bodyguards said to him: "You, me, us, we're all just skeletons with flesh on the bones, skeletons with flesh on top, skeletons in motion." And another guy interrupted him: "You're already drunk, Luján, you need something to pick you up." "Your sister, I need your sister. Skeletons with flesh on the bones," he insisted, and pointed at Taboada.

"Our colleagues just got here." El Negro cut them off; he had a walkie-talkie in his hand. "Barrios, Gutiérrez, and Fernández are waiting for you at the entrance. One of them is knocking on the door, with the subject. The other guy is waiting in the car."

"Good," said Licenciado Durazo, "you and you, take Mr. Clemente Morales to his brother's house so he can rest. Explain the situation to him and stay there to take care of him until the union people get there. Take the idiot who arrested him to solitary. Joaquín, you have good cells for solitary, right? I mean an isolated area, comfortable, preferably with running water, where sound doesn't get out. . . . Do you have a place like that?"

Taboada nodded. "There's the concrete room, but it's not used very much."

"Let's go there. That room's finally gonna be used."

"And the other guy, sir?" asked El Negro.

"What other guy?"

"The one who stayed in the car."

"Handle him like I explained earlier."

When they went into the concrete room, two bodyguards were holding Romero up. His eye was purple and his nose was bleeding.

"Taboada," he begged, "for the love of God."

"Shut up already, shut up." One of the bodyguards shook him by the arm. "The licenciado came to pay you a visit."

El Negro stood in front of the lackey and lifted his arm to punch him, but before hitting him he stopped and gave his boss the opportunity.

"Licenciado . . . would you do the honors?"

Durazo put on his brass knuckles, took two steps forward, and *boom!* Romero doubled over from the punch. Then he motioned to El Negro and they took turns hitting him: Durazo, Durazo, El Negro, El Negro, Durazo, El Negro again, Durazo. . . . When Durazo started to sweat, he took off the knuckles and motioned to his bodyguards:

"Now it's your turn, friends. He's all yours." He turned to El Travolta, "How far are you willing to go?" And he held out the brass knuckles.

Taboada remembered what his colleague said: We're skeletons with flesh on the bones.

When Romero saw him come up, he twisted in the assistants' grip "Not again, please, not my eye"—but El Travolta went after him and beat him mercilessly.

"Do you think that's enough?" Durazo egged him on. "Do you think that's enough, after what he did to us?"

That had been his first truly violent act on this earth.

Now, twenty-five years later, he remembered: We're skeletons with flesh on the bones, skeletons in motion. And he had a lot of things to do.

3

The day got off to a bad start: the congressmen were mad, the attorney general was upset, and the governor was furious. The situation with the journalist was posing a lot of problems. Taboada made a list of issues: the governor, the attorney general, the journalist's family members, my partner. . . . He examined each one of them, and in the end he decided to start with the most complicated.

He called Agent Chávez. The phone rang and rang but Chávez never answered. How strange, he said to himself, he never turns off his cell phone. After considering his options, he called Agent Cabrera's house, with the same result. Fucking Macetón, where'd he go? Then he called his secretary, Sandrita, at home, even though it wasn't seven o'clock yet. It was clear he had woken her up; she took a while to react. He asked her what she knew about El Chaneque.

"Nothing, sir. The last time I saw him was when he talked with you, yesterday morning."

"Go look for him at his house and tell him to report to me. I'll see you in an hour at the office."

Fifteen minutes later, after bathing and putting his clothes on, he opened the door to his car. He grabbed the latest edition of *El Mercurio*— the paper guy put it on his windshield—to find out that the dead guy's relatives had published an advertisement against him. Just what I need, he thought. They must have offered a lot of cash to the paper's editor to get him to publish that letter.

He got to his office at 7:30. The first thing he did was review the journalist's boxes. He found a small manila envelope with his property-tax receipt: Mile 31, Las Conchas subdivision. He saw the property was near the beach and asked himself what this journalist was up to. A little while later, he heard an old man's footsteps dragging down the hallway. It must be El Chicote, the old man is always the first one to get here.

"Good morning." The old man stuck his head in. "Can I get you anything?"

He had an intuition, so he sent the old man to buy all the newspapers, including the ones from the U.S. side of the border. As he suspected, Mr. Blanco's parents had put an insert in a newspaper in Mexico City and another one in the main newspaper in south Texas, in which they condemned his performance and demanded speedy justice. As if he didn't have anything else to do.

Sandrita arrived at eight o'clock on the dot.

"Where's Chávez?"

"I couldn't find him, Chief. I went to look for him at his house and he wasn't there."

"Cabrera hasn't come in either?"

"No, sir, he's not here yet."

"As soon as either one of them shows up, send him to me."

A few minutes later, the girl transferred a call from Licenciado Campillo, the governor's personal secretary. He was short and to the point.

"Turn on Channel Seventy. We'll talk in a minute."

He turned on the cable box and looked for the channel. A TV anchor in San Antonio, Texas, was talking about the state of affairs in the port. He condemned the death of the young journalist, Bernardo Blanco, and then criticized the shoddy way they were carrying out the investigations. The anchor, a young guy with a blond mustache, was asking ironically if the local police, who were known to have ties to the Paracuán cartel, would resolve the situation. Damn, Taboada said to himself, where'd he get that one from? Fucking dumb-ass reporters. Everyone expected great things from Bernardo Blanco. Just problems, he said to himself, the only thing he had accomplished was creating problems, like the one that for sure was ringing his phone right now.

"Chief, its Cruz Treviño on the line."

"Tell him I'll call him back."

Ever since they put Cruz Treviño in charge of the judicial police, Taboada hadn't had a good relationship with his colleague. Taboada didn't like it when someone beneath him got any power that made him look less important. He passed by the glass case where he kept his high-caliber firearms and stopped at his trophies hanging on the back wall: three deer heads and the head of a bear he killed in a nature reserve. *I need to take it to get fixed, the stuffing is coming out.*

At 8:15 Agent Camarena walked in.

"Have you seen Chávez?"

"No, sir. Not since yesterday morning."

Camarena was a very hard-working young man, but in El Travolta's opinion he wasn't mean enough or smart enough to do interrogations. He'd have to start learning how.

"Find Chávez for me."

When Camarena went out, the secretary came in. "Licenciado, they called you back from the state capital—"

"And why didn't you give me the call?"

"Because you told me not to. If you want, I'll call him back."

The chief shook his head and lamented the fact that Lolita had retired, his old secretary who knew all the criminals by name and nickname. Sometimes she could say who was guilty of a crime before the detectives had even left to investigate. But she had retired at the end of the eighties.

Taboada sighed deeply and told her to get him in touch with the state government.

"They say Mr. Campillo isn't available, he can't take the call."

Now he's the one refusing the call. Just my fucking luck.

He looked over the property-tax receipt again: Mile 31, Las Conchas subdivision. He was sure he had heard of that neighborhood, but he didn't remember the context.

Sandrita knocked on the door at nine on the dot and walked into his office. "Mr. Cabrera's wife called. She said her husband was run over last night. He's unconscious at the state hospital."

"Wait, wait. Which Cabrera? El Macetón?"

"Yes, sir."

What was Cabrera up to? And before the girl could give it to him, he noticed a telegram in her hands. The envelope was from Customs Agency Number Five, but he knew who had sent it before he even opened it. Only one person sent him telegrams, an impatient person. He worriedly read the contents. No fucking way, *cabrón,* there's a misunderstanding, and he fed the document into the paper shredder. Quite an invention, the paper shredder.

He looked around the back of the room and noted that the bear was still deflating. Everything's fucked, he thought. He was going to have to go in person. Chávez was normally the mediator for issues having to do with customs, but he was nowhere to be found.

"Sandrita, call the restaurant at the Customs House and make a reservation in my name."

Five minutes later, she told him, "Sir, they say they're all booked up for the day."

What the fuck, he thought, they've never told me that before. The situation had gotten out of control. He couldn't request backup and he couldn't go without protection, so he opened the display case where he kept the firearms and took out a .357.

4

The place to meet about customs issues was the restaurant Mogambo, the most ostentatious and expensive restaurant in any city in the region.

As soon as he parked, he noticed a woman waiting at the door. Instead of the normal bodyguards, a girl of incredible proportions was receiving the clientele. He was saying to himself that the lack of security was suspicious, when he noticed that two people working behind the counter in the store next door were watching him. In the parking lot, two pickups were idling, a man inside each one. Taboada noticed that all of them (every single one of them) was monitoring him. It wouldn't surprise him if one of them right at that moment were to point a high-powered gun at him. What have I got myself into? This place is perfect for a massacre, he said to himself. Against his better judgment, he left his gun under the seat in the car, so they wouldn't get violent, and headed to the front door of the restaurant. The hostess smiled at him.

"Good afternoon, sir, do you have a reservation?"

"I'm not here to eat. I'd like to speak with Mr. Obregón."

"If you'll just wait one moment, sir, what was your name?"

This girl must be new, he thought; for sure she's from somewhere else. The girl left and came back with Vivar, Mr. Obregón's attorney.

"It's not a good time, Licenciado Taboada, the boss has a really tight schedule." And he pointed inside the restaurant.

Vivar was almost six and a half feet tall and was wearing a dark blue suit that rippled as he walked. As they crossed the threshold, Taboada saw Mr. Obregon at the far end of the room, in front of several plates of goat meat. At the table, three stunning girls in low-cut dresses and an effeminate young man laughed at his jokes. Taboada started to walk toward them, but the bodyguard cut him off.

"Over here, please. Licenciado . . . please."

Vivar took him to the table farthest away, at the other end of the room. One of the bodyguards was smoking at a nearby table, his hand under the table like he was holding up the barrel of a gun. So this is the table for questionable visitors.

"I'd like to speak with Mr. Obregón."

"The boss isn't able to receive you, Licenciado. Please relay whatever you would like to say through yours truly. I'm at your service."

One had to recognize that Vivar was an educated man. There was a reason why he was the lawyer for the boss of the Paracuán cartel.

"He complained about an issue that I had nothing to do with. I'd like to explain the misunderstanding and ask him for a favor."

"Just a moment."

Vivar went over to Mr. Obregón and relayed the message as his lunch companions pretended to look away. How ridiculous, Taboada thought. Since when do I have to talk through messengers?

"Sir, it's Chief Taboada."

"I know who it is, tell him not to fuck around."

He saw his intermediary lean over and whisper in his boss's ear. Mr. Obregón looked very upset. His voice carried across the room.

"Tell him I said El Chincualillo is one of my people and ask what he locked him up for. I don't know how he'll do it, but I want him out."

Judging by his tone, he'd spent the night drinking. Taboada understood he'd picked a bad time, but it would be worse to postpone it now.

Vivar sat down in front of him again. Before he could convey the message, Taboada said, "I already heard; you don't need to repeat it. I'll look into what happened, but the investigation is already well under way. Best case, we could transfer him to the prison in the capital, where you already know the way things work."

"That's not going to be good enough for him, but I'll tell him. Something else, Licenciado?"

Taboada accepted his reprimand, but he still needed to find something out. "Was Bernardo Blanco in touch with your people?"

"Please don't insinuate—"

"Of course not. But I thought perhaps someone from your organization might have acted on his own, someone who wanted to make a good impression with Mr. Obregón."

Vivar sucked his teeth. "I can answer that one: we haven't seen Mr. Blanco in a year. We've had no contact with him since the day of the interview. If you're really interested, Mr. Obregón said last night that if you want to find who's responsible you should look around you."

"What's that supposed to mean?"

"You should know."

He thought about it for a minute, then stood up. "I appreciate your help. Tell him I'm very sorry and I am more than willing to—"

"I will, Licenciado."

Vivar shook his hand and led him to the door. Although Mr. Obregón did glance at him, he didn't say good-bye. The relationship was falling apart.

As he took the avenue back to the office, Taboada saw the white highway they had just finished. He remembered the receipt he'd found among the journalist's personal effects and told himself it wouldn't be a bad idea to take a look at the Las Conchas subdivision.

5

Chief Taboada took the brand-new highway and passed by the lagoon. A sign marked the turnoff he was looking for: GRUPO EN-LACE. BUILDERS. As he approached a barbed-wire fence, he saw a building emerging out of the dunes. He parked his car and continued on foot. A small bonfire was burning a hundred feet ahead of him, in the sand in front of the building, a bonfire like the ones that construction workers make to heat up their food. Next to it, they had tied up a German shepherd that still hadn't sniffed him out: finally, good luck, the wind's blowing in my favor.

A mountain of bricks and cement blocks was piled on the dunes. Taboada ducked down behind them to watch a man walking toward the bonfire; he was stooped over and wrapped in a dirty serape. At first, he thought it was a boy leading him by the hand, but soon he realized that what he had thought was a boy was actually a dwarf. The stooped man raised his eyes and his front teeth showed. I know that guy, he said to himself. It couldn't be . . . Jorge Romero! What is he doing here? Could he be the building's night watchman?

In front of the bonfire, there was a carpet of trampled beer cans. The dwarf helped Romero sit down on a stump, and they talked as the dwarf warmed tortillas. A little bit later, a girl arrived with a container of food and started to serve it on four plastic plates. Romero shouted something unintelligible to his right and another dwarf came out of the building. When they saw what was on the plate, the little men jumped for joy. The girl finished serving and the dwarfs attacked the food as if they hadn't eaten for a long time.

Right then, the wind must have changed direction, because the German shepherd started barking. One of the dwarves scaled the mountain of blocks with difficulty, and when he got to the top, he saw the policeman and jumped up and down and pointed at him. The other dwarf was jumping, too, and Romero immediately lifted the rifle the girl passed to him. As a reflex, Taboada reached for his belt, looking for his .357, which agitated the dwarves even more. He'd just seen the Blind Man lifting the barrel of the gun when the rifle blast tore through a bag of cement. Holy shit, he thought. There was no reason to fire back if he had no way to cover himself, and if he wanted to get to the car, he'd have to run at least thirty feet in the open. Fuck, he said to himself, there's nowhere to hide. From his spot in the dunes, Taboada saw the dwarves motioning in his direction, they were running toward him. A second rifle blast, even closer, forced him to jump to the ground. Shit, he said to himself, how can he be such a good shot? His eyes, *cabrón*. The dwarves are his eyes. When he tried to run away, he fell flat on his face right into a puddle full of mud. As soon as he could, he started to run down the slope and he kept on running until he couldn't hear the barking anymore.

6

He couldn't go back to his office looking like such a mess, so he went home to take a bath. As he took off his mud-covered clothes, he had the idea of calling Camarena.

"Find out who Grupo Enlace belongs to. Who owns it. And look for Fatwolf and the Bedouin. Tell them to come to my house."

He waited ten minutes, which seemed to last forever, and since they hadn't called him back he called the office again. The girl answered.

"Do you know who owns Grupo Enlace?"

"Yes, sir. Grupo Enlace belong to the governor's brother. My sister-in-law works there."

Damnit, girl, he said to himself, you're finally worth something.

"I'm on my way."

"Licenciado," said the girl, "Mr. Campillo just called for you. He says the governor wants to see you in the capital at eleven o'clock."

Taboada sighed deeply and collapsed on the bed. This is how it starts, he told himself: one day the governor calls you and it's all over. Back to the street, you fucking dog, thanks for your help. He had helped governors, mayors, secretaries of state, and even union leaders, but suddenly he wasn't needed anymore. What bullshit, he thought. The governor had wanted to put someone he trusted in the port, someone who could look out for his businesses. The way things were, he could choose to fight and win some time, stay on top of things, but he couldn't lose sight of the fact that the governor still had four years in office. . . . He could also negotiate for a good pension, some repayment for many years of loyalty.

"Thanks," he told her, "call them and tell them I'm on my way."

I'm on my way? he said to himself, no fucking way! He remembered an important detail: he had already seen a similar situation, a long time ago, when they got rid of Chief García. He wasn't going to let them do the same thing to him, so he picked up his cell phone and called his office.

"Licenciado?"

"Has anyone gone into my office?"

"Mmm . . . just Camarena, sir, when you went to eat."

Camarena? He didn't expect that one.

"And did he take anything?"

"No, I asked him what he wanted, and he said he was looking for you."

"But did he have anything in his hands?"

"Some papers."

Then he understood. The land they bought, Grupo Enlace, the journalist's murder, all of it was connected.

"Sir?"

"Lock up my office. Is the Bedouin there? Let me talk to him."

"What can I do, Licenciado? We're willing to do whatever you need."

"The next person who tries to go into my office, arrest him, whoever it is, especially Camarena. Understand? No one goes in there, nobody touches my files; you take care of that. I'm on my way."

7

He got to the state capital at eleven that night, after pressing the gas pedal to the floor for more than two hours. The attorney general called him three times, and he almost flipped his car over each time as he talked to him.

The lights in the state capital were still on. Everyone works at night here, he thought; that's when the most important things happen. He had never been so intrigued in his life.

"The attorney general will see you in just a moment."

They told him to sit down in a huge room, without anyone else around. Fucking hell, he thought, it could be anything, he didn't trust the new attorney general. Walking around the room, he found a copy of the most recent edition of the *South Texas Herald,* as if it were expecting him. The journalist's death and his father's insert stared him in the face. Suddenly, he felt something that wasn't exactly a pain, but more like a new feeling in his chest, like he was breathing knives. It must be the air-conditioning, he said to himself. I spent three hours driving in the sun's heat, and here the air is almost freezing. It's not good to switch from one temperature to another that quickly. As long as I relax a little while, I'll be like new.

As if she'd heard him, the girl walked in again. "This way."

They were waiting for him behind a large, round table: the attorney general, the governor, and the chief of the state police for Ciudad Victoria. Holy shit, he said to himself, fucking Sigüenza, fucking no good son of a bitch.

"Hello, Governor."

"Come in, Chief."

They held out three cold hands. The governor's hand was practically incrt, like he didn't want to touch him. Then, silence. They looked him over like one looks over a liar, or an unstable person who might do anything. It was obvious they had reached an agreement.

Sigüenza smiled. "How's the Bernardo Blanco situation going?"

"Good," he breathed, "good. We're looking into another line of investigation and I hope to get results."

"I can't understand how you allowed this to happen. It's hurting my administration's image. Did you see Channel Seventy?"

"Yes, sir."

"It's really bad. And you're on a different track now?"

"Correct."

"Looking inside the police force?"

Taboada felt a knife stab into him. How did he know that?

"Well, actually, I'm looking into all possibilities. I can't rule anything out."

And before he could continue:

The attorney general said, "We understand that you've been in your position since 1977, is that right?"

"Yes, it is." He nodded.

Not even a glass of water, he said to himself, they don't even offer me a glass of water to get me through this crap.

"I understand that you got there through a direct recommendation from the Federal Safety Administration, is that right?"

"Yes, sir."

"Can you explain how that happened?"

"Because of my experience."

"And your work on one case. Actually, for apprehending the Jackal, René Luz de Dios López."

Taboada nodded.

"René Luz de Dios López, who is now in prison in Paracuán. We're talking about the same case, right?" The attorney general handed him an old copy of *El Mercurio*. He didn't need to see the photos to recognize the girl, Karla Cevallos.

"Yes, Licenciado." He couldn't contain his shock.

"And the perpetrator is in prison. There is no reason to think that you could have made a mistake. Right?"

His heart beat loudly. "That's right, sir."

"Do you still have the evidence?"

"No, sir." He backpedaled. "We brought up charges and everything was presented to the judge."

"Fine," said the attorney general. "I understand you had the evidence in your possession quite some time, and in the end you got rid of it. Could you explain why?"

How did he know that? Only the people closest to him had access to his personal files.

He leaned both elbows on the table. He was trying to be convincing.

"For my own mental health. It's impossible to live with that case file so close by. I don't know if you understand what I'm saying." And he forced a smile, to which no one responded.

"So, there's no doubt that the perpetrator is in prison, right?"

"No doubt."

"Fine. Then could you explain this?"

He spread out half a dozen black-and-white pictures in front of him. Little by little, he understood that they were pictures of a girl hacked to bits.

"Look," Sigüenza pointed out, "the body in pieces, with her school uniform on top, with three initials. Just like the Jackal, right? It's the same system."

Taboada didn't understand anything. He looked at the attorney general, who stared at him unblinking.

"She was found this morning, on the outskirts of the city. They killed her the same way the previous murderer did twenty years ago, and according to you that would be René Luz de Dios López. But René Luz de Dios López is in prison—we confirmed that a few hours ago—which creates a real problem, a huge contradiction. So, Chief? How do you explain all this?"

Oh, he concluded, so this is it. Following his tortuous reasoning, with the intuition that had kept him in his position so long, Taboada understood that just one person could know all this, the person closest to Bernardo Blanco. Namely, Padre Fritz Tschanz.

"Chief? Do you feel all right?"

He was having a really bad time, but Fritz had it worse.

8

Statement of FritzTschanz, S.J.

It took me a while to recognize him, but it was El Macetón himself. "You knew," he said. "Why didn't you tell me?"

We were in my cubicle about eleven o'clock. At that hour, the school was empty and the only thing audible was the noise the eighteen-wheelers made as they braked their engines. The fact that Cabrera had put everything about Bernardo together surprised me, but I tried to deal with the situation.

"In the first place, it was the expressed order of the bishop. Second, professional ethics. And third, because you didn't ask the right questions. The Church Fathers concluded that one is not obligated to tell the truth if that puts one's life in danger. And since you came on Taboada's behalf. . . ."

Cabrera sat down in my armchair. He was wearing a wrinkled black suit and carrying a bag of bread. Because of his neck brace, he reminded me of a robot or a walking refrigerator. He had to rotate his whole body just to keep his eye on me, and I took advantage of that to protect myself and close the drawers.

"I heard about the accident. Do you know who it was?"

"Mr. Obregón's son," he explained.

"Hmm. Mr. Obregón is really dangerous. Why'd you get involved with him?"

El Macetón growled and adjusted himself in his chair, which creaked under his weight.

"What are we going to do, Macetón? Everybody's looking for you: the attorney general, your colleagues, and, now, Mr. Obregón's people. Don't you think it was unwise for you to come here? Do you know what Mr. Obregón would do to you if he found you in the street?"

"I took precautions," he said, and he showed me the shotgun he was carrying in the bag of bread.

"Don't use it. Why don't you leave town for a while, till things calm down? It's the smartest thing to do."

"And who's going to deal with the situation, El Travolta?"

"El Travolta, as you call him, turned in his resignation last night. He had a meeting with the attorney general and the state governor."

El Macetón tried to open his mouth, but his neck brace prevented him from doing it. A grimace of pain twisted his face, and then he charged ahead. "Padre, I don't have time, so I'm going to get to the point. You were the reporter's source, weren't you?"

That one surprised me, I admit it. How did he know I was the informant? I knew Cabrera was watching me through his dark glasses, and I felt my ears buzzing. "How did you find out?"

My former student fidgeted in the armchair. "You're the only one who could know all the angles: you work with prisoners and cops, and you've been here since the seventies."

Wow, I said to myself, El Macetón Cabrera solved the case, who woulda thought?

"The killer was someone named Clemente Morales?"

"Yes. His brother was the leader of the Professors' Union in Paracuán. He covered up the murders so he could pursue his career on a national level."

"And where is the murderer? They sent him to the United States?"

"They didn't have to, you can't imagine the power that man had. The killer could live in the same city in which he committed his crimes. . . . He could even live a few blocks away from one of the victims."

Then I took off my glasses and massaged my eyes. I'd never felt so tired before.

"The last time I saw him was in the psychiatric hospital. A little while after they came up with their scapegoat, his brother sent him to an appointment with me, to see if I could help him, and I found out he was the perpetrator in that first therapy session. A man named Clemente. I asked him to draw himself, and he drew himself with his body parts scattered around, separated from his torso: total schizophrenia. Draw a woman, and he drew a vagina. Draw a girl, and he drew four bodies. The first time he killed the daughter of the poor woman who rejected him, and at that moment something in him snapped. He kept on killing girls and scattering their remains around the city. At the end of the first session, his brother decided he didn't trust me and took him away from the port. I received threats and they beat up Padre Manolo because they confused him with me. If he's still alive, he would be sixty years old. Anything else?" I cleaned my glasses.

He showed me a page torn out of something that said *Vicente Rangel* and *Xilitla, Mile 18* on it. I didn't like where this was headed.

"Instead of bothering law-abiding citizens, you should solve Bernardo Blanco's murder, don't you think?"

My response upset him. I saw he was about to stand up, maybe to shake me, but his neck brace prevented him from doing it, so he just growled from his seat. "You know all of the murders are connected. Bernardo Blanco and the girls, the situation with the Jackal."

"We're going to resolve this once and for all. What year did you study with me?"

"In 1970."

It took me a minute to find it: Cabrera Rubiales, Ramón. To my surprise, I gave him an A as his final grade. An A, I said to myself, El Macetón got an A? How is it possible that I gave him an A and I can't remember him? And then it all came back. Of course. El Macetón was always very quiet; they called him the invisible man. Are you going to fight with the invisible man? Fritz, I said to myself, it's over; you have to know when to fold. An A, who would have guessed?

I opened the chess set clumsily and the pieces fell out all over the desk. A set of keys tumbled out with the pawns and bishops. El Macetón eyed them with curiosity.

"Take these," I told him. "Bernardo gave them to me months ago, when they started to follow him. I doubt El Chaneque has left any tracks, but with a little luck you'll find what you're looking for there."

Instead of thanking me, he pointed his finger at me. "People have died," he rotated his body. "If you're implicated, I'll be back for you."

Right then, something caught my eye in the street and I saw that two individuals were looking toward me.

"Are you driving a black pickup?"

"No."

"Well, there's one outside, and two people are looking over here. I suggest you go out the back door. Behind the soccer field, where the pine forest begins, you'll find a rocky path that'll take you to the Colonia del Bosque. I'm not going anywhere. I don't have any reason to be afraid."

Right then, a gust of wind blew through the window and I rushed to close it, turning my back to Cabrera.

"Bad weather's coming, you should go. You've been in one place for a while."

When I turned around, El Macetón was gone.

9

He opened his shotgun and made sure it was loaded. As he left, he heard an engine start. A black pickup, parked on the opposite side of the street was moving in his direction. He'd seen that truck before: it was outside the hospital when he left to stake out Fritz's office and get the keys. Holy shit! The priest is right, he thought, they're following me.

From the end of the street came a very strong gust of wind. It was a sign that the storm, the worst of the storm, was about to arrive. Well, he thought, that decides it. As he turned the corner, it started to pour. His shirt and suit coat were completely drenched.

He got onto a bus on Avenida Universidad. Every time he turned around, the pickup was still there. When the bus got to the Flamboyanes neighborhood, he got out in the middle of a group of people and crossed the avenue. The pickup had to stop at the light, so he took advantage of the opportunity, turning the corner and limping to the house. As he got out the key chain, his hands were trembling. Holy shit, he thought, holy fucking shit. The key wasn't working, and the pickup was getting closer. He could tell by the unmistakable sound of the tailpipe. When the truck turned at the corner, he made it inside. El Macetón waited for a minute, then stuck his head out the window and saw the pickup driving away slowly.

As soon as he had carefully locked the door, he went upstairs to look for a jacket, as he was trembling either from fear or from the cold. As he could see, Bernardo had set up his studio in the main room. A large simple desk, a book with photos from the seventies and another with film posters, but there was no sign of his papers and his report. They had taken everything, including the computer. As he got closer, he noticed that where the computer should have been, a layer of dust outlined the shape of the hard disk perfectly. A noise from far away caught his attention and he looked out the window. Because they had knocked down the trees, he could see the lagoon from an unusual perspective.

To the east, there was a long row of trucks parked: people drinking in their cars, boom-box car culture, volume all the way up, alcohol and beer. The ones who were most restless walked around in circles, checking out who had what car, what girl they were going with, what rims they had. To the west, where the lagoon ended, there was a huge highway stretching into the horizon. A straight highway, he could make out an enormous expanse of it but with no beginning or end, with no interruptions except for a group of palm trees and huisache. El Macetón watched as two eighteen-wheelers sped along and noticed a third, parked on one side of the road, that was having trouble. This third eighteen-wheeler had its hood up and the driver was looking over the motor. He thought: the truck is just like me, stalled. He stood there until he realized his mouth was dried out and went down for a glass of water.

There weren't many books in the living room, but they painted a complete portrait of Bernardo: chronicles of the recent past, political scandals, self-help and personal improvement books, the occasional legal thriller.

Next to the CD player, he found a small album with old photos. There was one of Bernardo's Texan girlfriend, but the most common were pictures of the young man alone. In a compassionate gesture, Cabrera took out the beautiful girl's picture, the same picture he had found in the bus station, and put it next to one of the pictures of the young man.

Right then, the telephone started to ring. Without knowing why, El Macetón picked it up. An unknown voice said, "You're going to die," and the line went dead.

The next thing he did was to call the bus station and ask what time the next bus to Mexico City left.

"At ten tonight, but there are no more seats."

"And the next bus?"

"Tomorrow at seven A.M."

In other words, he would have to stay there that night, so he went back to look at the lagoon. The truck was still stalled.

The wind howled all night long. About eleven-thirty, the window moaned like someone was trying to get in, but he got up to look out, and if there was someone, he didn't see any trace of them. It's going to be a long night, he said to himself, hopefully there's coffee.

He called his girl's apartment, but he didn't get her. He called his wife's colleague at work, but she hadn't made it in. Then he started to get worried. Shit, he said, I hope they haven't gotten to her. Mr. Obregón was capable of kidnapping her and taking out his revenge on her.

He put his rifle on the floor and collapsed onto the sofa in the living room. He fell asleep at the same moment he lay down. A while later, he opened his eyes and was scared it was past seven o'clock. Damn, he thought, I'm going to miss the bus, I have to get up, but he couldn't. The weather was perfect and the sofa was tempting him to keep sleeping.

A few minutes later, he had the impression that someone was circling around the outside of the house. He felt a presence look-ing in the window, walking around the backyard, and pulling on the doorknob. He knew that shape well. A second later, the back door opened and Bernardo Blanco walked into the living room and looked at him with surprise.

"Thanks for coming," said El Macetón.

"It's nothing," said the journalist. "You don't have to thank me."

He went straight to the album and picked up the picture of the blonde girl, or at least that seemed to be the case. He was wearing the same clothes as the first time El Macetón had seen him: light blue pants and a white shirt. A very soft light could be said to irradiate from him. The boy put the photo away in his shirt, and El Macetón got up the nerve to ask, Hey, Bernardo, just be-tween you and me, why'd you decide to write crime stories for a living? The answer was so simple, he couldn't believe it; he spread his arms apart to show how astonished he was.

Suddenly, he understood the whole mystery about Bernardo. This is important, he said to himself; I have to remember this. And despite that, as soon as he had the thought, he felt his resolve van-ish in thin air. Look, the boy told him, when you wake up, you're going to have a very important visitor. It's a question of life or death, so be ready.

El Macetón jumped up and decided he wasn't going to sleep anymore. He drank a cup of coffee, then another and another; he spent the rest of the night sitting on the sofa in the living room with the shotgun pointing at the door, ready to react. Dawn came slowly, and a clamor in the neighboring houses rose soon after. Beginning at 6:30, he heard a number of cars leaving garages and rolling down the street.

At 7:15, he heard someone knocking on the front door and opened it cautiously. A six-year-old girl, dressed in a school uniform, pointed to a black pickup.

"My dad says Padre Fritz wants you to have this book."

"I didn't think I'd find you," said the man driving the truck. "Fritz said you might be here."

"And you are?"

"Tito Solorio. They call me El Chícharo. But open the book," he insisted. "Fritz told me: 'Don't come back until you see the look on his face.'"

He took the book and opened it with curiosity. It was the lost volume from the newspaper library: June and July, 1978. As soon as he opened to the first page of the ancient, dusty tome, an almost musical feeling took over his body. Staying up all night was having its effects.

"Did Bernardo know about this book?" he asked. "Did he ever hold this book in his hands?"

"Yeah, that's what the catalog card says; look at it."

It was true. His name was on the card.

Wow, he said to himself, I can't believe it. He had the solution to the mystery. He was so excited he walked to the backyard where a tow truck seemed to be pulling away and a group of people were checking out the eighteen-wheeler's engine. That's good, he said to himself, it was about time. He stood there until the sun poked out and then he went to the edge of the yard.

A shiny object stuck out of the earth upturned by all the digging. Cabrera pulled out a bottle of Cola Drinks from before

World War II. What a coincidence, he said to himself. What a coincidence that it appeared right now, and he threw the bottle far away.

Well, he said to himself, I need to go back home, I have to prepare my statement. He told himself it had to be as succinct as possible, he needed to make himself disappear, take his own hands out of the story completely. But where do I start? And who do I write for? For Bernardo, he said to himself, answering his own question. I have to start with Bernardo. So he made an effort and imagined the journalist sitting at the desk.

He imagined him with a jumble of photocopies, maps, plans. He imagined him writing his book. The book dug deep into a crime that had occurred more than twenty years ago, when Bernardo was learning to read. He imagined that with his perceptiveness, it wouldn't have taken him long to figure out the conditions that, twenty years previous, had enabled a psychopath to kill four girls in the city. As El Macetón could attest, Bernardo's investigation suggested that they pinned the blame for the murders on an innocent man, and politicians were implicated in the farce.

As Bernardo was finishing his work, he received a series of threats that made him fear for his life. It had been a long time since he left safe ground, and he knew from a good source that the people implicated in the cover-up were out to get him. At first, he wasn't scared off, because the signposts weren't clear and he couldn't figure them all out, but one night they must have scared him, and from that moment on he stepped up his precautions. After getting the testimonies of Romero and the undercover agent and after reliving the girls' tragic ends, Bernardo knew that he was very close to unraveling the identity of the killer, and he thought it was his duty to locate him.

He imagined that Bernardo avoided going out of the house for a while and started to transcribe the interviews. He would wake up often in the middle of the night and it would take him hours to fall back asleep, a kind of lost soul, wandering around the house. He took to spending the afternoons sitting on his patio in an armchair looking over the lagoon, drinking beer as he watched the rustling marsh grasses, the occasional appearance of raccoons, nutrias, or fish, and the movement of the boats. But above all, he watched the highway, straight and unending as it disappeared into the horizon, with the tiny eighteen-wheelers rolling back and forth, busy crossing that landscape of palm trees and huisaches. Instead of finishing his report, Bernardo spent his time watching the water snakes slithering around a handful of white, deserted streets, built on land that twenty years earlier had seemed impenetrable.

He imagined his amazement the day he went to the newspaper library. Because a color photo on the front page was a reproduction of his own house, the house in front of the lagoon, the house where Bernardo lived his entire childhood. When he was able to move again, instead of reading on, he remembered what happened. In a nearby photo, he must have recognized the face of Lucía Hernández Campillo, his first playmate, his neighbor, that beautiful girl, his first love, and remembered the sense of expectation he felt before he would see her, this little girl who was a gymnast, with her black hair and her gorgeous smile.

Then, if his imagination was right, Bernardo must have discovered why writing crime stories had obsessed him his whole life.

El Macetón pondered the way that love lives on in one's memory, but that isn't important. Of course, he said to himself, one of the victims was his neighbor, a girl he played with. The journalist would have been five years old, and his obsession with her never went away. That's why he spent his whole life writing crime stories. Wow, he said to himself, who woulda known.

He went out to walk around and realized the eighteen-wheeler was still parked there. Without noticing, he stood there almost an hour, watching how a mechanic, hunched over the hood, made the final adjustments. The mechanic said good-bye and left, leaving the driver and his truck. A group of trucks passed by loudly for a few minutes, and finally it was just the driver and Cabrera, one on each side of the lagoon. From far away, he reminded him of Bernardo. Suddenly, he noticed that both of them were looking at each other with their hands in their pockets. Well, my friend—he looked at the truck—we can't spend our whole lives parked here; we've got to get moving and keep on going. As if he'd heard him, the driver got into the cab and accelerated down the highway. El Macetón stayed there a few minutes, watching as the truck faded into infinity.

10

Statement of Ramón Cabrera, AKA El Macetón

If you want to know what happened, keep quiet. I'm not going to start where you want or list the facts like you're used to. I'm going to tell it just like I lived it, in the same order that everything happened, which is the only order I can deal with. Later, if you act right, I'll give you a surprise. Yeah, I know I'm not in psychoanalysis, I know telling a story isn't the same as confessing and you only want to hear the dark parts of the story; the dark parts are always what interests you most. Why do you have to be so morbid? I was about to die, I passed through a series of life-or-death trials, I found something that could change my life . . . and that's not important to you: the only thing you want to know is if I slept with the social service girls and, above all, where I was at that time. I'm really sorry: I'm not going to start there. If you want to know what happened, keep quiet and listen to what I'm going to tell you.

No, I can't walk, everything hurts: my leg, my chest, my neck, my ribs— more than anything else, my ribs. That's why I'm going to sit on this sofa, in front of a TV that's turned off. If I'm willing to tell you everything, it's because I want to know what's going to happen to us. Now be quiet, and don't interrupt me.

It didn't happen the way they said on the radio, in the press, or on the TV news. I didn't want to get mixed up in the case, I want that to be clear. I'm like Rangel that way. Have you heard that name? Vicente Rangel, we know him better as El Músico. You don't know him? I think you do.

It all started with the case, remember? The case they put me in charge of. I didn't want to take it but I felt like I had to. I never look back, each person's past is private, just theirs, nobody else's. But I couldn't drop the case when I found out he was involved. That's why I kept investigating, even after they took the case away from me. That's why I insisted, and they sent me to the hospital.

They say I woke up a day after the accident. When I woke up I was numb all over, and it took me a while to understand where I was. Everything hurt, it was hard to move, I was more asleep than awake, like coming out of a long hibernation. The first thing I felt when I was born again was that the world had become incomprehensible, they'd translated it into another language, which isn't strange if you think about what happened to me. Mr. Obregón's son tried to run me over. I got away by the skin of my teeth. I was luckier than him.

I remember a mockingbird hiding in the pine trees was singing and singing and never stopped. Anyone else would have enjoyed the sound of the bird, but not me, I was trying to sleep. Damn. I said to myself, fucking stupid bird, we'll see if they make him shut up. I tried to get up to throw a rock at it, but the neck brace prevented me and I woke up.

The first thing I saw was Fatwolf. What bullshit, I said to myself, I'm unconscious for twelve hours and the first thing I see is Fatwolf; that doesn't make you want to live again. Excuse me, I said to him, but I'm going back to sleep. Don't fuck around, Cabrera, we found El Chaneque dead and you're the suspect. What happened?

He told me that every Friday at 6 P.M. Agent Rufino Chávez Martínez, better known as El Chaneque, would go to a bar in Ciudad Madera where *he'd usually spend a few thousand pesos. The waiters would greet him with total respect. Come in, sir, come in, your table's ready. He'd ask for a bottle of whiskey, the best they had in stock. Since he knew what he wanted, the manager purchased a wide variety of bottles, imported from overseas. What do you have today, Totoro? I have a Scottish whiskey, aged in oak barrels. Or some bottles from Northern Ireland that are twelve years old.*

El Chaneque would bring a girl with him, rarely the same one, and let her drink until eight o'clock; then he'd ask for the check. It was fun, and then they'd stay at the Subibaja Motel, aka the Seesaw Motel. Everyone knew his routine; El Chaneque was a creature of habit.

According to the waiters, El Chaneque arrived just like any other Friday with that week's girl, sat down at his table, and, before Mr. Totoro could approach to greet him, one of the waiters served him two tequilas. Just one second, I didn't order anything, the agent reproached him. The man at that table sent them to you, sir, and he pointed to a guy in a palm hat, sitting behind a column in the darkest corner of the bar. They say El Chaneque didn't drink from the glass, unlike the bar girl, who gulped her free drink immediately. To your health, mi amor. At the far end of the bar, the guy with the palm hat also raised his glass. What's going on, mi rey, asked the girl, you're going to let me drink all by myself? El Chaneque cut her off with a halting gesture as the man left the bar, leaving two bills on the table.

Good afternoon, Licenciado, the manager greeted him, it's so good to see you! They just delivered a few bottles from. . . .

I'll be right back, said El Chaneque, get the girl whatever she wants. The girl ordered a crab stew and three tequilas. At seven, she thought: He's taking so long, and at eight she realized he wasn't coming back.

So confess, fucking Macetón, tell me you did it and tell me why.

You're full of shit, fucking Fatwolf! I asked him what time it all happened, the fat ass told me, and I shouted: How could I kill him if I was unconscious! They ran me over at that same time. Honestly, you're full of shit, you fucker.

Well, OK, Macetón, but you're the main suspect for some people. Everybody says you're not doing so good at work, that the chief is trying to fire you, that you messed with El Chaneque and argued with him in front of everybody.

We argued? Damn, you're really beating around the bush: the asshole almost killed me.

They're also saying you're not getting along with your wife.

That's my business, I told him, and hers. Am I under arrest?

What do you mean under arrest, you're under protection. The state attorney general ordered us to take care of you until things calmed down. There are a lot of people who want you dead, starting with Mr. Obregón. And you know who you have to thank for your protection? Don Rubén Blanco, who's positive they tried to kill you because you were investigating his son's death. He worked his connections and they sent me to take care of you. Well, you didn't take such good care of me at headquarters, jerk. Chávez almost broke my leg. Yeah, I already heard you got into it with El Chaneque. . . . Your old lady's in the hall, you wanna see her?

Hell, yeah, I said, of course I do.

You were cold and distant and I told you: Okay, thanks a lot. Look I'm really tired.

You don't want me to stay?

No. You were acting really strange the last few days, almost like you were happy I didn't go back to work. That's the impression you gave me, don't argue. Then they brought breakfast: just some mush and a juice. You left.

Can I get you anything? The nurse asked. A glass of water, I said, a really big glass. I'm dying of thirst.

The next person to get there was the Bedouin, which was completely pointless, because we've never gotten along well. When he saw my neck *brace, he said: Fucking Macetón, that's a good look for you. Before he could move, I grabbed the glass of water and emptied it on his shirt. The Bedouin didn't react. He just dried off his shirt and said good-bye.*

I had other visitors that afternoon. Ramírez, who was proud of my exploits, and Columba, the kid with glasses. Ramírez said, Congratulations, maestro, you started a revolution. The attorney general says he's going to talk with you, that he needs someone like you in the chief's office. Finally they're going to recognize your work.

What? What are you talking about?

Nothing, Ramón, just that you're their candidate to take over the shop.

The kid with glasses looked at me like he admired me. I knew you didn't have anything to do with killing El Chaneque, he told me. We always knew you were an honorable guy, even though they did find your fingerprints at the scene of the crime.

Look, kid, my fingerprints are my own business, don't bother me with that.

Whatever you say. And Ramírez and the kid couldn't stop smiling. Damn, I thought, first I fight with my old lady and then I become a hero to the young people. Damn, don't I have all the luck. I had an upsetting premonition: And Rosa Isela? Why isn't she here, fighting it out with me?

She couldn't come, said the fat guy, Ramírez, but she sends her best.

She's going out with Camarena, said the kid. They're together now.

What? With Camarena? Holy shit, I thought, son of a bitch, he just waited till I was distracted to start flirting with the social service girls. . . . I didn't pay much attention to what the kid in the glasses was saying till I heard him say he was able to open the disk. What? I was able to open the disk, it was easy.

And so?

Nothing, I found the journalist's report.

What? Are you sure?

Well, yeah, that's right, sir, it has his signature.

Hmmm, I said to him, then I lowered my voice, who else knows about this?

Just me and Ramírez, he answered like he was confused.

OK, you and Ramírez can't say a word about this. Can you print the document?

Here it is—he handed me a huge stack of papers, printed and spiral bound— I thought you'd be interested.

Why'd you bring him that right now? Ramírez asked, he needs to relax.

Don't fucking worry about that, I said. Damnit, give me that, Ramírez, and you, give it here. Thanks, I told them, and don't tell anybody, especially not Fatwolf; this is between you and me. I got rid of them immediately and started reading.

It took me all night to read the manuscript, and I didn't stop even though my whole body was hurting. If Fatwolf or the nurses knocked on the door, I'd hide it away. When I finished, I said to myself: Wow, so that's what happened. No wonder the chief is so mean, and no wonder they went after Bernardo. These were serious allegations. What do I do? Do I take these allegations literally or do I read them like a novel? Damnit, they're really intense. Goddamn that Fritz! Why didn't he tell me he knew the whole deal? And what about me? Fucking reporter, I said to myself, didn't even mention me! He didn't put down one goddamn word about yours truly. I was there, too, I was already working there when this stuff happened, but he didn't mention me. It's true, nobody ever notices the pacifists.

I read the whole tome and I still had two questions: What happened with the killer? And what happened to Rangel? It was like there was another part missing. Where's the last part? I thought about it the whole night at the hospital and came to a conclusion: the second part doesn't exist because he was about to write it. The reporter was going to interview another person to find out the end of the story. And in the journalist's planner, there was just one word: Xilitla. And a name: Vicente Rangel.

The idea didn't come to me when I saw the planner, or when I found out the journalist was writing an article about the seventies. But when I went to the newspaper library and when I talked to René Luz, I had no doubt. . . .

Fatwolf wasn't very good at protecting me. Two times when I got up to go to the bathroom, I stuck my head out to see him and both times I found him nodding off. What a brave bodyguard they gave me, I thought, but it was all the same to me: it was actually better for me. I waited until he fell asleep and said to myself: I've gotta act fast, I can't lose any time, so I left the hospital and, pushing myself to my limits, I found an empty taxi. It was about a hundred degrees outside, perfect weather for breeding rattlesnakes.

I went to get clothes at my house. I got dressed, called a cab to go to the bus station, and went to Xilitla. I slept in a hotel and the next day I started to show the newspaper clipping to people. Soon, very soon, a boy charged me five pesos to show me the way to a place along the highway and he left me there. I had my pistol with me, just in case. According to the description of the person who killed El Chaneque, I thought it might be the accountant, Práxedes, the tracker for the Paracuán cartel, or maybe not.

Gun in hand, I crossed the street and only saw a small rusted trailer with a plastic table and beach chairs out front. A car from the seventies was on its side, abandoned to its fate. You wouldn't have thought anyone lived there, if it weren't for a battery-powered radio playing the blues. There was a hammock tied between two cypress trees, and a soccer ball. A neon-colored frog croaked in the lake. I tried to move forward and stepped on a mass of dried leaves. Immediately, I heard someone cock their gun. Hold still or I'll fire, a gravelly voice yelled, who's out there? No problem, I threw my gun on the ground, I'm not looking for trouble. You better not be, the person yelled, I've got a happy trigger finger. A shotgun was pointing at my stomach from inside the trailer.

What are you looking for? I'm looking for Vicente Rangel, I told him.

A man who looked to be about forty-something, wearing cowboy boots, with a long mustache, stepped out to look me over. He was the same guy as in the old clippings. Neither one of us said a word until the radio put on a Rigo Tovar song. I said, What a good song, and he said, It's shit. Then we started to talk. Fucking Macetón, he said, how long's it been? Twenty years? he said. They tell me you're still working with those guys. That's right, I told him, you got good information.

We talked for two hours. Then I understood why you got nervous when I was looking for some guy named Vicente Rangel, why you were so irritable then. They'd already told me you knew him, but I refused to believe it until I read the manuscript. My fears were confirmed.

I always imagined that something happened between you two, when you working for El Mercurio. *I know you've seen him recently. You ran into each other by chance in the city, when he came back, and you don't know what to do. That's normal, he was an important person in your life.*

I know you're going to leave; I know you're going to leave and I'll never see you. I'll have to make do with the social service girls—that is, if there's still time, if I can still find one who likes real coffee. If you'd like to know, that person who you're so worried about is waiting. I promised him I'd pass on his message and I'd respect your reaction. There's a sense of ethics, or there should be a sense of ethics, between honorable coworkers, between people who tried to do their job well. In the end, I've been with you since he disappeared.

Ever since we met, you've only had eyes for Rangel. When he went missing, you went to Mexico City for a while, and I missed you. If you ask if I went out with other girls, I did. I had to distract myself somehow, but I did miss you. I knew you'd come to the port all of a sudden, you'd stay a few days and then you'd go back. That's why, when I found you two years ago at that gas station, I didn't have to think about it at all. I went for you, and you know the rest.

I don't know what's going to happen with me. I might stay, accept the attorney general's offer, in which case I would have to be very careful, Mr. Obregón is dangerous. I might leave, live peacefully somewhere else. But things are going to heat up, there's no doubt about that. There'll be problems in Paracuán.

Now, my love, you have to decide: you can stay or you can leave, you have the right to do whatever you want. Thanks for hearing me out. I just ask you for one thing: if you leave, give me the remote for the TV. It's the least you can do for a pacifist.

Postscript

This is a work of fiction about an imaginary murder and an imaginary city, so any similarity or relationship to reality is courtesy of you, kind reader. Besides a novelist, a singer, and a detective who appear in the story with their real names and do things they never did in real life— though without a doubt they could have done them—the rest of the characters emerged out of a question heard in a dream. My novel is a response to that question and, at the same time, a *saludo* to the following people: Bernardo Atxaga; Ana Berta and Alejandro Magallanes; José Javier Coz; Jis, Trino, Alejandro, and Evelyn Morales; Rogelio Flores Manríquez; Federico Campbell; Élmer Mendoza; David Toscana; Eduardo Parra and Claudia Guillén; Horacio Castellanos and Silvia Duarte for the old man and the trip to Poland; Carlos Reygadas; Mónica Paterna; Raúl Zambrano and Sophie Gewinner; Guillermo Fadanelli; Luis Albores; Elia Martínez; Adela and Claude Heller; Rogelio Amor Tejada; Ricardo Yáñez; Daniel Sada; Karina Simpson; Rogelio Villarreal; Pedro Meyer; Adriana Díaz Enciso; Freddy Domínguez; Paulina Del Paso; Alicia Heredia; Juan José Villela; Coral Bracho and Marcel Uribe; Claude Fell; André Gabastou and the members of the Paris Workshop, specifically Jorge Harmodio, Miguel Tapia, Cynthia Rosas, Iván Salinas, and Lucía Raphael. I am indebted to each of them, just as I am to Luis and Mónica Cuevas Lara; Ignacio Herrerías Cuevas and Ignacio

Herrerías Montoya; Rosario Heredia Tejada; Gely and Luis Galindo; Taty and Armando Grijalva; Héctor and Andrea Rosas; Sálvador, Pablo, Rosa María, and Modesto Barragán; Silvia Molina; Juan Villoro; Sergio Pitol; Francisco Toledo; Guillermo Quijas; Claudina López; Agar and Leonardo da Jandra; Guita Schyfter; Hugo Hiriart; Guillermo Sheridan; Joaquín and Alicia Lavado; Ulises and Paty Corona; Tedi López Mills and Álvaro Uribe; Gerardo Lammers; Carlos Carrera; Francisco Barrenechea; Jorge Lestrade; Florence Olivier; Amelia Hinojosa; Svetlana Doubin; and Erika and Néstor Pérez Castillo.

For their interest and faith in my novel, Andrew Robinton, Lauren Wein, Amy Hundley, Morgan Entrekin, Christilla Vasserot, Dominique Bourgois, Junot Díaz, Mario Muñoz, Sara and Oswaldo Zavala, Aura Estrada, Miguel Aguilar, Claudio López, and Braulio Peralta share my gratitude with the first generous readers of the manuscript: Sylvia Pasternac, Luis Camarena, Valerie Mejer, Jorge Volpi, Vesta Herrerías, Augusto Cruz, and Francisco Goldman, who were the most critical friends and the most supportive critics, and to whom I owe the urge to write and rewrite this story.